To Suz
"Calm seas and a prosperous voyage"
Seymour

ASTREYA

BOOK I

THE VOYAGE SOUTH

ASTREYA

BOOK I

THE VOYAGE SOUTH

SEYMOUR HAMILTON

Cortero Publishing
An Imprint of Fireship Press

ISBN: 978-1-61179-190-7 (Paperback)
978-1-61179-193-8 (eBook)

BISAC Subject Headings:

FICTION / Action & Adventure
FICTION / Sea Stories
FICTION / Fantasy / General

Address all correspondence to:

Fireship Press, LLC
P.O. Box 68412
Tucson, AZ 85737

Or visit our website at:
www.FireshipPress.com

2.0

Dedication

Astreya is for my wife Katherine and my two sons, Benjamin and Robin, all of whom contributed to the story in more ways than they can imagine.

Astreya would not have been written, had not Mike Whitehouse taken me as mate of his traditional Nova Scotian schooner, the *Hakada*, when he sailed to Grey River on the South Coast of Newfoundland. This tiny outport on the fjord of the same name inspired the first paragraph of the book, and is where Astreya's story began, many years ago.

Acknowledgements

Appreciation and many thanks go to Jessica Knauss, the best of editors, for many corrections, suggestions and improvements that made the manuscript ready for publication.

In Memoriam

Tom Grundner, founder and senior editor of Fireship Press, who chose to publish *Astreya*, but who did not live to see the book in print.

The Village where Astreya was Born

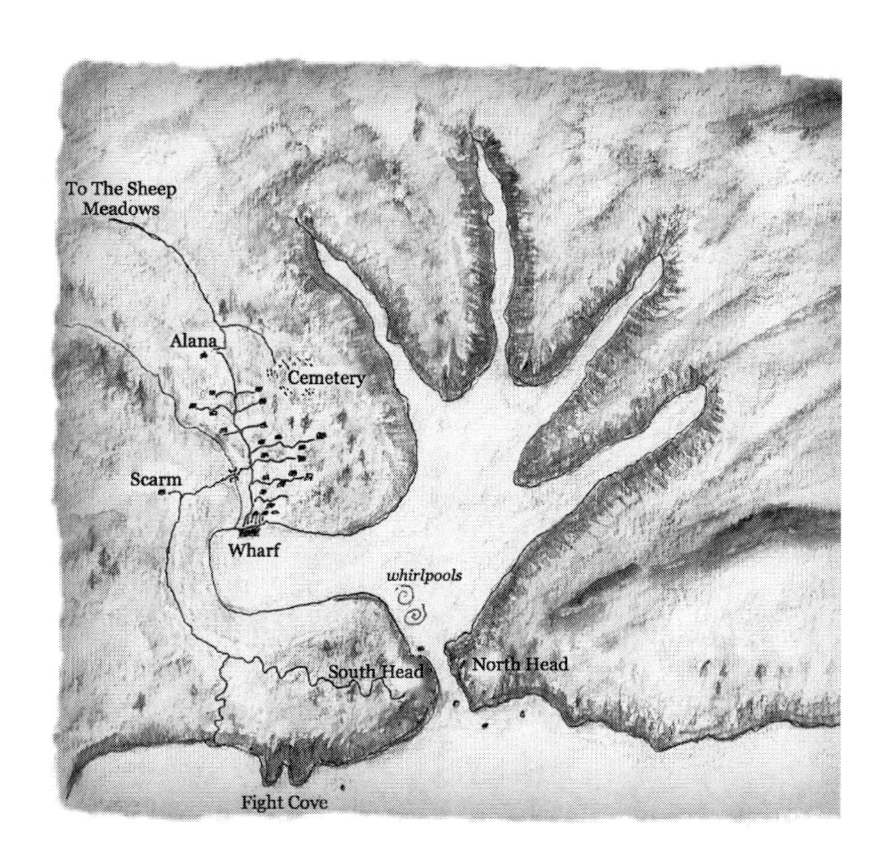

ASTREYA'S TRAVELS FROM TEENMOUTH TO CHARTON

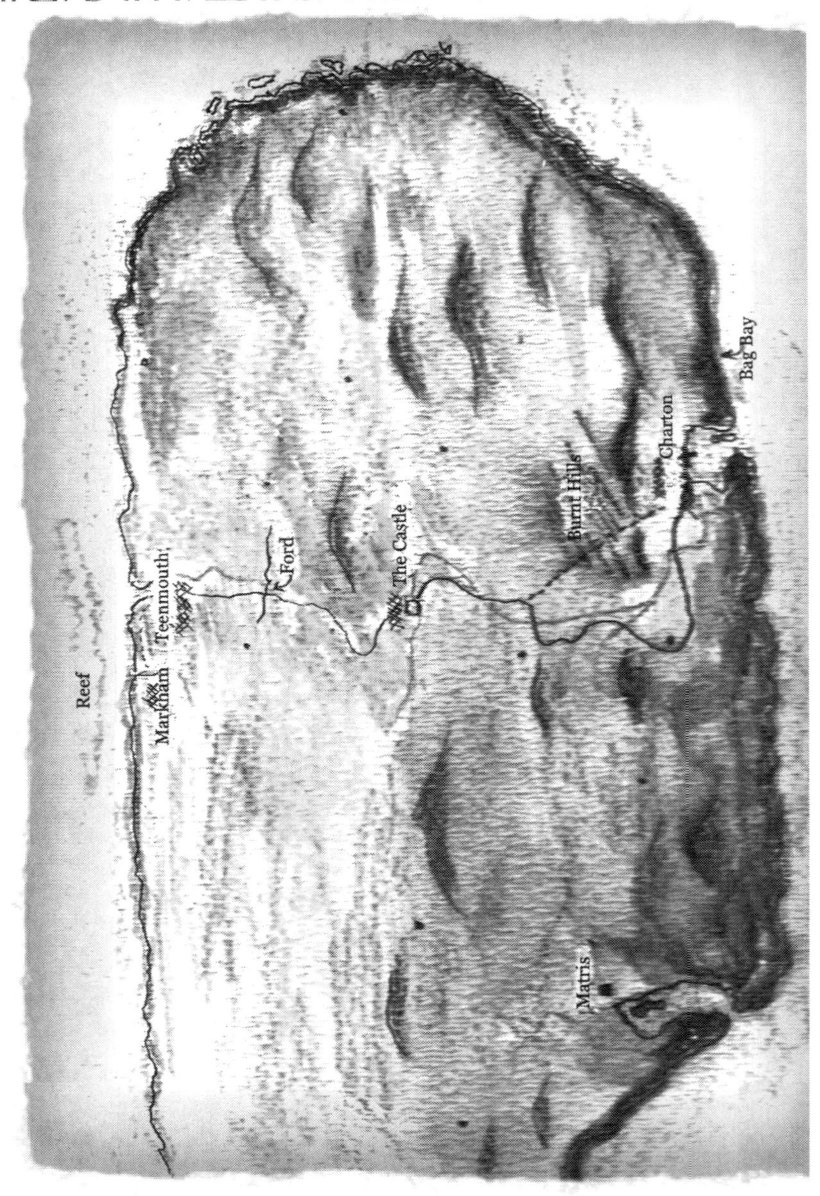

CONTENTS

Prologue 1

Chapter 1:
In which Astreya fights with Yan, and Alana passes on a gift 15

Chapter 2:
In which Roaring Jack discovers a use for Astreya's talent 27

Chapter 3:
In which Astreya prepares, and the skippers choose their crews 35

Chapter 4:
In which the *Mollie* sails south, and her crew makes a horrid discovery 45

Chapter 5:
In which they are storm-struck, and Astreya reaches Teenmouth 57

Chapter 6:
In which the *Mollie* sails North without Astreya 77

Chapter 7:
In which Astreya becomes a farmer 81

Chapter 8:
In which Astreya works for Jeb 95

Chapter 9:
In which Astreya leaves Teenmouth 109

Chapter 10:
In which the *Mollie* returns to the Village 129

Chapter 11:
In which Astreya meets Gar and Lindey 139

Chapter 12:
In which they are ambushed, and Astreya is falsely accused 157

Chapter 13:
In which Astreya arrives at the Castle 185

Chapter 14:
In which the *Mollie* sails south a second time 201

Chapter 15:
In which Astreya works as Gar's assistant 215

Chapter 16:
In which the hall burns down 255

Chapter 17:
In which Astreya and Lindey journey to the Sea 277

Chapter 18:
In which Astreya meets Adramin 293

A Sneak Peek at *The Men of the Sea* 309

About the Author 315

Prologue

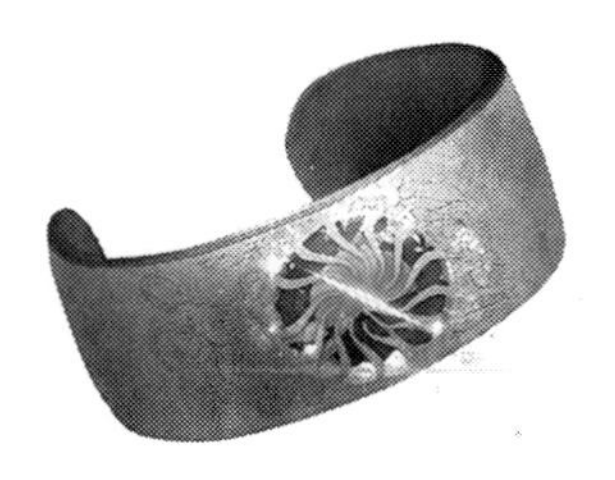

If you are in a hurry to get on with Astreya's story, you can skip the Prologue and go to Chapter 1. But if you do jump ahead, you'll find yourself wondering where Astreya came from, and why he was not like everyone else.

Ancient, round-shouldered mountains met the sea only a little south of where winter held the ocean ice-clad the whole year long. Along the coastline, where harbors were few and hard to find, jagged rocks combed the breakers, grinding at shards of wood that might once have been ships.

A double handful of small, blunt-bowed fishing boats worked their way across the wind towards a gap in the cliffs that only they knew was there. As each boat rose to the crest of a wave, the men aboard sometimes caught a glimpse of their companions' hulls, but more often they saw only dark sails, wind-bent on the same course. As they drew closer to land, the deep throated roar of breakers on the cliffs drowned the skippers' shouts when they turned downwind to thread a needle's eye of broken water between black headlands silhouetted against the evening sky. For a tense moment, each boat hung on the wave that its skipper had chosen to surf through the narrow gap. Then, one by one, they rode the breakers between the headlands, and were suddenly out of both wind and waves and only needed to avoid a tidal whirlpool before they were into protected water. Ahead of them was a bay the shape of a man's hand, with four narrow fjords like splayed fingers probing the forested mountainsides that fell steeply into the dark water below. The boats turned south into the fifth and broadest of the fjords where the mountains drew back, leaving a somewhat gentler slope where the fishermen had lived for so many generations that the first settlers had long been forgotten.

Within the shadow of the encircling highlands, the fishing boats eased through calm water, black as the rocky heights above. They slid towards the wooden wharves of the Village, heading for their allotted places, furling their homemade sails as they went. Where a stream made its final downhill rush into the salty bay, bait shacks and boathouses stood half on land, half on wooden pilings driven into the rocky bottom. As they neared the shore, the men glanced up at their cottages of stone and weathered grey wood that looked over each other's rooftops down to the water's edge. Smoke from the chimneys rose almost straight up into the evening air, until it escaped the lee of the sheltering cliffs, briefly caught the last light, and was swept away by the wind. It was near nightfall in the Village when the fleet was secured and the crews went ashore. Orange light from oil lamps spilled into the darkness as doors opened to receive the sailors home.

Inshore, higher than the last semicircle of dwellings, the stream chuckled over stones as it left the forest. There, high above the Village, within the sound of running water, was a level space where the Village cemetery grew a little larger every year to make room for the winter's dead. Higher still, the rocky crest was a black line against the twilit sky. In the shadows, where gravestones outnumbered the people living in the Village below, there were more markers in the ground than there had been bodies carried up the hill. "Lost at sea" repeated like a melancholy chorus echoing down the years, each of which had seen the little boats sail out of the harbor onto the ocean, some never to return.

If the fate of most men of the Village was to follow the sea until it caught them, the role of women was equally circumscribed. Their lot was to become a sailor's wife, and too often, his widow. Some would live to see their grandchildren, some would die bringing another sailor into the world—or a perhaps a woman destined to tend house and wait hopefully for her seafaring husband's return.

However, the sea yielded fish and the forest grew wood for boats in which to take the catch, and for most of the Villagers, there was security and even some contentment in knowing their fate. They were untroubled by the rest of the world, which had long forgotten them. Daily life within the cycle of the seasons was enough: few wondered about what might be *Away* or what could have happened *Before*, since none of them knew the answers. Their lives were not easy, but because they depended on each other in times of hardship, they also shared the brief moments of joy.

There were always songs in the Village, and dancing as well, both when the men came home, and for practice while they were away. Singers could rhyme the night away with so many songs to stir body and spirit that a tune was seldom repeated unless someone insisted on a reprise. There were songs of love, of longing, and of lovers parted by the sea; there were joking songs that grew longer with the doings of Villagers past and present; songs of mourning, and songs whose origin and meaning were obscure.

Of all the singers in the Village, none sang so sweetly as Alana. Unlike most of the Villagers, who were sturdy and fair- or red-haired, she was tall and slim, with long hair, as brown and shiny as a freshly peeled nut. Her eyes were by some lights blue, by others almost green. Alana grew from a thin, willowy girl blessed only with a voice, to a young woman who stood somewhat apart from the rest of the Village. Perhaps because her life had been darkened by the death of both her parents when she was young, there was a touch of sadness in the way she went about her life in an uncle's house, quietly helping her aunt with four children young enough to be her own nieces and nephews. Young men sometimes sighed for Alana, but they did not approach her. She was as much a part of their lives as the stream that ran through the Village, but she remained remote as its source in the forested mountains. They were all touched by the richness of her voice and the simple elegance with which she sang. When she was called upon to sing the long and difficult laments so much loved by the older folk of the Village, many of the men wiped the corners of their eyes, and women wept openly. When she sang of love, the young men's hearts were inflamed, and yet even the most boisterous of them became tongue-tied and awkward in her presence.

One evening, as she was watching the fleet return on the evening tide, a black-haired stranger was carried from the last boat. The skipper, Roaring Jack, Alana's uncle by marriage, had seen the man's dismasted and rudderless skiff being tossed by an onshore wind towards the cliffs, and it was Scar Arm Ian, known as Scarm, who had hauled the castaway almost lifeless from the sea.

At first, the Villagers thought the stranger dumb, or so shocked by his ordeal that he had lost the power of speech. Scarm, whose wife had died in childbirth many years before, cared for the sailor in his own cottage. The healers visited them daily, taking care of him despite his long black hair and dark complexion, so different from their own. When days passed into weeks, and he was able to walk down to the Village wharf where all could see him, it was apparent that he could speak, though with an accent and intonation different from the plain talk of the Village. With Scarm's help, he soon learned to understand and make himself understood, but he remained economical with words, even compared to sailors who spoke only when there was good reason for it. The Villagers called him "Stranger," since that was close enough the outlandish name he offered them.

"T'would be a foin t'ing if he could tell us from whence he came," remarked one of his crew mates, Red Ian, so named to distinguish him from his uncle, Scar Arm Ian.

"He has more to say than my relatives in the cemetery," said Scarm, "but not by a lot."

In fact, Scarm knew more than he told. He kept the Stranger's secrets because much of what he had heard were the whisperings and mutterings of someone at the edge of consciousness, making his way back to life. Scarm's silence was not difficult to maintain, because he was the keeper of many secrets, and had the habit of guarding his tongue. He kept the Village's *Born and Buried Book*, which, among other things, recorded who was related to whom, particularly when neither was wed to the other. He approved the relationships that he judged to be sufficiently separated, and discretely ensured that nobody inadvertently married a half brother or sister.

His own secret was a collection of books from both *Away* and *Before* that dated from a time when ships visited the Village regularly, coming across the seas and oceans, voyaging far from sight of land. Scarm and the Stranger soon recognized that neither gossiped, and so Scarm answered questions about the Village and its families, and gave the Stranger leave to read as he wished—even within the *Born and Buried Book*, where he had encoded much more than its name suggested.

Even though the Villagers did not accept the Stranger as one of their own, they approved when he fitted into the Village's work without friction or disturbance, first helping with the mending of nets and boats, then joining the Village boys as they fished for bait in the fjord, and then as he recovered strength, taking a place in the boat that had rescued him. Roaring Jack took him aboard the *Mollie*, where after a week's fishing, the big-voiced skipper declared, "He's handy." The few who did not hear Roaring Jack's approval knew his judgment in less than a day.

As the weeks passed, the mothers, aunts and the grandmothers of the Village conducted their own appraisal of the Stranger whenever they met for weaving, sewing and gossip. Though the Stranger and Alana were together no more than was explicable by the course of the day's work, their secret was revealed even before they knew it themselves, and after Roaring Jack's mother told her friends that she had seen Alana and the Stranger standing together much closer than was necessary for spreading fish on the drying racks, their love was hidden no longer.

So it was that the quiet man who seldom answered with more than the gleam of a smile began to open his mind and heart to the young, green-eyed woman, speaking to her in a different way from his conversations with Scarm. And because of her own apartness from the unmarried women, she guarded every word he said to her.

The season passed from fall to winter. The Village made all secure against the storms, pulled the boats up on shore, and prepared to endure the snow and cold. Ice formed on the fjord, and spray froze onto the rocks at the harbor mouth. During the brief brightness of the midwinter feast, Alana and the Stranger began keeping company in the formal manner of the Village. They sat together, danced, and stole glances as the Village wives and grandmothers kept them decorously apart in the decent traditions handed down over the generations—an arrangement that let the Villagers discuss the couple's every move.

Gradually, the Villagers began to see destiny in the union of the silent, black-haired man and the lonely young woman who sang. The two seldom spoke in the presence of others, but the couple's closeness warmed the hearts of those who remembered their own courtships, while the unmarried men envied at a distance too great for jealousy.

When the last icicles dropped from the eves and the grass pushed up its green spears, the Stranger and Alana exchanged vows. At the wedding feast, everyone tried to remember his foreign-sounding name, but none could get his tongue around it. Scarm, who conducted the ceremony, tried to copy the strange sounds, but even though the Stranger had written his name down for him, the best Scarm could do was "Astreya."

In the midst of the exchange of promises, the Stranger slipped a silvery bracelet from his arm and put it on Alana's. The elders' disapproving stares silenced the whisper of questions and comments that followed, but they, too were curious. During and after the feasting, singing and dancing that followed, most of the Villagers had something to say about the unusual marriage gift. When they asked Scarm what it might be, since he was the one who had had the best opportunity to see the shiny object, he only shrugged. Alana was proud of the gift, but did not display it to the admiring group of wives of which she was now a member. They had to content themselves with glimpses of a silver band as wide as a man's three largest fingers, in which was a dark green stone caged in a curiously wrought setting. No one asked Alana or Astreya directly, because even though their union had been duly blessed and approved by all, he still remained the Stranger and, consequently, she too was estranged.

All that spring and summer, when he went to sea, she never failed to climb to the headland at both his parting and return. When the little boats caught the morning wind and followed each other through the narrow passage between the headlands, she would stand on a rocky shelf below the cliff top, her shining hair blowing in the wind, one arm raised in farewell. Each evening after the day's work was done, they walked home hand in hand.

When he was ashore, the Stranger worked to patch and strengthen a cottage that had stood empty for many years high above most of the Village. Each time he returned he found that Alana had moved the work onward while he was away. By the end of summer, they moved into their new home together, where they completed the tasks of making it weathertight and well stocked against the coming winter. When the storms struck and the snow lay knee deep on each side of the trampled paths, they were happy together.

The year turned through the short days and bitter nights until another spring returned, bringing with it the preparing of boats for the summer's fishing. When the little fleet first ventured forth to replenish larders empty except for a few leathery salted fish, Alana was on the headland to wave farewell. When all but one of the fleet returned, she walked to her cottage alone and silent. When the last boat appeared through the gap in the cliffs, the Villagers heard a terrible scream in the twilight. Soon after, torches flickered on the Stranger's body laid out on the wharf between the baskets of gleaming, silvery fish. A day later, when Alana followed her husband's body to the cemetery, her once shining dark hair was streaked with white.

Since all had suffered a similar loss, the Villagers respected Alana's grief. However, their sympathy waned as the months passed and she showed no signs of abandoning her mourning and seeking a new husband. Those who came to share her sorrow were few, and when she would not rejoin the life of the Village, she found herself alone. Accordingly, hardly anyone noticed that she carried the Stranger's child until the birth was imminent. By chance, the year had seen an unusual number of pregnancies, so the midwife did not know Alana's condition until she was called to help with the delivery. She clucked her cheeks and shook her head because she had not been able to provide the charms and advice she gave the other expectant mothers in the Village. Fortunately, Alana's solitary life had not harmed her, and she delivered a healthy son with hair as black as the Stranger's, and as curly as his had been straight. Alana's aunt Mollie, Roaring Jack's wife, was present at the birth, and watched over mother and son with care and enthusiasm.

The months passed, eventually exceeding the year that the Village respected both as a time for recovery from childbirth and a proper period of mourning.

"Now," said the Villagers, "she'll be sensible and find herself a man to be father to her child."

They encouraged the few widowers to court her, but Alana politely and firmly refused their suits. The Villagers gossiped about this departure from time honored tradition and her female duty to bring forth as many children as she was able. Some older women bent their grey heads together and whispered words like "selfish" and "unwomanly." The men who once watched and admired her, now turned aside from Alana as she continued to refuse what all thought was her obvious destiny. Quietly, but with absolute finality, she ignored what everyone but she regarded as her obligation, and instead set about making herself indispensable to the Village as a seamstress of such skill that even though all disapproved of her solitary way of life, they nonetheless respected her ability. When festivals, weddings and funerals came, she was first asked to prepare the dresses, and then to sing. Eventually, her independence was ignored because it had no cure.

She named her son Astreya, after his father. She thereby earned the rebuke "stranger" from all those who could not pronounce it. As he grew, the Villagers were civil to the boy they called 'Streya. They were not vindictive folk, but they instinctively knew that he was not one of them, from his outlandish name to his angular face, to his grey-green eyes and curly black hair. Whether of himself, or from the solitary ways of his mother, or because of the Villagers' reaction to him, Astreya grew apart from other children of his own age.

As he grew up, Alana seldom spoke of the sea, as if she could somehow avert its threat by ignoring it. For her, the sea was both less and more fearsome than it seemed to the other women of the Village. Less, in that it had brought the Stranger to be her husband, more in that it had taken him away again. She lived in fear that it would also take her son. That fear gave power to the songs she sang about the salt spray and the heave of waves that tore families apart.

From her husband, Alana had heard of other destinations, other folk, different ways. She had kept his writings, even though she had never read what he wrote. Some of the more credulous women in the Village might have been afraid of the sheets of paper and pressed birch bark on which the Stranger had written and drawn. Others would have used the collection as a fire starter, unaware of its significance. A few might have held a more ceremonious bonfire. Death, fear, and the unknown were three strands of a dark rope that wound around the minds of almost all the Villagers, tying them to the past. They clung to custom lest they be overcome by terror of the sea that had torn sons, lovers and husbands from every family. Though Alana was much more independent of thought and action than they, she was nonetheless one of them, and thus affected by how they thought. Her compromise had been to keep her husband's writings, unread, in a leather bound oaken box where they were separate from her everyday life and that of her son. Year after year as Astreya grew, the lid of the box stayed closed, and her memories of his father became colored by the Villagers' increasingly distorted versions of the Stranger's short sojourn with them. At first, she tried to correct their impressions, then she fell silent, then she avoided them all as much as possible, and concentrated on raising her son.

While the other mothers cared for and minded each others' babies and toddlers, Alana kept Astreya apart. She knew that the older Villagers saw the black-haired boy as different from their own sons, and so she avoided both their glances and whispers. The distance between her and the other mothers increased as the Village children of his age began walking and talking, which meant that Astreya's infrequent meetings with other boys and girls were shaped by the behavior of their parents. The adults did not deliberately treat Astreya badly, but by drawing attention to the differences between him and other boys, they influenced their children, who turned looks into insults and words into bullying.

When Astreya was seven, a dozen or so of the Smiths came down from the mountains where they mined and worked the metal needed by the Village boats and homes, and the teasing took a new turn. The Smiths, who all seemed to be of the same family, were as black-haired as Astreya, though most of them were short and stocky. Unlike the Village sailors in hair and skin color, their way of life was apparent in their clothes and habits as well. Where the Village men stood tall, and looked up to the sky and winds they dealt with every day, the Smiths were bent from digging underground, and blackened from the charcoal with which they smelted iron into steel. Men and women alike wore leather clothes tanned almost black, and most were marked by fire or tattooed by fragments of ash and molten metal. The Villagers traded with the Smiths for their iron and steel, but made a show of being sea-scrubbed clean by ostentatiously wiping their hands after each transaction. The Smiths accepted both the trading and the insults with stolid faces, but Astreya, who had snuck down to the shore out of curiosity, could see that their resentment closely resembled his own dislike of being singled out for teasing.

"So, 'Streya, your folks are here!" said one of the Village sailors in a heavy-handed attempt at wit, and soon the joke had been repeated over and over.

"You goin' back up country wi' yer family, 'Streya? Or are they glad to get rid o' yer?"

The question was offered in the presence of the Smiths themselves, as they set out their wares on the wharf where skippers and wives alike could barter rope, cloth and salt fish for knives, shackles, pots and rowlocks. The eldest of the visitors stared at him, grunted something nobody understood, and turned away.

"See, 'Streya? Nobody wants yer. Yer dirtier than a Smith!" shouted a red-haired boy of Astreya's age.

A handful of Village children picked up the chant, "Dirty Smith, dirty 'Streya, dirty Smith!" and pushed him towards three of the younger Smiths, who were boys on their first trip down from the mountains. They promptly pushed back, sending Astreya reeling back and forth from one group to the other until he had fallen and picked himself up several times. Eventually, parents on both sides ordered all of them to stop, more out of annoyance than compassion.

When Astreya came home dirty and bruised, Alana was not convinced by his reply, "It was just a game." When she pressed him for more details, something in Astreya would not let him complain. When she cautioned him against fighting, he took the advice to heart, and determined that he would not to react to taunting. But in the months and years that followed, whenever the slights and insults focused on her, it was too much for words or even silences, and he threw himself at even the largest of his tormentors. Time and again he returned with grazes, cuts, dirty clothes and the same excuse in which neither of them believed.

When Scarm saw that Astreya was being constantly bullied, he first tried to remonstrate with the mothers and fathers of the boys who were making the boy's life miserable. When this proved ineffective, he realized that in saving Astreya the father, he had also incurred a duty towards Astreya the son. Scarm knew that to intervene directly would lead to more bullying as soon as he was out of sight, so he looked for another way, and found one that solved a problem of his own. Scarm's injured arm had worsened with the years until it kept him from pulling his weight at sea. Determined to be useful, he began the task of teaching the Village lads and girls how to read a little, to write at least their names, and to count enough to reckon the day's catch (if boys) and the tally of a knitted row (if girls).

As he warmed to his self-appointed task, Scarm found that Astreya thought differently from the other children. He had been conceived, born and raised apart from the community, but there was more than just the sum of these differences that distinguished him from those of his own age. Scarm saw curiosity and intelligence on the first day of school, but when the first class was over, he looked out his window and saw a circle of boys teasing Astreya, who struggled to follow his mother's wish that he refrain from fighting.

"Don't your ma make you wash your hair?"

Knowing that any answer would make them laugh, Astreya compressed his lips and said nothing, which made them sure that he thought them stupid, which made them resentful. They soon tired of repeating the question and found another.

"Wi' eyes like yours, does everything look green to you?"

Scarm recognized Astreya's dilemma. As he watched unseen, Astreya did not reply, which meant that they laughed anyway. The more he avoided them, the more they persisted, and the more unpleasant grew the questions.

"You as ugly as your da?"

Astreya's face set into a scowl, and Scarm guessed what would happen next.

"Why'd your ma have a stranger's son? She stupid? Or weird? Or what?"

Then the fighting began. They took turns, but because Astreya was lean and light and outnumbered, he was the one who suffered most. He lost that day, but the next, Scarm supplemented Astreya's schooling with private instruction in wrestling blocks, holds and throws. Astreya was unexpectedly apt, learning how to use his skill and speed to overcome their strength. Perhaps because fighting distressed his mother, maybe out of something that he found in himself, Astreya perfected the art of inflicting a stalemate on his oppressors. As time went on, none of the Village boys was willing to try a fall with Astreya, because though he never won a wrestling bout, he also never lost. Something in his nature or upbringing kept him from triumphing over another person. The Villagers found this reticence beyond strange. They understood fights where one won and another lost; they had no words for a third outcome.

If Scarm spent more time with Astreya's education than with the other boys, it was not only out of a duty to the man he had saved, but also because the boy had a hunger to learn, the like of which seldom affected the youth of the Village. Astreya mastered the basic skills faster than the other young people of his age, and when they left Scarm's tutelage, all of them convinced that they were adequately schooled, Astreya was unsatisfied. He consumed the few texts from which he was taught, and when he asked for more, Scarm introduced him to his private hoard of books preserved from *Before*, cautioning him that some of the Villagers would burn them, as their grandfathers and great grandfathers had done. Astreya learned the clean logic of mathematics, but he was captivated by stories of brave men who had amazing adventures on land and sea, and who won the hearts of beautiful women.

The combination of logic and romance distanced Astreya from the young people of the Village and made him long for nameless places—*Elsewhere*, he called them, although he never used the word to anyone. *Elsewhere* for Astreya held exactly the opposite feelings that the Villagers attributed to *Before* and *Away*—those places and times about which their forefathers had deliberately forgotten. Astreya's *Elsewhere* was a land of heart's desire, all the more attractive for the fact that he knew in the logical part of his mind that its perfection could not possibly exist. Astreya knew that the tales from *Before* came from a time deliberately forgotten. He learned not to ask questions of Villagers who did not speak or think about a long past age when ships had traded all manner of things and ideas, and people had traveled to and from the Village. Scarm let Astreya discover that long ago, the Villagers had rejected the outside world, thrown away everything that reminded them of it and thereby frozen themselves in time, along with their descendants. Astreya tried to understand what Scarm told him of their anger at being abandoned, but he tempered his criticisms when Scarm spoke of the way that the Villagers' ignorance and superstition were balanced by their courage, loyalty and steadfastness. When Astreya turned his attention to *Away*, asking Scarm about what was over the horizon, in particular where his father had come from, the old man was less helpful, both because he knew so little, and also because he was not sure about the truth of what Astreya's father had told him.

Neither Alana nor Scarm could or would answer Astreya's questions about the world beyond the horizon from which his father had come. As he grew, he still respected both of them, but he also became aggrieved at their reticence.

When it began to matter to Astreya that girls were different from boys by more than the length of their hair and the fact that they wore skirts instead of breeks, shepherds visited the Village. Each autumn for as long as he could remember, he had seen one or two men come down from the mountains carrying bales of wool on their shoulders to sell to the Village women. This time, a group of three, clearly a family, arrived at Alana's door early one morning when the wild geese were strung out across a windswept autumn sky. When Alana opened the door, Astreya stared at three faces he had never seen before, and they stared back. The man was stooped under a huge bale of wool, his face almost invisible under a shapeless leather hat. His wife beside him had a smaller load that allowed her to hold her head higher, showing a pleasant face darkened by wind, weather and travel. The face of the girl beside her caught and held Astreya's attention. Villagers' faces were oval, their heads roughly egg shaped, whereas hers was round, with a wide forehead and high cheek bones. She returned his stare out of large brown eyes that looked out between strands of dark travel-tangled hair held by a leather ribbon above her black eyebrows. As the focus of Astreya's eyes widened to take in the rest of her, he blushed to notice that the fastenings on her leather vest did not entirely close, revealing the hollow between her breasts.

"Lamb's wool for your spinning wheel," said the man, his voice slow and deep, like someone who spoke seldom.

"Enter, rest and we will speak of what we may exchange," said Alana politely.

The three looked first at her and then at each other, surprised by her hospitality, which was not what they had encountered from the other Villagers. The girl's brown eyes swiftly returned to Astreya. They all sat down at Alana's table and bargained her completed cloth garments for their raw wool.

The woman was entranced by the excellence of Alana's needlework, caressing the garments with her fingers as her man frowned lest her enthusiasm lessen his chances in the bargaining. Meanwhile, girl's eyes did not leave Astreya's face. Her lips were slightly parted, giving Astreya a glimpse of white teeth and the tip of her tongue.

When he asked whether her home was far from the Village, she nodded and went on staring at him. When he held the plate of Alana's cookies towards her, she solemnly took one and ate it, still regarding him without changing her expression. Unnerved by this attention, Astreya could think of nothing to say, so he sat, uncomfortably stealing glances at her, unable to wrench his attention away.

At last the bargaining was over. Alana shook hands with the shepherd and they parted, he with a handful of coins, his wife with a blouse and a skirt. Both she and the couple smiled their satisfaction. The girl and Astreya continued to stare at each other until the three shepherds took up their packs and went on down the path to try their luck in the rest of the Village, leaving Alana and Astreya with a pile of wool to sort, wash and dry.

Unnoticed by Astreya, Alana had seen how the girl's eyes had locked onto his, and she sadly recognized that she would no longer be the only female presence in his life. That she had long known this would happen someday did not make the end of Astreya's childhood any easier for her to bear.

For the rest of that day and for many after it, Astreya's thoughts were in turmoil whenever he thought of the girl. Even though he had seen her for only a few short moments, he had been ready to go with the girl to the mountains, to the place where the outcasts lived, shunned by the Village. He was shocked by the impulse, because it would have meant the end of his hopes to sail with the Village fleet. As time went by, he no longer was disturbed by his moment of irrationality. However, out of the encounter came a resolution that none of the Village girls would ever steal away his ability to think, as had the nameless girl from the high country. But he still cherished the memory of when their stares had gone far beyond mere looking, and from then on he no longer cared so much about being excluded from the community in which he lived. He had a conviction that even if there was no real *Elsewhere*, he would someday find his own *Somewhere*, and perhaps someone who would understand.

Eventually the Village boys' voices deepened, and hair grew on their cheeks and chins. Astreya had learned to jig for squid, cut bait, salt and dry the catch, row or sail a dory and tend main and jib sheets aboard a Village fishing boat as handily as the boys of his own age. He had also learned how to work with them, despite their ridicule and derision. Though he hated being called "Blackhead," "Outsider," or "Stranger," he also felt a fierce pride in being his own self—whatever they thought and said. He had grown up among the Villagers, but he was not one of them, and everyone knew it.

Chapter 1:

In Which Astreya Fights with Yan, and Alana Passes on a Gift

The young men of the Village pushed and shoved Astreya along the shoreline between outcroppings of rock at the sea's edge, and then into a little bay below the cliffs, where he could not escape. When they had formed a circle around him, Yan, the chief tormentor, shouldered his way into the wild-eyed ring. He was a heavyset, powerful looking boy with shoulders that began just below his earlobes. Solid muscles strained his shirt sleeves, and his thick forearms ended in stubby-fingered hands. His reddish hair grew almost down to his eyebrows, his youthful beard was patchy, and he breathed with his mouth half open, revealing widely spaced teeth. Astreya was as slim as Yan was bulky, dark as he was fair. He stood almost casually, but beneath the pose, he was as tight as coiled spring.

Yan lumbered forward; Astreya dodged, caught a big upraised arm, pivoted, pulled and stepped back. Yan fell face forward, and the ring of youths distorted into an oval. Yan scrambled to his feet, spitting sand.

"Fight like a man!" Yan shouted.

"Sure," replied Astreya. "If you can find me one. You're nothing but a boy."

He stuck out his chin and stroked his hand over his short, black beard, mocking Yan's pale tufts of facial hair. Yan growled wordlessly. Someone shoved at Astreya's back, but instead of falling, Astreya dived, rolled on his shoulder and came up face to face with Yan, so close that neither could hit the other.

"Where d'ya learn to do that?"

"Scarm."

"What kind of wrestlin' do you learn from a one-armed man? Hey, little Blackhead goody-goody? Spend a lot of time with Scarm do ya? Readin' stuff? An' what else do you do?"

"He's twice the man you are, with spare parts left over."

"Oh, he is, is he? So and how do you know? And what's he been teaching you about? *Before* stuff, that nobody cares codswallop to know? Tell me, Blackhead, what are you readin' about now?"

"Triangles," said Astreya. "Square corner triangles, and how their sides always work out to be three, four and five."

Yan paused just an instant too long before forcing a laugh.

"Some good that'll do ya. Tryin' to make yourself special. Well, Blackhead, you are special. Special strange. Son of a... a... stranger. Spendin' time with that crazy old one-armed man Scarm who's lost his grip." Yan paused. "One-armed man who's lost his grip. Hey, that's good, ain't it?"

Some of the boys laughed, whether they got the point or not.

"Very good, Yan. Very funny. A joke. And you got a laugh. Beginner's luck."

Yan fell back a step, half crouched, and readied himself to grab for the first hold.

"Yan," said Astreya, "this is stupid. Let's all go home."

"Are you calling me stupid?"

Astreya shrugged. Yan lunged forward to grab him in a bear hug, but Astreya dropped, crouched, and kicked at the back of Yan's knee, felling the big lad to the sand. Red-faced under his ginger hair, Yan scrambled to his feet again and aimed a roundhouse swing at Astreya's head. Astreya ducked and circled to his left, glancing over his shoulder for a weak spot in the ring of clasped hands.

"You—you stranger. You got no business speaking to my girl."

"That's her business, not yours."

"She's mine. And you're not going to steal her."

"I wouldn't want to."

Rob, a wide shouldered, long-armed boy just coming into his man's strength, grabbed Astreya from behind, pinning his arms.

"Yan, you goin' t'let this black-haired stranger mess with our girls?"

Yan glared at Astreya from under his thatch of unruly hair. Astreya slid down out of the hold, but two other young men snatched at his arms and hauled them in opposite directions. Astreya tried to brace on one and kick the other, but before he could do so, Yan charged head down into his unprotected middle, doubling him over. Astreya fell face down into the sand, gasping for breath, taking his two captors with him. Two more joined in to help, and a milling, grunting, sweat-and-sand-streaked pile held Astreya spreadeagled on the black sand beach.

"Turn him over!"

They tried to follow Yan's order, but Astreya kicked and struggled, knocking two back on their heels. But the two who held his arms did not let go. Astreya spat sand, some of which reached Yan's face, redoubling his fury. However, the pack's enthusiasm was waning. All but Yan found the victory unsatisfactory, since it had been at the price of breaking the Village's code of one-on-one wrestling. Fights among both boys and men ended when one person was pinned. There was no wounding or killing, because there never had been.

"That's enough, eh?" said Cam, the smallest of the group, who had been pushed aside early in the struggle. His mouse-blond hair stuck to a cut over one eye, and his oversized jacket was torn, even though he had not come close to Astreya in the confusion of hands and feet.

No one heeded, although Yan felt his followers' eyes on him. He shook his head, sweat flipping off the ends of his hair. His mind slipped to the work of killing fish, chickens, rabbits and sheep—the business necessary to eating and living in the world they all shared. He picked up a stone and advanced on Astreya, a matter-of-fact purpose in his eyes.

"Hold it," he said.

Indecision froze the minds of Astreya's captors as they saw the upraised stone, and they loosened their grip. Astreya squirmed convulsively, broke free, scrambled to his feet, stumbled backward and stood with his shoulders against the cliff that loomed above the tiny beach.

Yan advanced on Astreya like a sleepwalker, shrugging off Cam, who was too small and light to restrain him. His big, work-hardened fist came up. For an instant, all of Astreya's swiftness and agility ebbed out of him.

"Duck!" Cam screamed, breaking the spell.

Astreya saw Yan's hand tighten on the jagged stone, saw its sharp edges, saw the clumsy weapon coming at him, saw the ring of aghast faces, saw the encroaching sea behind them, saw the stone again, and knew he had ample time to sidestep before the stone smacked on the cliff close to his ear, crumbling in Yan's hand. The sound snapped the murderous sequence of events, leaving all them at a loss. Six attackers faced Astreya, unsure what to do next. Yan sucked split finger ends. Astreya scanned past faces as expressionless as if they had all been fresh woken from sleep.

"Take a look behind you," said Astreya calmly.

The incoming sea had more than halved the beach. Waves foamed over black, jagged rock on either side of the little bay.

Their footprints had vanished, and the marks of the scuffle were being eaten away by successive waves. They stared at the water in a horrified fascination, realized their peril, and shrank back beside Astreya, their backs joining his against the cliff.

"We can still make it back around the point," said Yan.

"In a goat's arse," said Astreya. "You'll be dragged out to sea with the first wave."

"We're going to be in deep, and soon," said Cam.

"We'll have to climb out," said Astreya.

The sea hissed on the sand as each wave pulled back from an ever higher watermark. The undertow rattled pebbles where they had walked dry shod.

Astreya alone was not hypnotized by the steadily approaching sea. While the others stared blankly, he turned towards the cliff.

"This way," he said, looking up at a crack in the black cliff. Above their heads, the crack opened to a fissure and then to a chimney that led up to where the roots of a pine tree knuckled over the cliff edge far above them, but the rock where he touched was slicked with green slime, and his fingers could not find a hold.

"You can't get up that," said Cam. "Nobody can. We're done for."

"No we're not," said Astreya. "Take off your belts and buckle them together," said Astreya. "Then lift me up. I'm tallest and lightest."

"He'll just get up there and leave us," said Yan.

"Don't be stupid," said Astreya. "It's the only way."

"Don't call me stupid!" Yan shouted.

"Well, don't say stupid things," said Astreya.

Something in his voice cut through their fear and indecision, and they did as they were told, even though under different circumstances, they might have sided with Yan, ignored Astreya, or told him in a few crude words not to think himself better than them.

"Right," said Astreya, as the sea herded them closer. "We need three to stand here against the rock and bend over. Cam, you're light, you can climb on their backs. Now if everyone braces against the cliff..."

"Rob and Yan, you're strongest," said Cam, who had seen what was to be done. "You be the bottom row." He clutched at the waistband of his breeks as they threatened to slip off his hips now that his belt was gone.

Yan placed his hands on the cliff, his head down, his mind confused by the succession of sudden changes. Blood dripped from his fingers onto the sand at his feet. Rob put his shoulder to Yan's hip, and Cam struggled up Rob's back onto Yan's shoulders. Then Astreya clambered up the clumsy human ladder. Cam's canvas jacket ripped again as Astreya got first one knee and then the other onto his shoulders. Steadying himself against the cliff, he stood and reached beyond the sea-slick rock to the first possible handholds of strong, dry stone. At that moment, the improvised stack of bodies disintegrated, and all but Astreya tumbled in a heap onto the sand below. For a moment, he dangled from his hands. He scrabbled with his feet and pulled mightily. First his forearm, then his chest and finally a knee made it to the first ledge in the widening cleft. He clung panting to the rock, felt his heartbeat pound in his throat, and momentarily was unable to move. Then as his breathing steadied, he recovered his calm. He looked up at the rocky scramble to the cliff top, and Yan's words came back to him. It would be easy to continue on up the cliff, leaving the others behind. He hesitated only for an instant, and then bracing his shoulders on one side of the crack, he planted his feet on the other, and unwound the rope of belts from his waist. He lowered one end down to the upturned faces below.

"Yan first, then Rob," he shouted, taking a turn of the belts around a spur of rock.

They all saw what had to be done.

"Good idea, 'Streya," said Cam. "We can do it."

Yan took hold of the dangling belts and scrambled hand over hand up the slick rock to the foot and handholds that began where Astreya braced himself. Avoiding Astreya's eyes as he clambered over him, Yan climbed up the widening gully. Sand and small stones rattled down on Astreya, bouncing off his shoulders and stinging the back of his neck.

One after the other, the rest half climbed, half hauled themselves up the cliff face. Without the improvised rope, they would not have been able to scale the water-polished, seaweed-slick stone, and every one of them knew it. They stared up at Astreya, climbed towards him, looked into his grey-green eyes, took his hand and accepted his help into the chimney of dry, firm rock, where climbing was easy.

Eventually they all stood at the cliff top, looking down on Astreya's head and shoulders as he scrambled up towards them. With sidelong glances at each other, and no words said, they collected their belts and set off for their homes. Cam was last to leave. He stood, fitting his belt back into his oversized breeks, looking quizzically at Astreya with his head on one side.

"'Streya, how did you do that?"

"What?"

"Why ain't you dead with a rock in your head?"

"I... uh... just was quicker than he was, I guess."

"Quicker? One moment you was a goner. Next moment, you're an arm's length away, Yan hit the cliff, and you were tellin' us what to do, like you were sayin' that the sun comes up in the morning."

Astreya could not explain, even to himself, how time had slowed for him, bringing with it complete confidence.

"Yan ain't goin' to say it, fer sure," said Cam with a grin, "so thanks for saving our lives."

Before Astreya could reply, Cam turned and walked away, his shapeless, torn jacket pulled around him. Astreya took a step back to the cliff edge, knelt, and looked past the grass they had crushed at its lip, down the steep gully to the water-darkened rock where the sea heaved and fell. Down there on the beach that was now under water, he had experienced something he had never felt before, and did not fully comprehend. He was proud that his strategy had worked, that he had organized and led young men who moments before had been ready to see him humiliated. But there was something more: for a moment, he could have left them all to drown. The realization made him giddy, as if at the last moment he had pulled back from stepping off the cliff top. Slowly, Astreya turned and headed towards his home.

* * * * *

As the last light faded above the rocky western ridge high above the Village, Astreya opened the door of his home. When Alana raised her head and turned towards the door, her white hair, loose for the night, flared in a candlelit blur. Her quick glance took in his ripped and dirt-caked clothes, and then the cut knuckles on the hand with which he tried to hide a bruised cheek. Silently, she pointed to a chair beside the table, and bent to scoop a bowl full of warm water from the iron pot above the fire. Astreya tried not to wince as she sponged dirt and dried blood from his face, forearms and hands. To avoid her eyes, he watched her shadow on the whitewashed walls. Eventually, when she had finished tending his cuts, he answered the question her silence had been asking.

"It was all because I drew a picture of Tina, and Yan saw it."

"Was it a good picture?"

"Well, you could see it was her. I caught the way she looks a little to one side, so she seems to be sweet on you, but it's really because she doesn't hear all that well."

"I didn't know that."

"You have to watch closely, just like she does to see people's lips."

"And you've been watching her?

"Only to draw her."

"Which you did today."

"Yeah. Down where they're preparing the boats for the season. She was sitting on the wharf, and I had my drawing stuff with me, and, well, it seemed like a good idea at the time. But Yan came up behind me and saw."

"And then?"

"He said it was stealing, and that she was his. And then I said something I shouldn't have."

"Yes?"

"I told him he was an idiot who didn't own anybody, least of all Tina."

"He was angry."

"Oh yes. He wouldn't take a run at me, because, well, I've stymied him before, and he didn't want to take the chance in front of her."

"And Tina?"

"She's the same as the rest of the girls. She knows that a man should be fair-haired, big-jawed and blue-eyed. I'm the green-eyed Blackhead with the dark curly beard. I'm a stranger."

When Astreya almost spat the words he hated, Alana spoke to move the story forward.

"So what did Yan do?"

"He got a few of the other fellows together. They followed me. I thought I'd lost them by going around the headland at low tide. My mistake. They caught me."

"And then?"

"We tussled a bit, and then we all got caught by the tide, and we had to climb up the cliff."

There was a long pause, as both of them contemplated what Astreya had not said.

"Stupid pictures. I never should have started. Now everybody knows I draw things."

"Secrets have a habit of getting out."

"Like Scarm teaching me to wrestle."

"You should call him Ian."

"Everyone calls him Scarm. He doesn't mind."

"He's been good to you. You should show him respect."

"Mother, I do. The last time I came home like this, it was a long time ago, and I was a lot younger. You remember, because you cleaned me up, just the way you're doing now. Next day, Scarm took me aside and showed me a few moves."

"Did you thank him?"

"Of course. And for the other stuff he taught me."

"The other stuff?"

"You know, the ciphering, the triangles, the puzzles, the stories. He said my... my father... would have wanted me to learn."

"So he would. Does anyone know he was teaching you?"

"I don't think so, leastways, not exactly. They know I've been into his books, but most of them can't read anything beyond a list of fish or their own names, so they don't know and don't care. Besides, Scarm keeps all but a few of his books secret, so nobody will know how many he has."

Alana looked into her son's eyes, and saw that there was no point in pressuring him further about the fight, or anything else he might have kept from her.

"Secrets," said Alana slowly. "I've kept too many from you."

"You've what? I thought I was the one who was keeping secrets..."

"You don't know enough about your father," she began.

She looked into Astreya's eyes for signs of rejection. Astreya stared back at her, noticing once again the contrast between her youthful face and the white hair that framed it.

"There's so much you don't know, Astreya, because I don't know, either. Or I'm not sure. I've never lied, but I have been keeping things from you. It's because I feared for you, what with people so unwilling to see what a good man he was. But it was wrong of me to hide your father from you—his strangeness, I mean."

The word hung between them, echoing the many times they had both heard it in the Village as an accusation and rebuke. This was why she had kept him to herself as much as possible when he was a baby and then a little boy, why she had tried to find ways of dissuading him from going to sea; and this was also why as he matured, they had slowly grown apart. They were both aware that over the most recent year or two, they had laughed together less often, and while they remained polite and even distantly affectionate, they were separated by Astreya's increasing need to become a man. Though they had not spoken of it, they both knew that a boy came of age in the Village when a skipper chose him as crew. The Villagers of his own age saw him as a stranger, he had responded by isolating himself, and this lessened his chances of being chosen, but he felt the need to go to sea, even though he knew that Alana dreaded the moment when he would sail onto the ocean that had taken his father's life. He was willing to be different, indeed, he took a perverse pleasure in it, but when Alana used the word "strange" of his father, a sudden anger hardened his voice.

"Strange, Mother? Foreign? Different? How strange? I don't think of my father as strange. Scarm doesn't think he was strange. Scarm always tries to get my—his—our—name right. If it wasn't for him—and you too, Mother—I wouldn't be able to read. I wouldn't have learned stuff people knew *Before* or..." he stopped as he saw the expression on her face, understanding for the first time that even to his mother Alana, he, too, was strange.

They stared at each other as if a cold wind had suddenly blown them apart. Alana deliberately stood up, went into her room and returned with the leather bound box that her husband had made. She put her hand on its domed top, and turned towards her son.

"I gave you some of what is in here, when you were younger. You've seen the pictures he made. I think maybe you started drawing because of them. Now...."

She undid the clasp, lifted the lid and stood aside, her head erect and her voice firm.

"You must follow your own way, my son," she said. "I cannot walk it for you. Forgive me if I have ever tried to hold your father's memory from you more than I should have, but... but I was not sure what to tell you. Some of what he said was beyond me. Some things didn't make sense. I couldn't explain them to you, because I didn't understand them myself."

Astreya took a pace towards the box, and then looked down at his mother, very conscious that he overtopped her height by more than a hand span. She drew Astreya to her for brief hug, and then deliberately released him. Blinking away tears, she busied herself with banking up the fire for the night. When she stood to go to her room, he was kneeling in front of the box, turning through bundles of bark and paper tied together with strands of wool that had not been undone in his lifetime. Silently, Alana moved out of the candlelight and went to her room, leaving Astreya alone, poring over the clues to his father's life.

That night, Astreya slept little, and so also the next. He already knew the plain words his father had written to help Alana learn to read and write, and which she had in turn used to encourage him when he first began his schooling. But what he read now was different, disordered and confusing. He had hoped to learn more about his father, but he was baffled by enigmatic references to a seafaring life unlike anything the Village could offer. There were pages of perplexing drawings marked only with symbols and numbers, interspersed with diagrams, some of them composed of interlocked triangles. They were bewilderingly unlike the triangles Scarm had shown him how to solve, first as mental exercise, then as a way of drawing charts. And then there were sketches of tall-sailed boats with many masts, the like of which Astreya had never seen or imagined. And then there were columns of figures interspersed with letters. And more inscrutable symbols. And always the sea was behind it all.

At the bottom of the chest, Astreya found a little leather bag and a small notebook. He emptied the bag onto the table, revealing about a dozen greenish pebbles, each about the size of the last joint of his little finger, and two larger stones, about the size and shape of an onion. He frowned as he examined them carefully, because he could see nothing that distinguished them from any handful of river stones. After a few moments, he put them back in the bag and dropped it into the chest.

The notebook was more promising. It had been made to be carried in a pocket, and it appeared to distill the cryptic notes that made up most of the writing in the trunk. Most of the pages were empty; many held sketches of boats, some of them with details of standing and running rigging unlike anything used by the Village fleet. Several pages reminded Astreya of the glimpses he had seen of Scarm's Born and Buried book, because they appeared to use the same shorthand or code, interspersed occasionally with the name of some important member of a Village family. He recognized one page as a map of the Village, the fjord and its seaward approaches. The last page held words that Astreya first thought might be part of a song.

Hand of gian far draws on shore
Star sets in song where stones roll in the tide
Son of or on plots a course to the city of the sea
Where dim clasps light no stones

The words were written in letters that had been gone over and over, as if the writer had wanted to carve them into the page. What his father had meant was not clear at all. Unlike the rest of the book, where words were complete though often obscure, this cryptic message was confused and apparently misspelled. He wondered if the third word lacked a "t," making the word into "giant"—but that made little more sense. The words were legible, but seemingly pointless. A star setting in the sea was possible, but in a song? Son of whom? Had he meant to write "off"? What was meant by "or on"? In which case, how could someone be a son 'off or on'? Had his father meant to write 'one' rather than 'on?' Had he just been a careless speller? Where and what was the city of the sea? Were there words missing in the last line? What was a dim, and how could it clasp light? The meaning of the riddle—if that was what it was—eluded him. He showed the verse to Alana, but she only shook her head.

The book fascinated Astreya, no page more than this one. Night by night, he pored over the legacy of words and drawings, and as he did so, Astreya grew subtly older and more distant in Alana's eyes. Although the moment of his parting from her hung ever heavier over both of them, neither could speak of it.

While the spring moon filled, they lived in growing discomfort. Each day, Astreya was part of the Village's preparations for the fishing season, and each night he sat silent, sometimes thinking, sometimes reading what his father had written, while his mother attended to her stitching, more often than not with the needle idle in her hands. When Astreya glanced up, feeling her eyes upon him, she turned her head away from the beeswax candle so that her face was shadowed. He returned to his reading, wondering whether all she saw in him was an echo of the man she had married but never fully understood.

CHAPTER 2:

IN WHICH ROARING JACK DISCOVERS A USE FOR ASTREYA'S TALENT

That same spring, there were other Villagers with decisions to make. The skippers of the Village's boats had to choose from among a dozen young men who would permanently join their crews. All had gone through their boyhoods learning to row and sail small craft in the fjords, fishing for and cutting bait, setting lobster pots, cleaning and drying the catch, as well as all the tasks of sailing and maintaining the seagoing boats. They had also been beyond the headlands for day trips when the winds were set fair, but now that their apprenticeship was over, they would join a boat and sail in all weathers, sharing the fate and fortune of their crew mates. The skippers took this task very seriously: they needed to balance their crews with respect to size, strength, skill and experience; they also had to take into consideration the intertwined families and the relationships among them. This was a political as well as a practical choice, and one that weighed on their minds as the day of choosing came closer.

Foremost of these was Roaring Jack, the skipper of the boat that had rescued Astreya's father. He was a broad-shouldered, red-bearded man, and a Village byword for luck and shouting. Like many big-voiced men, he could never be persuaded that he was noisy. He thought of himself as a soft spoken, quiet-loving soul, as he often told his family, in a voice that could be heard across the Village. People who would have feared violence from any other skipper who raised his voice so much and so often merely laughed and said, "There's Jack again, loud as ever."

After a particularly noisy morning that came at the end of an earsplitting winter, Roaring Jack climbed the southern headland, looking for peace and quiet, with only his big black dog, Skip, for company. Below in the Village, the other skippers were supervising preparations for the beginning of the new season's fishing—a task he had delegated. In a few hours, they would meet to choose the young men who would join their crews.

Reaching a little meadow at the cliff top where the sea winds blew everything except grass and a few sturdy crocuses out of the ground, Roaring Jack took off his jacket and sat on in it in the warm spring sunshine, where he was protected from the wind as it bowled over the cliff top in an invisible wave. He sighed, lay back, pillowed his head on a tuffet and closed his eyes. The grass was soft and springy, the creaking cry of the gulls overhead reminded him of the wind in his boat's rigging, the sea swished and grumbled at the foot of the cliff. First, he mused about how he would complete the crew he would soon be naming, then he yawned, and, lulled by the sounds around him, he slept.

Skip stood, nose to the wind, assessing the mix of sea and shore smells. Then he sat beside his master for a little while, until a scent, or perhaps the memory of one drew him to his feet and on down the zigzag path to where small brown furry creatures made their homes among scrubby pines and long grasses.

On his way down, he met Astreya going up, and they greeted each other with enthusiasm. Roaring Jack's big, black, curly-haired dog had been Astreya's companion since they had romped together as puppy and child. Their relationship was equal: neither owned the other, both enjoyed each others' company. So when Astreya's face had been slapped with a long, wet tongue, and Skip's ears ruffled and chin scratched, they both went on their separate ways.

Roaring Jack was asleep when Astreya arrived at the cliff top. He had brought with him some sheets of birch bark, stripped from logs destined for his mother's fire, and a handful of twigs he had carefully burnt to charcoal around her pots and kettles. It had been his intention to draw the gulls as they flew and hovered in the updraft of wind at the cliff's edge. He had seen a sketch of a pair of gulls in his father's little book, and it seemed reasonable to attempt the same task on the chance that it might give some insight into the indecipherable rest of the page. Besides, the climb away from the Village was Astreya's way of forgetting that tomorrow was the day when the skippers would announce their choices. Those chosen became men, those left behind stayed boys. Astreya knew he was neither popular among his peers nor well connected in the intricate web of families. Like some of the youths who had been with him on the beach, Astreya already had a short beard, but where the others' cheeks and chins sported blond or reddish hair, Astreya's black beard made him seem closer in age to the bearded men of the Village. If he were left on shore with the boys, he would be a painfully obvious failure. Astreya sketched so that he would not despair.

Astreya had made pictures when he could barely walk. Instead of spanking him for his first messy attempts executed in milk on the table, porridge on the floor and mud on the walls, Alana had encouraged him by offering different materials. His skills had grown with him. Perhaps because she enjoyed his pictures, perhaps because they both knew that the Villagers would not, Astreya's drawing had remained a secret between them until the fight with Yan started the rumor that Astreya had strange and worrying talents.

The Villagers were not enthusiastic about impractical pursuits—save for singing or playing the fiddle or flute, which had established places in their lives. Music was an entertainment in which everyone could join, if only by clapping hands and stamping feet. Scratching at birch bark with burned sticks was a solitary act, and thus suspect.

Few of Villagers saw the world as did Astreya. Most would have thought it more than half-crazed to climb onto the cliff tops to draw the image of a gull. For them, gulls were gulls. They picked up scraps when the catch was cleaned, soared and wove overhead before the weather changed for the worse, and served as guides to where schools of fish fed close to the surface. They had value only for these reasons, and were not a subject for further speculation.

Astreya saw gulls differently. For him, they spoke of freedom from the daily world of chores, duties and routine. Their flight drew him out of himself: he loved to watch them hang on the wind, soar around the cliffs or settle deftly on a stone. He had tried in the past to catch the sense of adventure they gave him, but the image had so far eluded him.

Astreya forgot seagulls when he noticed Roaring Jack. Seeing an unconscious model, Astreya immediately began to draw the bearded, bushy-browed skipper, his mouth partly open and his face relaxed in sleep. Working quickly, Astreya captured the determined set of Roaring Jack's jaw beneath a beard that erupted from his face, covering everything below his tanned nose and cheeks. Fine lines etched the corners of his eyes; a deep frowning notch above his nose splayed out into long valleys across his brow, but behind the exuberant beard and mustache was a mouth that could laugh as well as shout. Astreya crouched in the grasses out of the wind, his charcoal stick wriggling across the birch bark as he sketched with absolute concentration.

For a while, Astreya drew while Roaring Jack slept. Then when Astreya was drawing wrinkles around the skipper's eyes caused by squinting against harsh light, and tracing the lines etched by wind and weather, he glanced up from his drawing and stared into a single blue and wide awake eye. An eyebrow like a frayed paintbrush wagged up and the second steely blue eye opened as Roaring Jack frowned back into Astreya's green-eyed stare. Neither spoke.

Astreya was aghast at the situation into which he had placed himself. He knew full well that no skipper ever attained or kept command by being inattentive, and he guessed that even asleep, Roaring Jack must have heard a sound that had not been present when he had settled into the comfortable grasses. Then he had probably listened with his eyes shut at first, considering what to do when he decided to move with all the skill and speed necessary to trim a sail or tend the tiller.

At the same moment, Roaring Jack sat up and Astreya stood, shuffling his sheets of bark to conceal what he had been doing.

"Let me see the marks you've made, boy," said Roaring Jack in what for him was almost a whisper. "After all, if they're about me, Oi deserve to see 'em."

Astreya neither jumped nor shrank away, as people tended to do when assaulted by Roaring Jack's voice at close range. Astreya held out the sketch he had made. Roaring Jack took the bark in one big hand and examined it, the other hand absently stroking his red beard.

"So... that's me, is it?"

"I think so," answered Astreya.

The skipper's eyebrows almost met in a single bushy frown as he sat holding the birch bark. Now his left eye squinted and his right eyebrow rose. His free hand tugged at his beard as if to tear it out for inspection.

"Would m'wife see me in these markings?"

Astreya nodded.

"You're sure of yourself, m'lad," said Roaring Jack grimly. Scowling even more ferociously, he added, "Oi like that."

There did not seem to be anything he could say in reply, so Astreya stood silent. Suddenly the big man's mouth twisted below his luxuriant beard and mustache and his blue eyes opened wide. Astreya watched this transformation with growing alarm, wondering whether the skipper was about to throw a fit.

"Can y' draw things as well as faces?"

Astreya nodded.

"Do it. Show me the north head," ordered the skipper, waving a big arm at the cliffs and rocks on the other side of the gap between the headlands.

Closely watched by Roaring Jack, Astreya knelt, took a fresh sheet of birch bark and a new twig of charcoal, and went to work without a word. In a few quick strokes, he caught the outlines of the cliff, the rocky shore, the frieze of trees along the cliff tops, and the occasional pine that reared its head above the others to be bent by onshore winds. Then he added the fallen crags at the foot of the cliffs, where waves broke into spray. Soon, he was finished. His only thought was that he was spending a fine piece of birch bark on a subject that held no challenge for him.

Roaring Jack started to mutter as the first strokes caught the broad outlines. By the time Astreya was putting in final touches, such as the clouds and the set of the sea's eddies around rocks, the big man was stamping up and down, rumbling incomprehensibly to himself. Astreya held out the sketch for inspection. For a moment, it seemed that Roaring Jack would crush the fragile bark in his enthusiasm, but his big, sandy-haired fingers closed gently. He held it carefully at arm's length, sucked in his cheeks and snorted a couple of times before he knelt to put the bark on the springy grass so that he could follow the details of the sketch with a stubby forefinger. The wrinkles around his eyes puckered as he stared into the distance, then smoothed as he examined the drawing. Suddenly, he gripped Astreya uncomfortably close to his neck. The skipper's fingers dug in, yanking him painfully to his feet. Astreya felt a momentary stab of fear, but did not pull away.

Roaring Jack started to pace again, apparently forgetting that he still held on to Astreya. Perforce, Astreya walked with him, trying to match his strides. Back and forth on the tiny cliff top meadow the powerful, red-bearded man and the slim, black-haired youth marched and countermarched while Roaring Jack rumbled to himself. After a grumble of indistinguishable words, the skipper spoke at full volume.

"Now if only the boy could read and cipher as well as make his markings..."

Seagulls swirled overhead, tilting their heads to locate the sound.

"But I can..." began Astreya.

"If he could read and cipher—and a whole lot better than those young louts who can barely scrawl their names, then he's the one who can mark down me landfalls south'ards, so's I can find me way back, and...." He stopped, swung Astreya around to face him, and glared into his face. "What did you say, lad?"

"I can read and cipher. My mother got me started, and Scarm taught me from his books."

The sheets of birch bark fell from Astreya's hand. He had broken a promise to Scarm not to reveal the old sailor's private stock of books.

"You'd not be lyin'..." Roaring Jack began. "No. Alana's boy would tell the truth. Where did she find the art to teach you?"

"My father taught her," said Astreya. "We have my father's writings," he added hoping his lapse about Scar Arm Ian had not been noticed.

Roaring Jack nodded. "Oi mind now how the Stranger had a passion for anything wi' writing on it."

The skipper's free hand closed on Astreya's other shoulder. The skipper's mane of red hair shook in the wind, and words thundered out of him.

"You come with me, m'lad, we'll find a way south, and mark it down so's we can find our way north again. The last easterly of winter has come and gone, so we can hope for a fair passage south with a nor'west wind on the quarter, an' wi' luck, a sou'westerly to help us follow the fish back. We'll see if me old grandfer was ravin' in his dotage, or if the old squid jigger did see knives that don't rust and sails that always find a wind. He sailed south with his grandfer. He was nothin' but a boy then, and he never went again, nor said much about it, neither. Not a soul's taken the chance since. But I'll show them. They'll niver question me seamanship ever agin."

The big skipper searched Astreya's face for signs of fear, but the boy's grey-green eyes were lit with delight. This was his chance to find out where books came from, why no one would speak of anything beyond or before the Village, and most of all, what his father had meant by the enigmatic notebook. Amazingly, the very thing that marked him as different from the other young men was now an advantage, and a route to the understanding he craved. Astreya had hoped to go to the fishing grounds, because that was what everyone but Alana expected him to do. But he also wanted more. The things that made him different—his father, his mother's teaching, his newfound heritage—all told him that he should become more than a fisherman.

Amid all these swirling thoughts, he did not notice that Roaring Jack seemed to believe that people were questioning his seamanship.

Astreya and Roaring Jack stared at each other, enthusiasm flowing between them, and then suddenly Roaring Jack let go in embarrassment. Skippers did not allow themselves to sparkle with the eagerness of young blood, still less show it to their crew. Roaring Jack's eyes narrowed as he examined Astreya for any sign of ridicule or amusement. Finding none, he moderated his voice to a conspiratorial bellow.

"Now, m'lad, not a word of this—'cept to your mother. She's got the right to know. Oi'll be over to talk with her tonight."

The wind picked up a curl of birch bark and tossed it against the skipper's leg.

"Drop me bare arsed in a barrel of barnacles, they're gettin' away!"

They both bent to retrieve it, and then as more sheets were plucked by a shift in the breeze, they snatched low and high until they had recovered almost all of them. Roaring Jack's thunderclap oath turned into a grateful sigh when realized that he still had Astreya's two most recent sketches. The drawings clasped in one hand, Roaring Jack led the way back down the path to the Village, his voice somewhat muffled by the trees.

"So... two new youngsters... an' Ian fer strength... an' Scarm fer brains, ter make five in all."

Astreya almost ran into the big man's back as Roaring Jack stopped dead on the steep path.

"Scarm'll go for it. Sure to. Oi'll lick out the bait bucket if he don't."

Then the skipper was on the move again, this time singing as he walked.

"Oh she was round in the counter and bluff in the bow,
So Oi hoisted my yard and Oi took her in tow..."

A stone clattered under Astreya's foot, Roaring Jack glanced behind him, chuckled, and turned his song first into a deep, rumbling hum, and then a whistle. The seagulls long forgotten, Astreya followed him down to the Village.

Chapter 3:

In which Astreya prepares, and the skippers choose their crews

That same evening, Roaring Jack arrived at Alana's cottage not long after supper. The cottage grew smaller as he entered, its cramped space reduced by the skipper's heavyset body and filled by his booming voice.

"'Streya, Oi need to speak to your mother. Go."

Unable to think of what to say, Astreya silently left the cottage. He paused a little way from the door, listening to Roaring Jack.

"Oi'm here askin' you to keep me a secret, leastways, 'til the choosin'. It's about a t'ing Oi've been thinkin', an' it's not what you'd call popular in the Village."

Astreya smiled, imagining the expression on Alana's face as she tried not to wince under the onslaught of sound that the skipper thought was an intimate whisper. It would not have been difficult to stay within earshot, but instead he walked up the path towards the forest. Only a few steps away, the village stream rushed around boulders and down little waterfalls. He climbed past the turning to the cemetery where during the past winter three more graves had been painfully dug in the frozen earth, and four new headstones raised. He turned away from the well worn path to the burial plots, and scrambled over roots and rocks to where he could take a last look at the Village before the trees closed around him. Sitting within the knees of an ancient pine tree's roots, he leaned against the trunk. Moments later, he was joined by Skip. The old dog curled up at his feet and sighed.

To the north, the fjord mirrored the darkening sky, glittering faintly as puffs of wind ruffled its surface. Eastwards, where the Village looked towards the headlands, Astreya could see long rolling waves rising and falling like the flanks of a huge creature breathing in and out. Farther away, lay the notch between the headlands, where waves clashed together, competing to enter the narrow gap. Between the cliff heads, blue-grey sea stretched to an indistinct horizon where sea and sky merged. Higher still, a few mackerel-back clouds pinked as the last sunlight shone on their undersides. As he watched, darkness first claimed the sea and then climbed steadily into the sky.

Astreya looked down on the Village. Candles broke the gloom in a few windows. Lanterns swayed in the masts of fishing boats where men and boys were still loading food, water and gear against the next day's departure. Astreya wondered whether he should be down there working on Roaring Jack's boat, *Mollie*, but then he misgave. He had not yet been officially chosen by Roaring Jack before the whole Village; indeed, his going was not yet even approved by his mother.

Astreya tried to understand how she felt about his going to sea, but instead wondered whether she understood what it meant to him. Surely, she knew that the Village required men to fish the ocean, whatever the risks. However, he knew that Alana had hated to see him leave the calm waters of the fjord when he, like all the other boys, spent the occasional fine day apprenticed to different boats of the fleet. Those were an introduction to the ocean on days when the fish were close and the winds gentle. The boys chosen to become men would have to cope with whatever the weather sent for as much as a week's journey to the

High Islands, where good fishing was almost certain. But what awaited Astreya might be different. Roaring Jack wanted to sail south in a voyage of exploration so outlandish that it had not been attempted for more than a long lifetime.

Astreya confided his worries in Skip, as he had done many times before, hardly aware that he spoke out loud.

"What is he telling Mother? And if he isn't talking about what he said to me, is there something else I should know?"

Skip thumped the ground with his black tail.

"And what will the Village think, Skip? They're not going to like it if the *Mollie* sails in search of adventure instead of fish. And maybe they're right. Roaring Jack's got something about him that's... well, it's a bit scary."

Again, Skip's tail acknowledged Astreya, but offered no help.

"Most of all, am I really going?"

The evening sky darkened, Astreya's mood with it. Soon he could barely see the big dog at his feet. He became increasingly sure that he would be stuck on shore, condemned to be the eldest boy not chosen to take a man's place. Then the door of Alana's cottage opened, casting a shaft of yellow light, which a moment later was blocked by Roaring Jack. Then the door closed and the skipper's lantern bobbed and flickered down the path to his own cottage.

Trusting that his feet would find his way in the dark, Astreya ran down to his home. He threw the door open and stood in the doorway for a clenched handful of heartbeats, unsure whether he was about to celebrate his luck or rail against the unfairness of it all. Alana stood beside a table on which she had placed a kitbag and a pile of clothing.

"Shut the door, Astreya."

He kicked at the door with his heel, unaware that he had slammed it in the dog's face. His mother moved swiftly towards him. Astreya saw her blue homespun skirt sway and her white hair gleam in the light, just before she pulled him to her in a short, hard hug.

"We've got some packing to do."

* * * * *

Later that night, Alana rolled up the last item—a newly knitted sweater—and put it into Astreya's kitbag. He turned his father's enigmatic little book over and over in his hands, as if understanding could flow in through his fingertips. He did not notice when Alana left the firelight, disappeared into her room, and then returned to where he sat at the candlelit table. When he looked up, Alana took the book from him, slid it into a leather wallet, and then put it in the inner pocket of his oiled sailcloth jacket. Then from the pocket of her apron, she brought out a knife in its sheath and gave it to Astreya.

"Your father's."

The handle of the knife stuck to the sharkskin sheath for a moment, since it had not been used since his father's death, but when Astreya drew it out, he saw that the blade was still bright and keen. At first glance, it looked new, but when Astreya held it in his hand and examined it closely, he detected faint marks left by a sharpening stone. The blade was only a little longer than his middle finger, and it was blunt at the tip, like all the sailors' knives Astreya had ever seen in the Village, but its bone handle and shiny pommel distinguished it from the workaday knives he was used to.

Then Alana pushed back her sleeve to reveal the silvery bracelet with a green stone that she had worn since her wedding. Astreya saw her lips compress as she twisted the shiny metal out of the depression it had made in her arm. She held it near the lantern on the table, turning it so he could see the green stone in its cage-like setting. Then she showed him the inside, where the metal was rubbed smooth and bright. Three words were delicately engraved.

"Follow your star," Astreya read.

Alana pushed up his shirtsleeve and clipped the bracelet to his left arm above the elbow. Then they both gasped in amazement as the green stone began to glow. A fine spear of light appeared at its center, the color of new grass in sunlight. Astreya pushed a questioning fingertip through the raised wires that guarded the stone, and jerked his hand away as if he had touched hot metal. The bracelet tingled on his arm, but in a moment, both the sudden pain in his finger and the irritation under the bracelet ceased. He thought to take the bracelet off, so that he could examine it more closely, but amazement turned to pride, and he let it be. Instead, he cupped his hand over the stone, expecting it to feel warmth, but the light that leaked between his fingers was cold.

"It was almost as bright as that, when your father recovered his strength, but then it faded after he gave it to me, and stayed that way, like it was when they rescued him from the sea," said Alana.

"Don't you want to keep it, mother?"

Astreya's heart was not in his politeness.

Alana shook her head. They both stared until she broke the spell by rolling down his shirtsleeve to cover the glowing stone.

"I've often wondered whether I should give it to you. But it's come back to life on your arm. It has to be yours."

Astreya was so entranced by the gift she had passed on to him from his father that he hardly felt her fingers touch his hair as she turned away towards her room.

Later that night, Astreya fell asleep, his arms folded across his chest. A gleam of light escaped between his fingers from the jewel under his right hand.

* * * * *

Before sunrise the next morning, as wisps of wind-combed cloud blew across the brightening horizon, Astreya and Alana descended the steep path to the water's edge. By the time they reached the Village wharf, sunlight was greening the tops of trees along the ridge above the Village. The Village was still in chilly shadow, as were nine boats, rafted in threes, side by side at the end of the wharf. The sturdy craft rose and fell to the waves, jostling together as if eager to be at sea. Early as it was, the open space between bait houses and the wharf edge was already filling with people. They stood in family groups, some large, some small, each clustered around a young man with a kitbag at his feet.

The spring morning brought a cool wind off the water, so most wore heavy woolen sweaters, and many had added an oiled canvas jacket. The young men all knew how to sail, and most of them had spent a day or more on each of the boats in the fleet so that the skippers could get the measure of their abilities. Now they awaited the skippers' choices, after which they would be known not only by their names, but also by the name of the boat to which they belonged.

The boys expecting their first voyage as men wore trousers that stopped well above the tops of their feet, the color of rich brown earth. Those on most of the men were faded to grey by salt and hard wear. Around the older men's eyes were lines carved by wind and weather. When they looked about them, they did so deliberately and with judgment. The young men scanned about them constantly, now looking at the skipper they hoped might choose them, then at each other, then at the girls of their own age, and when they thought nobody would notice, at their mothers.

The women's dresses were ankle-length, save for younger and bolder girls whose shins and calves caught the young men's eyes. Married women, their hair in coiled plaits around their heads, draped their shoulders with scarves dyed brown from onion skin, blue from larkspur and yellow from rose hips. Grandmothers wore their shawls over their heads. The few unmarried young women let their hair fall free, or plaited it into braids, as did Alana. The young women were conspicuously animated when they were near the unmarried sailors—the first-timers in particular. One or two even cast glances at Astreya, but none came near him. Astreya adopted the wooden expression he kept on his face when dealing with everyone except Alana and Scarm.

"Hey, 'Streya. You got a berth yet? Bet'cha thought I wouldn't."

Astreya swung around to see that Cam was behind him, his hands deep in the pockets of his frequently repaired jacket, pulling the ample garment around him. He looked up at Astreya through mouse-colored hair that all but obscured his blue eyes.

"I'm t'be aboard the *Ronnie B.* You could join us. We're all sons wi'out ma's, da's, wives or sweethearts. Silver Don's skipper, now that his uncle's no longer with us."

"Ah, thanks, Cam. I hope... that is... maybe the *Mollie* will take me, but..."

"Luck, 'Streya. If you're aboard Jack's boat, you may need it."

He disappeared into the crowd, leaving Astreya wondering whether he had heard encouragement or sympathy in Cam's voice. He slid his kitbag off his shoulder and leaned it against his leg. Skip sat down so close to him that he could feel the warmth of the big dog's body. Alana had stopped to speak with Roaring Jack's wife Mollie, for whom he had named his boat. Astreya stood alone at the edge of the growing crowd. Resolutely refusing to be embarrassed, he focused his attention on Roaring Jack's boat, hoping he might soon be aboard.

"Think you'll be picked, Blackhead?"

Astreya swung around to see Yan, a sneering grin on his freckled face.

"Lookin' at the *Mollie*, are ye? Fat chance, Blackhead. I's the b'y that sails her. Roaring Jack's me father's cousin. We're kin. No strangers aboard *Mollie*."

Astreya's heart sank, and with it, his view of the world. He found himself staring at Yan's bare feet.

"What you lookin' at, Blackhead?"

"Your dirty feet, Yan."

"An' look at ye in yer boots! Don't know nothin' do ye? There ain't never no boots aboard *Mollie*, Blackhead. Oi've been hardenin' me feet up for weeks now. Bet yers 'll be soft like a girl's. Well, at least yer ready in yer boots for carryin' your kit back up to yer mother's cottage."

"My feet are are just as ready for sea as yours, Yan, it's just that mine aren't as stinky."

Yan took a belligerent step forward, but stopped when Skip growled a warning. Stepping around the dog, Yan shouldered his kitbag so that the canvas sausage swung towards Astreya's head. Astreya ducked, and watched Yan swaggering off through the crowd to where his mother was cautioning his five-year-old brother not to fall off the wharf.

Astreya turned towards Alana as she acknowledged a wave from one of the other mothers. As he looked eastwards, Astreya blinked at the masts of the boats while a flare of light from the first rays of sun poured through the gap in the cliffs. Even though he had the best of the exchange of words, Yan's needling had made him unsure. He was suddenly sure that Roaring Jack would not pick him, and he would soon be facing the Villagers' laughter. Only because leaving would be as conspicuous as running away, he stood his ground, his eyes lowered, planning that as soon as the *Mollie*'s crew was named, he would take his kitbag and climb back up the path, on past his home, into the forest and beyond to the foothills where the outcasts and misfits tended sheep, only coming down once a year to sell wool to the Village women. For a moment, he was struck by a memory of dark, expressive eyes looking fixedly at him. He shook his head.

"Roight, now. Ye'll all attend to Scarm—ah—Ian."

Roaring Jack's voice boomed around the Village, echoed against the cliffs and returned a second time, barely diminished in volume. Half a dozen seagulls flapped into the air and circled above the Villagers. Astreya looked up to see Roaring Jack standing at the wharf edge, a bait tub in one hand. The skipper turned the tub upside down on the ground and waved Scarm towards it.

Scarm, the oldest man present other than a couple of truly ancient grandfathers, stepped onto the upturned tub, and held up his good arm for silence. A puff of morning wind flicked a few strands of hair, more salt than pepper, out of its leather band on the back of his neck. He lifted his head to look out at the Villagers, and Astreya noticed how the old sailor's close-cropped beard had thinned and whitened around his chin.

"It's been a hard winter," Scarm began.

"'T'wasn't just the winter," said a voice in the crowd.

"And because some of us have faced grief and sorrow, we pause to remember the skipper and crew of the *Sarah Jane*."

The silence that followed was broken only by a muffled whimper, as neighbors embraced three women. The *Sarah Jane* had been lost with all hands in the first of the past winter's easterlies.

"But it was not the worst ever, by a long, hard windward tack," continued Scarm after a pause. "The Village is still here, the women's gardens are growing, the fleet will set sail, and, luck being with us, return with full holds."

"Aye," confirmed several voices.

"Last night the skippers met to choose their crews, as ye all know. And it took them a while, I can tell you. Eight young men to choose from, and each one of them ready for the sea. It doesn't happen every year. Last year, t'was only one youngster. The year before, none, and the year before that, as well. But there must have been something in the air back when all these boys breathed their first."

"It was a long hard winter!" shouted a voice from the back of the crowd.

Several men guffawed, and some women giggled.

"It was that," said Scarm, regaining control. "But whatever its cause, the Village was blessed with a mess of boys who today are becoming men. Now the skippers will make their choices known."

Scarm stood down from the bait tub, and almost everyone moved forward a pace or two. Well-wishers jostled the young men, clapping them on a shoulder or giving them an affectionate push. One mother clung to her only son's arm. Astreya took some bitter satisfaction that although Yan held Tina by the hand, she stood aside from him, unlike the girls who pressed close and looked up into the faces of their young men.

Roaring Jack stepped onto the bait tub and cleared his throat.

"Oi'm after tellin' you that Oi'm shippin' out wi' new crew an' a fresh purpose," he began. "Most of the skippers are content with their luck to the north, or in and around the High Islands. But Oi'm thinking of new fishing grounds to the south."

A murmur of conversation followed his announcement. Astreya overheard two men muttering behind him. One voice said, "Lots o' sound, not too much sense," to which the other replied, "There's times he ain't got both oars in the water." Astreya stole a glance around him, and saw two of the Village's skippers standing side by side. One of them had a hand hiding his mouth, and the other was nodding. Astreya was aghast. He had never thought that skippers might talk behind each other's backs. Were they jealous of Roaring Jack's luck at finding more fish than most? Or was there something else he did not know? He looked to see if Alana had heard, but she was intent on what was happening on the wharf. Anticipation drove the exchange out of Astreya's mind. He stood on tiptoe to see better.

"First of all, me crew from beforetimes. Red Ian, come forth."

A huge man in his twenties pushed his way through the crowd and took Roaring Jack's hand. Despite the extra height of the bait tub, the skipper's eyes were on a level with Red Ian's as they clasped hands. Astreya compared the two men's red hair, the skipper's curly and carrot red, and his crewman's bright as polished copper.

"Roight, Jack," shouted a voice from the crowd. "There's your first two choices in one man!"

"Next, Scarm—uh—Ian."

Voices asked questions, as Scarm and Yan moved forward for the handshake of agreement. Astreya heard the words "old" and "crippled," muttered more than once by people around him.

"And now for the new. I choose my kinsman, Yan."

"Yes!" Yan shouted, both fists punching air above his head.

As the first young man to be chosen, Yan was subjected to more or less friendly shoves and nudges from those who stood near. Discussions and congratulations mingled as the crowd shifted in anticipation of the next skipper's choice.

"And last, I choose Alana's boy, 'Streya."

Roaring Jack's voice blasted through the murmurs and left silence behind. Astreya's eyes grew very wide, and he stood unmoving as Alana embraced him and kissed his cheek. He searched for words, but could find none for her.

"Stay, Skip,"

He fondled the dog's big head before picking up his kitbag and walking towards the boats. The crowd parted, but no one spoke directly to him, and when he reached the bait bucket, only the tapping of halyards against the masts broke the quiet as the morning wind swayed the boats.

"Welcome aboard the *Mollie*, lad," said Roaring Jack in an almost conversational tone as he stepped off the tub and clasped Astreya's hand. "Take this and stow it with your kit."

He gave Astreya a square leather satchel as long a man's forearm and at least two hand spans thick. When he took it, Astreya discovered that it was lighter than might have been expected from its size.

"Birch bark," Roaring Jack tried to whisper, though most of the crowd heard him. "An' even some paper. Scarm put it together las' night for your markings. Now, get aboard."

On both sides of Roaring Jack and his crew, the other skippers' faces were dour. They all knew their fellow skippers' choices, and had heard the night before that the *Mollie* was not sailing with the rest of the fleet. Most of them were uncomfortable with the plan, and some were openly set against it. However, they knew that there was no point in arguing with Roaring Jack, since they could no more change his mind than they could shout him down. The women exchanged glances, but remained silent in anticipation of gossip later.

The big-voiced man led his crew to the boats, where all except Yan stepped out of their boots and climbed barefoot, boots in hand, onto the first, across to the second, and onto the *Mollie*, which lay outboard, ready to be first to leave.

"Y' take the main halyards, Red. Boys, get the jib up and drawing. Scarm, let go fore and aft."

Roaring Jack stood by the tiller as his crew went to work, and in moments the squeak of blocks, the flap of a sail and the slap of bare feet on the deck, together with the low chuckle of water under the *Mollie*'s bow all masked the exclamations, arguments and discussions that were taking place ashore, delaying the next skipper's announcement of his crew.

So it was that the *Mollie* set sail an hour ahead of the fleet, and none of her crew heard the nine days' worth of Village gossip that they left behind.

CHAPTER 4:

IN WHICH THE MOLLIE SAILS SOUTH, AND HER CREW MAKES A HORRID DISCOVERY

Astreya stood in the stern of the *Mollie*, sketching the outline of the cliffs he could see off the starboard bow. On his left, Roaring Jack held the tiller in one fist, his blue eyes roving up to check the set of his sails, then out to starboard, where rocks tossed up spray between his boat and the land, and then ahead to shape his coasting course. It was late in the day, and Roaring Jack was sailing the *Mollie* close to the shore in search of an anchorage for the night. In the leather bag at Astreya's feet was a series of sketches that recorded the other cliffs, bluffs, bays, islands and points they had been skirting during the days of their voyage south. He finished his drawing of the rocky fang around which they were sailing, stowed the sheet of birch bark with the others, and took a fresh sheet on which to record the headland once more, viewed astern, as the *Mollie* plunged onward under light but steady northwesterly winds. Roaring Jack insisted on an over-the-stern view, so that they would know what to look for on their return journey; however, Astreya was concerned that his materials would soon be exhausted. Back at the Village, Scarm had prepared what had seemed an endless supply of bark, and enough charcoal, ink and quill pens to last any voyage. But as he used his materials day after day, Astreya was not so sure.

Each evening, they found a bay or inlet where they could anchor or beach the *Mollie*. Then Astreya would ink the charcoal sketches, while Roaring Jack decided on the wording of notes to guide them back on their return journey. The skipper and Astreya worked by lantern light in the cockpit under a sail rigged as an awning over the boom, while Scarm, Yan and Red Ian clustered around a candle in the cabin. Recently, when they finally blew out the lights and Astreya looked up into the heavens, he saw new stars to the south.

Throughout the days, Astreya was so busy sketching that after he had done his share of getting the *Mollie* under way each morning, he had little time to think of anything but the continuous job of recording the shoreline. Occasionally, he wondered if Roaring Jack knew where he was taking them, so far from the Village.

From time to time as he sketched, his mother's face crossed his mind's eye, her hair blowing out to one side, a few strands streaking her cheeks, the way he had so often seen her when they had gone for walks along the high paths above the Village. These moments were more than mere daydreams, and quite unlike homesickness. Whenever they occurred, he felt sure Alana was aware of him, even though reason told him it was impossible.

Roaring Jack treated Astreya as a full grown man, as did Scarm and Red Ian. Astreya noticed that the young giant, who usually frowned at people in the Village, wore a face settled into a permanent grin now that they were at sea. On the other hand, Yan scowled at Astreya when the other men were not watching. Unused to the boat's lively action in the open sea, the red-haired youth had spent most of his first two days hanging head downwards over the side, retching back everything Roaring Jack insisted that he eat. Even now, when the worst of his seasickness had passed, he still winced when the *Mollie* punched her bow through the top of a wave and smacked up spray to sluice down her foredeck as she swayed and swung, her mast reeling dizzily overhead.

At the start of the voyage, Astreya's stomach had lurched whenever he was caught off balance by the *Mollie*'s dance among the waves. The first time they passed within a stone's throw of huge rocks lurking below the roiling water, he had swallowed hard not to throw up onto the sketch in his hands. But Roaring Jack's seamanship gave him a confidence that was stronger than nausea. At first, Astreya had barely been able to stand braced against the cockpit coaming, and his sketches were often smudged and uneven. But now he worked quickly and accurately, sketching as easily as on dry land. Yan clung unhappily to the cockpit edge looking gloomily at the waves.

"Watch the horizon, Yan, and you'll feel better," said Astreya.

"Get knotted," Yan muttered through clenched teeth.

"Yer think that there's an island?" Roaring Jack demanded.

Astreya glanced at his sketch, compared it once more with the shoreline, and decided.

"Looks like it, skipper," he said.

Something like a growl came from Yan as he frowned at Astreya.

A bellowed order from Roaring Jack brought Scarm and Red Ian up from the cabin.

"Ease the jib, an' we'll go in on a broad reach. Scarm, we'll need the lead."

They did not have to be told to keep a sharp lookout as the *Mollie* felt her way into the bay. Scarm climbed onto the foredeck to sound the depth of the water with a coil of light line, the lead weight at its end armed with a wad of tallow to sample the bottom. He stood with his injured arm hooked around the starboard stay, a coil of line in his otherwise useless left hand. His right arm swung the weight in a circle. The lead blurred in the air before flying ahead of the boat and splashing into the water.

Then as it dropped to the bottom and the *Mollie* moved ahead, Ian called out the depth when the cord was taught and vertical under his hand. Then he retrieved the line and the lead, checked the tallow for sand, mud or shells, and then repeated the process.

They sailed westward on a slackening breeze into a wide-mouthed bay that was completely unlike the narrow passage between the cliffs that guarded the Village. On either side were gentle slopes clad in forest, dark green with spruce, balsam and pine all the way down to the high tide line. Astreya drew a wind-blown pine that rose above the rest, and then as they sailed further, he made notes and corrections to his sketch of the island that sheltered the inner part of the bay. The *Mollie* forged ahead slowly, her sails hanging slack, a v-shaped ripple widening from under her bows. As they rounded the island that protected the bay, Astreya saw gentle, soft green hills rolling towards the skyline, where pink clouds veiled the setting sun. One by one, the crew of the *Mollie* took off their waterproof jackets to enjoy being out of the sea wind.

"Three fathom... two fathom and a half... just over two fathom... sand below... two fathom and good holding ground."

Scarm's soundings measured their slow progress around a point that proved to be a second wooded island, almost connected to the mainland by a line of huge boulders. Apart from the old sailor's voice and the occasional flap of the jib, the *Mollie* slid forward in the silence that had descended when they left the sounds of the open ocean behind them.

The land sloped towards them in the early evening light. Astreya began his last sketch with the outline of distant hills. When he glanced up, he frowned at rolling fields, grass green with spring growth. Closer, clustered along the shoreline and crowning the first rise of land were shapes he recognized with a quick, in-drawn breath of surprise. Roaring Jack had the same reaction, but louder.

"Sweet spirit of me long departed mother, that there's houses!"

Roaring Jack's exclamation shattered the silence. "... houses," echoed back at them a moment later.

"Good sized wharf, too," said Scarm. "No need to anchor or beach her, we can just lie alongside." He swung the lead once more. "Still firm sand at two fathom, an' that's at close to low tide."

Astreya's charcoal scraped across a fresh sheet of birch bark, picking up the shapes of houses, the sloping, rock-strewn beach and a wharf like a wall between the water and the houses behind it. When he started to draw the wharf, he saw what it was.

"It's a ship," he exclaimed.

"Fat chance," Yan scoffed. "It's far too big for that."

"No, look again. It doesn't go straight down into the water. It's a boat's side... bulging, and tapered at the ends."

"Y'r right, 'Streya. Dowse the jib, lower the main. Ready to fend off."

Roaring Jack's orders echoed across the still water, this time returning from the wharf that had once been a huge boat. As they drew closer, they saw that the deck of the wharf was more than head high above them. Quickly stowing his sketch, Astreya prepared to keep the *Mollie* from bumping against the black wooden wall.

"That's my job," muttered Yan.

"Fine," said Astreya. "You do the bow."

"I'm here. You go forward."

"Git yer arse for'ard, Yan," said Roaring Jack. "Red, take a line ashore."

Muttering, Yan started to climb out of the cockpit, but Red Ian was faster. He leaped up from the *Mollie*'s deck, his big hands grasped the gunwale of the stranded ship, and with something between a vault and a scramble, he was above them. Pushing against the dark shape with an oar, Astreya looked up and saw the big man's face crumple into a baffled frown.

"Dere's nuttin' in 'ere... nuttin' but rocks."

"Ease her aft a bit, Red, so's Oi can climb up."

The *Mollie* drifted astern towards a barnacled, weedy ladder nailed into the dark wood, almost invisible in the lengthening shadows. Roaring Jack climbed with the stern line draped over one shoulder. Astreya looked up at the broad backs of the two men silhouetted above him. Roaring Jack's voice rumbled into the evening.

"Well, Oi'll be..."

"Are you going to tell us, or do we have to guess?" asked Scarm.

"Come on up and look for yerselves."

"I could use a hand..."

"Roight y'are, Scarm. Toss up the end of your lead line."

The line flew through the air, Roaring Jack pulled, and Scarm half climbed, half walked up the blackened wood, the lead weight bumping on his hip. Astreya scaled the ladder Roaring Jack had used, Yan close behind him. They all stood on a strip of stained decking. At their feet was a ragged hole where once there had been the hatch of a hold. To their right were the remains of the deckhouse, one side stove in and splintered, its roof resting cockeyed on what remained. To their left, they saw the stumps of three huge masts, each thicker than Red Ian's big body. They stuck up like broken trees, one close at hand, another more than a dozen paces away, the third even farther beyond, where a broken cabin top ended and the deck tapered towards the bow. Astreya saw that the ship had been immense: he guessed it was more than five times the length of the *Mollie*. He looked down into the hold, and saw the sky palely reflected in dark water around huge rocks. As his eyes grew accustomed to the dim light, he saw that the rocks had smashed through at least one deck, portions of which were still visible on either side of the opening.

"Astreya was right. She's a sunk ship," said Scarm.

"I saw that before Blackhead opened his big yap," muttered Yan.

"Then why didn't you say so?" Astreya whispered.

"'Cause I'm not always sucking up to the skipper, that's why," said Yan, and stuck out his tongue.

"There must have been a hatch cover that they ripped off to throw in the rocks," Scarm continued as he, like Astreya, peered into the hole in the deck.

"I'd niver do that to a ship if she was mine," said Red Ian.

Roaring Jack looked beyond the other side of the ship, which met the land at a level with where they stood. Grass and weeds patched an area between the wharf and a line of barns, sheds and houses, which began a dozen or so paces from the water. The skipper's huge voice broke the evening hush once more.

"Is anyone there?"

"...one there?..." replied an echo.

"Nobody home," said Red Ian slowly. "No smoke."

"No boats, nor any sign of them. Not even a dory," said Scarm.

"Something's really wrong here," said Astreya.

The windows of the houses were dark and sightless, doors gaped open, what had been washing waved gently on a line, but it was so frayed and ragged that they could hardly distinguish shirts from sheets. The ground was even and smooth: no footprints marked the weedy pathways to and between the houses. Astreya shuddered. Roaring Jack glanced at him, and inclined his head thoughtfully. Yan edged around the open hatch to the narrow deck on the other side, and then stepped over what was left of the gunwales onto the land.

"What's over there?" Scarm asked, pointing with his good arm.

"That's the remains of a fire—a big one," said Astreya.

"Hey! The doors of the houses are open!" said Yan. "I'm going to take a look."

"Stop him, Jack," said Scarm quietly, but with an urgency that Astreya had never heard before.

"Belay that, Yan."

Roaring Jack's order echoed off the empty houses, as Yan broke into a trot.

"Stop where you're at!"

This time, Roaring Jack's voice was so loud that Astreya blinked. Yan continued towards the closest house, but before he reached the door a rope curved through the air, and Yan fell with his legs tangled in Scarm's lead line.

"Beauty," commented Red Ian softly.

Roaring Jack looked questioningly at Scarm.

"Maybe they had the plague. Could be they were tryin' to burn it out."

"It ain't safe, fer certain sure. An' they're all gone, one way or another. Nobody left," Roaring Jack muttered.

He strode towards Yan, who was trying to disentangle himself from the heaving line. In a few strides, the skipper stood over him, and in one smooth motion he lifted Yan by the shirt-front, dangling his feet a hand span above ground.

"Don't you niver, niver ignore me agin', b'y," he growled.

His face a finger-length from the source of Roaring Jack's huge voice, Yan's eyes first closed, then opened. Despite himself, tears slid down his cheeks. The rope around his ankles fell free, and Scarm retrieved it, the lead weight bumping over the bare earth. Roaring Jack started back, marching Yan ahead of him, one hand clenched into his shoulder. Then, apparently changing his mind, he walked towards the chest high charred pile of blackened wood. Astreya, Scarm and Red Ian heard Yan whimper, and a moment later, an explosion of sound came from Roaring Jack.

"Seethin' sclupins, there's bones here. 'Uman bones. Get back aboard. We're shovin' off. Roight flamin' now."

In moments, they were all aboard the *Mollie.* Astreya pushed at the black wood with an oar, and the gap between boat and ship widened. The wooden rings on the mainsail clattered against the mast as Red Ian hoisted quickly. The first puff of evening wind off the land scuffed the water into tiny ripples, and the *Mollie*'s bow swung eastwards towards the darkening sea. As he looked back over the stern, a last shaft of sunlight glanced on the water, illuminating the side of the half-sunk ship. Astreya saw a board at the bow, its letters highlighted in weathered white paint. In the instant before a cloud dimmed the setting sun, he was able to read the name: *Spindrift.*

"Steady, steady." Roaring Jack's voice was softer now, almost as if he were talking to himself. "We'll anchor for the night. No point in blunderin' around in the dark. Good holding ground, y'said, Scarm?"

Scarm nodded.

"Drop the killick astern, Red, pay out about ten fathoms as we go; we'll lay the pick ahead, shorten up, and lie between the two of 'em."

The killick was a crude anchor made of fire-hardened wood shaped into a rough cage around a heavy boulder, with a crosspiece below. Red Ian tossed it behind them as if it were a toy, then paid out rope while Scarm waited for the *Mollie* to slide a few boat's lengths through the darkened water, and then shoved the forward anchor off the foredeck. Moments after it splashed into the sea, Red Ian started to haul, and gradually the *Mollie* lost momentum, coming to rest between her two anchors.

As the light faded from the sky, they prepared for the night. They ate a cold and silent supper in the cramped cabin, seated on either side of the narrow table that dangled from four ropes set into the cabin top above them. Yan and Astreya had their backs against the forward bulkhead, the skipper sat on one of the steps to the cockpit, and Scarm and Red Ian faced each other across the table. A lantern swung gently above them.

Yan suddenly could not keep silent.

"You should' a seen it. There were bones in the fire. All mixed with beams an' logs and what looked like pieces of furniture. An' at the edges, there were bits of people. I saw two, maybe three skulls. And a hand—or what was left of it—on the edge of the burned wood."

"Animals, maybe, after the fire was out," said Scarm. "Pulling bones out the ashes. No knowin' how many bodies."

"Or how many were left in the houses," muttered Roaring Jack. "Could be, the ones that lived were tryin' to burn out the infection, an' were too late."

Astreya tried to imagine a grisly procession of people carrying or dragging bodies to the fire site, heaping whatever would burn on top and then torching the pile before going back to their houses to die themselves.

"Skipper, why did you think it was plague?" Astreya asked.

"Y'know the song, Astreya," said Red Ian slowly. And then he sang in a hoarse whisper:

"He must sail through storm and calm
His crew has done 'em harm,
He's left the dead ashore and he must sail forevermore:
He's the prisoner of an unforgiven curse."

Red Ian's words were half sung, half said as the lantern light cast shadows across the big sailor's face. Scarm nodded thoughtfully.

"'The Wanderer's Curse'," said Astreya. "I've heard the song, but mother—Alana—will never sing it."

"I can understand that," said Scarm quietly.

"It's just a song, a tradition. It doesn't say anything about plague..." said Yan.

"Can y' think of a stronger curse than that?" said Roaring Jack. "It was plague, sure enough."

"Even traditions have a beginnin' somewhere, sometime," said Scarm softly. "Words gets snarled up wi' fate, an' then it all repeats itself in a fresh pattern o' bad luck."

Astreya stared at Scarm, trying to unravel this lapse into speculation.

"Y' think it's still in the air?" asked Red Ian, voicing the thought that had occurred to all of them.

"Doubt it," said Roaring Jack. "We all stayed out o' the houses, an' didn't touch nothin'."

"No thanks to you, young Yan," said Red Ian.

Yan bent over the table, so that only the top of his head showed in the lamplight.

"Yan. You get first watch with me," said Roaring Jack. "On deck. You follow along too, Red, 'so's we can check how she lies."

Roaring Jack's order jerked Yan to his feet so quickly that he hit his head on the cabin roof. Not even taking time to wince, he scrambled up the short steps of the ladder to the cockpit after the skipper. Astreya tidied the remains of the meal, and set out rolled up blankets on the benches. Red Ian stowed the table and climbed up the companionway, closing the hatch behind him.

Scarm moved astern to sit opposite Astreya, the cabin lantern swinging gently above them.

"Scarm, you know more about this, don't you?"

Astreya saw Scarm slowly nod. "You guessed it wasn't plague back there."

"You didn't say it was plague, and it stands to reason that it wasn't," said Astreya. "If they had been trying to burn out the infection, they'd have set fire to the houses, instead of carrying bodies to a fire. And I can't imagine anyone doing that to the people they'd lived with—especially if they were family. Toss a torch into a house, maybe. Carry your mother or brother down to the shore and pile the bodies on a fire? Not a chance."

Scarm nodded. "I didn't want Yan fossicking around."

"If it wasn't plague, then why did you nod when Red sang 'The Wanderer's Curse'? What's that got to do with what we saw? What really happened?"

"Astreya, there are ships doomed to sail forever. I don't know how many there were, or are left. But that was one of them back there, scuttled."

"*Spindrift*," said Astreya.

"You saw her name. She must have come ashore with her crew and founded the village back there. There could have been as many as a couple hundred of them by the looks of it. Families, with children, some of them, I bet. But men came in another ship, they killed and plundered, and they left. It's likely that Men of the Sea did this, and they did it to their own."

Astreya felt his insides clench. He swallowed with a tight throat and whispered.

"Scarm, was my father a Man of the Sea?"

Scarm nodded.

"That's what he said to me when we fished him out of the sea. It made no sense at the time. I thought he was raving, 'cause he was barely alive. When we first saw him, we thought he was dead, and we nearly let him stay with the fishes. But Red Ian said we couldn't leave a man stuck afore we'd discovered if he was alive or dead, so we hauled him out. He was breathing—just—so we brought him home with us. I took him to my cottage. For the first few days, he could barely talk, and what he said was like he was dreaming. He told me, that is, I listened while he spoke, 'cause it wasn't like he was explaining to me—more like telling himself who he was. He spoke of being aboard a great ship, one of many. The ships of the 'Men of the Sea,' he called them. And he'd been a somebody, that was clear. I don't think he'd been the skipper, but he had been given an important job to do away from his ship."

"Why didn't they come looking for him?"

"I think maybe he expected them to, but when time went by and they didn't, he must have decided that his people had left him for dead. And then a bit later, he and your mother wed."

"But you talked with him. He must have told you all kinds of things. Scarm, you have to tell me..."

"I've said enough. He told me to tell nobody."

"Scarm, I'm his son."

The old sailor's mouth worked as if he was about to begin an explanation, but at that moment, the cabin hatch slid back, and Red Ian's feet appeared on the top step.

"Later," said Scarm as the big sailor descended into the cabin. He muttered a goodnight to both of them, and lay down on the bench opposite Astreya, endeavoring to curl himself up so that he did not take all of the space on one side. Soon he was snoring softly. Before Astreya could find words to ask another question, Scarm had adjusted a blanket to soften the bench for his withered arm, and had stretched out opposite Ian. Astreya sat watching the light from the swaying lantern slide up and down the boat's sides until his eyes started to close. Pulling himself awake, he blew out the lamp, lay down on the cabin sole, took off his jacket and rolled it up as a pillow. As he moved, his shirtsleeve rose above the bracelet on his arm and a gleam of green flashed in the dark cabin.

"Keep that green stone a secret, Astreya," whispered Scarm from across the narrow cabin. "It's like you brought it to life. When we found him, it was dull, just like one of those green pebbles he fished out of our stream. Later, it gleamed a bit, but nothing like now. And when he gave it to Alana, it went dull again. If I don't miss my guess, there's them that would take it away from you, and do you a heap of harm, besides."

"What did my father tell you about the stone?" Astreya asked.

There was no answer save for soft, regular breathing. Astreya looked up into the lamp lit shadows of the cabin roof his mind buzzing with unresolved questions. Just as he was expecting to spend the whole night awake and thinking about what he had heard, he suddenly fell asleep.

Chapter 5:

In which they are storm struck, and Astreya reaches Teenmouth

The dawn wind tugged the *Mollie* against her lines, waking Roaring Jack in an instant. Soon they had the anchors aboard and were heading out of the bay. At the skipper's word, Astreya had his sketching equipment in his hands from the moment they were under way, but he could see little ahead for the rising sun, which briefly lit the *Mollie's* sails before it was smudged by a band of cloud. Roaring Jack squinted through his bushy eyebrows, and then glanced down at Astreya's still hands.

"Well now, lad, give us one more look back at the mouth of the bay. We don't niver want to be goin' back there agin."

They cleared the headlands through which they had approached the doomed village, and turned towards the south in a beam reach. As the *Mollie* steadied to a freshening west wind, Red Ian passed out slices of twice-baked bread slathered with blueberry jam. Then, finding the cockpit too crowded, he climbed over the cabin top and sat with his back against the mast.

"Roight," announced Roaring Jack. "We're headin' south. There's got to be good fishin' somewheres near here."

"We're not going home?" Yan asked before he could stop himself.

"Not yet."

Astreya focused on sketching the view over the stern, now looking down at his work, now glancing up at the fast-diminishing headland to assure himself that he had seen correctly and recorded faithfully. This view was crucial, because it would identify their position when they made the return voyage, so he held the sketch at arm's length and examined it critically. Was there a rock he had missed? Suddenly, almost painfully, his bracelet tingled as if someone had gripped him just above his elbow. He would have peeled back his sleeve to find out why he felt it prickle his skin, but he was too busy, and besides, he remembered Scarm's advice to keep the bracelet secret. However, he was still acutely conscious of the circlet of silvery metal on his arm. Muttering about needing fresh charcoal, he ducked down into the cabin, and pulled off his jacket. The green glow from his bracelet was clearly visible through the material of his shirt, and dimly lit the cabin when he rolled back his sleeve.

"Here. Cover it with this."

Astreya turned to see Scarm half way down the companion-way steps, his arm outstretched. In his hand was what looked like a scrap of thick cloth, but when Astreya took it, he saw that it was a strip of hand-woven string.

"Ocean plait," said Scarm. "Wrap around and over your bracelet. Here. I'll tie it under your arm."

They stood swaying in the cabin while Scarm tied the plaited string around Astreya's bracelet. Only a faint light emerged through the fabric.

"It'll tighten if it gets wet. Make sure it stays around the metal and doesn't bite into your arm."

"On deck!"

Roaring Jack's voice brought them both out of the cabin in a rush. When they reached the cockpit, the *Mollie* was in bright sunlight, but a moment later, the light left them, gleamed briefly on the sea to starboard, and then disappeared into lowering dark cloud. The wind suddenly piped up from the northwest. Roaring Jack's eyebrow arched over his left eye as he squinted into the weather. Wind from over the land, gusty and confused by the headlands and cliffs, fought with the main force of the oncoming storm, whipping up white caps. Cats' paws of down-drafted air blackened the shoulders of rising waves. Overhead, the spar creaked and the sails strained as Roaring Jack spilled wind from the mainsail. Their eyes wide with anticipation, they awaited the skipper's orders.

"All hands to shorten sail," boomed Roaring Jack's voice. "We'll have the jib down, and a reef—no, two—on the main. An' put two boards in the companionway. We don't need any of the salt chuck below." Then more quietly, he added. "Not you, 'Streya. Finish yer markings. We'll need 'em on our way homeward."

"I'm done," said Astreya. "I can't go on now, anyway. I can barely see the headland."

The skipper looked over his shoulder to where the land was smudged by grey rain.

"Aye. She's come up roight quick. Get yer markings below, and batten down for a stiff one. She'll be on us full force 'fore you can sing a chorus of 'The Wanderer's Curse'."

Astreya looked up, startled. Had Roaring Jack been listening last night? Had Scarm and the skipper talked about him after he was asleep? He almost let go of the sketch on which he had been working as he went below into the tiny cabin, where he hurriedly stowed his sketching materials, staggering as the *Mollie* heeled alarmingly to port. He checked the cabin for loose gear, buttoned his oiled jacket, pulled a woolen cap firmly onto his head and climbed back to the cockpit. Once there, he slid the cabin hatch closed behind him and inserted two boards across the companionway to keep water from the cockpit from slopping down into the cabin.

"Luffin' up. Now!"

Astreya was thrown against the starboard side of the cockpit as Roaring Jack headed the *Mollie* into the wind so that the crew could shorten sail. The *Mollie* pitched up and down, one moment almost standing on her stern, the next plunging her bow into the waves. Huge gouts of spray flew over the *Mollie*'s foredeck, almost hiding Scarm from view. Water splashed into the cockpit, soaking Astreya to the knees. The mainsail flapped heavy whip cracks in wind that was still rising as Scarm eased the main halyard with his good hand, his other elbow hooked around the mast. Aghast at the forces around them, Astreya grasped the cabin top as the *Mollie* climbed another, even steeper wave. Spray flew into his face. When he wiped his eyes, Scarm was still there, thin stripes of grey hair plastered to his forehead. Astern at the tiller, Roaring Jack kept the *Mollie* headed upwind and luffing with the boom amidships. Yan climbed past Astreya onto the cabin top, and bent double over the boom. Red Ian stood in the starboard quarter of the cockpit, reaching up to where the canvas flapped above him. Astreya did his best to reach the boom between them. The sail bellied as it slid down the mast. All three of them strove to quiet the canvas by tying the reef points—the dozen cords dangling from both sides of the sail, which whipped back and forth as the sail jerked first one way and then the other. Astreya reached around the boom, grabbed sailcloth in both hands and bundled boom and sail together, smothering some of the flapping. Yan squatted on the cabin top with his knees under the boom. Astreya and Red Ian had to reach over their heads, past the bobbing and swaying boom, grasp a reef point in each hand and then tie the two ends around the boom with spray-numbed fingers. They staggered as the *Mollie* heaved and bucked, jerking Astreya off his feet to dangle above the cockpit sole. Red Ian's size and strength kept the boom from thrashing them all over the side, and after a few desperate moments, they each secured one, and then with increasing ease, the rest of the reef points. Astreya dropped back down into the cockpit. Above him, the sail still flapped and bellied, even though reduced to nearly half its original size. Red Ian clambered ahead to the mast where he and Scarm braced up the halyards to set the sail into its newly reduced shape.

Almost before they had finished, Roaring Jack yanked on the tiller, and the *Mollie* took the wind on her starboard side. Instantly, the lee rail was awash. Thanks to the reefs in her sail, the boat no longer threatened to lay her mast flat on the sea, but spray splashed over the cockpit coaming with each wave.

Whether from excitement or bravado, Yan came aft too quickly. He tried to get down from the cabin top in a single, slithering rush, but the *Mollie* heaved and shook as a breaking wave slapped her starboard quarter. Yan's foot slipped, and he fell face forward, his fingers clawing frantically at the smooth wood. Out of control, he plummeted headfirst into the water that was racing past the cockpit coaming.

Astreya reacted first. With only a bent knee under the coaming to hold him in the cockpit, he caught Yan's belt as he slid along the lee decking in a flurry of spray. The sea pulled at Yan's head and shoulders, and would have broken Astreya's grip, had the *Mollie* not swung to windward as she wallowed up the side of a wave. For a moment, the water no longer poured down the narrow side deck, and Yan's red hair dripped into the wave below him. Red Ian grabbed the slack of Yan's pants, and the two of them pulled him half into the cockpit. As the boat crested the next wave, the wind shoved the boat's lee rail back into the sea. Now the water slapped into Astreya's face, and again he almost let go. Then, as the *Mollie* ran into the trough between two waves, Roaring Jack hauled the tiller towards him, and Yan became almost weightless in Astreya's grasp as the sudden course change flipped him out of the sea into the cockpit, where he joined Astreya and Red Ian in a tangle at Roaring Jack's feet.

"Get a grip of somethin' and hold on," yelled Roaring Jack. "The wind's veerin' an' we'll have to run afore it. There's no chance of duckin' behind the headlands. We'd broach as we rounded the point, even if we missed the rocks."

The rain squall that had blotted out the shoreline now reached the *Mollie*, hissing into the sea around them as the first drops drummed on the taut sail. Roaring Jack took a turn around a cleat to check the mainsheet, and Astreya saw the rope twist and drip under the strain. When he could no longer manage the sail with one hand, the skipper passed the sheet to Red Ian, who controlled it almost casually.

Astreya had never imagined anything as impersonally terrifying as the power of the seas around them. He had been used to looking down on waves from the deck of the *Mollie*. Now their wind-torn crests were above his head, soaking all of them with spray. Through the spindrift, he glimpsed the horizon between waves like white crested mountain ranges. Water sloshed and splashed on his feet, the boat creaked ominously and her rigging wailed in protest. A paralyzing terror gripped him, and he breathed short. Moments earlier, his fear for Yan had made him quick to respond; now a chest-tightening stiffness possessed him. He was swung back and forth like a log, his chest thumping against the cockpit edge, his knuckles barked raw on the cleats at which he clutched. More by luck than will, he looked aft and saw Roaring Jack. The wind was blowing his red beard sideways across his craggy face, and his eyes were narrowed against the wind-driven spray, but the skipper's face was set in a grin. He glanced first upward at the sail, then from side to side, and then with a quick turn of his head, back over the starboard quarter to gauge the arrival of the next gust. Astreya saw that Roaring Jack was enjoying the danger as a sport, matching his skills against the uncaring storm.

The waves were now so high that the wind slackened when the *Mollie* was down in the wave troughs. Astreya saw that Red Ian also knew what he was doing and shared the danger equally with the skipper. With a long pull, he hauled the boom inboard as the clew of the sail touched the water; then a heartbeat later when they crested the wave, he eased the sheet to spill wind that would have split the sail or rolled the boat half over. Beside him, Roaring Jack stood at the tiller, his legs braced and his big shoulders humped. The two men alternately wrestled and coaxed the *Mollie* through seas that would have swamped her had their concentration wavered for an instant. Astreya's terror eased. He stopped fighting to stay upright, and began to swing back and forth with the boat's motion. Then he let out a breath that he had been holding for much too long.

"Get this slop out of here," shouted Roaring Jack, kicking a bare foot in the water that sloshed around the cockpit.

Astreya tugged a leather bucket out of the stern locker. Wedging himself firmly against the cockpit side, he started to bail. He scooped deep into the water surging around their feet, and the bailer came up almost full. When he tossed it over his shoulder, it hissed into a smooth, slanting wall of water above his head. Astreya was momentarily aghast at having to throw water upward into the waves. However, after a dozen or so bailersful of water had followed the first, his anxiety dimmed and he knew that he had begun a job that would have no end until the storm was over. Even as he bailed, more spray and rain added to what already sluiced back and forth among the crew's legs. He moderated his first heroic efforts at emptying the cockpit to the more realistic goal of keeping the water level tolerably low. His world shrank to the repetitive work. Scoop, scrape, throw; scoop, scrape, throw. Time was measured by the motion of his arm. Discomfort built to pain that numbed his shoulder; he changed hands, and discovered another measure of the storm: the number of hand changes. For a while, action kept him warm, then gradually his soaking clothes pulled heat from his body, and he shivered uncontrollably. He dropped the bailer, and stared at it stupidly. Scarm hooked his foot in it just before it went over the side.

"Change over." Roaring Jack's voice boomed over the whistling of the wind in the rigging and the water noises around the *Mollie* as she rushed through the waves. Astreya jammed himself into the starboard corner of the cockpit, and let his weary arms relax. All too soon, the skipper again gave the order to change, and later to change again. So it went throughout a long, dark, wet day, until Astreya could barely see what he was doing. As night fell, the skipper issued a new order.

"'Streya, go below. You too, Scarm. No point in everyone bein' wet and cold. Yan, get bailin'. Trade about when I call you."

Astreya and Red Ian opened the cabin hatch and struggled in one after the other, grateful to be out of the constant wind and slashing rain. Scarm reached into the boat's chest under the companionway and pulled out a lump of twice-baked bread, hard as wood, and a skin of Village whisky. Astreya had tasted the liquor before on a dare one midwinter feast, and remembered that he had coughed uncontrollably. Now, after one throat-searing swallow of the fiery spirit, he handed back the skin and swung himself into the lee of the mast.

"Your father did that," said Scarm. "One sip, then no more, even when we had a full hold to celebrate."

Astreya was so tired he barely heard the sailor's voice over the creaking of the mast beside him. The mouthful of whisky still burned in his stomach, but he was shivering, and his feet were numb. His arms ached as he struggled out of his jacket and stripped off his wet shirt. As Scarm had warned, the string had tightened around his bracelet, hiding both the silvery band and the green stone. With fingers that would not stop shaking, he dug out the new sweater Alana had given him, and put it on before draping a blanket around his shoulders and settling himself between the mast and the boat's side. One moment he was almost weightless as the *Mollie* fell under him; then, as the boat rolled and pitched, he felt the boat push him upwards all along his backbone. He rested his head against the curve of the boat's side between two wooden ribs, and heard the rush of water only a thumb's width away. The sound and motion that would have made him deathly sick only a few days earlier, now helped him relax. Water gurgled and sloshed in the bilge below him, the mast groaned in its step at his shoulder, joining a chorus of noises from all the many other parts of the *Mollie*'s wooden body. Nonetheless, Astreya slept.

What seemed moments later, he was roughly awakened.

"Back on deck. I don't have to do it all."

It was Yan, shaking him by the shoulder with a wet hand.

"Get up. You never do your share of the work," said Yan venomously, when Astreya did not move.

Scarm's voice came from the lee berth.

"That ain't so," he growled, his voice husky with sleep. "An even if t'was, it's small thanks you're givin' a man who saved you from your own foolishness in the last watch."

Yan turned and hissed a whisper more insistent than a shout.

"Don't take his side. Don't. You all do it."

Astreya crawled out of his berth and swayed to his feet in the darkness, steadying himself against the mast to get into his oiled jacket. Because he could think of nothing to abate Yan's anger, he simply pointed to the blankets before struggling into his wet jacket and tugging his wool cap down over his ears. Yan muttered something that was obviously not thanks.

Grumbling himself awake, Scarm led the way to the cabin hatch, pushed it open and scrambled out. Astreya paused, half in and half out of the cabin, transfixed by what he saw. A patch of star-shot sky gaped black between torn shreds of cloud, side lit by the waning moon. Then the *Mollie* lurched and the pin-pricked pattern was only a memory as he stood, one arm on the hatch cover, with the wind plucking at his still damp jacket. Astreya shivered.

Low, ragged clouds no longer rained onto the sea. Closer to him, Astreya glimpsed Roaring Jack's hand, gripping the tiller as if he was a part of his boat. Hunched in the stern, the skipper was silhouetted against the night sky, intermittently lit when the moon gleamed through wind-torn clouds. A silvery brightness came and went on the sea around them as moonlight shafted between the clouds onto the white splashes of spray that patched the water around the *Mollie*. There was no guessing where sea ended and sky began.

Astreya began to bail once more. Hunkered on the cockpit sole, he could not dodge the occasional wave top that burst over the coaming. His jacket protected him from most of the water, but spray found its way between his collar and his wool cap to run in a cold stream down his spine. Bilge water surged back and forth in the dark of the cockpit, sometimes splashing up into his face, but most of the time no longer rising higher than his ankles. He returned to counting the bailersful in order to forget the wind, the wet and a weariness that seemed unaffected by his rest below. Hypnotically he went through the motions: scoop, scrape, throw; scoop, scrape, throw.

When dawn began to contest with the moonlight, Astreya caught a glimpse of what he had been bailing by feel for hours. Then, looking up as he threw water over his shoulder, he saw Roaring Jack's face above him. The skipper's hair, beard and even his bushy eyebrows were flecked with salt and matted by wind and water, but his determined look had not changed.

Astreya returned to his bailing, gradually becoming aware that he could look forward to a finish. The *Mollie* rode easier. Spray no longer ran in rivulets from the cabin top nor splashed into the cockpit from the tops of waves. It had been some time since last he had been wetted. Seven scoops more, now five, now three; now only a succession of scrapes with a half-empty bailer. Astreya sat back on his heels and flexed his shoulders. Roaring Jack bent over him, salt glistening in his beard. His powerful voice was only a croak.

"Take the tiller, lad. Oi must stretch or crack."

Astreya scrambled to his feet and stood beside the tiller. As his hand closed on the smooth wood, he felt the twitch and heave of the *Mollie*'s life.

"Hold the wind in your right ear, and keep the sail full," said Roaring Jack.

The big man almost fell as he changed the position he had held all night. Scarm, hunched over the mainsheet in a half doze, moved as if to steady the skipper, but Roaring Jack regained his balance with a stagger. Cracking his knuckles and shrugging his shoulders, he faced the dawn's first glow with a prodigious yawn. He made a fist of one big hand and pounded on the cabin roof.

"Bring up food and whisky," he shouted, his voice husky.

Red Ian and Yan soon joined them in the cockpit. Roaring Jack seized the skin of liquor and took a long pull, coughed, and drank again.

"Where are we?" asked Yan, shivering in the dawn wind.

"We bin out o' sight of land all night," began Red Ian, and then stopped at Yan's look of terror and Roaring Jack's quick gesture for silence.

Village boats seldom ventured past where they could see land—never, unless they were sure that a simple course reversal would take them home. However, Astreya was not fearful. Like the rest of the crew, he knew that there was no guarantee that they had sailed in the same direction throughout the storm, let alone followed the unknown coastline. His glimpse of the stars had told him that they were heading south, and the predawn glow on the port horizon confirmed it. He saw concern, and, in Yan's case, fear, in the quick glances with which the crew searched the horizon for land, but strangely he did not share their anxiety.

Roaring Jack knew how to deal with the apprehensive mood. His orders soon had them hoisting the jib, shaking reefs out of the mainsail and tightening halyards. The work had the effect he wanted, as did the food and drink that followed it. Their fears abated, they sat together in the cockpit, chewing on hunks of bread and cheese washed down with water and, for the men, whisky. As the rising sun started to dry out both boat and crew, Astreya began to feel ready for whatever might happen next.

Roaring Jack had more orders.

"'Streya, you're lightest. Climb the mast and take a look about you. The *Mollie*'s not as frisky as she was."

Astreya glanced up, swallowed, and started forward. Yan whispered to him as he clambered onto the cabin top.

"Go on 'Streya. Fall over the side. I want to see you face down in the water."

Ignoring the ill wishing, Astreya gained the mast, pulled his knitted hat more firmly onto his head, took hold of the halyards and started to climb. Once his bare feet found the hoops of shaped wood that held the sail to the mast, it was surprisingly easy. He forgot the danger of letting go and being flung into the sea, and used the *Mollie*'s rolling motion instead of fighting it. He climbed when the boat was at the leeward side of her roll and the mast was like a steep, rounded ladder with widely spaced rungs; and then he clung as she rolled back. His climb became more difficult when he reached the gaff and had to work his way up and over the spar. Finally, he stood, the bare masthead in the crook of his arm, one foot on the jaws of the gaff where its leather padding sawed and squeaked against the mast. From this vantage, he could see in all directions, unhampered by the sail. He felt the wind pull at his clothes, flapping his pant legs and sleeves and tugging at his woolen hat. The horizon, which from the cockpit had only been visible in glimpses, now was a distinct line.

"...anything?"

Even Roaring Jack's voice was practically inaudible, making Astreya more conscious of how much height, air and wind separated them. He took a quick, nervous breath, and set himself to answering the skipper's question. Staring out over waves now only occasionally flecked with whitecaps, Astreya wished he could spare a hand to shade his eyes. Ahead, then to port, then to starboard, he scanned the ocean around them. At first, he saw nothing but the heaving waves. Then, as he looked ahead for the second time, it seemed that there was a whiteness he had not noticed at first. He bent his head to wipe his eyes on the arm he had crooked around the mast, and looked again.

"Breakers ahead!" he yelled, suddenly sure of what he saw.

"... less.... to port... or starboard?" The question reached him in fragments.

He reached a decision without even knowing he had made it. "Less to port," he shouted, and in the same instant wondered whether he was correct.

Below him, the skipper's voice boomed.

"Stand by to gybe... gybe ho!"

Astreya felt the gaff move under his feet as unseen hands below him sheeted in the sail to execute a controlled gybe. The *Mollie*'s movement changed: instead of quartering downwind in an up and down pitch and roll, interrupted by the occasional jolt when she punched her bow into a wave, she now surged slantwise across the seas, sliding into the troughs. As she heeled to starboard, Astreya could see the *Mollie*'s stem cut into the wave crests, throwing out a white bow wave. Elated by the speed, Astreya remembered gulls. Like them, he was poised on the wind, stealing movement from its power.

Soon the breakers were definitely less in the direction toward which they sped. Behind the white of the broken seas, Astreya saw green—vivid green, unlike the dark forests with which he was familiar.

"Land ho!" he shouted. "Low, green hills. Beyond the breakers."

He broke his message into sections to shout it down over the curved belly of the sail.

Red Ian's voice came from the foot of the mast, relaying messages.

"Is there a break in the surf?"

Astreya hesitated. How could he tell if a gap between the breakers would be wide and deep enough to take the *Mollie*'s keel? Would there be a gap at all? He searched frantically, tightening his grip on the mast as they drove towards a reef that grew nearer and more threatening every moment. The gaff creaked under him once more, and the *Mollie* was close-hauled, sailing roughly parallel to the breakers. Ahead, he glimpsed into the tube under waves that were cresting and breaking over the reef. He knew that the *Mollie* was at the mercy of a wind that could drive her into the lee shore. Before the thought could turn to panic, he noticed a change in the sea around them. The *Mollie* no longer sailed in blue-green sea, but was entering water discolored with reddish mud. Astreya's days of sketching at Roaring Jack's elbow made him certain of what he saw. Ahead and to his right, there was smooth-water gap amid the breakers.

"Take her alee, NOW!" Astreya shouted.

Fully expecting Roaring Jack to refuse his dangerous advice, Astreya's throat tightened as the *Mollie* altered course down wind, climbing the waves to their crests and then sliding down into their troughs. Astreya clutched at the masthead as the gaff under him changed position. The topping lift scraped his shoulder, so he put an arm over it to keep his balance. Astreya stood, dipping and swaying with the pulse of the wind itself. Like a diving bird that sights a fish, Astreya saw a ragged line of foam, weed and pieces of driftwood, and when next the *Mollie* crested a wave, he confirmed the gap where brown, muddy water marked the outpouring of a stream.

"Starboard! Wind astern!"

Moments later, Astreya felt the *Mollie* move to his will. He recalled Roaring Jack's fierce delight in the first squalls of the storm; he chuckled, heard himself, and was glad nobody else could. Then he clutched at the mast as the gaff swung out over the water. He glimpsed the top of Red Ian's head and shoulders as the sailor hauled on a jib sheet and the canvas belly of the sail cut off Astreya's view down to the fore deck. The jib filled to starboard, goose winged, balancing the mainsail, and the *Mollie* lurched forward through increasingly muddy water like a broad-beamed woman with her skirts billowing around her.

The passage was tighter than Astreya had guessed. The reddish water narrowed and narrowed between breakers. Roaring surf on either side drowned out even Roaring Jack's shouts. Weed lay along the surface of the brown stream, and the *Mollie* sailed through it as if in a field of rain-flattened grass. Long fingers of sand reached out towards them, and as quickly as they appeared, vanished astern. Suddenly, the waves that had plunged the *Mollie* up and down were gone, and the sound of rushing, crashing water was behind them. They were in a lagoon between reef and shore.

"Which way?' came Roaring Jack's shout from below, just as Astreya asked himself the same question.

Ahead, there was a beach of reddish sand, to which ran green, rolling fields dotted with clumps of maples, elms and beeches that were bigger than Astreya had ever seen.

"Which way?" he heard again.

Astreya risked his balance and pointed to port. Shortly after, he heard his voice crack in surprise as the unmistakable sign of human settlement came from behind a clump of trees.

"Smoke ashore!"

The boom and gaff swung, the topping lift cut at his armpit, and Astreya almost fell. As he was regaining his balance, Roaring Jack guided the *Mollie* up the slow-moving current of a winding river, scarcely more than a stream. To starboard side they could see heavy rowboats drawn up on shore. There was no need for Astreya to report; he could hear conversation below him.

"Who builds scows like that?" asked Roaring Jack.

"Lubbers, mostly," replied Red Ian.

The *Mollie* wound her way upstream towards the smoke, slowing as the current pushed against her. Astreya still tried to spy out rocks and shallows, but instead of the clear water of the ocean, there was only reddish river water curling around soft mud banks. As the last of the wind faded behind a line of trees that ran almost to the water's edge, he glimpsed a collection of houses. They were fewer than at the Village, but each was a different color, and some of them had contrasting windows, doors and trim. Astreya had never seen precious paint on anything but a boat, and then only black or sometimes dark green. The stone and wood houses of the Village were drab compared to the many shades that appeared through the trees. He wondered what the people who lived in these bright houses might drink. Here was no clear stream like the one that provided the Village with its water, but only a muddy river, slowly wandering down to stain the sea. To port, a green wall of forest slanted towards the muddy river; to starboard, Astreya saw a dike protecting a field.

The *Mollie* lost headway as trees blocked her wind, and the current overcame what little way she maintained. Below him, Astreya heard the anchor thump the deck and then splash into the water. The *Mollie* slid astern on the lazy stream and brought up with a gentle jerk. The spar on which he stood sagged as the sails went slack. For a moment, Astreya was busy keeping his balance. Then, just as he saw a party of men walking behind the shelter of the dike, Scarm's voice floated up from the deck.

"Come on down, now, 'Streya,"

Astreya climbed to the deck down a mast that now stood exactly up and down. When he reached the deck, he was both dryer and warmer than when he had first gone aloft.

"There's men coming," he reported eagerly. "Maybe a dozen or more. They're behind the dike."

As he spoke, two men crested the green mound and made their way to a rowboat pulled up on the muddy bank. They were both clean shaven and their hair was cut close to their heads, unlike the earlobe length worn by Village men. Their little boat was almost square at both ends, an unwieldy craft that would not have lasted long in the Village fjord, let alone in the open sea. The man who pulled at the stubby oars was no sailor, nor was the one who sat self-importantly in the stern. The rower had to stop and turn around every few strokes to keep his course, and each time he did it, one of the *Mollie*'s crew either sighed or snorted contemptuously.

"Look!" said Yan. "The man in the stern's got a sword!"

"Don't stand there gawpin'," ordered Roaring Jack, his voice once more a bellow. "Get this boat shipshape, and jump to it. Furl them sails neatly, coil the lines, let some air into the cabin—'cept 'Streya. Go get your markings and bring us up to date afore you forget what you've seen."

The boat from the shore came to within easy talking range of the *Mollie*, and the rower took short strokes to hold his position against the gentle current. The crew worked on, casting occasional glances at the two men. Roaring Jack stood tall in the cockpit, his folded arms proclaiming him the skipper. He peered down on the little boat as if he had just noticed its existence. Astreya quickly sketched the boat and its occupants, trying to catch the newcomers' faces and clothes. As he did so, he wondered what Roaring Jack might say later about "wasting good marking bark."

The men had expressions that seemed somehow smudged to Astreya, unlike the big-boned faces of Roaring Jack and the men from the Village. Here, noses, brows, chins and cheeks were rounded and soft—particularly on the tubby little man in the stern of the rowboat. He was wrapped in a brown cloak, despite the heat of the day. The rower wore shirt and breeks similar to Astreya's, save that they were much looser, the shirt tails hanging, as if the man had hastily borrowed his elder brother's clothes.

"Do you bring trade or trouble to Teenmouth?" asked the man with the sword in a curiously high voice.

"We're storm struck on our way south," returned Roaring Jack.

Neither entirely comprehended the other, since they were unfamiliar with the words and the accents in which they were spoken. Astreya wondered at the man's curious, almost singsong speech, while Roaring Jack scowled with the effort of understanding what he had heard. The two men in the boat conferred briefly, their heads bowed together. Then the rower let the sluggish current carry his boat away from the *Mollie*.

"If ye be raiders, know that there be men with weapons on the shore," shouted the man in the stern, half standing and showing them his sword. "If I but wave my sword, they'll be your destruction."

"Friendly little runt, ain't he?" said Red Ian.

Roaring Jack hissed him into silence.

Astreya looked at one shore and then the other. He was not sure whether they were within effective bowshot, but on the other hand, the *Mollie*'s crew had neither weapons nor defense against them if men came down to the water's edge and started shooting. The rowing boat trembled under the unsteady sword holder's weight. Astreya wondered whether it would capsize, and the *Mollie*'s crew be blamed for the accident. The man in the stern sat down just in time.

"We need water and anchorage until we have a fair wind," said Roaring Jack, moderating his voice as much as he could.

The two men bent their heads and talked agitatedly, rocking their small craft.

"Send two of your men for water. No weapons. The rest of you stay where you are," squeaked the fat man in reply.

The rowboat pulled awkwardly toward the shore, where five men appeared from behind the grassy dike. Aboard the *Mollie*, everyone had an opinion about what should be done next. Roaring Jack let Yan gabble at Red Ian and Scarm for a few minutes, and then drowned out conversation with a series of measured statements.

"They're afraid of us," he said, and Red Ian nodded. "But there are more of them than of us," he added, acknowledging Scarm's affirmative grunt with a tilt of his head. "So we'll not make them angry at us over any small thing."

Having established agreement, Roaring Jack gave orders. First, the crew unshipped and lowered the little dory that had been lashed ahead of the mast, then Astreya and Yan climbed into it and took the two small water casks that Red Ian handed down to them. Yan rowed towards the group of men at the water's edge.

"Why us?" he grumbled as he tugged at the oars.

"Because nobody's going to be afraid of the two youngest," said Astreya. "That way, if they think about it, they'll decide that the skipper is so confident that he doesn't need to send the strongest men on the boat." Yan frowned. "No one can know the future," Astreya added, unconsciously quoting his mother. "I'd do the same as Roaring Jack. It's a good gamble."

"Oh, I'm so glad the skipper's orders have the Stranger's son's approval," said Yan sarcastically. He tugged at his oars, making a splash.

"Come on, Yan," said Astreya, refusing to be needled. "Let's look as if we know what we're doing. You can row better than that."

Yan's scowl deepened, but he continued the short trip with more skill than the landsmen. When they grounded on the muddy beach, they hauled their boat up half its length, and stepped onto mud that squished between their bare toes. They slung the two water casks under an oar each, and shared the load on their shoulders as they climbed up and over the dike.

On the landward side, a path led through knee high grass towards a clump of big trees. Above their spreading crests, a skein of smoke trailed into the sky. To their right was the group of men Astreya had seen from the mast. They stood together, muttering among themselves, watching the two young men. The fat man with the sword had climbed a little way up the dike, from which point of authority, he waved to the two boys and pointed down the path. Reasoning that where there was smoke, there were houses, and where there were houses there must be water, Astreya led the way.

"Don't go so fast," grumbled Yan. "You're always putting on a show, and I don't like it."

Excited by the strangeness around him, Astreya ignored Yan's discomfort. Avoiding looking at the staring faces, they followed the path past the assembled men, some of whom followed them down the path. Hurrying, booted feet thumped on the path first behind and then beside them.

"Water!" shouted a man as he passed them, and then added some other words neither Astreya nor Yan could understand.

"We're out of sight of the *Mollie*," muttered Yan gloomily.

Astreya glanced back. "There's her masthead," he said crisply, impatience masking his own nervousness. "We still know where she is."

"But they don't know where you're leading us, and I still don't like it," said Yan.

"If you want to lead, go ahead," said Astreya. He heard irritation in the tone of his own voice. Yan kept walking, muttering indistinctly.

The path widened as they entered the shade of the big trees. Black branches laced together overhead blocking the sky with their broad leaves. Astreya stopped, and the empty kegs bumped together hollowly.

"What you do that for?" demanded Yan.

"They're oaks!" exclaimed Astreya when he saw the distinctive leaves up close. "But they're huge!"

"So what," grumbled Yan.

"They don't grow thicker than two hand spans at home," Astreya explained. "Here, two men couldn't get their arms around one of them."

"Who cares? Let's just get the water so's we can get back to the *Mollie*."

At first, the shade seemed dark after the bright sunlight, but within a few steps, they saw a stone-ringed well. When the casks were set up near the well mouth, Astreya looked around him, wishing for his sketching equipment. He imagined a picture of the light dappling through the leaves, through the crooked black branches onto the brown stone circle around the well, which was a destination for five paths. Between the trunks of the trees, Astreya glimpsed the green and red of the colorful houses he had seen from the *Mollie*. He looked back and saw the man in the brown cloak approaching, along with three or four older men. They stopped to watch from a cautious distance of about half a dozen strides. He noticed that they stood with their shoulders hunched, glancing first at Astreya and Yan, and then at each other, as if for reassurance.

The men became part of a picture in Astreya's mind—one of many he might draw to illustrate the tale of his journey. A second picture would be a more detailed view of the men in their loose, almost shapeless clothes. Unlike Village men, they were all beardless, although several had mustaches. Many of the faces were soft and plump with good living, although most of the older men were weathered by sun and wind. Something was different about these faces that puzzled Astreya at first. Then he realized it was what they lacked: their eyes did not have the lines common to every fisherman at the Village—the lines that come from staring out over the sea in all kinds of weather.

Then as he turned to look around him, Astreya saw three young men coming towards the well down one of the five paths between the big trees. By their size, they appeared to be somewhat older than Astreya and Yan, but their faces were beardless, which gave them a childish look. They were obviously sizing up the newcomers in case there was a fight. Then their heads turned as a group of four girls appeared down another of the paths to the well. The girls stopped at the edge of the clearing and whispered together in a group, pretending not to notice the glances that they were attracting both from their own young men and from Astreya. Like the men, the girls wore heavy boots that made their feet look clumsy. Astreya's eyes lingered on their blouses, bright with smocking that lifted their breasts in a way that would have been thought immodest in the Village.

"Help me, can't you?" demanded Yan, struggling with the bucket by the well while Astreya looked around. "Let's get the water and leave."

Yan was having difficulty working the unfamiliar windlass over the well's mouth, since at home in the Village, fetching water was done by dipping buckets into the swift flowing stream.

"It's simple," said Astreya. "Drop the bucket into the well, let it fill, and then wind it up again."

Taking the handle from Yan, he let the bucket fall and then turned the creaking spindle to haul up a bucket full of water. When he looked at Yan, he saw dumb hatred in the young man's eyes, so he put the bucket down and stepped back.

"So, now that smart arse Blackhead has shown me how, I get to do all the work," Yan muttered.

Astreya understood that anything he said or did now would be taken amiss. So, as Yan poured the bucket into the first of the casks, Astreya took a couple of paces towards the men watching the two of them. Smoothing a patch of earth with his foot, he knelt, picked up a small stick, and started to sketch a plan of the lagoon, creek and the houses he had seen. The men stepped forward to watch, turning their heads from one side to the other. While the brown-cloaked man from the boat stood importantly by himself, a heavyset man came forward to stand behind Astreya and see what he was scratching.

"Teenmouth," he said, pointing with the toe of his heavy boot. "River Teen," he continued, and bent over to track a winding course inland with his finger. Astreya looked into his wide and puffy face, but found it as inexpressive as his flat voice.

"Is there a city to the south?" asked Astreya slowly.

The man dug at the ground with his foot, scratching a rough map.

"Charton be in the south. Up river, then past the Learneds' Castle, and then on down to the great harbor. Couple days on a horse. Mebby a week on foot. Mebby less."

The hesitation about distances made Astreya wonder if his informant had ever been to the places. Hoping to get more information, he reached into his pocket for his father's notebook, but before he could use it, Yan interrupted him.

"Come on, 'Streya," said Yan. "Help me with these kegs. I'm doing all the work here."

"I'll be there in a moment," said Astreya, without turning around.

He put Yan out of his mind and focused on getting more information from the Teenmouth man, who went on speaking as Astreya scratched fresh marks on the ground. He found his ear becoming accustomed to the man's slow talk, even though some words were run together as if the man were bored, or hated talking. This was clearly not the case, however, becasue Astreya could hardly ask his questions in the spate of information he was given, most of it far too detailed and reliant on local knowledge to be useful. He did manage to catch what he took to be place names: Teenmouth, Mizzle, Markham, Charton; but he had difficulty in working out where they were, or whether they were inland or on the coast. The one-sided exchange continued until Yan finished filling the second keg. By that time, Astreya had learned that there were at least two more gaps in the sand bar edging the lagoon, more villages both east and west, and a harbor somewhere to the southeast. Distances remained vague, and so did the configuration of the shoreline, which he guessed ran east and then hooked around to the southwest.

The other men moved closer, and were quietly exchanging observations about Astreya as he talked to their spokesman. Yan muttered just loud enough for the two of them to hear.

"No help. Black-haired big head. Fart face. Suck up."

The man glanced at Yan, his attention broken. He frowned at Astreya, who decided to bring the confusing interview to an end. He stood and lowered his head respectfully.

"We thank you for the water, for your help and advice," said Astreya formally.

The man nodded briefly, and returned to his fellows, who were talking among themselves. Astreya caught a few words: "... black beard... strange... different... not like the others..." He shrugged off annoyance at words unwelcome even in strange accents, and turned to go, focusing on his pleasure that he would have news for Roaring Jack. As he picked up his end of the two oars, Astreya smiled broadly, completely ignoring the fear and misgiving in Yan's face.

"I've got some directions," he said. "I think there's a harbor to the southeast."

When Yan only grumbled to himself, Astreya felt his excitement turn to annoyance.

"Oh, all right," he said. "Be a punky old log in a bog, and don't say anything."

The rhyming insult from his childhood was out before he could stop himself. An apology was out of the question with the Teenmouth men watching, and anyway, Astreya did not feel repentant. The kegs dangling from the oars on their shoulders, they walked slowly from among the trees into the bright glare of the sun, Astreya in the lead.

When they were almost to the dike, Yan suddenly gripped both oars tight and stopped walking. The other end of the oars slid from Astreya's shoulders, bumping painfully down his back. The two kegs slid down the fallen oars, hitting Astreya in the back of his legs. He staggered and turned, a question on his lips, but before he had a chance to ask it, Yan pulled one of the oars free from its lashing to the keg, and swung it in a whistling arc. The blade of the oar struck Astreya on the neck. He fell heavily, and a second blow hit him in the back. Now all he could do was to roll into a ball to protect himself. Two more rib-cracking blows came down on his sides. Astreya tried to speak, but could only manage a grunt. Yan's voice reached him through the roaring in his ears.

"I hate you, I hate you, I hate you," repeated Yan over and over. "You're so clever, so smart. You make me into nothing. You help me. Me! You... you foreigner."

The final blow hit Astreya across the side of his head. Yan kicked him in the ribs, and ran towards the beach, dragging the oars behind him. Astreya struggled to his knees, saw black sliced with crimson and heard shouts diminishing into a huge dark distance. He did not feel his face hit the earth.

Chapter 6:

In which the Mollie sails North without Astreya

When Yan burst over the top of the green dike along the shore, the *Mollie*'s crew had stopped pretending to work, and even Roaring Jack stared at Yan's sudden return. One oar trailed from his left hand, and he clutched the other awkwardly across his body. He had no sooner crested the dike than he fell down the bank towards the water, landing on the mud in a tangle of oars and limbs. Struggling to his feet, he stumbled to the rowboat, threw in the oars, pushed at the bow until it was afloat, and then splashed aboard, nearly falling a second time.

"What's happening?"

"Where's 'Streya?"

"Here they come!"

Red Ian, Roaring Jack and Scarm all spoke at once.

Rowing splashily towards the *Mollie*, Yan could see the men running along the top of the dike, some readying their bows as they came. Confused shouting from the men on shore spurred Yan to redouble his efforts. He pulled at his oars with all his strength, jerking the little dory across the river. Still splashing wildly, he arrived at the *Mollie* with a thump. Red Ian reached down a huge hand and pulled him aboard by the back of his shirt, the oars still in his hands. Scarm reached with a boathook, scooped up the painter and secured the little boat astern of the *Mollie*.

"Where's 'Streya?" demanded Roaring Jack, holding Yan by the shoulders and shaking him.

"'Streya's... 'Streya's dead. They killed him."

"I'll have their balls for breakfast!"

Smacking a huge hand on the cabin top as he spoke, Red Ian swung one leg over the side to get into the rowboat. An arrow hit the side of the boat, and stuck there, quivering. They all froze.

"Don't let them kill me too!" whimpered Yan.

Roaring Jack reacted first. With one hand, he shoved Yan's head below the cockpit coaming, and with the other, he jerked Red Ian backwards into the boat. Ignoring the archers on shore, the skipper stood at the tiller.

"Scarm! The anchor!"

As Scarm started forward, a volley of arrows zipped overhead, one of them striking the mast and glancing off into the cockpit. Roaring Jack did not flinch.

"Red! Hoist the main. Scarm's got the jib."

The sails jerked upwards. Roaring Jack sheeted in, both shielding Scarm from view, and turning the *Mollie*'s bow towards the sea

"Ne'er mind the anchor. Cut us adrift!"

More arrows flew, most of them passing overhead. Two hit the *Mollie*'s side and one skipped across the cabin top.

"She's coming around to port. Stay low, Scarm!" Roaring Jack shouted.

Slowly the *Mollie*'s bow swung to the sluggish current.

"Get down yerself, Jack," said Scarm, as he slid, feet first, into the cockpit. "We're washing the anchor on the port side," he added calmly. "Seems a pity to leave it behind."

Roaring Jack put the tiller hard over, and the *Mollie* turned her stern towards the men along the dike. The wind freshened, the boom swung over with a thud, and the sail began to draw. Scarm stood to trim the jib. With both the wind and the current to help her, the boat gathered speed. Arrows splashed into the water astern, and the shouting on the shore faded as the river joined with the sea, and the wind strengthened.

"We've done it, lads," said Roaring Jack. "You can come up now."

Yan and Red Ian both stood up, cautiously scanning the shoreline. Scarm still stood by the jib sheet. An arrow pinned his crippled arm to the mast.

"Sliced squirmin' eels, Scarm. Yer hit."

"Just get me free of it," said Scarm between clenched teeth.

In the same instant, Red Ian had a hand on the tiller and Roaring Jack was pulling his knife out of its sheath. The skipper reached behind Scarm's back and cut the arrow close to its head. Scarm sagged forward, the shaft still poking through his arm, as the skipper eased him into the cockpit.

"Yank it out, Jack."

Roaring Jack hesitated. He gently pulled the shirt away from around the arrow, tore it back to the shoulder and then sliced the shirt sleeve free in two pieces. As he bunched the torn pieces together, he frowned at the blood oozing around the arrow shaft.

"Grit yer teeth, Scarm."

Scarm grunted as the skipper pulled the arrow out with one hand, and immediately clamped his wadded shirtsleeve around both the holes. Roaring Jack and Scarm both nodded approvingly as blood soaked into the improvised dressing.

"Could a' bin squirtin'," said Roaring Jack.

"But not for long," said Scarm softly.

"Yan, get me other shirt," said Roaring Jack. "Top o' me kit bag. Go now."

Yan jumped down into the cabin, rummaged around and came back up, the shirt held ahead of him. The skipper unceremoniously tore it into strips and bound up Scarm's arm.

"We have to go back for Astreya," said Scarm. "He may only be hurt."

"He's dead, Scarm. I saw them do it. His head's all broken in," Yan sobbed.

Tears streaked the mud that spattered his face. Secretly, he was amazed at how easily they came, and how well they reinforced his lies. He knelt on the cockpit sole, his head bowed, knowing that as long as he did not have to meet their eyes, his story would be believed.

"At least go back and talk to them," said Scarm.

He tried to get to his feet, but lost his balance. The skipper caught him and eased him back into a sitting position.

"Put me ashore, and I'll talk to 'em," said Red Ian. "I'll talk 'em right nice."

"They'll kill you, Red!" whimpered Yan. "They don't care."

There was a silence during which Yan saw his chance.

"Put me ashore, Skipper," he said, with a tremble in his voice that was only partly a show. "Maybe when they see I'm no danger to them, they'll listen."

Roaring Jack finished binding Scarm's arm. "It's enough that we've lost 'Streya without Oi send you to be killed."

Yan turned his sigh of relief into a carefully crafted moan.

"I should've..." he stammered.

"It's my fault, not yours, Yan," said Roaring Jack. "And now Oi've got to tell Alana her son's gone because o' me." His huge voice cracked; he cleared his throat and shook his head. "Now there's a load of work to do, and two men short. Stay where y'are, Scarm. Gi' me the tiller, Red; an' fetch the anchor aboard. We'll have to tack before we try for the gap in the reef. Ready about."

He brought the *Mollie* about close to the reef, and headed back towards the shore on the starboard tack. Red Ian bent below the boom and squinted under the belly of the jib with his head only a couple of hand spans from the water.

"Shoaling up, Skipper," he said. "I can see bottom."

"Roight, Red."

Roaring Jack took the *Mollie* as close to the shore as he dared, risking the possibility of grounding, but needing a good angle with which to attack the reef.

"Ready about... lee ho!" he muttered.

Red Ian tended the sheets, bringing the *Mollie* about to head for the gap in the breakers. The wind eased as they started into the narrow passage, and then as they sailed into the weedy stretch of water between the breakers, it strengthened again. With the skipper looking to windward, and Red Ian to lee, they drove close-hauled through confused water that swirled mud-brown and weedy, then foam-flecked and finally, sea green. The *Mollie*'s bow dipped and rose to the swell, then punched into the first real wave.

"Y'can ease her, Skipper. Y' got plenty room now."

With Red Ian handling both main and jib sheets, Roaring Jack coaxed the *Mollie* through two more waves, on into blue water. When the two of them looked down at their feet, Yan was holding Scarm's head as he lay the cockpit sole.

"He keeled over when we came about. I caught him. Is he alive?"

Roaring Jack knelt and put his fingers to Scarm's throat.

"He's alive, but he's passed out," said Roaring Jack. "Good work, Yan. Keep her as she goes, Red. Come on Yan, take his feet and we'll get him below. It's a lee berth for Scarm and double watches for us. We've run out of luck. We're headin' home."

Chapter 7:

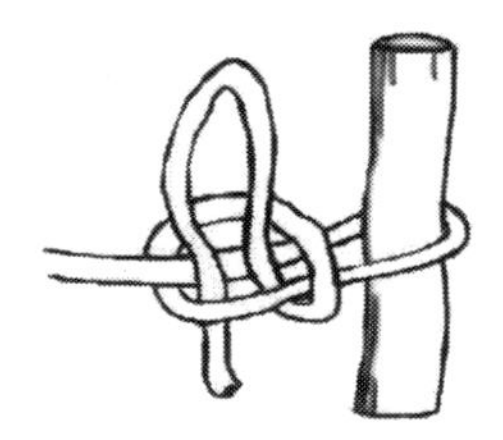

In Which Astreya Becomes a Farmer

Astreya looked up at clay-chinked beams he had never seen before. His head throbbed when he moved it, and cautious stirrings brought both pain and the realization that his head and shoulder were bandaged. When he tried to roll over and look about, he heard himself groan. Almost immediately, a woman's face looked down on him, and her hands pressed gently onto his bare shoulder. Astreya looked into dark eyes above a sharp chin and high cheekbones. Her brown hair was braided and coiled up high on her head.

"Just you lie still."

She frowned, and Astreya saw that she was older than he had first thought. The flat, almost expressionless tone of her voice awoke recent memories for Astreya, and he slowly came to the conclusion that he must be in a Teenmouth house.

"I have to get back to the *Mollie*—back to my boat," he said.

"Not now. You can't go anywhere."

She frowned, her lips compressing into the thin, firm line of a parent speaking to a willful child. Astreya struggled to rise, but when crimson-shot blackness blanked out his vision, he sank back. The woman was right. There was not much point in thinking about walking to the *Mollie* when he could not even sit up.

"What happened?" he asked, as his vision cleared.

"My man Jeb brought you here after you were hurt. Nasty mess of cuts and bruises you were, too, I can tell you. Good thing you were wearing that woolen hat: it saved you from a broken skull. But we patched you up, and you'll be all right soon."

"We?" Astreya asked.

"Eva, my girl, and me. You were lucky to be brought here to us who know something of the Healing Art. I was apprenticed to a Healer for two seasons before I became Jeb's wife," she said, her mouth softening slightly in self-congratulation.

"What is...?" Astreya began.

"No more questions now. You can talk to my man when he comes home. Rest. Eva will be here soon with some water for you."

Astreya persuaded himself to relax, which was not difficult when he thought about his attempt to get up. The promise of a drink made him thirsty, and so to be ready, he watched the doorway. Then a patch of sunlight on the wall beside him drew his eyes. The light seemed to move in jerks to a new position. Eventually, it diminished from a square to an oblong, to a sliver of light, golden with evening. At some time during these changes, soft footsteps came to his bed, an arm raised his shoulders, a cup was pressed to his lips, he drank, and then fell back into fitful sleep. When he awoke fully, a flickering candle lit the face of a girl. The candle dripped hot wax onto the blanket as she looked into his eyes, frowning. Astreya looked back into her brown-eyed gaze and saw a slender nose and a small, well shaped mouth, firm with attention to any telltale signs of a serious head injury. He blinked in the dim light, taking stock of her heart-shaped face, which was framed by wisps of brown hair that had escaped from two tight pigtails. He made an effort to smile at her, and she blushed, her concentration broken. Then her face became shadowed and indistinct as she lowered the candle and stepped backwards.

"Mother, I think he's better," she called.

Two faces hovered over him, the candle between them. Astreya smiled again, their mouths lifted at the corners in the same way, and they exchanged a glance of mutual congratulation. After a long silence, the woman nodded a couple of times, and spoke.

"My man Jeb's doing chores. You missed supper. Twice. Perhaps you can try some soup." She paused. "What's your name?"

"Astreya," he replied.

"'Streya," they both repeated.

Astreya accepted almost gratefully the echo of his own Villagers' mispronunciation of his name, and he did not correct them. As they stood looking down on Astreya, and he up at them, they heard the footfalls of heavy boots that thumped towards the outer door and scraped on a step.

"How's the boy?" asked a man's voice, without enthusiasm.

"He's awake," replied Eva. "He's going to be all right, Father."

Astreya rolled his head on the pillow to look at the newcomer. Though his temples throbbed menacingly, the dark threat of unconsciousness stayed at a distance. All he could make out in the light of Eva's single candle was the curve of the man's chin, dark with stubble. In the shadows, the man's eyes were dark circles above full cheeks.

"I have to go back to my boat..." he began.

"He doesn't know, Father," said Eva.

"Young fellow," said Jeb's slow, flat voice from the shadows. "You don't want to go back to those people. They don't care about you. You don't even look like them. The boy who hit you ran back to the boat. When we went after him, he wouldn't stop.

We shouted. We rowed after them. They pulled up anchor. Sailed away."

"No!" said Astreya, struggling to sit. "Roaring Jack wouldn't leave me. I know he wouldn't."

Jeb's voice did not alter. "I saw it all. We shouted. They paid us no mind."

His matter-of-fact, plodding way of speaking was more convincing than emotion-filled persuasion. Convinced against his will, Astreya slid down in the bed and turned his head away. Yan's attack came back to him in all its treachery, and each of his hurts throbbed, painfully recalling what had happened. Slowly, the pain ebbed to numbness, and he sank into something between sleep and waking. He could hear the family going about their evening duties, but his mind wandered. One moment, he expected to awake aboard the *Mollie* or even in the Village. The next, he was holding hopelessness at bay by refusing to think of anything save how he might draw a picture of the light and shadows of the dimly lit room. He fell asleep and dreamed of faceless men throwing stones at him, as the *Mollie*'s crew watched and laughed. He woke, sweating, and listened for a while to the sounds of Eva and her mother clearing up after the evening meal. He thought he was keeping track of what was going on, but he must have slept, because the next time he was fully conscious, the house was dark. The silence was broken only by the drip of dew from the roof. A patch of moonlight fell palely onto the blanket that covered his chest. When he rolled his head cautiously to his left, he saw that his bed lay in the corner between two outside walls, with a curtain making a tiny, triangular room.

Astreya's mind cleared, and he started to separate reality from his disturbed dreams. He recalled the scene at the well, and at first could think of no reason why Yan would want to attack him. Then as he remembered his irritation at Yan's complaints, Astreya heard his own voice giving orders, treating Yan as if he were a dunce, and he recognized what he had seen in Yan's eyes just before the oar swung for the last time. Belatedly, another memory of Yan with a stone in his hand rose in Astreya's mind, and he knew that ever since the fight on the beach the urge to kill had lurked in Yan like a worm in a nut.

"But I was right," Astreya murmured indistinctly to the darkness. "My sketching was more important than Yan's work. And I did my share of the bailing during the storm. And I saved his sorry arse when he nearly fell overboard."

He tried to justify himself out of a dark well of loneliness, but as he thought of how Roaring Jack, Scar Arm Ian and Red Ian had all accepted and even valued him, he could not understand why they had sided with Yan, sailed off and abandoned him. Slowly, Astreya began to ask himself if he had been deceived even before Yan's betrayal. If he had been so wrong about them, who could he trust? He blinked as tears distorted his view of the moonlit room, slid across his temples and soaked into the bandage around his head. He bit the insides of his cheeks, angry at having succumbed to childish weeping. Eventually, he slept.

Astreya was woken by a chorus of morning noises: chickens clucked and scratched outside his window, water sloshed in a pail, and on the kitchen stove a kettle clattered its lid before its contents glugged into a teapot. For a little while, he lay with his eyes closed, recalling memories of his mother's cottage in the sounds of the strange house to which he had been brought. When nothing came of this save a deepening sense of loss, he opened his eyes. The curtain had been drawn back, and the girl called Eva was looking down at him.

"Mother, he's awake again," she said. "Really awake this time." She bent over him and stared into his eyes, blushing when he smiled at her. "His eyes aren't dull anymore," she said, and stopped, embarrassed.

"I don't think I said 'thank you,'" said Astreya slowly, as memories of what he had heard and said came back to him. "How long have I been here?"

"More'n a couple o' days," said the flat, masculine voice, out of sight from the little room, which Astreya now saw was only the corner of the kitchen. Astreya sat up cautiously as the man came over to stand beside the bed. He saw a large chin salted with white stubble. Above the almost lipless mouth were eyes that glinted between puffy lids. Jeb had no expression at all: neither in his face nor in the words he spoke.

"First you were awake. You spoke, but you didn't say words. Then you talked a bit. The wife said I shouldn't tell you that your boat left. But before I did, you were restless. After, you slept."

Astreya knew he could not deal with the information Judith's husband was giving him if he let it touch his emotions. He nodded, forcing back despair.

"I'd like to get up," he said, and started to swing his feet over the edge of the bed.

He stopped when he discovered that he was naked under the sheet. He looked around and saw his clothes, washed and folded, on the foot of the bed. The knife that had been his father's lay on top. Worry drove out embarrassment as he clutched at his left arm, where his fingers closed gratefully on the bracelet under the woven string Scar Arm Ian had given him. The grey string glowed green above the jewel it concealed.

"There was no taking that off you," said Judith. "You thrashed about, so we left it alone."

"It was my father's. He's dead." Astreya spoke in a tone that discouraged questions. Then, not wanting to be rude to people who had helped him, he touched the bandage on his head and added, "You've done a wonderful job. I'm all right—apart from a tender spot above my ear, and a few bruises."

"Mother thinks you'll have a scar, but your hair will cover it," said Eva.

"You'll stay calm, 'til the wife is sure you haven't taken hurt inside your head." There was no compassion in Jeb's order.

Eva moved to the kitchen to help her mother, and Jeb went back to his place at the table. Astreya drew the grey homespun curtain and pulled on clothes no longer stiff with salt. As he did so, he became aware how much had been done for him. His body was clean, there was a white bandage around his head, another on his shoulder, but he was surprised that there was so little discomfort when he felt his cuts and bruises through the material. But when he pulled his shirt over his head, he winced as it caught on the cloth that ran around both his temples.

Moving quietly in bare feet, Astreya drew back the curtain. Just beyond one end of the pole on which it ran was a door that presumably led to a back room. Ahead of him was the main room. On his right was the window over his bed, and a little farther away, a second window over a table scrubbed white by many cleanings. An outside door was open in the far wall, through which he could see a couple of brindled hens scratching in the red earth path outside. To his left was a brick and metal stove between two more windows. The far corner held a set of shelves for dishes above a closed cupboard.

Astreya took all this in quickly, and then focused on the three people. The man named Jeb sat in the one chair, with his back towards Astreya. He was powerful, work-hardened, stoop-shouldered and callous-handed. Graying stubble obscured deep lines on either side of his thin-lipped mouth. He moved as if he sensed that he was being observed, so Astreya turned his attention towards Eva's mother. She was tall and so slim that the bones of her forearms were visible, and she walked with a slight stoop, as if she was carrying a burden on her thin shoulders. She wore a loose white blouse above a brown skirt that fell to her ankles. As he watched, she carried an earthenware jug and a loaf of bread to the table, where Eva was already seated on a bench under the window. While Eva had been all alertness and swift motion, her mother moved with a tired efficiency born of countless repetitions. His eyes lingered on Eva's sleek brown hair, which today flowed loose down to the middle of her back, held by a ribbon over the top of her head. Eva blinked up at him in the sunlight from the window under which she sat, her eyelashes throwing tiny shadows onto the bridge of her nose. Astreya wondered how he might draw so fine a detail. Eva blushed at his intense stare, and pointed to the stool opposite her. She smiled as he sat down, and then after a quick glance at her father, focused on spooning porridge from the bowl in front of her. Her mother joined her on the bench below the window.

"Eat," said Jeb, pushing back his chair. "Eva, you're finished. Go tend to your chores. Don't be chattering to him." He spoke as one who expects to be obeyed, and though his voice was low, his tone was harsh. Astreya thought of Roaring Jack's huge voice, and then banished the memory before he could dwell on how he had been deceived and abandoned. When Jeb pushed back his chair, stood and walked to the door, drew on boots he had left at the doorstep, and strode off into the morning, Astreya noticed that both women visibly relaxed. The tension faded from Eva's face, and even her mother's firmly pursed mouth relaxed somewhat.

For a while, Astreya had no consciousness of time. He ate his breakfast as much with his eyes as by its tastes. Milk in a deep brown earthenware jug, golden butter on a blue-ringed plate, a crusty loaf on a breadboard of black hardwood, all lying on the white wood of the table, its grain raised by repeated scrubbings.

He took a bite of bread, and was amazed by the taste.

"Is something wrong?" Judith asked.

"Not at all," Astreya answered. "It's just that it's so good."

"Don't you have bread where you come from?"

"Mostly we eat oatcakes."

"Oats?" said Eva. "Like we feed to horses?"

"No wheat, then?" said Judith.

Astreya shook his head. They both looked at him pityingly, and he felt himself blush.

When he had finished eating, Astreya stood to carry his plate and mug to the little washstand beside the stove, where

Judith was cleaning dishes. Eva and her mother both seemed surprised. They refused to accept any help from Astreya; indeed, they seemed to take it amiss when he suggested that he could make himself useful around the house. Astreya did not insist, but sat a little uncomfortably at the table while they worked around him. He plied them with questions about Teenmouth. Eva was glad to oblige him as she helped her mother with the chores, and if she talked more than she worked, her mother took no official notice.

Astreya discovered that Teenmouth was made up of a dozen extended families, more or less interrelated, most of them with several children. The men were all farmers. None of them used boats except to paddle across the little river, or to set nightlines in the estuary. He had the impression that Eva thought Teenmouth and all its people were deadly dull. On the other hand, Judith's interests were intently focused on the doings of neighbors, as well as familiar topics such as rain, sun and the growth of plants and animals. Astreya found himself wishing to be back in the Village, where women's gossip was about familiar people he had known all his life, and the men's talk ran to speculating (and sometimes boasting) about where and how to fish.

Since he had little interest in the doings of people he did not know, Astreya asked about what lay around where the *Mollie* had brought him. He learned that Eva knew little about nearby communities, nor did she have much curiosity about any of the ones which were close, all of which she spurned even more than Teenmouth. However, she was fascinated by what and who was further away. When she asked Astreya why the *Mollie* had adventured to the south, he explained as best he could, and she was curious why Roaring Jack would want to leave the land and sea he knew. He took a breath to explain, but in that moment, he remembered that most people in the Village had opposed the journey south. He abruptly changed the subject to hide how he had lost faith in his skipper. Forestalling questions, he looked into Eva's brown eyes, and she was suddenly silent.

"What do you want to do with your life, Eva?

The enthusiasm of her reply surprised him.

"I want to be a somebody," she said earnestly. "I want to go to the Learneds' Castle, and study from books. I want to read, to know how to make people well. I want to be a Healer."

Blushing, she gave Astreya a challenging look that he had not seen before. She put both her hands on the table and leaned towards him. Astreya was momentarily distracted, because girls in the Village did not wear their bodices so colorfully embroidered, so tight or so low. He dragged his eyes up to look into hers.

"Why don't you, then?" asked Astreya, focusing on her face and the urgency in her voice. "Didn't your mother tell me that she had...?"

"Mother was apprenticed to a Healer. He only taught her what he was too lazy to do himself. And then he died, she became my mother, and then she could learn no more. I want to go and learn it all at the Castle."

"Hush now, the Castle's only for boys," said her mother.

"It wasn't always that way," said Eva. "You told me there used to be women Healers... even women Learneds."

"That was a long time ago, girl, and things change."

"But if I could go, I think they'd accept me. If only father would let me..."

"It's not up to your father. You know that. Teenmouth has only one place to fill, and you know it's got to go to Seth or Jacob or nobody."

"But they don't want to go!" Eva said, stamping her foot. "The fools don't even care!"

"What's the Castle, and who goes there?" Astreya asked.

"It's up country to the south. Every few years Teenmouth gets to send someone to the Castle. They stay there for two years, and when they're finished, they're sent to places like Teenmouth that need a healer. Places that don't send someone, don't get one. They teach you how to read and write. And of course, that makes you different when you get back. That's why neither Seth nor Jacob wants to go. They're stupid."

"Can none in Teenmouth read, then?" asked Astreya.

"'Course not. Well, nobody but a few elders, and they aren't about to teach farmers' sons, 'cause if they did, they'd lose their authority, wouldn't they? Some of the older men, like my father, can make out a few words. But not read to learn. Why should they? I mean, can you?"

Astreya nodded, and as he did so, realized that she'd thought she'd known the answer to her question, so he nodded again. She drew back from the table suddenly, her dress swirling around her ankles.

"You can read?" she asked incredulously. "You're scarce more than a boy."

Astreya nodded again. Eva called to her mother, who had gone outside the house to tend her bread oven, and then rushed out to tell her. Astreya was left alone in the kitchen, pondering what seemed to him an excessive reaction. In the Village, not everyone could read, but most could spell out simple, plain words on paper, make lists, or write down important instructions. The kind of reading that Scarm had helped Astreya achieve might have seemed odd or unchancy to some of the older women of the Village, but certainly would not have awakened the wonder that Eva's face expressed.

Thinking about the Village reopened the night's pit of despair. He closed his eyes, breathed deeply, deliberately opened them and looked around as if he were about to sketch the room and its contents. For a few moments the distraction worked. He noticed that there were neither pictures nor texts nor woven hangings on the walls, as there would have been in the Village. Though only a few men like Scar Arm Ian or Astreya's father were "eager for words" as the Village called it, nonetheless, almost all the cottages had texts worked in needle and thread or with a poker on wood, or even carved on whale bone. "Haste makes waste," was a favorite, but there were also phrases with no apparent meaning, such as "Remake now thy creature in the dew of the hearth," which hung over Roaring Jack's fireplace, almost obliterated by the smoke from winter-long fires. This train of thought brought him back to his skipper, and the pit yawned once more.

Eva and her mother came back into the farmhouse, curiosity showing on their faces. Judith wiped her hands on her apron, and then shook it out the doorway to remove fine ash and flour from her bread oven. Eva was at her side, flipping her hair back over her shoulder.

"You can read and write," said Eva. "Go on. Tell her yourself."

Astreya nodded, embarrassed by the unsought admiration. He had never spoken about books with any of the Villagers of his own age, because Scarm had asked him not to, and also because he knew that his accomplishment would make him seem even more strange and foreign. He suspected that the adults would have been just as unimpressed. But things were different here. Apparently, Teenmouth people—other than the two strangely named young men—revered those who could read, because nothing would satisfy Eva and her mother until Astreya had written their names—Eva and Judith—on a scrap of paper with a twig of charcoal. Judith nodded her head approvingly.

"The Master of Healing from the Castle did it just so when he made a visit here. I was little more than a child," she said.

"Mine's less than yours, Mother," said Eva. "What does that mean?"

Eva was fascinated as Astreya explained how the letters stood for sounds. They barely heard Judith leave. Eva leaned on Astreya's arm, her head next to his, looking at the letters he was making. When he glanced at her, he saw her brown eyes narrowed with concentration, her lips parted, and she held the tip of her tongue between her teeth. Astreya was captivated.

Neither noticed how much of the morning passed with the two of them side by side, her hair occasionally tickling his cheek when she nodded her head, his hand guiding hers as he showed her how to form letters. Judith interrupted them from time to time, and even found more scraps of paper on which they could practice writing, but they soon returned to their fascinations: Eva with words, Astreya with Eva. Judith stood for some time watching them in thoughtful silence before she shooed them away from the table so that she could prepare the evening meal. When evening came and Jeb returned for dinner, Astreya again found himself being shown off like a rare and valuable animal. Eva showed her father her careful attempts to write her own name beside Astreya's.

"You see, father, you see," she said eagerly. "Girls can learn to read and write. I could go and learn, be a Healer, come back and be able to read... and everything."

Jeb looked at her narrowly, his slit eyes almost invisible, as if his daughter was a bright light.

"Don't you think, Husband," said Judith softly, "that Teenmouth has maybe had its problem solved by providence? Just when the elders can't find a young man to send to the Castle, out of nowhere comes a boat bringing one to us. And who knows, Daughter, perhaps he'll return when he becomes learned. If he is as generous natured as he is now, he might teach you to read and write."

"But Father, it's I who should be going..." Eva began.

Her father jerked his forearm upright, hand open, his elbow still on the table. Eva fell back as if he had struck her. She shook her head, and Astreya's cheek was first whipped by her hair, and then splashed by a hot teardrop.

"Father, it's not fair," she said, getting control of herself.

Jeb closed his hand. His fist was lumpy from years of plowing, seeding and reaping. Eva was silent, and Judith's face tensed.

"Your place, Daughter, is here. Your duty is in Teenmouth. No girl should speak of the Councilors' choice of a Scholar. Nor you, Wife."

Slowly, Jeb lowered his hand until it lay on the table, the fingers loosely clenched. He tipped back his head to look down at both of them and as he continued to stare down his somewhat bulbous nose, Astreya saw Judith's eyes focus on her lap. Eva tossed her hair, caught a strand between her fingers and pulled hard. Her eyes were wide and watery, but she made no sound, even though her breasts rose and fell as if she had been running.

Astreya was shocked by the intensity of the moment. In the Village, he had often overheard couples arguing with each other. Indeed, almost everyone at some time had heard Roaring Jack and his wife Mollie when they were launched on one of their occasional shouting matches. But the general opinion was that these were like summer storms: loud and angry, but soon passing. He looked at each member of this Teenmouth family in turn, seeing something much more bitter and lasting.

Without thinking, Astreya intervened to protect the two women from Jeb's humiliating stare.

"I have to get back to my boat... to the Village... to find my..." he stammered.

"Put that out of your mind," Jeb ordered. "The lad who struck you must have lied. Told his people we murdered you. Reason why they wouldn't listen. When the big one looked like he would attack, we had to scare them off. They didn't care for you. Small wonder. You don't even look like them."

Astreya felt his last hope slapped down by Jeb's words. He bowed his head. Behind his closed eyes, he saw whitecaps to the horizon as if from the *Mollie*'s masthead, headlands circled by gulls, the foaming stream in the Village, Alana's hair in the wind. Astreya hugged his chest, holding himself together against the ache of loss. His fingers found his father's bracelet under his shirt, and the images faded slowly before his mind's eye. A tingling started below the silver band on his arm. He felt the hair on the back of his neck move, he raised his head and met Jeb's gaze.

"If I can't get back..." He almost stopped, but hurried on. "Then I'd like to go and see this Castle place. Maybe they'd know how I could..."

"You too, 'Streya?" cried Eva. "I thought you were different." A stool crashed to the floor as she turned and ran out of the house, her skirts flaring behind her. Judith righted Eva's stool, and started to serve Jeb his evening meal, her face inscrutable.

"You'll ask for nothing," said Jeb. "You owe me your life. You'll pay for it working my land. Now eat your food."

Astreya tried to eat, but his stomach was in a knot. He wanted to object, but everything he could say foundered because he had no alternative, no bargaining position, no power at all. Opposite him across the table, Jeb put food into his mouth and chewed stolidly, occasionally taking a swallow from a mug of dark beer. Judith lit two small oil lamps, placed them on the table and served herself small portions of food that she did not finish. At the end of the silent meal, Jeb pushed back his chair and cleared his throat judicially.

"Young man, you've sat and eaten at my table. If you're obedient and useful, you may again. You're healed enough to be in the barn, not under the same roof as my daughter. It's not seemly."

Jeb's slow speech ended. He emptied the earthenware jug into his beer mug, drank deeply, and sighed like a man who has finished a heavy task.

Astreya could stand it no longer. He took a breath to protest, but before he could speak, Judith caught his eye. She was standing behind her husband, reaching for his empty plate while his eyes were focused on the inside of his beer mug. With a small gesture of one hand, she pleaded for Astreya's silence and agreement. He would have ignored the request had she not followed it with a glance at her husband. Distressed to see her fear, Astreya sat silent. In the quiet room, Jeb's mug gurgled as he drained the last of his beer. He wiped a face with lips so thin that his mouth looked as if it had been cut with a knife, grated his chair back and stood.

"Come now, young stranger. I'm going to make a farmer of you. Wife, give him bedding and send him after me. I'll deal with Eva later."

Taking up one of the lamps, he strode out the door.

Judith found a couple of blankets, much rougher than those under which Astreya had slept, and handed them to him.

"What does he mean, 'I'll deal with Eva'?" Astreya whispered.

"She'll get the sharp side of his tongue and the flat of his hand," said Judith softly. "He won't use a stick, or harm her so it shows. But he's set in his ways."

Astreya stared at her. Growing up in the Village, he had never known parents who struck their children, save for a mother delivering the occasional smack on the bottom of an erring toddler. In rare cases, when a boy had done something mean, disrespectful or dangerous to others, his father might led him by the ear to the woodshed where he would administer a green switch to the offender's behind. That a father would strike his almost-grown daughter was an idea entirely foreign to Astreya.

"Why did you stop me from speaking? Maybe I could have..."

"Stopped him from correcting Eva later? No, 'Streya. It's a kind notion, but it won't work. Once she crossed him directly, that was that. The fat was in the fire. I know."

Her voice fell so that Astreya barely caught the last two words.

"It's best if you bend with the wind," she said slowly. "You'll learn. Now hurry after him."

Astreya stumbled out the door into darkness. At first, he could see nothing under the trees that stood around the cottage.

Then he glimpsed yellow light from Jeb's lamp just before it disappeared around the corner of a building. Astreya's bare feet felt his way down an earth path to where a tall barn blocked the stars. He turned the corner to where Jeb was waiting for him, silhouetted by the lamp in his hand. The farmer thumbed a latch, opened a door and pushed Astreya inside. He struck his shin on something unseen, and fell onto a low bed, cushioned by the blankets in his arms.

"No lights in the barn, sailor boy. Ever. If I catch you..."

He slammed the door, leaving his threat unspoken. It did not have the effect he wanted.

"He thinks he's smart, but he's a stupid brute," Astreya whispered between clenched teeth as he rolled himself into his blankets. "He's not going to scare me."

In his moment of anger, his arm tingled under his bracelet. Astreya pulled back the blankets, shoved up his sleeve, eased the woven string so that enough light pulsed from the stone that he could look around his tiny wooden cell. In the mysterious greenish light, he could make out a small window in the wall on his right, a door at his feet, and the stool over which he had fallen, all surrounded by rough sawn wooden walls.

Astreya had broken Jeb's first rule, and he enjoyed doing it.

Chapter 8:

In which Astreya works for Jeb

Something knocked loudly on the other side of the wall close beside Astreya's head, jolting him awake. Before he could take stock of where he was, the door of his cell-like room was thrown open, and Jeb stood silhouetted against a sky brightening towards sunup. He threw a shirt onto Astreya's bed.

"Put these on. Y' can't work in them sailor clothes."

He stood in the doorway while Astreya pulled on the coarsely woven shirt. It was little more than a large sack with a slit for his head and loose sleeves that flapped at his elbows. He was going to tuck his shirt into his trousers when he noticed that Jeb's shirt hung down to his thighs, so he did the same.

"Get on with it. Chores. Muck out the horses."

"Horses?"

"Two. Jonah's knocking on the wall. Sally's the quiet one. Shovel out their boxes, give them two forks of hay each, fill their water tubs. They get their oats in the evening. Don't eat their supper."

Again came the twist to his lips that was Jeb's version of a smile. Astreya ignored the jibe as Jeb looked him up and down.

"Y' need boots. Come. Can't tend horses barefoot. Yer no good to me with broken feet."

Astreya followed Jeb around to the other end of the hip-roofed barn where double doors gave entrance to the horses' stalls. Jeb disappeared into the dimness of the barn, and a moment later two well used heavy boots thumped on the ground by Astreya's feet. He was stooping to put them on when he saw the heads of two horses looking expectantly out of their stalls. Astreya stood still, amazed, the uncomfortable boots forgotten.

"Never seen horses before?"

"Only in books."

Jeb grunted scornfully. "Go easy. Call 'em by name. Don't take no guff. There's the shovel and the barrow: get started."

Astreya picked up the shovel, took a deep breath and walked slowly towards the first horse's head, which was outside the shoulder high door of its stall. Astreya looked up into a large brown eye. The horse stretched his neck and blew warm breath out his nose into Astreya's face. It was a pleasant smell that reminded him of the dog Skip, who would greet him by putting two front paws on his shoulders and breathing heavily. The memory gave him confidence, and he took a step closer. The horse huffed again, and then deliberately sniffed Astreya's hair. Astreya stood still until the big head shoved against his shoulder.

"Hey, there, Jonah," said Astreya, with more confidence than he felt. "Time to clean out your stall."

He was about to open the door, when Jeb appeared at his side. The farmer seemed disappointed that Astreya was not terrified.

"Put on his bridle, lead him out to the hitching post, and then get to work."

"His bridle?" asked Astreya.

Jeb snorted again disdainfully as he took down a bridle and lead rope from a peg beside the stall, and bucked it onto the horse.

"Watch, then you do Sally."

Astreya did as he was told. The second horse seemed quite willing to accept him, now that her partner had checked him over first. With a bit of fumbling, Astreya got the bridle on correctly, in time to see Jeb open the door of Jonah's stall and walk with him into the open air.

Gripping the bridle at Sally's cheek, and holding the lead rope in a tight coil as Jeb had done, Astreya opened the door cautiously. The horse led Astreya rather than the other way around, but since she knew her routine, they arrived alongside Jeb in good order. Reasoning that this was a big, valuable animal, Astreya tied the halter rope to the hitching post with a quick bowline.

"What in tarnation are you up to, sailor boy?"

"Ah... tying up the horse?"

"Where did you learn that?"

"From... everyone ties their boats up like that."

"Well, sailor boy, we don't tie up horses that way." His voice was condescending. "Not like that. Never. Like this."

Astreya watched, and then copied a simple hitch that the Village women would have been ashamed to use on a laundry line. Prudently keeping the thought to himself, Astreya turned back towards the barn and began removing what he had smelled in the stalls. While Astreya shoveled and barrowed straw and horse droppings, Jeb busied himself in the corner where he kept the horses' tack, watching Astreya work. After the stalls were clean, Jeb gave further laconic instructions, and Astreya pulled down hay from the loft above the stalls, filled water buckets at a pump, and brought both to the horses. When the horses were champing on their hay in the morning sunlight, Jeb told him to start the grooming. Astreya was somewhat apprehensive at first, but when he saw that the horse enjoyed the process, he scrubbed with more confidence, and was rewarded with a snort that he took for gratitude. Jeb left him grooming the second horse. He was finishing Sally, when the farmer reappeared.

"Ever milk a cow, sailor boy?"

"No."

Jeb only grunted as he led the way to the cowshed, which stood separate from the horses. Collecting a bucket and stool at the door, he handed them to Astreya, pointed to the cow, and stood back, obviously expecting to be amused. However, Astreya knew what to do. He stood for a moment in front of the cow to let her sniff him, then set up the stool and bucket and started drawing down the milk. The cow swung her head around to look at him, he murmured wordless noises to her, and she turned back to placidly chewing her cud.

"Thought you said you'd never milked a cow."

"Only goats," said Astreya, concentrating on what he was doing.

Jeb watched him until the job was done, growing increasingly grumpy from having been cheated of another chance to make fun of Astreya's ignorance of farm ways.

"Wash up for breakfast," Jeb grunted.

After taking his turn under the pump by the kitchen door, Astreya took off his ill-fitting boots and entered the kitchen. He was immediately greeted with a stream of questions from Eva, who seemed to have completely forgotten the ugly scene of the previous evening.

"Tell me about your Village, your family. Where do you live? Does your family have a farm, like Father's? Does everyone fish? What do the women wear? Do you really eat oats? I mean, aside from in porridge. When can you teach me some more reading and writing?"

Before Astreya could choose a question to answer, Jed silenced both of them in a voice so stern that Eva winced.

"Sit, Daughter. You'll not talk to the lad. Eat your breakfast."

Eva lowered her head and began to eat her porridge, but she did not stop peeking at Astreya whenever she thought her father was not looking. For his part, Astreya did not know whether to acknowledge her glances. Judith frowned at Eva as she served up porridge, bread and steaming mugs of tea—not that her daughter took much notice of her disapproval. Astreya ate silently, remembering the night before. Instead of talking, he carefully memorized the braided arrangement of her pigtails, the curve of her cheek and the way her small hand held her spoon. He waited until Jeb's attention was on his food, and acknowledged Eva's glance with a wink.

"Husband, I'm concerned about his head. It was a shrewd blow he took."

"He's had rest, now he must work."

"May I not just check under the bandage?"

Jed sighed and nodded. Judith stepped behind Astreya's back, and carefully undid the bandage around his head.

"Well?" demanded Jed.

"There may be a scar, but his hair should cover it from view."

"Can he work?"

"Does your head spin when you stand up?"

Astreya shook his head.

"Did that hurt?"

"No."

"Then he's ready," grunted Jeb.

Judith placed a bowl tied up in a square of cloth in front of both Jeb and Astreya.

"For midday," she murmured, when Astreya looked up at her questioningly.

"Get your boots, sailor boy."

While Astreya sat on the doorstep, putting on his boots, he heard Jeb's low-voiced set of commands.

"He will not come in this house except for meals. You will not go near him. Do, and you'll feel my belt."

Moments later Jeb came outside, as if nothing had happened. While tying up his boots, he asked Astreya, "Ever cut cedar rails?"

Astreya, swallowing the urge to demand why Eva should not speak to him, shook his head.

"Well, can you use an axe without cutting your feet off?"

Astreya nodded.

"We'll see," Jeb grunted. "Now get Sally."

Jeb attached a bewildering collection of straps and chains to a horse collar, and grumbled when Astreya asked what they were for. Eventually, the horse was ready, with the hauling chains looped up on either side, a leather bag of tools to the left, and a basket for their midday meals on the right. At Jeb's impatient gesture, Astreya opened the gate, and the horse clopped out of the yard, the equipment jingling. They cut across a field that seemed to Astreya to be growing only weeds, up a cart track beside a little stream under oak, maples and birch trees many times larger than those that grew near the Village. After walking under intertwined boughs, they went down a short, green trail and arrived at a second field, striped with regular green lines of new growth. This time, Jeb led the way carefully around the crop, following a snake fence of cedar to where it ended at the edge of the forest.

Astreya recognized a style of fencing similar to what the Villagers made of driftwood around their kitchen gardens, and felt confident enough to ask the question that had been in his mind as they walked.

"About Eva and me..."

Jeb stopped, swung around and stepped so close to Astreya that he felt the man's breath. The movement was so sudden, Astreya could only stand, mouth ajar and eyes wide.

"Get this through your head, lad, or I'll put it there with my fist. There is no Eva and you. I know what you're up to, trying to teach her to write. I have what you wrote, and there'll be no more of that. You do not speak to her, visit with her. You do not look at her save to stay out of her way. Is that clear?"

Jeb's voice held a note of menace that took Astreya by surprise. He nodded.

"Answer me. Do y' understand?"

"Yes," Astreya gulped.

"Now you know." Jeb turned and pointed down a hoof-scarred path into the woods. When he spoke, it was as if nothing had happened. "Down in that swampy bit there's cedars. Cut 'em, haul 'em up here, and set 'em up like the rest of the fence." He heaved a deliberate sigh. "I suppose I'll have to show you."

Leading the horse, Jeb followed the hoof marks downhill into a cedar bog. On their way, they ducked branches, stepped over rocks and fallen trees, and slapped at the flies that attacked horse and men alike. They stopped in a small clearing where there was a pile of freshly felled cedars, and a mound of branches beside them.

"I'll only show you the once," he declared. "The horse knows its job. All's you got to do is put the chain on the rails, an' tell her to go."

Jeb tugged on the horse's collar and backed her towards the pile of poles that were the width of a man's thigh at their base, and more than twice a man's height in length. The farmer unhooked one of the chains that had jingled at the horse's side and secured it to one of the poles. At Jeb's peremptory gesture, Astreya secured a pole on his side of the horse, with Jeb watching him critically. Sally the horse stood, flicking flies with her tail and nodding her head up and down.

"Hey—YA!" yelled Jeb.

Astreya barely had time to leap out of the way, as the horse lunged forward to break the poles out of the wet earth. Clods of wet earth flew from her hoofs as her huge rump disappeared among the trees, the poles thumping after her. Astreya and Jeb followed more slowly. When they reached the end of the fence,

Sally was standing waiting for them. As they pushed through the last of the trees, the horse slowly turned her head to watch, as if to ask what had taken them so long.

Astreya smiled at the big animal and rubbed its nose.

"Talkin' to the horse, sailor boy? Get over here and do some work."

The fence on which he was to work zigged and zagged its way along two sides of the field of some shin high crop that Astreya did not know. Jeb stood beside the last four poles from the previous day. Behind him, the fence angled back and forth across what otherwise would have been a straight line. Following Jeb's curt directions, Astreya uncoupled the chain and dragged over one of the new poles to where the last set of poles lay fanned out on the ground, waiting for the load the horse had just delivered. Jeb had him lift one end of his pole onto the first log in the fan. Jeb lifted the end of the next pole in the fan onto Astreya's, and waved him off to get another. Astreya's next pole went on top in line with the others below it, so that the joined ends formed an angle like that of a man's two hands laced together at the fingertips, the palms wide apart. The ends of the four poles that made one section rested on the beginnings of four more piled up poles that started the next. The result was a fence that needed no posts.

"Now get another load," Jeb ordered.

Numbed by the way he was being treated, Astreya did as he was told.

For the rest of the morning, he cut fresh lengths of cedar for the horse to pull through the woods. Jeb hoisted the poles into place, and rested while Astreya cut and fetched more. Each trip ended with a callous admonition to work faster. When they stopped, eight more zigs and zags were complete.

At midday, Jeb walked the horse back to the cart track so that she could drink from the stream. While the horse sucked huge draughts of water, Astreya sat on a stone in the dappled shade, eating the thick cheese sandwiches Judith had made him. Jeb stood by himself to eat, drinking beer from a stone jug he had hung on the horse's trappings. He neither offered any to Astreya, nor looked at him throughout their meal. When he had done, he gave orders to Astreya in his customary monotone.

"You work 'til the field's in shadow. Do six more before that. Get on with it."

Without looking back, Jeb strode off towards the farm. Astreya waited until he was out of sight, then stood and held out a hand towards the horse.

"Come, Sally. We've got work to do."

The horse swung her big head slowly around and looked solemnly at him, as if commiserating, and then picked her way towards him out of the stream in which she had been standing. With Astreya at her head, they started back up the cart track to where the fence grew painfully longer.

* * * * *

Astreya threw himself into the task, determined to show that a sailor could work as hard as any farmer. The day wore on, the work was repetitive, and he had time to think. The more he reflected on the way Jeb treated him, the more he was reminded of how he had been taunted as a child until Scarm had taught him how to fight back. He wondered how he would fare if it came to a fight with Jeb. The farmer might be slow, but Astreya had seen brutal strength in the way he manhandled logs into place, which was not comforting. And even if he won such a contest, what would come next? He could hardly fight the rest of Teenmouth. He did not know where to go on land, and he could not get far in one of the flat-bottomed rowboats. Besides, these were people who had looked after him. He did owe them, even if Jeb's idea of repaying a debt was close to slavery.

The day brought him no solution, but he became proud of what he had accomplished. He had only Sally the horse for companionship, but she seemed to respond to what he said and did. He found that she could be coaxed into pulling poles into the best position to be lifted into place, and that she seemed to be grateful when he waved away flies with a cedar frond. He looked forward to telling Eva about how many trees he had felled, trimmed, skidded and maneuvered into the fence. Then he recalled Jeb's threats, and he misgave.

When the shadows of the tall trees on the other side of the field had crawled across the bright green crop, he found himself talking to the horse as they started wearily back to the farm, just as he had done so many times with Skip.

"What do you think of him, Sally? Does he boss you around the way he does me? Does he rule your life, right down to who you can talk to?"

The horse offered no answer. The fence cast long shadows on the hoof-marked ground as they skirted the field. When they entered the wood, Astreya looked up to see the tops of the trees still bright with sunlight, while the path at his feet was darkening towards evening. The horse's hoofs clopped steadily as she walked, head down, along the packed earth of the cart track, with scarcely a jingle from the traces that Astreya had looped up on her back. They both plodded wearily on for some time, until the horse raised her head. Moments later, Astreya heard another horse approaching behind them. Thinking to give whomever it was plenty of room to pass, Astreya shouldered Sally to the grassy edge of the track. She stopped and scratched her neck on a low branch. The skin around his bracelet tingled and he felt a wary tension overcome his tiredness.

The other horse approached at a steady walk, then slowed and stopped. It was a big black and tan gelding, festooned with packs on either side of a thin rider who slouched from a long day in the saddle.

"This the way to Teenmouth?" he asked.

Astreya looked up at a man whose face was shadowed not only by the trees, but also by a broad-brimmed hat. A shaft of light fell on the man's hands holding the reins, and Astreya noticed that they were thin and knobby at the joints, the skin blotched with age spots.

"You'll be at a farmhouse in a few moments. Leave it to port, and you'll be there in..."

Astreya hesitated, because he had no idea how far the center of Teenmouth was from Jeb's farm, and he was still looking for words when the man kicked his horse into a trot and was soon out of sight around a bend.

"That wasn't polite, was it, Sally?" Astreya coaxed the horse back into the track. "Tell me, horse, do you ever think of running away?"

The rest of the way back to the farm, Astreya reflected gloomily that to run away was pointless unless there was somewhere he could run to. He was met by Jeb's dour face as he was hitching Sally outside the barn.

"Rub this horse down, give her a scoop of oats from the bin by the door—don't steal any for yourself—pump her some water, hang up her tack, don't come near the house."

He turned his back and walked swiftly towards the kitchen door. Astreya set slowly to work, determined not to let Jeb humiliate him. He took off the horse collar, unbuckled the traces and then fetched a tub of water from the pump, an armload of hay from the loft above the barn and a scoop of oats. While Sally ate and drank, he began to brush her down. The horse's skin shuddered when the brush scratched the fly bites she had endured during the day, and she turned her big head slowly so that she could see him, as if to indicate where next to scratch. When Astreya walked around her to work on her other flank, he turned his back to the house and looked past the barn to the road towards Teenmouth. In the deepening evening shadow of the barn, he saw four men, and they were all facing him. When he stopped grooming to look at them, they huddled briefly together, muttering. Astreya felt sure that the newcomers had been staring at him, but he had no idea why. Then one gestured towards the house and the other three followed him to the kitchen door, leaving Astreya wondering if he had imagined that they had been watching him. He finished grooming the horse, led her into her stall beside her mate, put away the gear, and walked to the pump to wash. As he did so, he glanced towards the open door of the kitchen, where he could see lantern light on the table. The doorway darkened when two or more bodies blocked the light as they went inside, and while he was shaking the water off his hands and brushing his hair back from his wet face, the door closed. Since he had been banned from the house, there was no point in going to ask for something to eat, so he went to his tiny room at the other end of the barn from the horses, and lay down on his bed. On the other side of the wall, he could hear the occasional thud of a hoof as the two horses settled for the night. After his companionable relationship with Sally during the day, the sound was somehow comforting.

Astreya lay on his back and looked out the small window at the blackening sky, wondering where the *Mollie* and her crew might be. His mood darkened with the fading light. He was about to pull the blankets around him and try to sleep when there was a soft knocking that was not from the horses. He sat up, and greenish light glowed from the bracelet on his arm. The door gently creaked open.

"It's me... Eva," she whispered. "I've brought you some food."

Astreya pushed back the lacings to get more light from his bracelet.

"Oh... don't... they'll see."

Astreya doubled a blanket and hung it over the window. The light from his bracelet now dimly lit the side of the room to his left, and he was able to see Eva, a basket held in both her hands.

"Does that light come from the bracelet on your arm?" she asked.

"It does. It's not dangerous. You can come in... and thank you," he said. "Here, put the basket on the stool."

"All right," she said. "It's stew. Careful, it's hot. Mother made it. I... she... we were worried about you working all day after what you've been through."

"I was all right," said Astreya. "The horse did the hard work."

She sat beside him on the bed as he took out a big bowl. When he untied the napkin and lifted the plate that covered it, a mouthwatering smell of chicken stew reminded him that he was very hungry. Eva rummaged in the basket and found a thick slice of bread and a spoon. He dug into the food gratefully. As he ate, she whispered to him, the words tumbling out as fast as she could say them.

"The Council has come to see Father. They're deciding what to do about you. There's been an attack from the sea on Mizzle—that's to the west, past Markham. It's awful. People killed, women kidnapped. Needle Nick the peddler brought the news. And 'Streya, he saw you on the road and he thought you were one of the Men of the Sea—that's what he called them—'cause he said he'd seen some of them, and their big boat, and they looked like you."

Astreya tried to swallow a mouthful of hot stew so that he could tell her about the rider that had stopped to question him, but Eva did not give him a chance.

"The Men of the Sea had black hair," she paused and looked at him. "And they just took what they wanted—food, water, and he says they took some of the boys and the younger women, too."

"How does he know? Did he see it happen?"

"I don't know. I only heard what the Mayor told Father. I guess the peddler took off on his horse to save his skin. Anyway, the thing is that some of the elders think you're a spy. It's 'cause you were asking all kinds of questions, before that boy hit you. And 'cause you don't look like the others on the little boat, and Needle Nick thought you looked like one of the Men of the Sea. And they don't know you like I do. They're scared, 'Streya. They think that if they drive you away or kill you, then all of us could be in bad trouble if the men from the big ship attack Teenmouth, and they don't find their spy—you. If they let you stay, which is what Father wants, because he says you're a good worker, then the others are scared that maybe you'll bring the black ship down on us somehow."

"So what have they decided?"

"They're just talking and talking, getting nowhere. They aren't bad men, 'Streya. They wouldn't kill you... I hope... but if they all knew about... that thing on your arm, they'd be even more scared, and then who knows what they'd do. I have to get back. Mother told me not to be long."

Astreya wolfed down the last of the stew, and wiped up the gravy with the bread. "Maybe I can sneak up and listen..."

"All right, but be very careful. And don't let them see that light, or for sure they'll think that's how you'll call the men from the sea to kill us all." She leaned closer to him, her dark eyes glinting in the light from his arm. "You wouldn't, 'Streya, would you?"

"I couldn't if I wanted to, and I don't," said Astreya. "I'm not..."

She put her hand up to his face. "I believe you, 'Streya. Now come softly behind me. I don't need a light to find my way to the house."

Astreya covered his bracelet with Scarm's string, and then with a rolled shirtsleeve. Barefoot in the dark, neither of them made a sound as they walked towards the lit window. When they were only a few paces from the house, Astreya felt Eva's hand touch his arm, and then slide down to his fingers. She drew him off the beaten earth of the path onto short grass that surrounded the house, and bent almost to a crawl to get below the light from the window. Astreya crouched beside her.

At first, he could only hear a confusion of voices interrupting each other. Then he was able to pick out the high voice he remembered from his conversation at the well.

"... writing... suspicion... black hair... spy?"

The high voice silenced the others, and then after a short silence, began again more softly, so that Astreya could make out only a few words. "...solution... useful..."

Then he heard Jeb's voice. "...solves your problems. Not mine. I lose a worker."

A deep voice spoke slowly and emphatically.

"It's a problem for all of us, Jebediah. If men come to Teenmouth in one of those great ships the peddler saw, we're all in danger. Your plan only works if they listen to us. What if they just arrive and start killing people?"

"We can make sure that doesn't happen, because they'd start at Markham..."

Another voice interrupted. "And Markham doesn't have our reef."

"That didn't stop the boat that brought the black-haired boy."

"The peddler saw a black ship—much, much bigger."

"So he says."

"Peddlers' stories is wild stories."

"You're right about that."

"But a whole village gone last year, he said. Killed, stolen, raped, burned..." The voice rose in horror.

Astreya suddenly thought of the grisly scene at the empty village where the *Mollie* had planned spend the night. Had that attack from the sea been by the same people?

The high voice now spoke without interruption.

"Councilors, we must decide tonight. It would be easier if we had more time. But tomorrow's the day we have to send one of our lads to the Castle. And there's our answer. We send him on to the Castle to do his spying there. They're not on the coast."

"What will our lads think about losing a chance to go?"

"Like your son, maybe?"

"My son Joshua is smart enough to go anywhere he wants..."

"Sure he is, Hezekiah," said the deep, confident voice. "But what he wants is Jeb's Eva, and if he were to be chosen as our Scholar, for which he is amazingly unsuited, she may take a shine to my Samuel, and then the adjoining lands..."

"You'll not discuss my daughter before my face, Daniel."

Jeb's voice harshly stopped the exchange. Astreya and Eva held their breath. The high voice broke the silence.

"Then it will be tomorrow, at the hall. I'll have the writing. Jebediah, you go around the farms and get the money. We'll choose him officially at the meeting, then there'll be the food and the dancing, and next day we'll send him on his way."

"It's an awful expensive way to solve the problem," said Jeb.

"Who knows, Jeb. Perhaps he'll come back in a year and be our healer."

"When pigs fly," said Daniel softly in his deep voice, and then louder. "Listen, men, we've talked enough. The beer's done, and so are we. Thank you kindly, Jebediah and Judith, I'm sure. Now let's get home to bed."

"Mayor, let me walk with you to your house," said Jeb. "I have a thought about how we can reduce the expense."

Eva tugged Astreya's hand and breathed into his ear.

"Quick, quick, back to the barn. I'll go in through my window. Hurry!" She let go of his hand, crouched even lower, and scuttled below the window ledge towards the back of the house.

Astreya's toes felt cool grass, and then packed earth. Glancing upwards, he saw the brightest star of late spring above the roof of the barn. A few silent steps, and he was letting himself into his little room. Looking out of the half-closed door, he saw figures start down the darkened road, their lanterns casting swooping patches of yellow light onto the tree trunks. He watched them until the last light from their lanterns flickered into darkness, and then lay down on his bed. He stared into the dark, trying to make sense out of the fragments he had heard. A greenish glow lit his left arm, and when he pulled back his sleeve, the strong light from his bracelet softly illuminated the little room. Strangely reassured, Astreya pulled the blankets around him, sighed, and fell asleep.

Chapter 9:

In which Astreya leaves Teen-mouth

Astreya's next morning began like the first. Horses' hooves knocked on the wall by his head and, moments later, Jeb's boot kicked his door open.

"Chores. Now."

Astreya yawned, stretched, pulled on his clothes and walked around to the horses' end of the barn. They greeted him with huffs of air blown out of their nostrils and more knocking of hoofs. One by one, they pulled him in an enthusiastic clopping surge to their hitching post in the yard, where he fed, watered and groomed them before returning to muck out their stalls. He was barrowing a stinking pile of manure and straw to the midden when Jeb returned.

"Wash up. Breakfast. Kitchen. Now."

As Astreya undid his boots and climbed the steps to the kitchen, he thought about the conversations he had overheard the night before, and wondered if there might be a way out of servitude to Jeb. The men had been in agreement when he last heard them; but Jeb, who had not been happy with the decision, had conferred alone with the mayor, and there was no way of telling whose opinion had prevailed. Astreya reasoned that being invited into the kitchen augured well, but he was not sure, and he still felt dominated by the man who believed that rescuing Astreya conferred the right to own him, body and spirit. The emotional up and down of the past few days had left him irresolute, balanced between hope and fear as circumstances threw him from betrayal, to rescue, to slavery, and perhaps now to an uncertain chance of escape. He stopped in the doorway, took a deep breath, and just in time stopped his right hand from feeling his bracelet through his sleeve.

He looked at Jeb, who sat with his shoulders hunched, resting his forearms heavily on the table. Eva moved light-footed across the kitchen, her bare feet appearing and disappearing under her swaying blue dress. She put a pewter mug by her father's right hand, and backed away quickly. Moments later, Judith was a more deliberate and slower echo of her daughter, as she carried a plate of food and laid it in front of her husband.

"Sit, eat, listen," said Jeb.

Astreya did as he was told. He ate the porridge Judith spooned into his bowl, welcomed its warmth, but hardly tasted it. As he ate, he could feel Jeb's eyes on him, watching his every move. Eventually, he laid down his spoon, took a deep breath and deliberately returned Jeb's gaze.

"I'm to be robbed of your services for the good of Teenmouth. You're to go to the Castle as our scholar."

Astreya was amazed both by the words and the change in Jeb's voice. He had gone from barking orders to a conspiratorial, almost wheedling tone.

"Don't thank me—I was agin' it. The Mayor and the other Elders decided that you're to go, because none of our young men want to go, or could go, or their parents don't want them to go. And if we don't send someone, Teenmouth will not have another chance at either getting a Healer, or sending another scholar. So, you're in luck, boy."

"Uh... thank you."

Astreya, wondered why Jeb should sound as if he were persuading him to go, even though the farmer wanted his unpaid labor.

"Tonight, the Elders will give you their blessing and the gifts. You'll be our Scholar, and even if you don't come back, we will be considered for a Healer, and, in time, there'll be other young lads from Teenmouth who'll go to the Castle."

"Why don't you send Eva?" asked Astreya. The question popped out of his mouth before he could consider that if Jeb agreed, he would continue to be Astreya's master.

"Don't you worry yourself about Eva. She's a good girl, but a bit headstrong. That's why most o' the young fellows are all bespoken to other girls, or have no time for her. She'll soften in time. 'Muddy boots,' she says. There's no shame in muddy boots for a farming man. My boots get muddy. And I take 'em off at the door, don't I, woman?"

Judith nodded.

"'Course, the lads she could fancy aren't swift like you, sailor boy. She'd wait for you, I can tell you that. No competition."

Astreya frowned. Where was the jealous father who had told him never even to look at his daughter? Jeb scraped his chair back, walked to the door and started to pull on the boots he had left on the doorstep. His voice changed back to the tone he used to issue orders.

"Wife, I'll be to the Elders now. I'll deal with Eva later," said Jeb. "Now, sailor, even though you're going to be our scholar, you owe me another day's work on my fence before you come to the meeting hall at sundown."

He strode away without waiting for an answer. Astreya and Judith listened to his footsteps receding down the path before they looked at each other. Astreya could not understand the contradictions in the man's behavior. He had just spoken as if he owned his wife, his daughter and Astreya. But moments before, he had been sounding more like a conspirator.

"What's he up to?" Astreya asked.

Judith shrugged. "He's seen some advantage for himself and none other. Don't take it for a change of heart."

"What should I do, then?"

"Go to the Castle. There's nothing keeping you here... or there."

"What about Eva? And what did he mean about 'dealing with' her?"

"He knows she took you a meal last night. But she's her own self, 'Streya, and I'm proud of what she did, even if it causes her pain. And I'll tell her you cared for her, and wanted no part of a forced exchange of favors."

"I think she's wonderful, but..." Astreya searched for words that would not somehow be insulting.

Judith nodded. "You don't need your whole life's road walked for you," she said. "No more does she. But the Elders don't think that way, no more do the Learneds. So have a care about how you show yourself."

She smiled unexpectedly, and for a moment, Astreya thought of Alana. It was not that Judith and Alana were alike, save that each had told him in her own way that he had a right to live his own life. In that moment, Astreya was transported in memory to the moment of leave-taking from his mother.

The memory triggered a shower of questions. Would Roaring Jack be able to follow the sketches he had made? What would he say to Alana? Would she believe that he was dead? Or would she somehow know, despite what she was told? Either way, there was nothing he could do. They were cut off: their lives separated. It seemed to him that distance and death were almost the same. The room swam for a moment, and Astreya sniffed. Village men did not cry; at least, he had never seen one do so.

"There's nothing wrong with tears," said Judith gently. "Don't upset yourself trying to dry them from the inside. When they're finished, they'll stop on their own."

"But..." Astreya choked.

Then her arm was around his shoulders, and he was able to take control of himself again. For days, he had been alone among strangers, from whom he had discovered that the people he thought of as friends had deserted him. Judith's understanding seemed to flow from her, and her arm was like rescue from a slow, lonely drowning.

"You must get on with your own life, 'Streya," said Judith. "No compromises. No easy way out. Don't ask me how I know. I have feelings about what'll happen, and sometimes..."

"My mother has such feelings," said Astreya, his voice firmer. "She'll know I'm alive." Against reason and the black thoughts only a moment past, he believed what he told her. "She knows things before they happen sometimes."

Judith nodded, held him at by his shoulders at arms' length, and looked into his eyes. She stepped back as if suddenly embarrassed.

"I'd better go work on the fence," said Astreya, feeling his cheeks hot.

"I'll have your midday meal for you when you've made Sally ready."

When Astreya had prepared the horse and picked up a parcel of food from Judith, he walked back up to the snake fence, where he and the horse went to work together. The day, which had begun cloudless, warmed quickly, but white puffy clouds were forming, from time to time offering a few moments of shadow. Towards noon, when he stopped for his meal, he led Sally to the stream, where they both drank, and he ate cold chicken and greens between thick slabs of fresh bread. In the afternoon, more cloud shadows dappled the field, and a steady wind kept most of the flies away. The day before, Astreya had worked to numb himself against the thought that he had been both abandoned and enslaved. Now the task was a challenge, and at the end of this second day, he looked back on what he had done with satisfaction. The snake fence wound its way almost to the western side of the field, dark in the late afternoon light. On his way back along the path, the horse plodding beside him, he felt a sense of achievement in what he had done that had nothing to do with Jeb.

When he had returned to the farm, rubbed down Sally and given both horses their supper, he took the cloth that had wrapped his midday meal to thank Judith in her kitchen. On the table was an armful of clothes topped by a pair of boots that looked almost new. She picked them up and gave to him.

"You need to be seen as someone who does Teenmouth credit," she said.

Astreya thanked her as best he could, but she would not meet his eyes. She turned her back while he pulled on brown trousers that almost brushed the top of his feet, in the manner of the farmers of Teenmouth. Then he sat on the doorstep to pull on new socks and surprisingly comfortable boots. When he stood, she gestured for him pull off the shapeless garment Jeb had given him, and handed him a shirt. It was made of much finer fabric than the sack-like one he had just removed. Pale yellow, and tapered towards his waist, it fastened in front in a line of bone buttons, and was full in the sleeves. When he admired the stitching, she smiled at the compliment and helped him put on a green, sleeveless vest and fastened its buttons so that the shirt showed almost to his waist.

She stepped back and looked him up and down. "You'll turn all the girls' heads."

He smiled, but shook his head at the flattery. "Thank you, Judith."

"I only made a few adjustments to the clothes sent by the Elders."

She waved away his thanks without meeting his eyes, and pointed his way.

"Follow the road and keep to your left. You'll see the hall. It's red, and by the time you're there, there'll be lights inside."

Astreya followed the cart track, overarching trees darkening his way. When he looked through gaps between the tree trunks on his left, he saw the sunset gilding hay fields to the west. The trees on his right blended into a forest. Following Judith's directions, he turned onto a wider track of hard-pounded red earth between hedgerows that blocked the view of anything but the next bend. As he walked towards what he presumed would be some kind of community gathering, Astreya remembered how the Village celebrated the turn of the seasons and the bounty of the sea, and he wished he were going back, instead of onward to a task he had not chosen. Wondering how he might untangle the next twist in his fate, he slowed to little more than a shuffle.

There was a rustling in the hedgerow. He opened his eyes to see Eva step out of the bushes. She stood in the middle of the road, her head on one side, looking up at him. Astreya looked back. He noticed that her eyes were red, she had a smudge of dirt on her cheek, and hair had been teased out of her braids by twigs. They stood a couple of paces apart, each made awkward by the questions they wanted to ask.

"'Streya, are you going to the Castle?" she asked.

Astreya nodded.

"I spoke to your mother," said Astreya. "She said it would be best if I went."

"She said that?"

"She said we each had our own roads to walk."

Eva nodded. At first, she had stood as if poised to run, but now she relaxed, stood with her weight on one leg and tossed her head, making her pigtails flip back and forth. Her lips, which had been compressed into a thin line, curled into a smile.

"See you at the celebration," she said. "I'll show you how we dance." She brushed past him, and when he turned, waved her fingers as she ran off down the track towards her home.

Astreya's return wave came too late. Bewildered by her sudden change of mood, he stared after her in the fading light, catching a moment when her dress brushed a tuft of grass as it swayed jauntily from side to side. He stood transfixed by the curve and sway of her until she disappeared around a bend. None of the girls in the Village had been as fascinating; none had made his mind slow and his mouth go slack.

A dog barked farther along the track, as if summoning him to what he had to do. Astreya shook his head to clear it, and continued along his way. Soon the rough hedgerows around the fields turned to trimmed cedar hedges with occasional gaps through which he could see houses framed by big oaks and maples. The first buildings Astreya passed were made of logs like Jeb's cottage. Then, as the road lost its center stripe of grass, he passed houses clad in sawn planks, crisp and sharp at the corners, some of them rearing up to a second storey. The sun was now set, but the western sky still glowed, allowing him to admire doors and windows painted in vivid greens, blues and yellows, standing out against contrasting tones on walls.

In the front yard of one of them, three small girls let their skipping rope fall and watched him go past with their mouths open. An adult's voice called them into the house, but they did not move. Once he had passed, Astreya heard a spate of chatter from all three, not one word of which could he understand.

When he reached the crossroads, Astreya saw the meeting hall. Judith had told him that it was red, but nothing in her words prepared him for the way the building glowed in the evening light, its walls surmounted by a bell spire whose shadow fell aslant the square where three roads met. He stopped walking without deciding to do so, and stood wishing there were some way to capture what he saw on paper. Slowly, he became aware that he was no longer alone. Men, women and children were making their way to the meeting hall from all sides of the open square in front of the glowing hall. The men were in sober black trousers and jackets over white shirts, and the women wore smocked blouses and full, ankle-length skirts that were bright in the last rays of the sun. Astreya thought to wait until they were all ahead of him, but even though he had stopped walking, he was already committed to crossing the open space in front of the meeting hall, and there seemed no way of turning back. Acutely conscious of being watched by many people he did not know, he walked up the steps to the white doors of the hall, which rattled open in front of him. Astreya froze. Inside, it was dark after the sunlit evening.

"You're late." said the high voice in the shadows. "Come on in, young fellow."

Suppressing the desire to turn and run, Astreya stepped into the darkness. He felt his heartbeat throbbing in his throat. As his eyes adjusted to the dim light, he saw three men sitting on a dais at the other end of the hall, silhouetted against a tall window. Jeb moved out of the shadows to his left and stood beside Astreya.

"Go forward now," he whispered.

With the farmer an uncomfortable presence at his left shoulder, Astreya paced down the center of the hall between rows of benches. He felt the muscles of his neck and shoulders tighten, and his bracelet tingled. One of the figures ahead of them raised a beckoning hand. Out of the shadow that was his face came the squeaky voice of a petulant old man.

"Get on with it, boy."

Astreya looked from one face to the other, wondering what to say or do. As he came closer and looked up at them, part of his mind noticed that all were beardless. He saw fleshy wattles shaking under the chin of the oldest, whose head trembled above a thin, black-clad frame. To his left sat a shapeless body topped by a fat, bald-headed face poised on a staircase of double chins leading down to a well filled black waistcoat. In the third chair, a tall lean man in a white, puffy-sleeved shirt smiled down at Astreya.

Jeb whispered behind Astreya's shoulder.

"That's the Mayor. Beside him's our parson. The tall one's Councilor Daniel."

Jeb pushed Astreya with a hand on his shoulder towards the three men.

"The young fellow's a newcomer, and does not know our customs. But he's civil, and he can read and write," said Jeb. "I brought you proof of what he had written."

"Is this the truth?" demanded Daniel in a deep voice that Astreya remembered from the night before. "Or is it only that you can make out a few words and write your name?"

"I can read and write plain words, sir," said Astreya. "But there is much that I don't know."

"Well answered," said the fat man. "Jebediah, you've turned this meeting from a wake into the celebration it should be."

He nodded several times, his chins wobbling.

The ancient one rose out of his chair with shaky care. He stood, swayed slightly, arranged his shin length coat around him with thin fingers, and began gabbling a string of memorized words in a nasal drone punctuated with occasional gasps.

"Will-you-now-go-to-the-place-of-learning, (wheeze), and-devote-your-days-to-study-for-the-good-of-all? (wheeze, wheeze).

"Say 'yes,'" whispered Jeb.

"Yes," said Astreya.

Before he could say more, the wheezing voice continued.

"Then-by-my-power-as-spiritual-leader-and-temporal-guide-of-Teenmouth, (wheeze) I-call-you-Scholar, (wheeze) and-I-wish-you-well (wheeze, wheeze). Now take your Scholar's letter. (Wheeze.) Where is the wretched thing? (Wheeze.) Have you filled in his name, Councilor?"

The councilor named Daniel stood in a single fluid motion and leant forward to offer Astreya a roll of parchment. Looking along the arm extended towards him, Astreya saw amused eyes above a quick lean-faced smile. The mayor, who had slowly levered himself upwards on his elbows with the awkwardness of the very fat, waddled down the three steps one leg at a time, like a little child. When they reached the floor, all three held out their hands towards Astreya.

"Take their hands," Jeb prompted.

A fleshy, moist palm pressed Astreya's hand, then dry, bony fingers squeezed him briefly, finally Daniel's rough, strong hand enfolded his hand almost to his wrist. He looked into a face lined by laughter as well as age and weather.

"Good luck, young man," said Daniel. "You're saving us a heap of trouble, and we're grateful. Take these."

He held out what looked like a folded green blanket and a leather drawstring bag equipped with shoulder straps. Astreya accepted the armful, and then struggled to free a hand to take a fist-sized cloth bag that Daniel handed him. He started to offer thanks, but before he could speak, he had to step out of the way as the old man teetered towards Jeb.

"You've done well, Jebediah. (Wheeze.) Join us for the festivities. Walk with us."

The four men walked around Astreya, passing him two on each side. He turned and stood with the gifts in his hands, looking at their backs as they moved slowly towards the doorway, where the last light streamed in onto the white scrubbed wood of the floor. Astreya followed them wondering as he did so whether he should or not.

"Here's our scholar!" shouted Daniel.

He turned, took Astreya by the shoulder, and pushed him in front of the four of them so that he stood on the steps of the hall, looking out at the open space below. Indistinct in the evening shadows, the people of Teenmouth looked up in silence. Astreya stared back at the crowd, not knowing what else to do.

"Let us find somewhere to sit... and soon," wheezed the old man.

The Elders went back into the meeting hall, and the crowd surged up the steps behind them. Astreya stepped inside the door to let them pass, feeling their glances, some curious, some smiling. One or two offered him a handclasp that nearly caused him to drop his new possessions. A tall, well-muscled young man of about Astreya's age stepped out of the flow of people and looked at him solemnly out of eyes so dark that they seemed to have no pupil at the center.

"I wish you joy of it, Scholar," he said, glanced at the bundle under Astreya's left arm and disappeared into the crowd in the meeting hall.

Astreya did not know whether he had been congratulated or insulted. He was acutely conscious of being the only stranger among people who all knew each other, and who were meeting and greeting with an enthusiasm he could not share. As a few stragglers pushed hurriedly inside, he stood alone just inside the doorway. Lamps were lit, a fiddle creaked and squeaked its way into tune, and benches were scraped and bumped out of the way to make room for dancing. An aproned woman of huge girth carried a tray of food to a table near the door, and behind her came a man with his hands full of mugs, closely followed by two lads rolling a sizable barrel. Couples held hands waiting for the dance as a second fiddle joined the first in the squeaky business of tuning up.

"Go on, silly, it's your party!" said a voice beside his ear.

"Eva!" said Astreya.

He turned towards her expectantly, and then stopped to stare. She wore a white-trimmed green dress that clung tight on her hips and then flared out past her knees. Her hair fell loose to her shoulders in brown ringlets, held back by a strip of green ribbon tied on the top of her head. Her shoulders were bare above sleeves that ended near her elbows. Below a line of red and blue cross-stitching her blouse swelled attractively. Astreya noticed that the material began a very long way below her chin, and then blushed as he became aware that he had been staring.

"Um, that's a pretty shirt. Nice, er, stitching."

Having now completely embarrassed himself, he was prepared for her to turn and leave him. Instead, she poised her head on a slight angle, and smiled up at him provocatively.

"Here, give me your bag, cloak and papers," she said, and when he held them out to her, she knelt to thrust them under a bench.

"That's a cloak?" he asked, trying to cover his embarrassment. He resolutely looked only into her eyes as she stood up in front of him.

She swung her chin upward in something more than a nod, and laughed up into his face.

"Don't they have girls where you come from?" she teased.

"Yes," said Astreya. "But..."

"They dress like the women of Markham. I know it from the way you look at me."

"The women of Markham?" asked Astreya.

"Never mind. Come on."

A new and even livelier Eva took Astreya's hand and led him into the middle of the hall, her toes flickering back and forth in a dance that was yet to begin. Lanterns hung from the rafters, the fiddles were ready, and the hall pulsed with excitement. Although he was once again at the center of many strange people, Eva put her small hand in his, and he no longer felt alone.

"A toast to the scholar!" shouted a voice. "A toast! A toast!" echoed others.

Daniel waved a large hand over his head as he used his height to wade through the crowd and stand beside Astreya.

"Friends, you know how much I hate talking," he began. A gust of laughter put the lie to his seeming seriousness. "But I've got to tell you that we're lucky to be here tonight celebrating our scholar. He's not one of us, but I want you to make him at home. His name is 'Streya, and though he doesn't know us, he's going to do us all a great service. Teenmouth will not only send a scholar this year, but will be able to send scholars in the future. And I don't mind telling you that we came close to losing both opportunities. Teenmouth needs a Healer, and now we can petition for one. No offence to our young men, mind you. If you're not a scholar, then you're not, and shouldn't waste everyone's time trying. Now it certainly looks as if we've found our man, because 'Streya, here, can already read and write. Maybe in a few years, should he study the Healing Arts and take a fancy for us, he'll come back. So, I give you a toast to 'Streya, our Teenmouth scholar!"

Mugs were raised and voices mumbled Astreya's name. A drink was pressed into his hand, and Eva pushed his arm upwards to encourage him to drink. It was beer—good beer, Astreya decided. It had a nutty flavor like beer brewed for the Village's autumn celebrations, when parents looked the other way while the older boys filled their mugs.

"Reply! Speech! Speech!" shouted several voices.

Eva stood on tiptoe to speak into Astreya's ear. "Tell them you're glad to be going and that you thank them all for what they've done."

Astreya spoke into the waiting silence.

"Um, you have given me a chance to learn, and I thank you. I owe much to your kindness... especially to Judith, Eva—and Jeb—who have looked after me so well. Again, I thank you."

His reply seemed both inadequate and inaccurate to his own ears, but the shouts and clapping that followed were loud and enthusiastic.

"Wonderful," said Eva. "They liked that."

The crowd parted in front of them, and Jeb pushed his way forward, his hand outstretched to Astreya. Eva took a step backwards. Astreya took Jeb's extended hand, very much aware that the gesture contradicted the events of the last two days. Then he saw that Jeb's eyes were focused past Astreya at the tall man behind him, and his expression was of deep dislike. He gave Astreya's hand one quick downward pull, far too strong to be friendly, turned to face the crowd and deliberately usurped the role as spokesperson.

"Thank you, young fellow, on behalf of us all. Elder Daniel has spoken well, but there is something I would like to add..."

Astreya saw with some satisfaction that Jeb's intervention had come too late. Attention had turned to food, drink, dancing and merriment. Daniel waved a long arm at the musicians, the fiddlers started to play, and people began to clap and stamp in time.

Suddenly Jeb was beside him, his hand closing on his arm, the fingers digging between his muscles. The farmer's voice was low in his ear.

"Listen. You just remember I saved and sheltered you, sailor boy. Tell your masters that when they come back. I, Jebediah, took you in. Not the weak-minded Elders I talked into it. Me. Make them know I'm the man to deal with here."

Before Astreya could think of a reply, Jeb let go his arm and turned furiously on Eva, speaking in a harsh whisper.

"Daughter, do as I said. Get him out of here tonight."

Astreya wanted to explain that he was no spy, but to do so was to admit he and Eva had eavesdropped on the previous night's meeting. He hesitated, and the opportunity passed. Jeb's frowning face disappeared into the crowd.

"Take your place, young scholar," shouted Daniel.

Eva grabbed Astreya's hand and led him into the widening circle of people both young and old, all waiting for the dancing to begin. The music began in earnest and Astreya caught the rhythm as Eva led him into the dance, prompting him with eager little tugs and shoves. Astreya's feet recognized patterns like those he knew from the Village, and after they had followed a line of couples for a turn around the hall, collecting others behind them, somehow he and Eva was one couple in a circle of eight people. When he glanced over his shoulder, he saw other circles.

The steps of the dance were similar enough to those he had learned at the Village so that with few pushes and pulls from Eva, he was able to follow the figures. Partners changed in a chain of hands around; then there was swinging in pairs, elbows locked; then, knees up prancing back to back, and then another chain of hands led to fresh partners with whom to repeat the figure.

At first, Astreya had to concentrate to keep his place, but soon he was able to take his part confidently and even smile at the girls with whom he high stepped and swung. Most looked up at him somewhat nervously, and then as the spirit of the dance took hold, each brief encounter became more intense. As partners met and exchanged, he was surprised by the way that the young women tried to catch his fancy. In one of the twirls, a tall girl with a freckled, upturned nose and chestnut hair pressed herself against him. "I'm Becky," she whispered, but a few quick steps later, Eva's hand was on his shoulder and the touch of her hip against his, as she reclaimed him. She pulled away for a moment, and Astreya saw Becky stumble, and then Eva's satisfied look. Astreya recoiled as much as was possible in the swift movements of the dance. Then Eva looked up at him, her lips parted. His disapproval melted, and he felt accepted, even courted. The feeling went to his head more than the beer he had drunk. At the Village dances, he had always felt that he was at best tolerated, never really taken into the company of those his own age. Here, he was not relegated to completing a set of pairs with the Village grandmothers and their youngest granddaughters. Astreya felt an enthusiasm that went beyond the music and rhythm. Dance succeeded dance, some slower, some faster. The rhythm of the music and the colors of the girls' and women's swirling dresses held Astreya entranced. Occasionally dancers and musicians alike paused to catch their breath and raise their mugs of beer, but each time, before the exuberance could fade, the music began again, and Eva led him back into the dance once more.

At last, the music stopped and did not start again. Astreya found himself standing with one arm around Eva's waist, laughing with pleasure rather than at any one thing. Eva unwound herself from his arm and disappeared. He gradually became aware that the party was drawing to a close. Like a sailor reaching land after days at sea, Astreya's view of the world took a little while to steady and come back into everyday focus. He saw older women clearing up the remains of beer and food, noticed that the fat mayor had fallen asleep with a beer mug balanced on his ample stomach, and watched as the fiddlers wrapped their precious instruments while the last of the beer was brought them by a buxom girl. She glanced sideways towards Astreya as she passed him, and he recalled that her well-filled blouse had tilted towards him during the dancing. He was looking after her when Eva reappeared in the doorway with a basket in one hand. She had changed into her everyday clothes. The young man who had spoken to Astreya before the party began was at her side, whispering something he could not hear. Eva stamped her foot and almost shouted.

"Get away from me, Seth. I don't ever want to see you again!"

Seth shrugged and slouched off into the night. Eva tossed her head as if to shake something out of her hair. Then she beckoned to Astreya, and they went out the door together, where her mother waited with the gifts he had received from the councilors. When they were out of the light that spilled from the open door, Eva hung the cloak over his shoulders, turning him into a black pillar in the gloom.

"The parchment is in here," whispered Judith, handing him the leather pack. "Start tonight. You can rest later, on the way. Take the south road. Don't wait about. There are some who feel that it was all done too quickly, and would like to do it again, but different. Do you understand?"

Astreya nodded because it was expected of him. There was no time to ask her what she meant. From the top of the pack, she he pulled the little bag, heavy with coins. She hung it around his neck by a leather thong, and dropped inside his shirt.

"This is money for your fee at the Castle. My man Jeb raised it from the people of Teenmouth—with much complaint. Keep it close to you."

"But I don't know where...." Astreya began.

"I'll show him, mother," said Eva.

"Don't worry. Things will turn out well for you. Leave now."

Judith turned and disappeared into the night before Astreya could ask her any more questions. Almost as soon as she had gone, Eva took his arm.

"Come on, 'Streya," she said. "We have to make up for the time we lost dancing—'cept that it wasn't lost, was it?"

Her hand slid down his arm and she entwined her fingers in his. Astreya was so surprised that he could not think of an answer. He stood still and looked up, reading the heavens with a sailor's eye. A prickling of stars was overhead, and a bright planet shone through the branches of the trees around the square. He oriented himself with the North Star and read the circling constellations' positions, estimating how much of the night remained before dawn. The air was cool and fragrant with spring, welcome after the evening's dancing.

"Come on, 'Streya," said Eva, tugging at his hand.

She led him across the square and down a lane between houses. Astreya felt the ground under his boots soften from hard packed earth to close-cropped grass. Not long after, they passed a candlelit window in the last house. He shrugged the pack he had been given into a more comfortable position on one shoulder, bundled his cloak and threw it over the other. Beside him, he heard Eva's dress rustling gently against her legs. He breathed deeply, smelling pine trees. He felt pleasantly cool after the hours of dancing, and not the least sleepy. Now that his eyes had adjusted to the dim light, he could see their path ghosting ahead of them as it skirted a tongue of forest. Eva suddenly pulled at his sleeve and led him into the woods. A few paces among rough-barked pines, and she stopped at the edge of a starlit clearing, put down the basket she had been carrying and sank to her knees on a springy bed of pine needles. When he looked down at her, faint light gleamed on her hair. She shrugged a shoulder, and a bundle fell from under her cloak.

She whispered something that was lost in the night wind among the pines. He leaned forward to catch her words. In the shadows of her face he could see stars reflected in her eyes. Around them, the world was grey and black, indistinct and mysterious. Then her hands clasped behind his neck, and she kissed him.

Astreya felt a totally unexpected shiver run down his backbone. Her lips and tongue were teaching him to taste her mouth, but the whole event was so unexpected that he felt the need to stop, think and analyze what was happening. At the same time as his mind seethed with questions, he felt energy building within him. He returned her kiss softly at first, then experimentally and somewhat awkwardly put his arms around her. Her hands slid from the back of his head down to his chest, pushing him gently but firmly away. She drew back her head. "Food," she whispered, and knelt beside her basket.

Astreya took several deep and calming breaths, his heart pounding. She spread out the cloak he had been given, and he kneeled beside her to let his hands do duty for his eyes in finding a soft spot between the roots of the pines. His fingers met Eva's in the darkness and lingered. She found his face with one hand, and put a drumstick of chicken into his mouth with the other. He chewed, swallowed, and realized how hungry he was. They began to investigate the basket of food together, passing a flask of cider back and forth, and growing increasingly sticky-fingered. Eva produced a cloth on which they wiped their lips and fingers, and then they were kissing again. They lay back on Astreya's new cloak and she drew close to him, so that their bodies warmed each other.

For a while, kissing was enough, then gradually, it was not. On the one hand, he felt the insistent urge for more than mere tenderness; on the other, he remembered the injunctions with which he had been brought up. Alana had taught him that casual lovemaking was an affront to the ways of the Village, where young people were supposed to choose each other with the keen knowledge that their pledge would be broken only by death. Moreover, in the Village he had always been the

Stranger, and thus the one left out when hands were held and kisses exchanged, so lack of opportunity had guaranteed that he follow custom. Now, with Eva close against him, he was very aware that this was not the Village.

His hands somewhat awkwardly posed a question. Eva gasped as he touched her breasts, and her fingernails bit into his arm. They both tensed, and the moment was lost, along with Astreya's brief rejection of Village customs. In that instant, all of his earlier questions seethed in his mind, ending whatever might have been. Even though his face was close to Eva's, he was suddenly transfixed by the thought that he had no idea what she was thinking. He wondered why she had suddenly been so bold. He asked himself whether she was enjoying what was happening or whether she was manipulating him. He remembered her father telling her to get rid of him, and he recalled being puzzled by the way she had so publicly disdained the young man called Seth. All these thoughts tumbled through his mind, making him unable to decide what to do next. They lay still for an interminable moment, then Eva suddenly sat up. In the darkness, he heard her attempt to stifle a sob.

"I'm sorry," he said, feeling his words to be both inadequate and not entirely true.

She sobbed again. He stretched out his hand in the darkness and touched her shoulder. She flinched away. His gesture rebuffed, Astreya suddenly found himself talking, blurting out thoughts and feelings without a pause to wonder what he meant or how his words might be received.

"I don't know whether you're crying because we stopped, or because we should have stopped earlier. I don't know whether I should get up and walk away into the night. We've only known each other for a couple of days. I don't know what you want. I'm supposed to go south to the Castle, but I don't know where I'm going and I don't know if I'll be back."

She laughed harshly. "There's so much you don't know, 'Streya," she said. "And yet you're so wise in some ways. So wise, and so foolish."

Astreya frowned in the darkness, trying to unravel the contradictions.

"'Streya, I brought you here to let anything and everything happen. I hoped you would go ahead, take your pleasure, not think about me. Then I could hate you for it, and blame you if I had a baby. But you ruined my plans. You were gentle, and thought about me, and... and... well, it didn't work."

"What didn't work?" Astreya asked. "And why?"

"Don't you know? Oh, 'Streya. Don't be insulted. I like you. I really do. And it isn't your fault that you're a man and that means you get picked to go to the Castle, even though you're a complete stranger and I'm from Teenmouth and could go, and want to go, and..."

"Why don't you?" Astreya asked. "I know the folk around here don't think you should, but perhaps they'll accept you at the Castle."

"That's the worst of it," said Eva with a sniff. "The Castle will sometimes take women, Mother told me so. But Teenmouth people don't want to know that. Jeb won't even hear, 'Streya. Do you know what that's like? To talk to someone and they look at you as if they were deaf?"

Astreya thought of the confusion and hurt he had felt at Yan's treachery, and decided that he could guess at Eva's feelings. "It doesn't seem fair," he said.

"It isn't fair. And then along you come, and you get the money, the cloak, the party—and my own father made it happen."

"But I still don't understand why."

"Why he did it? To get ahead without working, same as always."

"But why..."

"Why did I bring you here? I'm not sure, now. I thought maybe if I couldn't do what I want, then I'd do what they want me to do, but so that they don't like it. You saw Jeb, pushing me at you to get you out of Teenmouth before they could change their minds. It almost made me hate you, 'Streya. Maybe he wants me to go with you and then come back alone, with the money. But he doesn't want you to lie with me and leave him a pregnant daughter with no husband. Maybe he wants you to like me so that you'll go back to your people and he will profit if they come to Teenmouth. I don't know, and I just don't care. So, I decided that if I can't go, I'll do anything... anything that happens. And if I have a child, then he won't beat me. That would be the beginning. I'd be the girl with a baby and no man. And then, no one will have me."

Astreya was unable to follow the contradictions and misunderstandings behind what she was saying, still less to calm her with an explanation.

"Eva," he began, "I'm not... you mustn't..."

She continued as if he hadn't spoken. "I'll go back. What else can I do? I can't live in hopes you'll return, because sure as fate there'll be no Teenmouth boy interested in me after tonight—not that I want their muddy boots around me."

"Come with me to the Castle," said Astreya impulsively leaping at a possible solution to all the confused facts and emotions that surrounded him. "You know the way, and I don't. They must have room for an extra scholar or two. Besides, I want to know what I'm getting into before I join, and I need someone I can ask questions. I need to make my own decisions based on what I know, not on people who make them for me, people who I..."

He had been going to say, "who I don't trust," but checked himself lest she think he doubted her.

"Make my own decisions," echoed Eva slowly. "That's what I want, too. Mother says to think for myself, but every time I do, it only makes matters worse."

She sniffed, and Astreya wondered if she was going to cry again.

"When Mother said goodbye, she said people do the unexpected. What did she mean, Astreya?"

"Well," said Astreya, "I guess she's right, because unexpected is what keeps happening to me."

"She knew! She knew!" cried Eva in the darkness. "'Streya, she guessed I'd come here, and she knew you'd be different. Oh, 'Streya, it's going to be all right!"

She grabbed him around the neck and kissed him vigorously, if somewhat inaccurately. Astreya was too surprised by the sudden change in her mood to react before she had let go and was again a part of the darkness around him.

"We have to leave," she said as she repacked the basket.

"Your mother told me to go tonight," said Astreya, "And that means now. The Hunter's Belt set a little while ago while... um ... while we weren't looking. And there's the moon beginning to rise."

Eva chuckled. "It was nice, 'Streya, so nice. I thought it might be, but I didn't know how much."

"For me, too," said Astreya, choosing to forget his misgivings. "I never..."

"You never had a girl?"

Astreya nodded in the dark.

"You seemed to know what to do," said Eva.

"So did you."

"I'm not ignorant," said Eva with dignity. "Just inexperienced."

"Me too," Astreya agreed.

There was a long silence in which Astreya started to review all that had happened until practical questions crowded out speculation.

"Will they follow?" he asked.

"Not far. They'll walk to the edges of the fields and shout a bit, but they'll only make sure that there are no bodies lying around. Once they decide that I went with you willingly, they'll sit around and tut-tut about it."

"What about your father and mother?"

Eva was silent for a while, and then whispered very quietly, "She'll understand," and then much louder, "And I don't care about what he thinks."

Astreya fumbled for his pack in the darkness, and folded up his cloak. "Can you find the right road?" he asked.

"We're close to it," said Eva. "A few steps out of these pines, and we can be on our way. The first part is between fields. We'll not go very fast in the dark, but we can make a start."

As they picked up their belongings, Eva's voice came to him in the darkness.

"I never kissed a man with a beard before. It's a bit prickly, but nice."

Chapter 10:

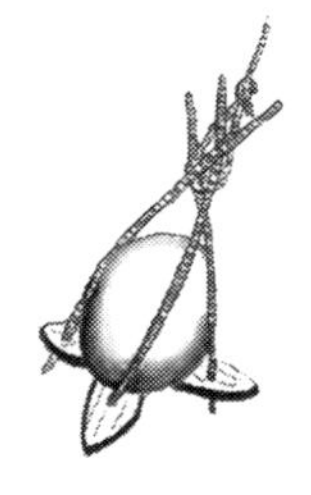

In Which the Mollie Returns to the Village

Scarm woke in two kinds of pain. A fire was burning in his arm, but his memories of Astreya were just as painful. He reached for the skin of whisky and lit a third fire in his gullet. He hung the skin on its peg against the boat's side, and levered himself cautiously into a sitting position. His head throbbed, then settled down into a dull ache.

"Air," he muttered as he braced himself with his good arm and stood up.

His four steps up to the cockpit were hazardous as the *Mollie* dipped and swung to a quartering wind, but eventually he stood with one hip braced and an elbow crooked under the cabin top.

"Scarm, what in blazes are y' doin' out of yer bunk?" demanded Roaring Jack.

The old sailor's gaze took in Red Ian on the weather side of the cockpit, the main sheet in a huge hand, and Yan slumped drowsily in the lee. He looked up at the sail, now bellying full above them, glanced first starboard to the weather side where high cloud masked the sun, then to port where lay a darker line that told of land on the horizon. Then he focused on Roaring Jack's face, his red hair and whiskers pushed sideways across his face by the wind.

"I'm better in the wind. Takes my mind off... off what happened back there. Tell me, Jack, what's the plan?"

Roaring Jack jerked his head to the landward side, and he hesitated momentarily before answering.

"We've gotten a landfall, prob'ly a bit south o' where we lost sight of it when the storm blew up on us."

"It's a lee shore. That's why you're standing out this far."

Roaring Jack nodded and glanced around him. Scarm had the odd sensation that the skipper had not thought of this obvious strategy.

"Get some northing, hope the wind eases, drop to loo'rd in a bit, look for shelter."

"Could be turning into an easterly."

"Could be. Hope not."

Scarm wondered what he was hearing in the skipper's tone, because it certainly was not the usual confident bellow.

"How long we been going?"

"You slept the night, an' the day's more'n half over."

Scarm shook his head in disbelief, felt dizzy, and let himself sink down into a sitting position on the cockpit sole. There would be no turning back now. He would have to live with his conviction that they had not done enough to rescue Astreya—or worse, to find his body. His respect for Roaring Jack dimmed, but he deliberately spurned that thought, and looked for a reason to excuse the skipper.

"Did anyone get any sleep—besides me, that is?"

"Red and Yan took us some o' the way through the night."

"Jack, you've been at the helm for the best part of three days, then."

Roaring Jack shrugged. "Thinkin' about me foolishness in sailing south. Tryin' to make up me mind what to tell 'Lana 'bout 'Streya."

Yan's head jerked upward. Neither Roaring Jack nor Red Ian noticed, but Scarm, seated at the same level, saw a gleam of eyes before the boy slumped back into counterfeit sleep. A few moments later, when Roaring Jack called for food from the cabin, Yan put on an unconvincing show of waking up. Protecting his arm, Scarm hauled himself painfully out of Yan's way, and took the boy's place on the lee side. Yan avoided his eyes as they passed.

Throughout the rest of the day, Scarm took his mind off his pain by covertly watching Yan. The boy was quick to respond to Roaring Jack's orders, earning the occasional "Good lad," when he finished a task. However, Scarm saw a puppy dog, fawning kind of obedience, deliberately contrived to say, "Look at me being brave after all that's happened to me." Roaring Jack appeared to be taken in. Scarm decided that the skipper was probably so numbed with tiredness and grief that this was not the time to talk about his uncomfortable conviction that Yan was concealing something.

Later in the day, they cautiously dropped downwind towards the shoreline, which changed from a blue smudge to a hard dark line against an afternoon sky patched with puffy clouds. Then just when they were close to afternoon-shadowed cliffs, the wind freshened, pushing them constantly closer towards outlying rocks, each marked in white by waves exploding into spray. Scarm hung on with his good hand and looked for anything that would signal a cove or inlet, knowing that Roaring Jack, Red Ian and Yan were doing the same.

The *Mollie* was skittish in the troubled water, demanding their best efforts at the helm and sheets. Looking ahead as the *Mollie* poised on a wave, Scarm saw one cliff edge apparently moving against the line of farther headlands. He waited until the next time the boat rose out of a trough before confirming what he thought he had seen.

"Ease her a bit, Jack, there's a break in the cliffs ahead."

"She'll lee shore... an' if you're wrong, we'll be fresh out o' luck an' I'll be..."

Roaring Jack bit off his words as they turned into a whine. Scarm frowned in disbelief at the uncharacteristic display of uncertainty. Moments later, as the *Mollie* rose to another wave, Scarm saw the gap he had noticed opening like a doorway, and he was looking through to see low hills in the distance.

"Just a bit, Jack. Hold her now. There it is, a beach. No breakers, either."

"Better be right, Scarm," he said accusingly, and then continued in his habitual bellow. "Mind the sheets, boys, we'll be on the point of a gybe all the way in."

They were lucky. The *Mollie* threaded between spray-splashed rocks, long skeins of foam painting the waves down wind, but no rocks or shoals barred their way. Roaring Jack altered course, and as the cliffs cut off the wind that had threatened to run them ashore, they saw a curve of sand and pebbles that had been invisible from the open sea.

"We'll beach her, boys," said Roaring Jack as he used what was left of the wind to urge the *Mollie* onward.

* * * * *

A rainy easterly blew past them in the night, drumming on the cabin roof and soaking the *Mollie*'s furled sails. When they awoke the next day and looked up, a watery, yellowish sun had thinned some of the mist, and the sky was clear only immediately above them. Out between the headlands was a wall of white. All that day, a fog clung to the sea, coiling into their bay.

"We ain't goin' no place today, lads," said Roaring Jack. "Best spend our time gettin' ourselves shipshape. Yan, find us some fresh water."

Yan dragged out the remaining water keg, the other two having been left behind in his mad rush back to the *Mollie*.

"Here, lad, I'll take the other end of an oar for you," said Scarm.

Yan was not enthusiastic, but could hardly refuse the help. They slung the keg below an oar and made their way up the beach beyond the tide line to where the stream ran fresh. While Yan pressed the keg into the stream to fill it, Scarm affected a nonchalant examination of the scrubby pines that grew to the stream's edge.

"It's not going to be easy to tell Astreya's mother what happened. Would you like to try with me now, so's you know what to say?"

"Uh... all right," said Yan, unable to think of a way out. "We... um... 'Streya and me beached the tender, and headed up over the dike. There was a path that led to a well. So, we hauled up the water and filled the kegs. An' then... an' then..."

"The men..." prompted Scarm.

"Yes. The men came and they killed Astreya."

"Just like that?"

"Yeah. While I was hauling up the water from the well."

"They left you alone?"

"I... I guess they didn't notice me."

Scarm bit back the obvious question why Yan had been spared, and left the story unquestioned for the time being.

"I know this is difficult for you, Yan, but how did you know he was..."

"Dead? I could see the blood. He was on the ground, his face in the dirt, an'... an'... blood..."

"Where?"

"All down his cheek... from his ear to his chin... into the ground."

"He was hit on the head?"

Yan nodded, looking at Scarm for the first time in his recitation.

"With what?"

Yan's mouth remained open briefly, he swallowed and took a big breath.

"With hammers. Three of four of them. Big hammers, like... like..." he paused, and then rushed on. "Like for drivin' posts into the ground."

"And so you...?"

"I grabbed the oars and ran."

"Smart of you to think of them. You must have been scared."

Yan nodded. "They yelled after me, too."

"Good thing they didn't have their bows."

"Uh huh. I guess the ones with the bows were back at the dike."

"But you didn't see them."

Yan shrugged. "I was kinda' busy running with the oars."

"Of course you were. Now shall we get the keg back to the boat?

They returned to the *Mollie*, where Roaring Jack was preparing to set sail with the morning tide. Scarm was unconvinced by Yan's story, but Roaring Jack was so eager to sympathize, and Yan stayed so close to him, that here was no opportunity to broach the subject with the skipper, much less have Yan retell his obviously fabricated account.

When the next morning produced a southwest wind under a sky brushed with high, wispy cloud, they were on their way north once again. Around midday, Roaring Jack identified a distinctive cliff face that marked the abandoned village. All were glad when the entrance to that bay was astern, even though it meant spending the night bobbing at anchor in the lee of a tree-clad island further along the coast, close to a rugged shoreline where the waves surged between mounded up boulders.

Over the next few days they had good weather, with light but persistent southwesterly winds that carried the *Mollie* northwards in a comfortable reach. Scarm tried to find a moment when he could talk to Roaring Jack without Yan hearing them, but when such opportunities arrived, Roaring Jack was either unwilling or unable to speak about anything to do with their ill-fated arrival at Teenmouth. Scarm gradually came to the conclusion that by refusing to talk about what had happened, the skipper was putting off his task of returning without Astreya by living in denial. Roaring Jack's remorse was clear from his long, moody silences and over-concern for Yan, who basked in the attention and became as voluble as the skipper was silent.

"When are we going to fish, skipper?" he asked every morning, and when Roaring Jack just shook his head and shaped a course northwards, Yan pestered both Red Ian and Scarm with questions about likely spots to find fish. When neither would answer to his satisfaction, he took to sitting on the bowsprit, humming monotonously to himself. When the third day started with the very same question, Roaring Jack told Yan to sling a line over the side if he wished, but made no alteration of his course northwards. Yan immediately set the largest hook he could find. All three men let him be, since it was clear that the skipper was humoring the boy. Throughout the day, Yan watched a long line that led from a bucket in the cockpit, over the stern and into the *Mollie*'s wake. To nobody's surprise, the day ended with nothing caught. Yan was losing interest, but more to cope with boredom than any hope of catching anything, he set the line again as they began another day's run. Scarcely had he paid out enough line to clear the wake when he gave a yell as the line cut into his hand.

"I got one! Skipper, I got a fish!"

"Haul it in, then, boy."

Yan pulled, and then was nearly tugged into the water himself. He yelled as the line cut into his hands.

"Here, put these on," said Red Ian, handing him a pair of gloves.

Somehow, Yan pulled the gloves onto his cut hands without either letting go of the line or being yanked into the sea. He was just in time, because the fish made a long run that took most of the line.

"Haul in!" said Red Ian.

Yan needed no encouragement or instruction. He had been hauling fish all his life, first from the shore or the wharf, then from dories in the bay, but nothing had prepared him for the size of the one that he had hooked. Roaring Jack glanced shoreward to ensure he had plenty of sea room, and brought the *Mollie* head to wind.

"We'll heave to and let him have his fish."

Scarm and Red Ian backed the jib and hauled the main while Roaring Jack watched Yan indulgently. It soon became clear that this was no ordinary fish. Again and again, Yan hauled in slack line, only to have the fish make another plunge for freedom. Red Ian helped keep the line clear and untangled, but Yan shrugged off any help to work his fish. Finally, when he thought his arms would take no more, he saw a huge grey shape rise towards the surface near the *Mollie*'s blunt bows.

"Here he is!"

Roaring Jack caught Yan's enthusiasm. "Gaff him, Red."

Red Ian locked his knees under the stern decking and jabbed downwards, his big shoulders straining his canvas jacket drum taut.

"Missed 'im. He's big. Hold me feet."

Yan was about to protest when the fish rolled on its side, showing a body that even Red Ian could not have put his arms around.

As Scarm braced Red Ian's feet, Roaring Jack pulled out a harpoon and prepared to join in. One knee on the narrow deck, he leaned over the side, looking for the right moment. Once he started only to check his thrust, then he drove his harpoon deep into the back of the fish's head. The water streaked red as it thrashed wildly and eventually floated still beside the boat.

"Roight. Now all we have to do is get 'im aboard."

This proved to be a major undertaking, because although the fish was dead, it was still occasionally twitching, and weighed more than they could lift. Finally, they secured lines around its body, ran a block and tackle half way up the mast, hauled it up the boat's side and lashed the creature along the starboard gunwale against the cabin. The *Mollie* listed to one side as if pressed down by a strong wind.

"That's some thunderin' great fish you've caught, Yan," said Roaring Jack when they all climbed back into the cockpit and set the *Mollie* back on her course. "I never seen a bigger one. We need t' celebrate."

Red Ian fetched the whisky skin from the cabin and passed it around.

"Just one swig, young Yan," said Roaring Jack.

Yan managed to avoid coughing, though his eyes widened and he had to take several long breaths before he could talk. Then he could not stop talking. He relived every instant of his struggle with the fish, pausing only to look at the results of his luck. The three men, all of whom remembered their first big fish, let him run on, but they eventually stopped listening.

The next day was spent sailing in light airs on gently rolling seas towards the Village. The time hung heavily on Roaring Jack, who spent many hours with the tiller in one fist, and his other hand tugging at his red beard until one side was noticeably shorter than the other. He answered all questions with grunts, and turned away when Scarm tried to open a conversation.

They reached the approaches to the Village in the late afternoon, as the cliffs threw their shadows onto the sea. The gap between the headlands was a dark opening onto the fjord, hidden until the *Mollie* was sliding down the last of the ocean waves into the calm water that led to the Village. As they approached, it was clear from the crowd on the wharf that someone had seen them coming from the cliff top. When lines were tossed to willing hands ashore, and the *Mollie* was alongside, the crowd moved forward to wonder at the size of the big fish lashed along the starboard side.

"Where did y' find a great fish like that, Jack?"

"How big is that?

"Who caught it?"

"I did!" Yan yelled.

Instantly, he was at the center of attention. He climbed onto the cabin roof and stood over his prize, drinking in the admiration. He waved and grinned, then started into an account of how he had caught the fish singlehanded. Roaring Jack cut across Yan's self-important account.

"Where's Alana?"

"She's at her cottage," said Mollie. "Go see her, Jack."

"See to the lines, Red. Scarm, Yan, come wi' me."

He vaulted ashore and started for the steep path up to Alana's cottage. Mollie caught his arm, but he yanked his arm away and scowled at her.

"Streya's dead, Mol. 'An it's my fault."

Leaving his wife without the embrace that had ended every voyage since they married, he strode up the hill.

"Is it true, Scarm?" she asked.

Scarm nodded as he passed her, Yan following uncertainly behind. The three of them walked up the hill in silence except for their plodding footfalls and the steadily decreasing murmur of the crowd at the wharf. Roaring Jack reached the cottage door, took a deep breath and raised his fist to knock on the weathered wood. The door opened before his knuckles touched it. He looked down on Alana's upturned face, her eyes steady and her mouth firm.

"'Lana, Oi have to tell ye that young 'Streya's dead. There it is, said. An' it's my fault. 'Lana, he's gone, but...

"No he's not, Jack. Astreya isn't dead. And it certainly isn't your fault."

Roaring Jack's mind latched onto her last words, and his guilt diminished. He looked at her gratefully, his hunched shoulders relaxing. Behind his back, Scarm wondered at Alana's certainty. He glanced sideways at Yan, and caught a look of something close to terror in the boy's eyes. Scarm felt his disbelief in Yan's story suddenly grow into conviction.

"It's true, 'Lana. Come, boy, tell her."

Yan looked first at Roaring Jack, then at Alana. His mouth opened and closed several times, his hands came up to his face, he turned and fled down the path.

"The poor lad can't hardly bear it, 'Lana. He was there when they killed 'Streya. An' it's 'cause Oi sent them ashore for water."

Ignoring the skipper, Alana turned to Scarm.

"What do you say, Ian?"

"Alana, I didn't see it. I..."

Roaring Jack talked Scarm down.

"Scarm got shot by the rotten bastards. He was out of it when we left. Oi should'a gone back, but there was Scarm wi' an arrow in him, and near to bein' a goner. So we left without 'Streya's body. Oi know you can't forgive me, 'Lana. Oi'd do anything to make it better, but..."

"Jack, you must go back for him, that's all there is to it. Now come into the house where you can tell me the whole story of your voyage. You too, Ian."

The big skipper meekly ducked his head under the doorframe and followed her into the cottage, Scarm behind him. Yan, who had stopped a little way down the path, saw them go in. He turned and ran down the hill to revel in the Villagers' admiration of his fish.

Chapter 11:

In which Astreya meets Gar and Lindey

It was noon when Astreya and Eva reached the ford. The river Teen had shrunk to a stream that wound its way through mixed forest. The road was now only pair of red earth ruts on either side of a ragged green strip of grass, scarred by horses' hooves. At first, the road kept to the valley bottom, running just far enough from the river to avoid spring flooding, then it headed more directly south, crossing and recrossing the meandering stream on increasingly ramshackle bridges until it ran so shallow that a bridge was no longer necessary. Where the road met the water, it was joined by another that was little more than a track, overgrown with ferns and almost blocked by fallen branches.

At the water's edge, Astreya and Eva sat to take off their shoes before wading to the other side. They had travelled for most of the night, their way lit by a late-rising moon. Somewhere in their journey, they had passed through tiredness into an unreal state in which they walked side by side, neither of them wanting to be first to stop. Sitting under the overhanging trees, they took their time to soothe their feet in the smoothly flowing water. There seemed no good reason to do anything more than sit, perhaps lie down and sleep, drugged by tiredness and the silken sounds of water.

As they dawdled in the green shade, a creaking and rumbling came down the disused track from the east. They looked up at the sounds of a horse's hooves and the squeaks and rattles of a wagon bumping over stones and stumps. Two voices alternately gave brief warnings and assurances. The branches swayed aside, and a wagon lurched down towards the sun-dappled water of the ford.

Tired as he was, Astreya stared at the vehicle in delight. Behind a piebald horse was a wagon on which every available space had been painted and ornamented. The body of the wagon was a tall, boxy affair painted bright yellow. It was roofed and sided with canvas spread on hoops, and painted to look as if it had windows, in each of which there was scene so cunningly detailed that it seemed a glimpse into a different world. The wagon lurched to a stop beside them, letting Astreya clearly see the two mock windows on the side nearest him. He saw a horse that galloped away and a lone figure who stared out at the sea. Below, the wagon's yellow sides were decorated with fantastically convoluted faces of people and animals, some grim, some friendly, some with mysterious and haunting looks. Even the spokes of the wheels, now muddied and dirty, were etched with curlicues and scrolls; and from each hub a whirling face stared either down at the ground or up at the paintings.

The driver of this wonder was a man with a close trimmed white beard and a fringe of equally white hair. The shirt he wore had once been brown, but had been splashed and wiped with all shades of colored paint. As he bent forward to loop the horse's reins on the rail in front of him, Astreya saw that the top of his head was perfectly bare and darkly sun-browned. A young woman, taller and more substantial than Eva, strode around to the horse's head. She had twisted her shoulder length hair into a loose knot at the back of her head, but twigs and branches had pulled some of it loose. Her russet-colored skirts were kilted to mid thigh, and the sleeves of a loose shirt were rolled above her elbows. In her hands was a stout staff, tall enough to reach her shoulder, muddied at one end from levering the wagon over obstacles.

Astreya stared, because it seemed to him that both the man and the woman had some special meaning to him. Against reason, he had the overwhelming feeling that this accidental meeting was destined to reveal something about them—and him.

The man, woman and horse were working efficiently. All three were all loose jointed with tiredness and intent on their tasks, which allowed him to watch them unobserved. However, when Eva stood to greet them, their reactions were quick and purposeful. All three stopped dead in the trail. The horse's head jerked up, the man's right hand swept downwards and reappeared holding a short cudgel, and the young woman grasped her staff around its point of balance, transforming it from tool to weapon. Their determination was obvious, but as Astreya looked into their faces, their eyes were calm. The man evaluated him, turning his head slightly so that first one and then the other of his grey eyes met Astreya's. He felt himself respond to the man's stare as if commanded. He returned the look until the man frowned and turned his attention back to Eva, letting Astreya observe the young woman. His first thought was how blue her widely spaced eyes were, and how steadily they held his gaze. Then he noticed that the hair that framed her face and fell almost to her shoulders was a distinctive shade of honey blonde, with a couple of leaves caught in it. He felt an unexpected need to remember her exactly as she stood before him. He studied her carefully, memorizing a slightly upturned nose and her calm, alert expression that contradicted the belligerent way she held her staff.

"We're friendly," said Eva, extending her hands in a gesture of peace, somewhat confused by the fact that she still held her shoes.

"Are there any more of you?" asked the man, and then answered his own question ruefully. "Of course, if you're up to no good, you wouldn't say."

He sighed, put his cudgel on the seat beside him, and shrugged one shoulder to his companion, who grounded one end of her staff.

"If there are any more of them, we've no position to defend anyway," he said wearily. "Besides, I've never seen footpads with shoes in their hands."

"We're traveling to the Castle," said Eva.

"Scholars, are you?"

"We hope to be," said Astreya. "Did you do the drawings on your wagon?"

"So, the young man has a voice after all, though with an accent I don't recognize."

"We're from Teenmouth," said Eva.

"You are, but your inquisitive companion, no."

"Can we help you cross the ford?" asked Astreya.

"A friendly offer, wherever you're from. We accept."

He clicked his tongue at the horse, and the wagon started forward, brushed by the branches of a willow that hung over the water. As it lumbered past them, Eva and Astreya put their shoes, his pack and her basket beside the driver, and walked behind the rear wheels, feeling their way through the water in their bare feet. In two steps the water reached Astreya's knees. The bottom was a rock ledge slick with mud, and although the water got no deeper, the horse started to lose its footing. Astreya pushed and heaved at his side of the wagon, curling trails of mud darkening the water beside him. Ahead, he could see the young woman leading the horse, one hand on its bridle. The wagon slowed and slid sideways. Rattling and banging noises came from within as it tilted towards Astreya, threatening to leave the ledge and fall into the pool downstream. Eva's shoes slid into the water. Astreya scooped them up, tossed them into the wagon, and then braced his back against the tailgate, and shoved as hard as he could. He succeeded only in driving his feet into the mud.

"All together, now," said the driver.

Horse and helpers all pushed or pulled at the same moment, the wagon lurched, Astreya lost his footing and fell. Beside him, Eva staggered, splashing herself from head to foot. Ahead of them, the young woman fared little better as the horse thrashed heavily through the shallows onto dry land, its hoofs spraying water and mud. They were successful, but at the price of a wetting.

Astreya trudged out of the stream, his clothes clinging to him. Eva, only slightly less wet, wrung out her dress as best she could, while the young woman lent on her staff and stared at the stream that had filled her boots and soaked her skirt. Astreya saw her lips move, and knew that she was cursing silently. His own lips twitched in sympathy. She saw him observing her, and one of her eyebrows rose. He quickly looked away.

"It seems hardly fair for me to be the only dry one," said the driver. "But if you can all manage a hundred or so paces, there's a good place to build a fire and dry out."

His face softened into a smile, which he tried to suppress. Astreya looked at the dripping, disconsolate figures, saw the driver's point of view, and chuckled. Eva stopped trying to shake water from her sodden clothes, and looked at him with irritation.

"You have a weed in your hair," she said brusquely.

"You've a face full of freckles," returned Astreya cheerfully.

Eva wiped her face, producing a brown smudge. Ankle deep in the stream, Astreya laughed, as he had not done since leaving the Village. Still laughing, he waved his hands in an effort to convey that he found the entire situation funny, but Eva turned angrily away from him, trying unsuccessfully to wipe her face clean. Astreya strove with his mirth, realizing that Eva thought he was laughing at her, but a deep chuckle from the driver set him off again. He saw the blonde woman's lips curl upwards. At that moment the horse turned its head to look at the humans, then snorted and shook, spattering them all with mud, including the driver. Once he had wiped his face on his sleeve and run his fingers through his circlet of white hair, his weathered face was as blotched as his paint-spattered shirt.

"I'm Gar, and this is Lindey," he said cheerfully.

"I'm Eva."

"Astreya."

"Sure you are."

Astreya frowned at the strangely worded response, and decided it was a question. "Of course I am," he replied.

Gar's eyebrows almost came together in a deeply notched scowl. For a moment, he stared at Astreya with the same calculating intensity that had made him almost forbidding at first meeting. Then his face softened into a smile so pleasant that Astreya almost forgot what had just happened. Gar nodded and repeated both names. Expecting the usual abbreviation, Astreya was surprised when Gar pronounced his whole name easily, albeit slightly accented, as if the name were longer. Lindey nodded at each of them, her expression polite but neutral.

"Well then," said Gar. "Any wetter, and you'd look as if you'd been lost at sea."

He paused, glanced at Astreya, expecting a reply, but when none came, he shrugged and flicked the reins on the horse's back. Astreya briefly wondered whether he had heard a special emphasis on the last three words.

They followed the creaking wagon along the tree-lined track, leaving a trail of wet footprints behind them. The sky was cloudless, but big-leaved maples and spreading oaks shadowed them in green gloom until Gar led them to a clearing. Only a few sun-warmed strides more, and they stood beside a ring of fire-blackened stones. When Gar slid from the driver's seat and reached into the back of the wagon for a handful of dry kindling, Astreya noticed that his breeches were as painty as his shirt. Bold stripes of different colors crisscrossed his thighs where he had wiped paintbrushes or fingers. The paint marks camouflaged him, making it difficult to guess at the man within the paint-daubed, baggy clothes. Judging from the nimble way Gar moved, Astreya guessed at a strength belied by his fringe of white hair. When he helped unharness the horse it became clear that they were approximately the same height, and though Gar was by no means thin, he was certainly fit.

From inside the painted wagon, Gar and Lindey produced food and drink, to which Eva contributed what remained in her basket. Soon, wet clothes festooned the upturned wagon shafts and flapped in a light wind. Astreya gratefully accepted a clean, paint-daubed shirt and cutoff breeks from Gar while the yellow shirt Judith had given him dried. Eva refused Lindey's offer of both shirt and skirt, and instead wrapped herself in a blanket. Lindey watched with a faintly quizzical expression as Eva attempted to keep it around herself while they knelt or sat around a cloth spread for their meal.

Their shared experience at the ford encouraged explanations and histories, spurred by Gar's smiles and grey-eyed attention. He encouraged them to speak by his silences and nods rather than with questions, and seemed to understand more than the mere words they spoke. Lindey, having unobtrusively prepared the food, sat quietly a little apart, her blue eyes watchful, her expression pleasant but neutral. Astreya found himself speaking much more freely than he had intended, and after the meal was over, he wondered whether he had said too much to complete strangers, no matter how generous they were with their food. After giving a brief account of sailing from the Village to Teenmouth, he fell silent, determined not to speak of Yan's or Roaring Jack's treachery.

Gar refrained from asking Astreya what happened next, but his encouraging looks soon had Eva explaining that her father would not accept that a girl could want to learn to be a Healer. Astreya noticed Lindey's eyebrows rise slightly, as if irritated by what she heard. Gar continued to nod attentively as Eva described Astreya's arrival, how he was attacked and then abandoned by the *Mollie*'s crew, and then chosen as scholar. Astreya did not correct or embellish her account with how or why he had been betrayed and forsaken, and neither Gar nor Lindey questioned the gaps in their story.

Astreya grew embarrassed as Eva continued to talk enthusiastically about his reading and writing skills, so to stem her flow of superlatives, he stood up from the log on which he had been sitting and pulled his shirt from the wagon shafts. He shook off a few remaining specks of dried mud, shrugged off Gar's paint-specked garment and put his own back on. As he tucked it into his waist, he was aware of Gar's gaze sharpening from a casual look to intent curiosity. Astreya's hand felt for the silver bracelet on his left arm, and the leather pouch of money around his neck. When he looked at Gar again, the man's face had undergone a subtle change, and there was something in his tone of voice that Astreya could not fathom.

"Astreya, Eva, now it's our turn," said Gar "Or at least, it's mine, because Lindey isn't as talkative as I am. I'm a painter. I travel. I visit places in search of work. Never to return, or at least that's the way it's worked out so far. Lindey joined me many months and a handful of villages ago. We, too, are on our way to the Castle, where I am to paint, ornament, embellish and otherwise beautify the walls of their hall. I'll be there for some time: the hall's as big as this clearing."

Astreya looked at Gar incredulously. A single building into which Alana's cottage would fit three or four times? The thought of producing a drawing on the wall of such a place struck Astreya as a task requiring years, if not a lifetime. Gar gave him a knowing look, and answered his unspoken question.

"Once you've decided what to paint, getting it onto the wall's only a minor problem," he said.

"But the materials," said Astreya. "You're going to need so much charcoal, and paint, and..."

"I have the strange conviction that you can draw as well as read and write," said Gar slowly. "Well, come and take a look."

He stood up and rolled back the flaps at the rear of the wagon. Inside, Astreya saw a traveling painter's workshop: rolls of canvas swung from the wooden hoops that held up the roof, stretched canvases on frames were tucked into racks, tools and brushes were clipped to a paint-daubed folding table or dangled from strings above it, and under the two benches that ran along either side of the wagon were pots, pails, canisters, jugs, beakers and bottles of paint and pigment, each patched with a splash of color to mark its contents. For the first time in his life, Astreya looked at another man's possessions with sheer envy. To be able to work with such a range of shades and colors made Astreya remember with disgust his own attempts to use the natural dyes that the women in the Village cooked up to tint their wool. Unlike the soft tones suitable only for cloth, Gar's pigments offered shades that could be vivid or subtle, strong or muted.

At Gar's invitation, Astreya pored over the sketches and finished paintings that were ready for sale. Most were landscapes of the kind that looked familiar until he saw that they were all cunningly vague and generalized variations on a handful of themes such as a river in morning mist, a single tree at sunset, a small boat sailing across a bay.

At first, the older man was cautious lest Astreya's interest was one with so many of the young men and women who were attracted by his brightly painted wagon, but who then dismissed his work as useless, or suspected that it was magically dangerous. However, he soon saw that Astreya's appreciation was not only for the finished product, but also for the skills that went into the paintings and drawings.

"These are what I do for me," said Gar eventually, as he climbed into the back of the wagon to reach a leather case from which he pulled several thin-planed boards.

They were all portraits sketched in charcoal and highlighted with paint. They captured a person, and most spoke of the mind behind the features, as if the artist had recorded them to make a collection of the characters he had met. Here was a mean-spirited man with an avaricious twist to his mouth; there was a woman whose gossip was spiteful; and there was a girl who, though pretty, was not as beautiful as she wanted the world to believe. Astreya turned through the canvases, admiring the artist's skill and technique, wondering how the landscapes were so sweetly appealing and the portraits so cunningly observant. Gar leaned out of the wagon with another handful of drawings.

As Astreya handed the others back, his shirtsleeve slid, and the silver bracelet gleamed through the strands of woven string. Gar's eyes locked onto it.

"Where did you get that?" he asked softly.

"The bracelet? My father. He's dead."

Because his attention was on the paintings Astreya did not notice Gar's intense scrutiny. He was absorbed by meticulous drawings of animals, each in its natural setting. Although the detail was finely executed, it was not the mere exactness that fascinated him. Life and movement were caught in the still colors and lines, as if at any moment each animal might disappear from the board on which it was painted. Astreya held up a small drawing of a squirrel and stared at it, still oblivious that his blunt response had not satisfied Gar's curiosity.

"You like it?" Gar asked.

"It's not just any squirrel," said Astreya slowly.

"You're right. I called him Chatters. He visited me almost every day and tried to steal my lunch for nearly a month. Since he didn't care to travel on with me, the best I could do for the little fellow was to paint his picture."

Astreya turned through more drawings, stopping at an unfinished sketch of a woman with a heart-shaped face. There was something puzzling about how Gar had drawn her. Without thinking what he was doing, Astreya held the drawing above him, and the answer became clear. The woman's dark hair hung down from her face, shadowing her cheek but revealing intensely focused eyes. Whoever she was, Gar had drawn her from below as she looked down at him. He was about to ask about the unusual point of view, when Gar took the sketch from him and slid it into the back of the satchel.

"Unfinished. I should have gone back," he said, as if speaking to himself. Then he continued in his usual confident tone, "Let that be a lesson to you, young lad. Never interrupt your work—whatever she says."

Eva frowned disapprovingly at his last three words as she walked over from the fireside to find out what they were talking about, her blanket still draped a trifle uncertainly around her. Astreya looked up only when one arm, bare to the shoulder and a little below, reached to take the next drawing he was about to examine. Standing a couple of paces away, Gar's eyes twinkled as he watched Astreya's concentration transfer to the round softness just below the top of Eva's blanket.

"Astreya can draw too," said Eva, hitching the blanket higher. "As well as read and write."

Gar's bushy eyebrows rose slightly.

"Show him, Astreya. Go on. Draw something for him, the way you said you did for your skipper."

"I don't have bark, charcoal, ink...." Astreya said with a shrug.

Gar considered the reply. There had been no self-deprecation in Astreya's tone. Gar reached into the wagon and brought out a sketching satchel, equipped with charcoal, wafer thin boards and inks.

"Use what you need," he said.

"These are very fine," said Astreya as he drew out a board and a wooden box of charcoal. "Are you sure?"

Gar nodded.

"What would you have me draw?" asked Astreya.

Gar pursed his lips again. Perhaps he had been wrong, and would have to face his own and the lad's embarrassment, or worse, a mess of scrawled lines that appealed only to the one who had made them. Gar had met young people who had no idea how badly they drew, but he could recall none who had shown Astreya's singleness of purpose.

"Draw her," said Gar, waving an arm at Eva.

Astreya looked about him, then took Eva's hand and led her to the front of the cart.

"Can you stay still, if you're comfortable?" he asked.

Eva nodded, blushed, and then held his eyes as she nodded again. She half leaned, half sat on the wagon's shafts, the blanket across one arm, her other hand catching its edge from slipping off her shoulders. Astreya took two steps back, knelt in the grass, and stared at her fixedly for several long minutes. The redness of her cheeks eventually subsided. She stayed very still.

As the moments passed, Astreya's concentration only grew more intense, so much so that even when the wind flicked a damp curl of black hair across his forehead, his expression did not change. Astreya continued to look at Eva, who eventually frowned as if she thought he was embarrassing her. Lindey watched from a distance, her head slightly tilted, and raised one eyebrow at Gar, who took a step forward to bring the awkward charade to an end. But before he could speak or move more than a step, Astreya began to scrape the charcoal in long strokes across wood, making a smooth, hissing sound. Quick tapping and scratching noises followed. Gar stood still, nodding slightly. There was control and sureness in the first bold strokes of the charcoal, and the rhythm had not been broken as Astreya worked on detail. He looked up only occasionally. Lindey walked quietly to where she could see over Astreya's shoulder. She caught Gar's curious glance and again raised one eyebrow at him, this time in wonderment.

Eva sat as if carved in stone, the center of attention. A biting fly found her shoulder, and the blanket slid far lower than her mother would ever have let her wear a blouse. Eventually, her Teenmouth training was stronger than her will to remain still. The wind caught the blanket and tugged it low enough that she broke out of her pose in a scramble to preserve her modesty.

"I'm sorry, 'Streya. I'll try to go back to the same position."

Astreya looked up blankly at her confusion. "It's all right," he said. "You can move if you want to."

He worked on for several minutes, then stopped and regarded what he had done with his head on one side. Eva went impatiently to him and looked at what he had drawn. For a moment, she stood agape. Astreya had drawn a young woman, not the little girl who had looked back at her from her mother's battered metal mirror. When he looked up at her, he saw her standing more confidently, holding her head proudly.

Gar smiled at Eva's unconscious preening. His own examination of the drawing was more professional. He approved the likeness Astreya had caught, but he seemed more impressed by the vigor of the sketch, and he looked with even greater approval at the sureness and economy of the lines. He narrowed his eyes as if seeking to find fault as he might in his own work, and then he suddenly shrugged and smiled at Astreya's apprehensive expression.

"Who taught you?" asked Gar.

Astreya shook his head. "It's like feeling the shapes with my eyes. I look, then I look at the blank sheet, and I see the picture. Then I shape it with the charcoal—except that things get a bit changed." He paused. "Does that mean that I'm lying?"

Gar chuckled and ran his fingers through his circle of white hair, fluffing out tufts over his ears.

"If you didn't change things, you wouldn't be making a picture. Look, here, where you shadowed under her arm to bring it a little higher than it was: that's good, because it accentuates her breasts; and here, where you highlighted to tilt up her chin a bit, you've caught that... um... delicate look she has when she glances up at you. But here your line got a bit lost and you had to fudge it with a second stroke. Up here, you have good balance between..."

Eva stepped back during the flow of commentary to which Astreya listened attentively. She hunched her shoulders under the blanket, drew it around herself tightly and frowned at Gar.

"Spoiling my picture with words," she muttered. "He's saying I'm not really the way 'Streya drew me."

Astreya recognized the voice of someone speaking partly to herself, partly to be heard and apologized to. As he searched for suitable words, Lindey resolved his problem.

"They'll talk about you now as if you were a tree," said Lindey. "They're alike. They look silently, but once they've drawn something, they have to talk."

Eva stared at Lindey, whose face was as inscrutable as her voice had been.

"And what do *you* do for Gar?" Eva asked, lifting her chin for emphasis.

"I take turns driving the wagon, cooking, looking after the horse. Sometimes I mix paints, and from time to time I help him stay out of trouble."

Eva sniffed and turned away after Lindey's matter-of-fact comments.

Astreya was suddenly fearful that the chance meeting that held so much promise might be about to end.

"Lindey," said Gar suddenly. "Would you set about pitching camp here for the night? I've got a lot of talking to do with this young man."

As Lindey nodded and set to work unpacking the wagon, Eva flounced away from all three of them. She pulled her still damp clothes from where she had spread them, and went behind the bushes to change.

"How did you...?"

"Where did you...?"

Astreya and Gar spoke at the same moment, stopped, and laughed. Astreya answered Gar's question before it was completed.

"Roaring Jack was the only person—besides my mother, of course—who thought there was any use in my 'markings,' as he called them. He took me south to draw where we'd been, so that we could find our way back."

"He had you sketch his landfalls?"

"Yes. And because we stayed close in sight of land, I made a whole lot of sketches. You could say that I made one very long sketch of our way south."

Astreya was dimly aware that Eva was listening to their conversation, as if about to demand, "What about me?" He noticed that she had started to comb out her hair and replait it into pigtails, casting glances at the two men, and then at Lindey, who was preparing a stew.

Astreya's concentration returned to Gar when she strolled off along the road, kicking her shoes into the dust. He wondered briefly if he should say or do something about her, but then she returned almost immediately, went up to Lindey and stood, her hands on her hips.

"If you want help, just tell me what to do," he heard Eva say.

Lindey's face softened into a surprisingly gentle smile. "Memories?" she asked softly.

Astreya saw Eva put her head on one side, as if looking for signs that she was being patronized.

"I don't want to go home," she said. "But at the same time, I wish... I wish..." Eva could not finish her thought.

"You wish life was a little more predictable," completed Lindey.

Eva's mouth fell open. She nodded. "How did you know?"

"I knew I had to leave my home, but that didn't make it any easier," said Lindey. "At first I was lonely a lot of the time."

"You were by yourself?" asked Eva incredulously. "You can't be much older than I am."

Lindey nodded as she slid chopped onions off a cutting board into a pot.

"I had trained for it, of course," she said. "You're learning all at once. But for certain, you've been lucky."

"Lucky?" asked Eva.

"You had Astreya, and then you found us. You could have been robbed, raped and murdered."

Eva swallowed, then deliberately refused to be impressed. "While you, of course, wouldn't have been."

"That's right," said Lindey calmly.

"You don't need a man to look after you," said Eva sarcastically.

"That's right," said Lindey, as if stating a simple fact.

Astreya watched as Eva shook her head again. He saw that she was unable to reconcile Lindey's perceptive awareness of her problem, and her emotionless statements about dangers Astreya knew terrified Eva. He was struck by the differences between them that went so much further than the fact that one was diminutive and brown-haired and the other full-figured and blonde. He reflected on the way Lindey continued with what she was doing, answering questions simply and directly, while Eva reacted to what she said as if she needed a more emotional response.

"What lamb stew needs is herbs," he heard Lindey say. "My supply has run out. Mother always said you can't make stew without herbs."

He wondered how Eva would respond, fearing that she might reject Lindey's overture of companionship.

"I smelled mint at the ford," said Eva. "I'll go get some."

"... and so I stayed ashore and turned my hand to painting, which was something I'd always wanted to do."

Gar's words snapped Astreya's attention back from the two women. Rather than confess that he had not been listening, Astreya hazarded a request.

"Would you show me some more of your drawings and painting?"

"Thought you'd never ask," said Gar cheerfully. "Come into my perambulating painter's store of wonders."

Astreya and Gar went back to his cart, where their conversation continued. While they talked, Astreya was strangely conscious of Lindey. When she came over to the cart for a crock of sourdough starter he watched the way she moved, and his gaze lingered when she returned to the fireside to start the process of making bannock. He was also dimly aware of Eva, who did not even glance in his direction as she first sat on, then leaned against a log that someone had placed near the fire, and combed her hair once more. When Astreya looked again after Gar had completed a commentary on a couple of his sketches and was reaching for a third to demonstrate the point of his monologue, tiredness had overtaken Eva and she had slid sideways onto the ground.

As the afternoon drew on, and Gar talked about painting after painting and sketch after sketch, Astreya listened with part of his attention still on Lindey as she silently fed the fire and prepared their meal. Eventually, the shadows slanted across the little clearing and Astreya saw her take up her pot of stew, and then she dug a second lidded pot that was acting as an oven from under the red coals. When the lid clinked open, the smell of fresh bannock joined the aroma of stew.

"Time to eat," Lindey called.

Gar was still talking as he and Astreya walked towards the fire that was now bright in the shadows at the close of sunset.

"Be grateful for the times when you are ignored," Gar was saying as they took their places. "I've left two villages in the past year where the good people were convinced I was a witch, and they were anxious to do their souls good by dismembering my mangy carcass. The second time, they would have succeeded if Lindey hadn't appeared just in time, and cracked a couple of heads with her staff. Of course, because she's a woman, they were convinced we were in league with the powers of darkness, and they went back to their houses, in search of firebrands, pitchforks and spiritual uplift. While they were seeking supernatural aid, we got Nora, the queen of all horses, hitched up to the shafts and we stole away by moonlight."

The horse, hearing her name, whinnied softly and then went back to champing at the grass.

"They thought you were a witch?" asked Eva incredulously. "Witches are..." she stopped, glancing back and forth between Gar and Lindey.

"They recognized their faces in a few sketches I had done, so they decided I must have stolen something from them. Since they hadn't felt anything being cut away, they decided I must have relieved them of their souls." Gar chuckled. "It didn't do any good for me to tell them that I wouldn't know a soul if it came up to me and bit me in the rump. The more I said, the more testy they became."

"Testy!" said Lindey, looking up from the stew pot she was unloading into earthenware plates. "Irrational. Unreasonable." She pronounced the last word as the ultimate condemnation.

"Lindey has this charming belief in reason," said Gar. "She also has a disconcerting willingness to resort to violence when she thinks that reason alone will not prevail."

"Force can be a reasonable response, if used for self-protection or to avert imminent violence," said Lindey calmly.

Astreya and Eva stared at her.

"There she goes again," said Gar.

Lindey was an enigma to Astreya. Bent over the stew pot, her hair curtaining her face, there was something about her that made Astreya pause and watch her with quiet delight. In some ways, she could be taken for the kind of girl of whom the people of the Village would say, "She'll make some man a good wife." But when she spoke about the use of force, her pronouncement did not sound like a girl repeating a lesson, but more like one of the older women, or even a skipper. When she stood up, holding the heavy iron stew pot in one hand, Astreya saw that she was as strong as he. The image of her stance at the ford came to his mind: her staff at the ready, her skirts kilted above her knees, her blue-eyed gaze steady, she had been both essentially feminine and surprisingly dangerous. He warmed to Lindey's capability, just as Eva unconsciously shrank away.

"I've been trying to teach Lindey how to disappear in a crowd," said Gar. "But I haven't got very far. Smile vaguely, Lindey. Slouch."

Lindey's face moved obediently. She raised the corners of her mouth, but achieved only a travesty of a smile. The muscles responded, but the result was disturbingly false. She rounded her shoulders and let her hands hang, but only managed to look like a bad imitation of an idiot. Gar shook his head sadly. Lindey's face relaxed, a fleeting smile curling the corners of her mouth before her calm expression returned. She stood with the competent poise Astreya remembered from their first meeting, and he stared at her, suddenly conscious of the difference between her level gaze and Eva's ingratiating upward glances.

"It's no good," said Gar. "Lindey can't see the funny side."

He spoke pleasantly and Lindey accepted his words without rancor, but Astreya had seen Lindey's fleeting, subtle smile, and he was sure that she both appreciated Gar's wordplay, and also had a droll humor of her own.

"I wouldn't be so sure," said Astreya.

Lindey turned to him slowly.

"He's always sure. He's even sure of opposites. He can tell one of his customers that he is the greatest painter in the universe, and then a day later, he's crumpling up good paper and canvas and saying, 'It's no good, I can't catch it, I can't paint.'"

She mimicked Gar's voice and intonation cleverly. When both Astreya and Eva chuckled, Gar stared at her, his eyebrows raised. Lindey's usual dispassionate look softened. The corners of her mouth drew back and her teeth gleamed between lips that were usually firmly held together.

"Well, I'll be pounded flat and rolled into a pie crust," said Gar. "All this time you've hidden your talent for mimicry from me. And now you have an audience, you use it to pour scorn and derision on my innocent head. I'm doubly hurt and dismayed." He roared with laughter, stopped, fluffed his hair over his ears, and laughed again. "All this time I thought she had no sense of humor."

Lindey's smile flickered again, and Astreya silently clapped his hands.

"My trouble is that I'm never there at the right time," said Gar, as he ladled out stew. "Why, once a man wanted me to paint his cow, and I said I would, and then he told me she'd been dead for two years, but he'd tell me all about her. Sure was difficult to catch a likeness. Now, if I'd been there to see the cow.... If I'd been there to see Lindey smile... Except, this time, I was there, but I missed it."

Astreya stared at him thoughtfully. He guessed that there was bitterness to Gar's comedy, as if behind his words were other, more serious events that he regretted. Noticing his expression, Gar launched into a series of entertaining reminiscences, each more improbable than the last, each making himself the butt of the joke.

All through the meal and on into the evening, Gar entertained an entranced audience. As the light faded from the sky and firelight warmed their faces, Gar talked on. Sometimes he pulled out a painting to illustrate where he had been and what he had seen. Eventually, as eyelids started to droop and stares into the fire grew longer and longer, Gar told his last tale. Leaving the three young people sitting in that indolent state that comes when it is too much effort to get up and go to bed, he went to the wagon and pulled out hay-filled pallets which by day protected his belongings from the jolting of the wagon, and at night could be used as mattresses. Soon all four were lying under blankets around the fire.

"Astreya," said Lindey in the darkness. "Thank you for helping me show Gar that I do find some things funny."

Astreya was taken by surprise and could think of no answer. He turned on one elbow and looked at Lindey across the dying fire. Her light hair gleamed softly in the flickering light.

"My mother has a saying: 'You had it in you all along, it only needed a little help to find the way to let it out.'"

Gar's white fringe of hair appeared out of the shadows as he sat up to contribute to the exchange.

"That's what the first girl I ever bedded told me—except she didn't put it quite so nicely."

His chuckle mingled with a crackle in the fire. Astreya heard a little snort from Eva that he took to be of disapproval, but when he looked in her direction, she had turned her back and was tightly curled up under her blanket.

Chapter 12:

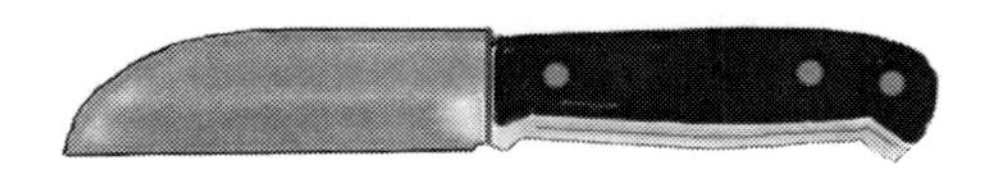

In Which They Are Ambushed, and Astreya Is Falsely Accused

The next day they walked the road southwards, Astreya, Gar and Lindey at the horse's head. Eva, whose shoes were still too wet to wear, drove the wagon. As the morning went on, Astreya found himself talking more freely to Gar. Lindey dropped a few paces behind them, a floppy cloth cap covering her hair and shadowing her face. If he had been asked, Astreya would have said that he knew Lindey could hear everything he said, but at the time, her silent presence just over his shoulder neither encouraged nor inhibited him, even when he tried to explain his relationship to Eva.

"She, um, wants to be a Healer. Always has, she says."

"But you're to be the Teenmouth Scholar, you said yesterday."

"Yes, but it's not like that. I didn't steal it from her. Nobody wanted her to go, except maybe her mother. She's the one who patched me up when I was..."

"Go on."

"When Yan hit me in the head and left me behind and the *Mollie* sailed without me."

He stopped talking, and for many paces, there was only the clop of hooves and the rumble of the cart. Then, slowly, with many long pauses, and often out of order, Astreya told Gar about the journey south. The previous day, he had set out some of the facts, this time he let himself talk about his surprise and delight at being chosen by Roaring Jack, about the excitement of the journey south and the adventure of the storm. Astreya was aware that Gar, and Lindey behind them, were listening intently to his attempt to evoke a series of pictures in their minds: the skipper bent over the tiller, a glimpse of stars through wind-driven clouds, the spreading trees at Teenmouth, the moment when he chose the passage through the breakers. When he finally reached the point when the *Mollie* had abandoned him, his words trailed off and he walked in silence. Gar had let Astreya talk, but when distress halted the story, Gar searched for a way to restart the flow.

"You never knew your father, then?" he asked.

Astreya nodded. He nearly complained about how his mother had always wanted to keep him safe ashore, but as he thought of her, he understood a little better how much she feared lest he be lost at sea like his father before him, and he wished that his realization had come when he could have shared it with her.

"All I know about him is some writing in a little book, a knife..." Astreya remembered Scarm's warning in time to avoid mentioning the bracelet.

"He left you his name," said Gar.

"Yes. The name of the Stranger. And muddy green eyes and a head of black curly hair that's not like anyone I ever met."

"Well, it's better than having white hair, you know," said Gar lightly.

Astreya grinned, and suddenly the future seemed more important than the past.

"I'd like to think I'm walking down this road because I chose to do it myself," he said.

Gar glanced at him before replying. "Because I'm such a clever person, I guess that this particular red earth track we're on is not really all that you mean. And I won't insult you by asking a silly question such as whether anyone really chooses anything, because I know you don't need a whole pile of logic-chopping words. You want to feel that you're the one who's making up your life's story as you go along, and, what's more, that you're the hero of it."

"Something like that," said Astreya.

"Good," said Gar firmly. "Stay with the feeling. It's the wanting that counts."

Astreya looked at Gar, who strode down the road with a slight roll to his walk, as if he challenged it to bring him anything with which he could not deal. He glanced over his shoulder to see Lindey at the horse's head, her easy stride conveying much the same confidence. She smiled at him, and the rhythm of Astreya's walk subtly changed.

He was briefly aware of Eva behind the three of them, the reins in one hand, the other tugging at her braids, looking as if she were frustrated that she could not overhear what they said, or perhaps angry at all three of them for excluding her.

Putting Eva and her moods aside, Astreya concentrated on the landscape through which they were traveling. The road now ran almost due south through mixed forest increasingly marked by human activity. Astreya saw stumps among the undergrowth, and from working with Jeb's horse Sally, he knew that the gouges in the earth were from logs skidded down to the road. Occasionally, lesser tracks and trails joined them. Gradually, the green center strip of grass faded into earth that had been packed hard by the passing of many wheels and horses' hooves. Tree branches no longer met overhead, and the sun beat down so strongly that he wished for clouds. Astreya undid a couple of buttons on his shirt, and was about to roll up his sleeves until he remembered his bracelet. Biting flies pestered all of them; Nora jingled her harness and swished her tail. When they stopped under a big tree for their midday meal, they all were hot and what wind there was only raised dust in their faces. Walking was tiring, but at least it drew them nearer their goal, so they did not slacken their pace during the afternoon.

As the shadows began to lengthen, the road bent westward almost imperceptibly, but enough that it was not possible to see far ahead. Every few miles, there were spaces among mature trees where aspens and scrubby bushes had invaded long abandoned fields. As they reached the end of just such a break in the forest, where the sunbaked road was particularly dusty, the road curved towards a little bridge. Something that was not wind stirred the bushes near the stream. Gar's stride slowed and he glanced back to Lindey and Eva.

"Well, let's all lie down in the shade of those big trees up ahead, and play chuckle belly, folks. This old man could do with a little rest."

It was clear from his tone that he did not mean what he said. Eva's head jerked up, and Lindey changed her grip on her staff. Beside Astreya, Gar tucked in the right side of his loose shirt, revealing a knife in a sheath on his belt. A moment later, four young men emerged from the ditch just ahead of the bridge, knives in their hands.

Astreya saw them run towards him, their loose brown shirts flapping around their bodies, dust kicking up behind them, sun glinting on their knives. In the same instant as he was imprinting the scene on his memory it seemed to him that the men slowed as they neared him, the first coming at him with a knife held blade uppermost. Astreya sidestepped the lunge that would have opened his stomach, and kicked into the back of his attacker's knees. While the man was still staggering, Astreya shoved him into his companion's way, and both collapsed in a tangle, scrabbling in the dust for the knives they dropped as they fell.

"Finish them off, Astreya," Gar shouted as he scrambled to his feet.

Astreya kneed one man in the ribs, keeling him over into the ditch. Gar lurched forward, and stamped on the other's knife wrist.

"Two at the cart," he grunted. "They got by me."

Astreya took one stride, kicked the fallen knife out of the road and ran towards Lindey. She was leaning calmly on her staff, its other end deep in the midriff of a man who was pleading for mercy.

"I've got this one," said Lindey. "Help Eva."

Astreya ran on to where Nora the horse was rearing and kicking at a man trying to drag Eva from the cart.

"Eva! Under the seat!" yelled Gar, still bent over the downed man.

"'Streya! Help me!" Eva screamed as she snatched up Gar's club.

She swung the weapon and her attacker staggered away from the cart, his hands across his face. With an incoherent shout, he turned and ran down the road that they had just traveled. Another ran after him, drops of blood falling into the dust from his left arm.

"You'll live," Gar called after him, and wiped his knife on his thigh.

Astreya grabbed the horse's bridle to stop her kicking the front out of the cart, but she bucked, lifting him off his feet. While in the air, he glimpsed a movement to his left, let go and dropped into a crouch. The last man had emerged from the ditch where he had found his knife, and he was charging a second time, the blade held waist high. As the man lunged Astreya dodged, seized his wrist and pushed down, and the man's own forward motion sent him face forward into the dust. The knife flew through the air, glinting in the sunlight. As the man tried to get up, Gar grabbed him by the back of his breeks, jerked him to his feet and then propelled him, still off balance, past the cart where Eva was still waving the club.

"Keep going, son," said Gar.

Astreya heard wheezing, painful breathing, turned and looked down. Lindey's staff held her man prone, his legs doubled up. Both of his hands were unsuccessfully trying to relieve its pressure on a point just below his breastbone. Gar bent down and held his knife so close to the man's eyes that he squinted.

"See, son? A girl flattened you, and now an old man is wondering whether to slit your ears, your nose or your throat." He paused, as if to make up his mind. "Now, tell me, before I reorganize your face, would you prefer to run away, like your friends?"

The man nodded his dust-caked head, still unable to get enough air to speak.

"Right then, Lindey, let him up." She stepped back, her staff held crosswise, ready to strike. The man looked from one face to the other, panicked, and ran after his companions.

Lindey grounded one end of her staff and leaned on it. Her face was flushed as she picked up her cap, which had fallen off in the fight, but her expression was calm as she tucked tendrils of blonde hair back out of her face.

"What happened to you, Gar?" she asked.

"I got an elbow in the gut," he answered. "Took my breath away. I caught a glimpse of you two as I went down. Saw your staff take out one knife very nicely, Lindey. Saw Eva batting at her black-eyed attacker. Missed your part of the action entirely, Astreya. Both times."

"So did I," said Lindey slowly, "and I was watching. I've never seen anybody move so fast."

"Fast?" Astreya asked. "I was just lucky to have the slow one to deal with. And then, stupidly, I didn't get rid of his knife properly."

Lindey shook her head in disbelief.

"You were so quick, 'Streya," said Eva, still standing in the cart. Gar stared thoughtfully at Astreya as he sheathed his knife and readjusted his shirt to cover it.

"You all were amazing," he said. "Now about that rest I was mentioning... I think we have some cider in the cart, don't we, Lindey? And Nora could do with a drink, as well."

They stayed in the shade by the stream to rest and refresh themselves for more than an hour. All four had been more shaken by the attack than they would admit, and they needed time to wind down from the excitement. Eva talked compulsively, describing how she had fought off her attacker, embellishing her story with a lively account of her own fears and hopes at the time. Lindey handed out mugs of cider, her gaze resting longer on Astreya than was necessary. Gar thoughtfully examined the inside of his mug.

"You have a knife, don't you? Couldn't you find it in time?"

"I didn't think of it," said Astreya slowly. "In the Village, knives are for fish, not people."

While they were fighting off their attackers, Astreya had been completely calm. He had felt invulnerable, moving as if he were stepping through a complicated but predictable dance. But now that it was all over, delayed shock washed over him as he recognized that the consequences could have been fatal. He sat quietly, very much aware that the Gar he had just seen threaten to cut a man's throat was not the jovial itinerant painter of animals and people he had seemed until that moment. The thought preoccupied him as they went on their way again. This time, Gar held the reins, Eva sat beside him and Astreya and Lindey walked silently ahead, glancing warily from side to side as they passed through the last of the forest.

Lindey watched Astreya closely as she scanned the road ahead. She could see that he was thinking uncomfortable thoughts, and she guessed that they concerned the fight. She had been impressed by Astreya's speed and agility, which was that of an experienced fighter. But when he had not pressed home his advantage, she knew that the black-haired, green-eyed man walking beside her was no ruthless killer, even if he had the skill and capacity to be one. This contradiction fascinated the logical side of her mind. She speculated about Astreya, wondering why he was so unlike anyone she had ever met, even as she deliberately ignored the unexpected excitement she was feeling at being near to him.

As he walked at her side, Astreya noticed that he had caught Lindey's attention. He guessed that she was curious about him, but her thoughtful glances were not like anything he had ever experienced. In the Village, women and girls had scrutinized him, but only as a stranger and person apart from them. Eva's attention had moved so swiftly from amazement to unexpected and confusing intimacy, to the flattering need to be protected that he felt a responsibility for her, even though a voice inside him said, *Too much, too soon*. In contrast, Lindey's interest was cool, un-possessive, almost distant. Lacking the context of family and shared upbringing that were always present in the Village, he could only guess at what might explain her unusual character. He was surprised and impressed with the skill with which she had bested one of their attackers, and he liked her independence. Moreover, he enjoyed walking in step with her in ways that were new to him.

There came a moment when their glances met. Astreya looked into her eyes, and saw her mouth open just enough for him to glimpse the tips of her teeth. Lindey felt his grey-green eyes look into hers, and she saw more than the sharp features and black hair that marked him as extraordinary. She smiled at him, and in doing so, she lowered a carefully crafted mask of objectivity and reason.

They both looked away, surprised by the intensity of the moment. Behind them on the cart, Eva saw their swift interaction and clenched her teeth. Then he saw her compose her face into its most pleasing shape and favor him with a brilliant smile.

For Astreya, it was as if the day had started afresh. All his tiredness forgotten, he became more aware of his surroundings, in particular, Lindey walking at his side. At each gentle rise, he observed that the land was more tended, with fences in better states of repair with each field they passed. The hay was higher in the fields than it would be so early in the year at the Village, and there were yellow and red wildflowers in the fields that he would not have expected for a month. He was still thinking about how much more fertile this soft country was than the rocky land around the Village, when the road rounded the edge of a small hill and he caught his first glimpse of the Castle.

Astreya was immediately disappointed. He had been looking forward to seeing a wondrous building befitting a place of study and learning. He had imagined a school even more marvelous than he had read about in books. Instead, he saw a collection of big, heavy, crudely built brick buildings standing randomly in a large field. A spider's web of paths connected them all to the central building made of quarried stone, standing twice the height of all the others, with a domed roof unlike anything Astreya had ever seen. His eyes followed the broadest path back to a massively ugly gatehouse set into a red brick wall, which was topped by jagged shards of flint that flashed in the sunlight.

Beyond the enclosed space to the west and south, low wooded hills rolled towards the horizon. A stream flowing from them caught the light where it widened into pools. The water became invisible behind trees, and then reappeared within the Castle wall, where a few old and twisted trees marked its winding course among the buildings.

On the near side of the wall was an untidy town, so unimpressive that he had overlooked the confused huddle of dusty houses and sheds, their tilted slate roofs and leaning walls supporting each other like drunken men shambling home arm in arm. Houses and hovels, barns and sheds clustered with no apparent plan, under a haze of smoke from many chimneys, not one of them straight. Astreya scanned his companions' faces, guessing at their different moods. They stood looking down on their destination, thinking their own thoughts.

"Not a place where you'd expect to find highly-tuned artistic sensibilities," remarked Gar. "I'll be pounded flat if there's a man there who ever made anything for the simple joy of it."

Astreya glanced at Eva, and saw from her bright, expectant expression that she saw none of the ugliness. Her eyes shone at being near the place on which her hopes had been fixed for so long that he guessed that she would have made her home in a dungeon. He almost envied her reaction. When he had heard of the Castle, he had imagined soaring towers, frowning battlements and cloistered courtyards where the Learneds exchanged wise words. What he saw were uninspiring buildings scattered in a huge field, with a clumsy brick wall separating one side of the random collection from a slatternly town. Astreya felt as depressed as Eva was excited. He glanced at Lindey, but if she had any thoughts or misgivings, she shared none of them. She clucked her tongue at the horse, and they all moved forward.

The road bent first one way and then the other as the little town at the bottom of the hill closed in around them. Sheds, outhouses, homes, inns and shops clustered together, served by a warren of narrow streets and alleys running in every direction, so that when Astreya looked back, he could no longer see the low hills through which they had walked. Above the clutter of slanting roofs, he caught occasional glimpses of the domed building, and when they passed some of the blind alleys to their right, he could see the Castle's wall rising more than twice a man's height.

They turned a corner, and found themselves in an overcrowded square fed by many roads and streets. It was market day, and carts, riders, cattle, pigs and dogs contested noisily for a share of what little space was left by men, women and children carrying every kind of burden. The street smelled of excited people, frightened animals, dung, cooking fires, dust, and, as they passed each of many taverns, beer. When people and animals halted Gar's cart, Astreya stood and looked around. Immediately, a woman with a baby on her hip jostled him, then when he backed away, he was bumped his other side by a man dangling a pair of squawking chickens from each hand.

"So many people," Astreya muttered.

He had never seen so many strange faces, each absorbed in his or her own concerns. He stepped aside from a butcher in a bloodstained apron carrying a tray of sausages. A huge horse with a farmer astride its broad back clopped through the crowd, threatening everyone's feet. A man with a barrow-load of potatoes would have hacked Astreya's shins if he had not moved back quickly onto a doorstep, his shoulders against the door. Temporarily out of danger, he caught his breath, overcame his momentary panic, and stood fascinated by all he saw. Here were two housewives with waist high children clinging to their skirts, carrying baskets of bread, vegetables and a live trussed chicken. There was a man carrying a piglet upside down and squealing over his back. A farmer with two large, panting dogs at his heels directed three young men who struggled under the weight of bulging sacks. A tinker clattered by pushing a wheelbarrow, his pots and pans clanging like cracked bells. Beneath an overhanging window on the other side of the street, a dark-haired man, cloaked to the ankles despite the heat, drew trinkets out of concealed pockets for an audience of young men and girls, occasionally selling a ribbon, a paper of pins or a broach. Several women, some of them young, and some trying to appear so, stood by the doors of taverns, where the crowd was thickest. They wore bright dresses and tight, scoop necked blouses, many of them with their waists nipped in and their busts thrust out by broad, brightly woven belts. Some people were already tipsy, while others waded thirstily through the crowd in search of their first ale of the day to wash away the dust of travel and bargaining.

Astreya stood on the edge of this flood of people, studying faces intent on buying, selling, exchanging and seizing their own pleasure. Nobody noticed him, and even those who jostled him treated him only as an obstacle. A little smile raised the corners of Astreya's mouth, as he became aware that here in this kaleidoscope of humanity, for once he was unremarkable.

He became entranced by the variety in the faces of the people around him. Unlike the people of the Village, whose faces were all similar in shape, the people around him were of all shapes and sizes. Some of the men had faces that were snub-nosed and scant of hair, even though they were of an age with the skippers at the Village. Here a young man had an oval face and a curved nose above a mouth thin-lipped as a knife gash, there was another who had a head wider than it was tall with dark hair that curled down across his forehead. There were two young girls whose faces were circles centered on snub noses, bracketed by tight chestnut ringlets. Their smocked blouses and full skirts covered equally rounded bodies. They shook their heads primly as they first assessed and then ignored the slatternly clothes of the women at the tavern doors. When one of the girls saw that Astreya was looking at them, they whispered together, and deliberately turned their backs, shaking their curly brown hair so that it rippled over their shoulders.

A pair of tall, lean men with skin even darker than Astreya's strode through the crowd, something in their manner causing people to move out of their way with sidelong glances. Each had a long, serviceable knife belted on top of his well-worn leather jacket. As they passed Gar's cart, Astreya's arm tingled under his bracelet. One of the men checked his stride, turned and glanced towards Astreya, who shrank back into the doorway. When his companion spoke, he shrugged and they both walked on.

In the doorway of the house across the road stood a man round as an egg. Double and treble chins ran down to his greasy shirt, and his feet were splayed apart at the end of legs thick as tree trunks. On the other side of the narrow street, an aged woman scowled at Astreya. Her nose was only a finger's width from her chin, and her toothless cheeks were hollow. He could have drawn her to illustrate a fairy tale. She glowered at him with a wrinkled malevolence, made a quick gesture with a handful of knotted fingers, and then spat. A thickset man in a knee length blue coat bore down towards Astreya, making no attempt to swerve. Astreya glimpsed a white shirt above tight-fitting trousers before the man pushed him aside, shoving him back into the doorway where his head knocked painfully against the wood.

"Watch your wretched self," said the man over his shoulder as he urged his horse through the crowd.

The door opened inwards behind him. He turned to look down into a pair of squinting, mud brown eyes. Straggling grey hair framed a woman's scowling face.

"I'm sorry, but I was..." Astreya began.

The woman raised both her fists and pounded him in the chest. "Get your arse out of my doorway, Blackhead."

Astreya winced, more from the name than from the blow. He stepped into the press of people once more, trying to see Gar's cart. Eva's wave caught his eye, and he made his way through the press back to stand with Lindey beside Nora's head. The horse was as uncomfortable as Astreya.

"All right, Nora," said Lindey softly into the horse's ear. "We'll be out of here very soon, so just stay calm until we can move again."

Nora bobbed her head as if agreeing. Astreya also nodded assent to what seemed like good advice, even though delivered a bit late. When he looked past the horse's big head, he saw Lindey looking at him. He shrugged.

"Avoid looking them in the eye," she said. "They don't want to know you."

Astreya thought back to the Village, where nobody passed another person without some acknowledgement in the form a word or at least a nod. He looked around again, avoiding eyes, but continuing to observe the people around him.

Making their way through the crowd were groups of young men in threes and fours, all wearing dark green cloaks like the one that had been presented to Astreya, which now lay rolled up in the back of the wagon. He guessed that they must be the Castle's scholars. They all had a certain air about them that was as distinctive as their cloaks, which they had turned back over their shoulders in the heat of the day. They elbowed their way arrogantly through the crowds, making sure that everyone noticed their apartness from the clamor of commerce. A tall scholar whose brown hair curled to the shoulders of his gown called out to Gar as he came near the wagon.

"Hey there, uncle! Yes, you on the painted cart. You have two girls with you, but only one boy. Which one warms your bed, uncle?"

"Or do they all?" asked one of his companions, a heavyset young man whose dark hair fell so far across his eyes that his nose and even his mouth were only intermittently visible. His black cap and broad shoulders might have confused him with the farmers, were it not for the disdain with which he pushed people out of the way to get a better look at Gar's wagon.

"Do you paint them in their clothes, or out of them?" asked a third, whose hair stood out from his head like a wiry, carrot-colored bush.

Astreya bristled at the questions, but before he could attempt a reply, Gar turned the innuendo aside with a smile. Imperturbably ignoring the blushes on both Astreya's and Eva's cheeks, he beckoned the three scholars closer. Lindey's face was expressionless, but Astreya noticed she had shortened her grip on her staff, subtly changing it from walking stick to weapon.

"Lead us to a quiet tavern," said Gar. "Show me where to stable my horse without being robbed, and I'll answer all your questions over a mug—perhaps a jug."

The tallest of the three smiled with an unexpected grace that took the sting out of his earlier jibes and made him look like the curly headed boy he must have been when he was a few years younger.

"Follow us, uncle. We'll look after you. All of you."

Astreya and Eva wondered why Gar should have thrown in with the loudest and most aggressive threesome they had seen. As the scholars pushed to the head of the painted wagon and started to clear a way ahead of them, Gar clucked at the horse and they followed the swaying green gowns into a narrow, twisting and grimy alley. The press of people thinned, and they soon arrived at an inn only two or three houses from the Castle wall. A faded sign depicting a jug and a bottle swung above a low door that stood invitingly ajar. Gar negotiated with the burly, red-faced hostler who lounged by the steps that led down into the taproom, and handed Lindey the reins. Astreya glanced a question at Lindey, wondering whether he should go with her. She raised one shoulder to him, pinched her nose in a quick gesture that anticipated what she might find in the stables and waved him towards the inn. Deciding that she was probably more capable than he for the task, Astreya joined Eva, Gar and the three scholars as all but Eva ducked their heads under the low lintel before disappearing into the dim interior of the inn.

Eva lagged back, shrank against Astreya and seized his hand. He guessed that she had been brought up to believe that no decent woman would enter a tavern. Astreya was apprehensive, because he knew taverns only from stories he had read in Scarm's books, and his knowledge was both fragmentary and confused. Although he was as inexperienced as she, Astreya was more curious than apprehensive. When his eyes adjusted to the lamp lit gloom, the taproom of the Jug and Bottle was reassuringly quiet and orderly, reminding Astreya of a snug cottage at the Village—only considerably larger, and with a far richer assortment of smells. People sat at heavy tables on equally heavy benches, hunched over beer and food. Conversation was as muted as the light that filtered through bottle green windows or gleamed from lamps hung below smoke-blackened rafters.

At the head of an empty table nearest the back wall was a chair with arms. Gar moved smoothly into the comfortable seat, just before the tall, curly-headed scholar took possession of the authority it represented. Astreya found a place at the table with

Eva beside him, where he could look across at the leader of the three scholars. He had a full mouth, brown eyes, well-kept curly brown hair that had marked him from first sight, and a small mustache of which he was evidently proud, because his fingers strayed to his lip as he spoke, as if reassuring himself that it was still there.

"I'm Damon," he said. "And these are Sandy and Enoch—Nock, to his friends—and his enemies, too. Who are you?

A small man appeared at Gar's shoulder before he could answer. He leered at Eva out of one brown eye, and Astreya saw that the other was pearly white. The good eye winked and he twisted his face into a professional smile when Gar chinked money and ordered beer. As the taverner headed off to fill the order, Astreya saw him nod at a large man with a lumpy face and huge hands who stood by the door. The big enforcer of the inn's peace subsided into a chair, his services not necessary as long as the guests' money held out. Gar caught Astreya's eye and nodded approval of his observation, and began introductions.

"These two are here to become learned. I've learned enough already. I'm a painter, as you may have guessed."

Astreya noticed that Gar concealed that only one of them would become a scholar.

"New to the Castle, eh?" asked Nock, staring at Eva from under a thatch of ginger-red hair. "What's your interest?"

"I want to be a Healer," said Eva.

"You're in luck," said Damon, also looking her up and down with unabashed frankness. "There's room for a few more women, so I hear. What about you, 'Streya?"

Astreya felt the need to assert himself. "Astreya," he corrected.

"Astreya," Damon mimicked accurately. He laughed. "You'll be wanting to become a philosopher, with your attention to names."

"I haven't decided yet," said Astreya, raising his voice to be heard over the sound of incoming guests behind him.

Fingers dug painfully into the top of his shoulder, and a voice spoke above his head.

"Then decide now, while you have chance to be schooled by an expert."

Astreya twisted, stood and turned in the same movement, shaking off the hand that had grabbed him. He was in a space among the tables, facing three young men with scholars' cloaks turned back over their shoulders. The foremost was tall, broad shouldered, and powerful. Astreya looked into a face that might have been handsome, had it its lips not been set in a taunting smile. He stepped forward, and when Astreya did not retreat, snatched the knife from Astreya's belt and threw it into a corner. Slowly and deliberately, he drew his own long knife from a sheath on his belt.

"Where are you from, new boy?"

The other two started to close in on their victim. Time slowed for Astreya. A part of his mind decided that he had been abandoned, this time by Gar, Lindey and Eva. Whatever they were doing, he had to solve his problem on his own.

At the leader's peremptory gesture, his companions grabbed Astreya from both sides. These were not Village fishermen's sons but accomplished tavern brawlers. They caught at clothes first, and then shifted their grasp to Astreya's arms and neck. Recognizing that struggling was futile, he stood still and waited for an opportunity. The leader crouched, brought up his knife and sliced air in front of Astreya's face.

Astreya knew nothing of knife fighting, but he refused to be mesmerized by the blade glittering in front of his face. He stared back through the arcing steel. The taunting continued, interspersed with pulling and shaking by the two who held him.

Something behind Astreya fell with a crash, followed by a series of thuds. When the grip on his right wrist relaxed momentarily, Astreya kicked into his captor's armpit, and when the man let go with an oath, threw himself shoulder first towards the floor, breaking the grip on his other arm in time to lessen his fall. He rolled and twisted, but before he could get to his feet, he glanced up just in time to see the hand with the knife above him. He kicked up at the man's wrist, his boot connected, and the knife jangled to the stone floor at his feet. Astreya snatched it up as its owner was suddenly shoved aside by the tavern's enforcer, along with two more men of the same size and determination.

Astreya stood his ground, knife in hand. Half the lamps had gone out and the others swung crazily above tables and benches overturned by the other drinkers when they hastily made room for the fighters. His original assailants were nowhere to be seen in the gloomy taproom, but out of the corner of his eye, he saw a side door open and close. Before he could take any further notice, a short club swung expertly, and Astreya was empty-handed, numb from forearm to fingertips. Two enforcers closed in, each as strong as all three of the young scholars Astreya had just faced. He was grabbed and frog marched out of the tavern by hands as hard as the heel of a boot.

Astreya's nightmare continued outside. One arm twisted behind his back, he was pushed along the alley, towards the thoroughfare, into the marketplace that they had skirted on their way into the town. Soon he was in the thick of townspeople, travelers, farmers and scholars, through which his burly captors forced a way. Some of the onlookers shouted obscenities as his captors marched him past. With casually efficient brutality, they shoved him towards a wooden platform at the center of the square. Every step he took, his captor wrenched his arm higher; every time he stumbled, the other kicked him in the muscles of his calves.

A few staggering steps up a flight of wooden stairs, and Astreya stood on a platform, shoulder height above the crowd. A man with a bulbous nose sat in a massive wooden throne-like chair. A sweat-stained broad-brimmed hat was pushed back on his head, revealing his receding hairline, from which runnels of sweat ran down to his collar. Around his neck was a silver chain that descended to a gold medallion the size of a small plate, which rested on the straining buttons of a red shirt stretched over a stomach thickened by middle age and indulgence. Astreya was given another push that brought him to his knees; close enough to smell the man's sour sweat. He looked up into pale blue eyes narrowed to wrinkled slits against the sunlight.

"Caught 'im knife fighting, yer eminence," said the largest of Astreya's captors, and produced the knife. "Took this 'ere off 'im."

He handed the long knife to the man in the chair, who tested its edge with a cautious thumb. He sucked in his cheeks, blew them out again, and lowered his gaze to Astreya.

"Your name?" he demanded.

Astreya looked from one face to another. He was alone, surrounded by people in whose eyes was only curiosity about what would happen next. He was as helpless as an animal about to be slaughtered.

"Astreya," he replied, hearing hopelessness in his own voice.

"Well, whatever you said your name was, these men have you dead to rights. You're a scholar? Where's your cloak?"

Astreya shook his head.

"Of course you are. You deny it?"

"Not yet sir. I'm supposed to become a scholar. That's why I was sent here."

"Another reluctant student." The man pursed his lips together. "And since not yet a scholar, entirely under my jurisdiction. You are the worst kind, you enforced learners. You terrorize my town, waste the time of the Learneds who try to instruct you, and fail to return to your miserable little hamlets, even if you do finish your studies. I can think of no reason why you should not become an example to others, since you are clearly no use for anything else. Do you know the penalty for fighting with a weapon such as this?"

Astreya shook his head, and tried to explain that the knife was not his. As soon as he made a sound, one of his captors pushed him down until his face was almost on the fat man's dusty boots.

"The punishment, my young friend, is not pleasant at all. First, I will have you beaten, and then I shall have you locked up until it pleases me to have you run out of town by whichever of these fine, if somewhat boisterous people wish to pursue you. Meantime, that is, until next market day, you will be doing constructive work to make good the expense to which you have put us. The beating can take place now."

The man licked his lips and settled his hands on the central mound of his stomach below the medallion. Astreya felt leather straps curl and tighten around first one and then the other wrist. Then two men who grasped Astreya's arms each went down on one knee, pulling his arms apart and holding him doubled over. His fingers started to throb as the leather straps cut off the flow of blood to his hands. The third man slit the back of his shirt from hem to neck and tugged the two sections apart, exposing his back and shoulders. Astreya bit his lip. Whatever happened, he would not cry out. He held his breath and closed his eyes.

Instead of a blow, a confused shouting came from behind him, which resolved itself into Gar's voice, echoed by at least three others.

"Your eminence," shouted Gar from the edge of the platform. "Your estimable justice is misguided... by circumstances that are no fault of yours or your watchmen."

"Who are these importunate people?" demanded the man, rising from his chair. "I know none of them to be my townspeople."

"Get on with the whippin'!" came a horse shout.

Another voice behind him added to Astreya's confusion.

"I'm one o' your townsman, yer eminence. I saw the whole thing. This young lad was set upon, defended himself bare-handed, and disarmed the man who attacked him. 'E was standing, innocent, threatening nobody, when the Watch arrived."

"Is that Robert the Taverner? You're making long speeches, Bob, and I can't hear you properly. Come up here where I can see you."

He waved to delay the whipping, and the two men holding Astreya relaxed somewhat. He no longer felt that his arms were being pulled out of their sockets, but the straps on his wrists still held him from twisting away. He turned his head and saw the wall-eyed innkeeper climbing the steps onto the platform. The fat mayor settled back in his chair and raised a finger to deflect the sweat trickling through his thin eyebrows into his eyes. When Astreya looked under his left arm, he saw the heads of Gar, Damon, Sandy and Nock looking over the edge of the platform.

"Tell it to me again, Robert. Do you allege that this young ruffian is innocent?"

"Aye, and the one that jumped 'im goes free. See 'im for yourself at the edge of the crowd."

Everyone within earshot turned in time to see the scholar who had held the knife on Astreya turn his back and hurry down an alley, his green cloak flaring behind him.

Gar's voice was loud, confident and yet also deferential.

"You see, sir, I mean your eminence, the guilty are escaping at this moment. But you have the weapon, and that speaks for itself."

"What is this nonsense? A knife can't speak."

"If it please you, your eminence," said Gar as he clambered onto the platform without bothering to use the steps. "You know, of course, that the knife given you by the Watch is so large that it can only be carried in a hand, or in a sheath. Now, would you be so merciful as to ask your Watchmen if they took anything from the young lad that's big enough to hold this—this small sword?"

"Well?"

The two men holding Astreya shook their heads. Repetitions, questions and discussions rippled through the crowd.

"A nice point, whoever you are, I am amused by your ingenious defense. Clearly, the knife does not belong to our black-haired friend here, and Robert the Taverner's story rings true. Release the prisoner."

Gar shepherded Astreya off the platform in a daze, amazed that he had been freed. As Gar guided him down the steps into the crowd, the mayor stood up and launched into a speech in a loud, carrying voice. He commended the Watch, the innkeeper, Astreya, Gar, and everyone who stood around; and then launched into a diatribe against all knife fighters, particularly the one who had been chased from the marketplace. The crowd responded by cheering and clapping at appropriate moments, their ugly mood turned inside out. Hands reached out to pat Astreya's shoulders or to shake his hand as Gar elbowed through the crowd. Astreya barely had the presence of mind to clasp his torn shirt to his chest to conceal his money pouch.

Gar pushed Astreya towards Damon, Sandy and Nock, who formed a wedge around the two of them and thrust a way back to the Jug and Bottle, which was now filled with curious and thirsty folk. Gar picked a fresh table, this one in a corner where they could avoid attention. His fringed head gleamed under the light of a hanging lamp as he again claimed the armchair, this time with no competition. Damon, Nock and Sandy took the outside bench while Astreya leaned gratefully against the wall at his back. They were no sooner sitting than Lindey and Eva appeared through a side door. Eva carried one of Gar's less painty shirts. Lindey held her staff in one hand and his father's knife in the other.

At that moment, jugs of ale thumped onto the table, and all three young men began talking at once. As drinks were poured, Astreya ruefully stripped off his yellow shirt, now in two pieces. In the dimly lit tavern, he could see the stone in his bracelet glowing through gaps in the string. Seeing that Gar and Lindey had also noticed, Astreya pulled on the fresh shirt as quickly as he could, grateful that his left arm was away from Damon, Sandy and Nock. Both Gar and Lindey sensed his concern and looked away, Lindey in silence, Gar by drawing attention to himself.

"Astreya, you are probably wondering why we didn't help you when those peculiarly unpleasant people grabbed you. Well, we were being forcibly restrained by some of their friends who I don't think you saw, either then or later. We didn't see them any too well ourselves, because Damon, Nock, Sandy and I were being held by the hair, which in my case is as painful as it is difficult to locate." He ruffled his white fringe as he spoke.

Eva whispered, "It was horrible," in Astreya's ear. Sandy demonstrated on Nock, who objected, exactly how he had been held. Damon explained in detail exactly what he would have done had he been able. Gar silenced them all by pounding his tankard on the table, and when he had their attention again, refilling it from an earthenware pitcher.

"We might all still be watching Astreya get ventilated if it weren't for the subject of my toast. I give you our rescuer, Lindey!"

He raised his mug and tossed back a healthy swig. Other mugs waved in the air and were drunk with enthusiasm. Lindey nodded her head in appreciation and gave a little shrug as if to say she had really done very little.

"You probably were a bit too involved in what you were doing, Astreya, but if you heard a couple of thuds, it was Lindey's staff cracking heads."

Astreya stared, wondering why there were no corpses on the floor. That must have been the sound that gave him a momentary advantage. The struggle came back to him, and his heart pounded as if he faced the waving knife a second time. It was not fear, but an onrush of reaction to his time-bending readiness during the fight. Now that action was out of the question, his body shuddered, and he panted in quick, shallow breaths. Seeing his eyes lose focus, and his head droop, Lindey put her hand on his arm.

"Breathe deeply, Astreya," she murmured. "Know that you did well."

Astreya took the breath she commanded, and felt his pulse slow and steady.

"That was quick," Lindey murmured, as Astreya once more took an active interest in what was going on.

"After that," said Gar, "Our friends Damon, Sandy, and Enoch acquitted themselves handsomely. Of five who came, only Carl, the one with the knife, was able to leave on his own. Foolishly, he then went to the marketplace, and had to take to his toes."

"You should have seen Gar," said Eva eagerly. "He had a mug of beer in one man's face and his elbow in the ribs of another before he was even standing up."

"Experience born of a misspent youth," said Gar, fluffing his hair over his ears. "I begin to understand how Enoch's name got shortened to Nock. You have a skillful way with your fists!"

Nock grinned, showing a gap between his front teeth that could well have been the result of learning his craft.

"Where did you learn to fight?" Damon asked Astreya.

"I wrestled at the Village... where I come from," said Astreya.

Damon fingered his mustache, looking at Astreya thoughtfully.

"Why didn't you follow through?" he asked. "You had Carl, and you stood there with the knife held all wrong. I couldn't believe you were the same person who had taken it away from him so fast nobody saw you do it. And he's good with a blade, or he wouldn't have the following he does. How did you break their holds? And how did you get to the knife without getting cut to shreds?"

Astreya shrugged. He had never tried to explain his reticence about attacking anyone; indeed, he did not know the answer himself. Damon leaned towards him, his brown eyes earnest.

"Listen, Astreya, you show me that trick, and I'll teach you how to hold a knife as if you meant to do more than slice a loaf of bread."

"You could do a lot worse, Astreya," said Gar softly.

Astreya's protest that he had no secret was forestalled by the arrival of a fresh jug of ale, supplied by Robert the Taverner as his tribute to the young man who had outmaneuvered Carl, the celebrated knife fighter. The innkeeper presented the drinks with a flourish, making sure his generosity was noticed by all those crowded into his taproom.

"It was good of the innkeeper to speak on my behalf," said Astreya.

Damon snorted.

"It had good results," he said. "But don't give Bob the Swab any marks for virtue. Gar paid him a handful of money, and I told him that I'd get the Learneds to bar his tavern if he didn't support you. And now this place is filled with thirsty people come to take a look at you, Astreya. And that's more than it or he deserves. Fear and greed were the source of his performance in the square, not a love of justice."

Astreya's eyes widened.

"Oh dear, an innocent," said Gar at his astonishment. "You have a lot of disappointment ahead of you."

"I'm not disappointed in anyone around this table," said Astreya firmly.

"It will happen, nonetheless," said Gar. "Disappointment, that is. With which warning in mind, I've got news that will take some sorting out. Damon, here, is an expert on the rules by which the Castle functions..."

"Break enough of them, and you get to learn them," Damon interjected.

"... and he tells me that it is possible to get a position as a scholar if you're a woman, but there's only one person taken from each community."

Eva's face rose and fell.

"Astreya, you've got the purse and paper that says you're the one they chose..." she began.

Astreya cut her off. "Eva, you go. It's what you've always wanted."

Gar's face blended wry amusement with a judicial stare.

"I'm impressed with your generous natures, both of you, but I haven't explained that there really isn't a choice to be made. Eva's the one, and that's that. It seems that the Castle expects all its new scholars to be beyond reproach, whatever they might do later. Nobody can be a scholar if he's ever been publicly accused of a crime. That's right, isn't it, Damon?"

Damon nodded, and spread his hands expressively.

"It's ridiculous, of course," he said. "It might be understandable, if not particularly fair, if it said convicted of a crime, but the rule says 'publicly accused' and there aren't many more public places than the town square on market day. Carl knew that, Astreya. He wasn't interested in carving you up, although he would have done so cheerfully. He only had to get you accused, and he would enjoy his idea of fun. He's done it to several would-be scholars."

"Why doesn't someone stop him?" Lindey asked.

"Because as a scholar, he's immune to any discipline except from the Learneds. Somehow, he always manages to get away with it because of some technicality or another, and he even gets praised for his knowledge of the weasel words in the rules that let him off."

"That is neither logical nor just," said Lindey firmly.

Damon, Sandy and Nock stared at her. Astreya and Gar exchanged glances, amused by the trio trying to reconcile what they had seen and heard with their preconceptions about women. Astreya was briefly aware that Eva was oblivious to everyone in her delight that she would get her fondest wish.

"Where are the bodies, Lindey?" asked Gar. "Carl's following never made it to the marketplace."

"Resting peacefully in the stable midden, unless they've woken up and walked away," said Lindey evenly.

"Well done. Very tidy," said Gar.

The three scholars continued to stare incredulously at Lindey, who drank her ale with the air of one who knew she deserved it. Astreya fell silent. Once again, decisions were being made for him. He was about to sink into gloomy contemplation when he saw Gar and Lindey, sitting side by side, smiling at him as if sharing a secret. Gar's smile was not the public display he flashed on those he wished to impress, but a gentler version that drew lines around his mouth and tilted his eyebrows. Beside him, Lindey's mouth became generous and her blue eyes caught the lamplight. Astreya warmed to them both. They had saved him, fought for him, spent money for him, and he had not even thanked them. Poised between an uncertain past and no future he could discern, Astreya suddenly felt favored by life. He smiled back, took a swig of beer, and grinned around the table. Here, he was certain, there was no treachery.

"Astreya, how can you be so happy?" asked Eva. "You're not going to the Castle."

Astreya took another mouthful of beer, conscious that they were all waiting to hear what he would say.

"I didn't choose to become a scholar. It was wished on me, whether I wanted it or not. Now, whether I want it or not, it's been taken away. I'm back where I started, except that the next choice will be mine."

"But Astreya, you can read, you're suited to study."

"Eva, did you say he can read?" asked Damon.

Eva nodded, and when Damon looked at Astreya, he nodded as well.

"That's incredible," said Damon. "None of the poor scholars can read. That's why the Castle only trains them to do something more or less useful, before sending them back to their villages."

"You can read, then?" asked Eva, bridling at being called a poor scholar.

"Quite a bit," said Damon airily. "But then, I'm not a poor scholar. Besides, most of what we do in philosophy is through discussion. The ancient tradition, you know."

Astreya did not know, but instead of asking the question Damon wanted to answer, he asked one of his own.

"Does the Castle have many books?"

"Thousands and th - thousands," said Sandy, around a hiccough. "Most of them are in the Great Hall."

"That's what you're supposed to fancy up, isn't it?" Damon asked Gar.

"Say 'paint,'" said Gar with dignity. "I'm not the man who whitewashes the walls or carves little knobs on the rafter ends."

"Paint, then," said Damon, sketching a deferential gesture that almost sent Sandy's ale into his lap. "But anyway, you'll see the books when you go in. I bet some of them haven't been touched in a lifetime."

"I would've thought that books would be at the center of a Learned's life," said Lindey.

"Most o' them don' bother much wi' books," said Nock, his voice slurred. "They teach what they've learned. 'Course, now and then, one of them writes something, but..."

"My Learned's writing a book," said Sandy, whose words flowed from beneath his dangling hair as quickly as Nock's had been slow. "He's talked about it many times. It's something to do with filling in the gap left when a book was destroyed by accident about seventy years ago. He's been studying the books on either side of it, and he's working out what the missing one must've been about."

"I'd like to see if some of the books say anything about *Before...*" began Astreya, and then stopped as he discovered he had to shape his words with care.

Gar interrupted him by clearing his throat after a prodigious swig of ale.

"Astreya, I have a proposition to put to you. And I make it in front of witnesses, all of whom I conjure with strong oaths to absolute secrecy. You may not be able to enter the Castle as a scholar, but how would you like to go there as a painter's assistant? The Learneds promised me food and lodging for two helpers, and their offer still stands to be taken up by me tomorrow morning. I think they expected me to show up with a party of eight or ten, you see, so they stipulated two, not knowing that at the time, there was only Lindey and me. Are you following me? What do you say, Astreya? Will you join up with us?"

"Do you suppose I could fool them into thinking me a painter's helper?" asked Astreya.

"Fool them?" echoed Gar, with a snort. "You could fool me. You're a painter, my lad. Not that there aren't a few things I can show you, mind you."

"You'd teach me?"

"You'll learn," replied Gar.

"Then I accept!"

Astreya half rose in his seat as he reached for Gar's hand and shook it warmly. Most of Damon's ale poured into his lap, and the rest flowed across the table so there was only a moment's touch between Astreya's and Lindey's fingers as everyone grabbed their beer and tried to remain dry.

"I hope you won't be this clumsy around the paint pots," said Damon as he wrung out his sleeve and waved at the Taverner for more ale.

"You don't drive much of a bargain," said Gar. "I can see that there are a lot of other things I have to teach you. Now tell me, Astreya. What are you going to make out of this deal?"

"I'll have what I can learn from you, and my board and lodging from the Castle," said Astreya. "Won't I?"

"Of course you will."

"But you'll be associating with a villainous, black-haired, curly bearded, green-eyed..."

"Supernaturally powerful warlock," Gar completed. "So, until people forget about today's little scene in the marketplace, you'll wear a hat over your black hair and shave off that beard."

"All right. I mean, if you insist. Especially because you saved me this afternoon. Perhaps there's some way I can pay you back for the money you spent today on me. I'd give it to you now, but I don't have any. I mean, I have this money they gave me at Teenmouth, but Eva's going to need it for—oh, whatever she needs it for."

"Fees. Food. Lodging in the Castle," said Damon.

"I thought you said poor scholars..."

"She is—or will be—a poor scholar. Unless Teenmouth stumped up the kind of money my stepfather spent to get me out of his house."

Astreya looked at Damon for a moment, sensing a story behind his words. Then, somewhat cloudily, he returned to his first thought.

"Here, Eva. You take the money."

He reached into his shirt and ducked his head under the leather strap that held the moneybag. Her eyes wide, Eva took it from his outstretched hand.

Gar rolled his eyes upward and spoke pleadingly to himself.

"What can you do with innocence like that?"

"Take care of it, teach it, let it be," said Lindey. "Most of which you're doing."

Gar looked at her sharply. "You're not supposed to hear me when I talk to myself, young lady. Much less understand the wise words of the ancient man with whom you are journeying."

Lindey allowed one eyebrow to rise, keeping her face otherwise expressionless. Gar's chin fell.

"I'll be pounded flat. In more than a year we've been together, you've never done that before."

"You haven't been watching," said Lindey.

Gar let himself slip down in his chair so that his head came to the level of his mug. He shrugged elaborately.

"I am pounded flat," he said to her, and then straightened up. "But not for long. Food! Drink! Merriment!"

Gar ordered. Bread, cheese and cold meats came and were soon consumed. Eating steadied them, and conversation began again. Astreya looked around the table, freezing each face in his memory. He watched Gar and Damon competing to tell the most improbable story, encouraging each other to greater and greater liberties with the truth, Nock and Sandy laughing and applauding vigorously. Eva sat in an oblivious cocoon of satisfaction. Nock's gap-toothed grin, Sandy's explosion of red hair, Damon's index finger caressing his mustache, Gar's leathery brown face with its fringe of white hair, Eva's half-smile—all of these he memorized so that he could draw them later.

When Astreya looked at Lindey, her face was subtly animated, as if words ran through her mind too quickly to be spoken. He wondered at first if it was a trick of the light, or his own wandering attention; then he saw her glance at Gar as he concluded a story, and affection, concern, exasperation and amusement moved across her face like gentle wind across water. Astreya was sure he had understood the expressive sequence, and was also certain that there was no way he could ever draw what he had seen. Each minute change in Lindey's face had been clear and meaningful, and yet she remained enigmatically silent.

"If you get inside—when you get in—I'll find you and we'll arrange a time when you can show me how you ducked out of that hold," said Damon to Astreya, and then turned away to speak to Eva.

Astreya was suddenly conscious that it had been some time since he had been attending to what people were saying. Eva was leaning towards Damon, listening, but there were too many other conversations going on for him hear what they were saying. Then Damon stood up, and announced that the three scholars were about to return to the Castle over the wall, since the gates were long shut. Gar was on the other side of the room, bargaining earnestly with the innkeeper. He wove his way among empty chairs and tables back to their alcove.

"If you young people care to spend the night under a tap room table, you may, but I'm older and much too wise to repeat that dispiriting experience."

After wishing Damon, Sandy and Nock a good night, Gar led three young people to the rooms he had engaged. Astreya found that he had to take unusual precautions against bumping into the furniture as they made their way across the taproom. Eva, who had sipped cautiously all night, looked only tired. Lindey appeared unaffected, despite having matched the men mug for mug. Gar took the lead with a stub of a candle in his hand, and they climbed a narrow staircase that led to a narrower passage in which Gar's flickering light was almost useless to Astreya, who brought up the rear. Gar indicated the door of one tiny room for the two young women and fumbled with the handle of the door next to it. Eva lingered for a moment after Lindey and Gar had both gone through their respective doors.

"Thank you so much," said Eva. "I hope you're not too disappointed at not being a scholar."

Astreya searched for words to help Eva understand his satisfaction with the way things had worked out. In the long pause, Eva felt for Astreya in the darkness, pulled his face down and kissed him on the forehead, clearly enjoying being generous to the underprivileged. Before he could react or even wonder, she was gone, leaving him to find his way into his room by feel. Inside, the nub of the candle flickered on the floor between two pallets, on one of which Gar was already snoring.

Astreya shook his head. The day had held too much to be ordered into any coherent pattern of meaning, especially after all the ale he had consumed. He sat down and unlaced his boots slowly, thinking that some new part of his life was opening up before him, one in which he might be able to take hold of his own destiny. With one boot half off; he decided that he had to relieve himself before sleeping. The candle stub dripping wax on his hand and his bootlaces flapping, he fumbled out the door, along the passageway, down the stair and outside to the outhouse. On his way back from the evil-smelling jakes, he met another figure, candle shielded, making its way towards him across the tavern yard. As they were about to pass, Astreya saw it was Lindey. She was grumbling to herself under her breath about the grubby tavern, the distance to the smelly outhouse, and the guttering candle in her hand. Her unusual wordiness was Astreya's first clue that she, too, had drunk more ale than she had planned.

"G'night, Lindey," he said. "Thanks for all you've done."

"You deserve better than this, Astreya," she answered. "And so do I."

Astreya continued back to his room, wondering at her remark. Companionship and ale had made him optimistic, and there seemed so much for him to anticipate, that it was strange that she should be offering him something akin to sympathy—so entirely unlike Eva's patronizing. Puzzled, he pulled off his boots and sank onto the pallet. He rolled over and saw a faint light from his bracelet gleaming through the white fabric of his shirt. Turning back his sleeve and separating the woven string, he studied the green stone curiously, wondering why he was not made uncomfortable by its strange behavior. As he watched, the stone gradually dimmed until he asked himself whether it ever had been so bright.

He scratched vigorously, suddenly aware that Gar and he were not alone in their beds. Before he could either wish for better or regret what he had left behind, sleep claimed him.

Chapter 13:

In which Astreya arrives at the Castle

Early the next morning, Astreya woke to hear Gar stropping his razor-sharp pallet knife on his belt.

"Say goodbye to that beard, Astreya. You'll grow a better one when you're a bit older."

Astreya opened his mouth to protest, and then recalled their agreement.

"Don't worry, I won't cut your throat. I'd let you shave yourself, but we're in a hurry."

A short time later, they joined Lindey and Eva, who were waiting with the horse and cart. They set off for the Castle, Gar and Eva in the cart, Astreya and Lindey on either side of Nora's head. Gar wore a cleaner, but no less paint-daubed shirt, while Eva had hauled her smocked blouse up to a compromise position between provocative and modest. She had braided her hair on top of her head like her mother, hoping to suggest a maturity that her eager face contradicted. Lindey wore a pale blue skirt that fell to just above her boots, and a blouse the color of a brown egg. She had reshaped the soft cap she had worn on the road, wearing it so that most of her hair was concealed. The effect was as neutral as Eva's was attention-getting. Astreya had pulled on the same clothes as he had worn the previous day, but it was his face that attracted the two women's eyes.

"Astreya, you look... you look like your younger brother," said Eva.

"I don't have a... Oh. You mean I look childish."

"You look fine," said Lindey. "Although I liked the beard."

"Now put this on, and nobody will recognize you," said Gar, handing him a floppy brimmed leather hat. "It's amazing what a good disguise it is to take off a beard. Much more effective than growing one."

"And quicker," said Astreya.

As they were walking from the tavern towards the Castle gate, Gar suddenly stopped, pinched at his shirt and rolled his fingers together. Astreya tried the same maneuver the next time a flea bit him but without success. To ignore the occasional fresh bite, he concentrated on the people in the street. Ahead of them, a farmer was shouting at a peddler whose horse was trying to steal from a cartload of cabbages and carrots. A dog barked at a pair of chickens that had escaped through an open gate, and Nora shied away from two elderly men carrying scythes over their shoulders, the gleaming blades providing them with plenty of room from perhaps a dozen young men behind them, fussing with scholars' cloaks that they had never worn before that day.

Eva slid down from the seat on the wagon. "I... um..."

"You'd better go in alone," said Gar. "It will do you no good to be associated with riffraff like us.

"I'll see you soon, 'Streya, won't I?" she asked, her words encouraging, but her smile forced.

"Good luck, Eva," said Lindey.

"Yes. Me too. Of course," said Astreya, feeling inadequate.

Eva smiled vaguely at all of them without looking into anyone's eyes. Astreya noticed a slight twitch to Gar's lips and Lindey's raised eyebrow, and was both amused and a little sorry at how quickly Eva turned away from them and towards her new life.

Seeing her trim figure, one of the young men nudged his companion, and in moments, they were all staring at her, whispering. She was carefully looking anywhere but towards her admirers as they pushed past Gar's cart and surged around her.

The students crowded into the entrance to the gatehouse, some of them glancing over their shoulders at Eva. As they reached its shadow, they all stepped back onto each other's feet as the heavy oaken doors ground open towards them, pushed by two elderly men bent over with the effort. The green-gowned scholars milled through the doorway, into the dark tunnel in the middle of the ugly building, and out into the bright sun on the other side.

"We're next," said Gar.

Lindey clucked her tongue, and Nora clopped obediently forward through the echoing tunnel. The dome of the main building lay ahead of them, framed by the black shadows of the gatehouse, like a picture.

"Well, they got the composition right," said Gar. "Must have been an accident."

As they walked into the sunlight, the picture book illusion vanished. They stopped on a broad, packed earth path, their way blocked by the new scholars. Seated at a table beside the path was a man with a thin beard that straggled to the middle of his chest. He glanced up briefly, frowned, waved the three of them on past the students, and pointed to where they should wait. Nora took the necessary few paces, lowered her head and cropped at the turf, giving the three of them a chance to look about them.

Two middle-aged men stood in the shade of an awning that had been set up beside the path, their clean-shaven faces registering aloof boredom. Green cloaks with gold trim at the collars fell from their shoulders, folded back to reveal clothes so sober and dark as to turn their owners into silhouettes. Three or four strides from them stood a stocky woman holding a tally stick in one hand and a small knife in the other. She enjoyed none of the shade from the awning that protected the men. Her green and gold cloak was like those of the men in design, but where theirs set off their clothes, hers was all-enveloping and severe, turning her into a short, plump green post surmounted by a face soft as a dumpling, gleaming with perspiration.

Astreya looked around, wondering what had become of Eva. She had waited until Astreya, Gar and Lindey had been admitted, and then advanced towards the table, her scholar's parchment in one hand, moneybag in the other, and her green cloak over her arm. The bearded man glanced up at her and jerked his thumb. Thinking he meant her to approach the two Learneds, Eva stepped forward and stood respectfully. When the men ignored her, she stepped forward again with a little cough. They turned to look at her as though noticing a dog.

"Tally woman, one of yours," said the taller of the two, and with a contemptuous wave dismissed Eva towards the woman.

"Bold little wench should mind her place," Astreya heard him say before bending his head again to his colleague, and continuing their conversation.

As she walked over to the woman, Astreya saw Eva's shoulders rise and fall. He hoped that the cause was controlled deep breathing, not tears. The woman clucked instructions at her, and Eva put on the cloak Astreya had been given at Teenmouth. With a sniff, the woman tugged it closed across Eva's chest and buttoned it at the neck. The cloak reached the ground; however, it was clear that to the woman who led her away, wearing the cloak was more important than whether it became dirty. Before they went between two of the blocky buildings and were lost to sight, Eva turned and waved. The woman plucked at her sleeve, admonishing her severely.

Astreya looked after Eva as she trailed out of view. There had been no time that morning to do more than give her the cloak and the parchment, with his name cunningly replaced by hers, thanks to Gar. Now he wished he had taken time to say he did not quite know what.

Gar cleared his throat meaningfully, and Astreya saw that while he had been standing in the dusty path, staring after Eva, the straggly bearded man had been giving instructions, which Gar was repeating to him.

"We'll leave Nora under the tree over there with her nosebag to keep her happy. Apparently she shouldn't be here at all, but when I suggested that I could whip up our noble steed and charge the people coming through the gate, the weedy fellow at the table over there relented. Come on."

While Nora chewed contentedly under her tree, Astreya and Lindey followed Gar past large barn-like buildings with few windows. They were on a well worn path past broad-branched trees, where the grass thinned to brown earth. Soon they reached the largest of the halls that they had glimpsed through the gatehouse. It was not so awkwardly proportioned as the buildings, but its effect was more imposing than beautiful. The walls were constructed of quarried stone, massive at the bottom courses, and then reducing to grey chunks set with no consistent pattern as they rose to more than three times a tall man's height. Astreya noticed as they approached that the building had no corners or angles; because it was so large, the walls curved almost imperceptibly. Curiously shaped windows, pointed at both top and bottom, were set into the stonework at regular intervals, their curved wooden frames holding clear glass set in leaded panes. On top of the walls, what had looked like a domed roof from a distance proved to be a bulging, multifaceted pyramid made of heavy radiating black beams, none of them perfectly straight. At the top was a crown-like cupola sheathed in greening copper. The triangular spaces between the beams were sectioned by horizontal cross members, creating irregular cells, which were filled with off-white mortar. A squat, square entrance jutted out towards them, as if patched on as an afterthought by people who had forgotten to plan a way in and out.

"Whoever built that wanted to impress," said Gar. "What he achieved is impressively hideous."

He paused, shook his head, and then walked on. Lindey strode imperturbably beside Astreya, carrying a light satchel containing some of Gar's paintings, the only item he had wanted them to bring. Since it did not seem likely that they would be allowed to drive Nora and the cart to the hall, Astreya's resentment of the Learneds, kindled when they had been so short with Eva, grew more intense and personal as he reckoned the many trips back and forth it would take before all the equipment would be ready to begin work.

They passed groups of scholars on the pathways among the buildings. The young men sweltered under their green cloaks, but none of them had turned them back over their shoulders as Damon, Sandy and Nock had done the day before, or as had the Learneds at the gate. Astreya was relieved that the scholars' traditions did not extend to him.

A group of four Learneds walked towards them on the path, so intent on their discussions that the green-clad men almost ran into Gar. Two were bent with age, but the two younger men were walking with the same stoop-shouldered, plodding gait.

"Every one of them has his eyes on the ground and his head bowed," said Astreya, after they had passed on their argumentative way.

Gar turned, smiled and slowed to walk between Astreya and Lindey.

"Why did you notice?"

"My people... the people at the Village... are sailors," said Astreya. "They have to know what the wind and sky are doing, and they're always looking up."

As he spoke, he felt a sharp desire to be home, among people who lived as close neighbors to wind, sky, sea and mountains, where nobody wondered about the meaning of everything around them. His own shoulders stooped, and he dropped his eyes to the ground.

"It must be catching," said Gar. "You're plowing the path with your nose, like those foolish cloak wearers."

Gar's cheerful lack of respect for the solemnity around them brought Astreya back to himself. Squaring his shoulders, he looked around. Lindey returned his glance, her eyes steady and direct as ever, and he smiled at her. Two fingers on the hand that held her staff waved at him quickly, and her lips curled slightly in swift wordless movements that Astreya read as approval and encouragement as clearly as if she had spoken at length. The shadow of his loneliness passed into memory, and his mood brightened to match the early summer morning.

A gathering of Learneds waited for Gar at the entrance to the hall. Six men encircled him and then escorted him towards the heavy doors, showering him with conflicting opinions. The green-clad men were so busy interrupting each other as they told Gar what to do that they clogged the doorway, making it difficult for any of them to enter. When Astreya and Lindey tried to follow, a short, squat little man impatiently waved them away. They waited in the sunshine, listening to voices that paused, restarted, paused again and then spoke less between longer gaps in which they heard Gar's voice, although they could not distinguish words. Lindey grinned at Astreya.

"Gar's getting to them," she said. "This is fun. Let's get a bit closer."

She cautiously pushed the doors wide enough for them to squeeze inside. When their eyes adjusted to the gloom of the windowless entrance, they saw another pair of black, wooden doors, only a couple of strides away. Lindey cautiously pressed down the latch and pulled them ajar so that they could both hear and catch a glimpse of what was going on. They saw that the building seemed larger than it appeared from outside, and also much brighter than Astreya had expected. When he looked up, he saw why: a nearly perfect spherical ceiling, smoothly covered in white plaster, reflected light from the pointed windows they had seen from outside, as did the plastered walls between the windows. Shafts of sunlight lanced down through fine dust into the lower part of the hall, falling on rows and rows of head high shelves laden with old, leather covered books. The bookcases fingered out from the walls like the spokes of a wheel, each containing more books than Astreya could estimate.

They looked down a central passage between the bookcases to the open space in the center of the hall, where the green-gowned Learneds clustered around Gar. Lindey had wanted Astreya to hear Gar negotiating, but now he was close enough to hear, she saw that instead he was fascinated by the spaces available to paint. His head back so far that his neck ached, Astreya looked up at the center of the dome, where there was a cunningly jointed circle of black wood, wider than twice what a man could span with both arms. He wondered what Gar might decide to paint there, and how it could be done.

Gradually, Astreya began to notice the exchange that was going on below the dome. The green-gowned men had no objection to repeating themselves, which seemed strange to Astreya, who was used to the economical speech of sailors. As he listened, he noticed that each Learned had a favorite expression, which he used constantly. As they spoke, the wall of green-gowned backs gapped and reclosed, giving Astreya and Lindey glimpses of Gar as he listened to a succession of harangues. One, a small, fussy man with nervous fingers, spoke repeatedly of "conceptual purity." Another, whose more substantial build bulged his green gown at waist level, held forth about "intellectually sophisticated discourse for the cadre of elite thinkers." The moment either paused for breath, he was instantly opposed by a younger man who, unlike the others, sported a patchy beard. This one insisted on the importance of "intuitive assimilation of the thematic material." No sooner had he begun to elaborate than a short, stout man, whose gown flapped as if a wind instead of a man were under it, vigorously argued against all of them, waving his hands as he held forth on the "intellectually perceived formal reality commensurate with the geometric challenges of the structure." Astreya frowned with concentration, trying to wring meaning out of the many words that tumbled from the Learneds' mouths and echoed softly in the dome above. He had almost decided that he was simply too stupid to understand, when Lindey caught his eye, shrugged and glanced upwards as if to say, "Who cares?" Astreya grinned back at her gratefully, and began to listen to the exchanges as an obscure game that he had no intention of joining.

A Learned, who so far had been silent, abruptly took charge of the debate. He was a tall man with a lined face that was clearly visible to Astreya and Lindey above the green-gowned shoulders of shorter men. Astreya memorized him: deep etched frown lines fanned up from the bridge of his bony nose, turning his eyes to slits, while another set of furrows carved onto the lower half of his face bracketed a downturned, lipless mouth. He took two measured steps forward, his expression conveying impatience and disgust. When he spoke, he accompanied his remarks with glances that momentarily widened his hooded eyes in a sudden stare. The trick was like an accusation, at which his opponents fell silent, unable to interrupt him as they had their other colleagues. His words flowed smoothly, evenly, constantly, and, to Astreya's mind, unintelligibly. When he had finished, each arguer unconsciously stepped back, and the group no longer pressed in on Gar. The supercilious Learned raised his head to stare down his thin nose at Gar, who alone had not moved.

Astreya, who had long since stopped trying to follow the man's words, looked a question at Lindey. She raised one finger from her staff, and her lips soundlessly told him, "Just wait."

"I've given you the essence of your task," intoned the Learned, his words clear for the first time. "Now you can..."

He got no further. Gar stepped towards him so quickly that their faces were less than a hand span apart. He spoke with aggressive cheerfulness.

"You can't do it, can you?"

The Learned stepped back, despite himself. "What do you mean?"

"You can talk up a storm, but you can't do, can't make, can't realize, can't create. That's why you've hired me. Now, in order for me get on with it, I need several things. Not ideas, not concepts, not advice—things. Also money. And the quicker you give them to me, the quicker I can get started."

Gar's directness worked so well that Astreya almost laughed out loud. The Learned shrank within his green gown as if he were a bladder of air that had suddenly sprung a leak. His mouth opening and closing like a freshly landed fish, he shuffled backwards at precisely the same moment as the other Learneds, who were clearly delighted at his discomfiture, moved forward towards Gar again. This time, Gar did not let himself be surrounded. He led the way out of the center of the hall, the Learneds muttering among themselves. Lindey glanced at Astreya, nodded, and the two of them ducked between the first two rows of bookshelves.

Gar strode confidently along the central passage with his characteristic chin up, slightly rolling walk. The Learneds followed him more hesitantly until they saw that he was leaving the hall. Then they all hurried forward, milled around the inner doors, pressed through and recreated the confusion in the darkness between the two sets of doors.

As Learneds hurried towards the confusion at the door, Astreya and Lindey took a step backwards between two rows of bookshelves, looked at each other and chuckled. Then Astreya stretched out a hand to examine a leather bound book whose ornate cover had caught his eye. Lindey's hand stayed his arm.

"I think you're about to do something that's forbidden," she whispered, nodding her head towards the last Learned, a narrow-faced man who had seen them as he hurried towards the doors, his green cloak ballooning behind him.

"Keep your hands away!" ordered the man, aghast. "Who are you and what are you doing here?"

"We're Gar the painter's assistants," said Lindey.

"Silence, girl," said the Learned, ignoring her to glare at Astreya. His head poked forward like a pecking bird. "Who are you?" he asked again, his forehead notched with a frown above eyes set too close together.

"As my friend said..." began Astreya.

"Her place is to keep silence. Indeed, she has no place here."

"What she said was true," said Astreya.

"I advise you, young man, to explain to me instantly what you are doing here, and why you are not properly cloaked."

"We are Gar the painter's assistants," said Astreya, echoing Lindey. "We are not scholars."

"You, perhaps. But she is a woman."

"Lindey is Gar's trusted assistant who prepares colors for the paints he will use on your building. She has special skills that..."

"Oh. Yes. Colors. Woman's work."

The bird-like face frowned and his green cloak swirled as the man shrugged and rejoined the group around Gar.

"Women are not considered fit to speak here," Lindey said in her matter-of-fact tone. "He wouldn't even hear me. Most unreasonable behavior for those who claim to be learned."

Astreya looked at Lindey in amazement. They waited until the green gowns had flapped past, and then emerged from between the bookcases into the main aisle, and headed for the door, where they found Gar, who had stepped into a dark corner of the entrance to let the Learneds precede him into the sunlight.

"There you are," he growled. "Let me tell you that these Learneds have a lot of learning to do. They hadn't expected that I would need to set up staging, and would require more paint, and money to live on in advance of the final payment."

Astreya misgave, wondering whether Gar's next words would be that they had to leave the Castle. Gar guessed his thoughts and grinned broadly. The scowl that moments earlier he had worn for the Learneds turned into a look of confidence and cunning as he confided in his two young assistants.

"Don't worry," he whispered, in contrast to his earlier, fully voiced comments. "Another thing they haven't learned is how to bargain. They'll come running after me. Watch."

It was as Gar predicted. He led Astreya and Lindey out the doors, still grumbling loudly. He pushed through the cluster of green-gowned men who were asking each other where he had gone, and walked purposefully down the sunlit path under the big trees, Astreya and Lindey a few paces behind him. They heard the Learneds' voices pause for a moment, and then begin to blame each other. They had not gone more than a dozen strides before they heard quick steps behind them. The middle aged, tubby, gown-flapping Learned trotted past, upset and out of breath. His gown encumbered his arms and impeded his legs, and his shoulder length hair was stuck to his forehead and neck, but he hurried on, soon getting several strides ahead of Astreya and Lindey. Gar was approaching the gate when the little Learned, his dignity in shreds, caught up with him and plucked at Gar's sleeve.

Gar allowed himself to be drawn into the shade of a tree, where he and the Learned talked for some time, while Astreya and Lindey watched the remaining members of the group slowly catch up, still in agitated, hand-waving debate. Eventually, Gar and the fat little man returned to the sunlit path, along which came his peers, sweating copiously and casting accusing looks at each other. They regrouped in front of Gar, who stood firm and unyielding. His demands, punctuated with a stabbing finger, produced incredulous noises and shaking heads. The little Learned backed away, flashing nervous short-lived smiles until he was beside the tallest, whose sleeve he pulled until he was able to mutter something up to his ear. The tall man drew his gown about him and raised his chin. As if this was a signal, the whole group withdrew a few strides and huddled together, leaving Gar standing, hands on hips, contemplating the hall with unshakeable equanimity. After a short but obviously anxious period of consultation, the Learneds straggled back towards him. Brief discussion followed, concluded by much hand shaking, after which, Gar broke away to rejoin his companions.

"At last, a modicum of sense," he said softly. "Can you believe it? They wanted us to work only at night, behind draperies. How they expected us to see what we're doing, they didn't know. But they're starting to learn, even though they are a bit slow. Now, you two unload the stuff. There's a good deal of negotiation still to do, but you can be bringing equipment into the hall. I haven't got them to pay for the staging and our lodgings yet, but I will. And another thing: leave the wagon where it is. They won't let us move it closer, so you'll have to hump the stuff by hand. Have fun."

He returned to the group, taking the arm of the plump Learned who had run after him. They all started in the direction of one of the smaller halls.

"There's beer in there, for sure," said Lindey. "I don't know how he does it, but Gar can find drink and someone else to pay for it faster than a needle slips through cloth. Come on, we have a lot of fetching and carrying to do."

Several times during the many trips in the hot sun, Astreya wondered whether Gar had forgotten them. Lindey remained cheerful, sharing the loads evenly. The noon hour pause for food and drink came and went, and still the pile inside the hall grew as the wagon emptied. At last, Astreya and Lindey sat on the tailgate of the empty wagon beside the Castle gate, dangling their tired feet and wondering when Gar would return. Nora whuffled in her nose bag and tapped a hoof on the cobblestones, looking sideways at the people leaving.

"I hope I never see another sack of pigment or one more pot of turpentine," said Astreya.

His words were purely for effect, and he knew it. He was lazily watching the dapple of light through the leaves of big maple that overhung the Castle wall and wondering whether it was possible to catch its subtle colors with the help of the paints he had been carrying.

"You don't mean that," Lindey replied. "You can hardly wait to start painting."

Astreya looked up, surprised. In a world wherein it seemed he was constantly misunderstood, his thoughts seemed to be transparent to Lindey, and, to a degree, hers to him. Her lips curled in her subtle smile, and her head tipped very slightly to one side. Astreya raised his eyebrows encouragingly.

"I was wondering how Eva's getting on," she said. "It'll be hard for the Castle to live up to hopes as high as hers. And it's not as if they're receptive towards women."

Astreya nodded and swung his legs, thinking that while Eva had often embarrassed him by her earnest admiration for accomplishments that he took for granted, Lindey consistently treated him as an equal. This was the kind of relationship between the sexes with which he had grown up—and yet it was not, because she had a physical confidence that the Village reserved for men. Try as he might, Astreya could not imagine any of the girls with whom he had grown up carrying a staff, let alone using it so efficiently on the men who had attacked him.

"Who taught you to fight with a stick, Lindey?"

"My uncle," she answered. "Grandmother insisted I learn before I left Matris."

Astreya stared at her, hoping she would go on talking about herself. When she did not continue, he tried another tack.

"Where's Gar from?"

"He doesn't say. I've tried several times, but all I got was interesting stories. In the end, I was none the wiser."

There was another long pause, in which Astreya looked for a way to get Lindey talking about herself.

"What do you hope for, Lindey?" he asked.

Before she could answer, Gar appeared in the gateway, still surrounded by Learneds. His swagger was pronounced, and he wore a self-congratulatory grin. He turned and waved cheerfully at the green-cloaked figures. The little fat one responded with a half-hearted wiggle of his fingers before they disappeared into the shadows of the gatehouse. Gar headed towards the wagon, his white hair standing out stiffly over his ears.

"I've arranged us a widow's house to live in," he announced. "And the Castle is paying for it, and providing the scaffolding, and keeping the Learneds and scholars out of our hair while we work. I've put in a good day, so far."

"While we sat about and did nothing," said Lindey.

"Brain work," said Gar with dignity. "It's much more taxing and important than mere labor with the hands and body."

"Yes, but is it doing anything, making anything, realizing anything, creating anything?" asked Astreya.

Gar looked at him sharply.

"So... you heard that did you?" he asked softly. "Did you also hear what I said the other day near the ford when I told you that getting the paint on the wall was the easiest part?"

Astreya nodded.

"Do you detect a contradiction?"

Astreya nodded again.

"Brace yourself for more. The world's a contradictory place."

"Contradictory if not understood," said Lindey. "The Learneds don't understand making things because all they do is talk. What people can't do, they don't value."

"The people of Teenmouth valued the ability to read," said Astreya. "And yet none of them could."

"The people of Teenmouth have no power," said Lindey. "Therefore reading is a mystery to them. The value they place on it is the result of their envy for the power it confers."

"Profound," Gar said, and sniffed. "It must be something in the air. You two aren't supposed to be deeply thoughtful. You're supposed to fetch and carry for me and quietly admire my wondrous intellect. I'm the one who provides sage advice, wise counsel, philosophic insight and practical experience in the ways of the world."

Astreya decided he was supposed to laugh. Gar appeared serious, but his exaggerated self-importance was too ludicrous to be genuine.

"And now you laugh at me."

"Are you sure that you have a promise from the Learneds that will hold?" asked Lindey, totally unimpressed.

"You're doubtless thinking of our little disagreement with that scruffy hamlet six days northwest of here. Well, this time, I'm dealing with educated men—much easier to fool. I have paper with a detailed contract written on it. They sent for pen, paper and someone who could use them, and we all composed fine words. I'm willing to bet they don't know how much they're going to pay for."

"When does the part about the food get honored?" asked Astreya.

Gar looked at him, and then at Lindey.

"You've been having an evil effect on each other. First you question my ability, then you usurp my role as wise teacher of youth, and then you make callous requests for food and drink."

"He didn't say anything about drink. Obviously, you've already had our share," said Lindey.

"Insubordination!" shouted Gar. He turned on Astreya. "See what you've done, my lad? Turned a perfectly amenable, reasonable and biddable girl into a shrew." His voice dropped to a conspiratorial whisper. "Quick work. How did you do it?"

Astreya was still a little unsure how much of the exchange had been humorous, because he had never bantered with anyone old enough to be his uncle. Wondering whether he might have gone too far, he tested the situation with a small smile, and was rewarded with hearty thumps on the back.

"Up! Up! Into the wagon! The Widow Amy awaits!" declaimed Gar as he climbed into the driving seat and slapped the reins. Nora the horse turned her head to look at him, snuffled what might have been a sigh, and they set off out the gate and down the road.

The Widow Amy lived on the outskirts of the town. Her house was a last outpost, situated beyond the debatable area where the town street became a country road. The nearest neighbor was much more than a stone's throw away, while further down the road fenced fields were green with early summer crops. Opposite was a fallow field, bordered on its far side by the lumpy stones and bricks of the Castle wall. The Widow's house was old, but it had weathered well. It was made of the same dusty, faded red brick as some of the better buildings they had passed, but because it stood on its own patch of treed land, some distance from the huddle of houses that made up the town, it seemed almost to be a little farmhouse. A slate roof with low eaves gave it a cottage-like look that reminded Astreya of the Village. Unlike the houses in the town, whose doors opened onto the street, it sported a garden outside the front door, in which grew a confusion of plants. Herbs and vegetables intermixed with clumps of flowers that bloomed blue, yellow and pink.

A woman wearing a white apron over a blue skirt and bodice welcomed them. Her body, hands, fingers and several chins all were comfortably rounded. Nonetheless, she moved surprisingly quickly when she ushered them into her house.

"Always pick a plump landlady," whispered Gar to Astreya. "They're usually good cooks, and they're invariably more cheerful than the scrawny ones. It helps if she's a widow, too." He winked hugely at Astreya and smoothed down his circlet of white hair with both hands. Lindey was looking approvingly at the garden as she followed Nora the horse along a track past the house towards a hip-roofed barn. If she heard Gar, she gave no sign.

Not long after, Gar's wisdom was apparent to them all. The Widow Amy accepted Astreya and Lindey as if their mothers had asked her to take good care of them. When she heard that they had spent the previous night at the Jug and Bottle, nothing would content her until they all took turns in her outer kitchen where they soaked in a big barrel of hot water into which she added bunches of astringent herbs. When they had washed and changed into their declining stock of spare clothes, they found that their travel-stained garments were boiling in a huge pot at the back of her stove.

Damp-headed, scrubbed and combed into a sense of wellbeing they had not enjoyed for days, they sat down to a meal of ham roasted with raisins, fresh bread and soft churned butter, washed down with mugs of beer and followed by rhubarb pie and mint tea. Conversation was limited to sighs of approval and full mouthed requests to pass dishes and mugs. The Widow Amy plied them with second helpings, particularly Astreya, whom she had decided was far too slim. She kept an eye on Gar's mug, refilling it throughout the meal.

"That's enough, you wicked woman," said Gar at last. "You're tempting me beyond all measure."

As he spoke, he patted her ample behind. She slapped at his wrist with a pleased smile.

"Oh, but you're a forward one," she said archly. "At your age, you should know better."

"Oh, but I do," replied Gar.

She chuckled, hiding her smile behind dimpled knuckles.

It was not long after dinner and the conversation that followed that they were all ready for bed. Each told a brief version of his or her story for the Widow, who was amazed to have such well traveled people in her house. Lindey gave an economical version of her journeying with Gar. Her account of herself was the shortest of all, leaving Astreya wondering once more why it was that she was alone, so far from a home that he guessed she must have loved. Astreya tried to copy Lindey's brevity. He was not sure whether Gar's watchful glances were encouraging him to say less, or looking to learn more. Gar offered a spirited account of people he had met and places he had been, which was amusing, but not particularly informative. Later still, in the room under the eaves he shared with Gar, Astreya sat on one narrow bed and stared over the candle at the bald top of the painter's head.

"Where are you from, Gar?" he asked as he undid his boots.

The words were out of his mouth before he could consider them. Gar shrugged and grinned, but when Astreya continued to stare at him, his expression softened.

"I'm not a rapist or a murderer, and I don't cheat, lie or steal any more than is necessary to stay alive in this wicked world. As for the rest, it's all so long ago, I've forgotten."

Astreya saw that this was the only answer he was going to get. Even though his words told Astreya nothing, He was pleased that Gar had not tried to argue, cajole or persuade him, as he had done the Learneds. Gar's words refocused attention on what he had seen and heard the painter do, and it came to him that he already trusted Gar, and had done from their first meeting. Astreya was still curious, but if Gar wanted to keep his secrets, that was his business.

Astreya was about to blow out the candle, when Gar stopped him.

"Give me the light, Astreya. I have some exploring to do." He paused in the low doorway, eying the room approvingly. "I don't mind sleeping rough when I'm traveling, but when I work, I surely do love to rest my bones between sheets laundered by a cheerful widow."

As the door closed behind Gar, Astreya snuggled into bed under sheets and blankets that smelled of herbs. As far as comfort and cleanliness were concerned, Astreya could only agree.

CHAPTER 14:

IN WHICH THE MOLLIE SAILS SOUTH A SECOND TIME

After the *Mollie* returned, Alana found herself even more isolated from the rest of the Village. News traveled quickly in the small community, and it was only hours after she had spoken with Roaring Jack and Scarm that everyone knew she had denied Astreya's death with unshakeable conviction. Since everyone had lost a father, brother, husband or son to the sea, they at first understood her refusal to believe in the finality of death, and most of the women (and some of the older girls) sympathized when they came to pay their respects, bearing traditional gifts of food. However, as the days lengthened into weeks, conventional understanding waned into barely concealed impatience, and finally to avoidance. Only Roaring Jack's wife Mollie continued to visit Alana. She was a generous woman with an engaging smile, good humor seemingly unaffected by her husband's shouting, and a kindness for all needy children, animals and birds. Throughout the summer, she regularly puffed her way up the steep path to Alana's cottage. Once there, she sank into Alana's rocking chair, drank rose hip tea and told Alana about the doings of her four married daughters and their children, and all the details of Village gossip—excepting only the Villagers' increasingly frequent allusions to "the crazy lady" who had married a strange man and given birth to an even stranger son who had come to a bad end. Alana knew of the other Villagers' opinion, but she never spoke of it.

From Mollie she learned that Roaring Jack was having a season of fishing so far beyond even his luck that the other skippers would have been jealous, had they had not also been exceeding their own expectations. The Village fleet returned early from every voyage loaded to the limits of safety. The drying racks groaned under the weight of fish, and the Village's cooper could not keep up with the demand for barrels in which to store the unexpected bounty. When Mollie suggested that this was a good year for Alana to look for more opportunities to trade needlework for the fish she would need in the winter, there was no response, so as midsummer came and went, Mollie grew concerned for Alana's welfare, as well as with her persistent refusal to accept that Astreya was dead. When no amount of persuasion had any effect on Alana, Mollie recruited Scarm.

"Scarm, you get your arse up there and tell 'Lana she's got to look after hersel'. She's talkin' wild stuff 'bout sailin' south, an' I can't put no sense in her."

When Scarm reached her door, Alana was ready for him. Before the old fisherman could more than sip the mug of ale she offered him, and long before he was ready to open the conversation he had been dreading, she spoke in a voice as calm as someone observing that the weather was clearing.

"Ian, you're sailing south with Roaring Jack again, and I'm going with you."

She was interrupted by a gurgle as Scarm choked on his ale.

"You remember, I told Roaring Jack he had to go look for Astreya, and he said he had fishing to do first, and I said when the catch is in, and he nodded."

"This is going to be news to Mollie," said Scarm cautiously.

"I told her, but I don't think she was listening. She's so worried about me that she won't listen to what I'm saying. Whenever I talk, her eyes glaze over. Then she tells me what everyone's doing, and slips in a suggestion or two about how I should be doing likewise. I love her, but she's driving me a bit crazy."

Scarm twitched at the last word.

"That's what they say I am, isn't it?"

Scarm took a long pull at his mug. Alana nodded.

"So when do we sail?" she asked.

"We had good luck again, so...."

"Thanks to Yan?"

"I don't know about that. Yan is... There's something he hasn't told us."

"That Astreya's alive."

"I hope what you say is true, Alana, but what can I do, short of calling him a liar? And Jack, too, because he believes Yan. All they have to say is that I was in no shape to know what was happening at the time, which is true. But that means Yan can say anything he likes and be believed by most everyone. He's a hero, what with the big fish and the way he told his story."

"I know that, Ian. I don't know how to face him down, either. And to make him seem even more lucky, the *Mollie*'s brought home more than any of the other boats, every time."

"Full hold every trip, and deck cargo as well."

"But he's going south, isn't he?"

"Roaring Jack keeps his promises," said Scarm loyally, but his tone was dubious.

"Is Yan aboard for the voyage south?"

"I don't know, Alana," said Scarm uncomfortably. "I can't get Roaring Jack to say one way or the other, let alone when. He mutters about the catch, and turns away."

"As you said, Scarm. He believes everything Yan says."

"He's filled with guilt, Alana, and he can't think clearly."

"I gathered that, from the way Mollie won't say anything about his state of mind. She never does."

"They're private people," said Scarm. "Leastways, when they're not shoutin' at each other."

Alana nodded.

They sat in silence broken only by Scarm taking the occasional swallow of ale. Then Alana casually dropped the question she had been holding in her mind.

"Is it two or three days until the *Mollie* sails?"

"Three."

The word was out of his mouth before he could stop himself, and then there was nothing more to add. Scarm finished his ale with Alana smiling pleasantly at him in a silence that neither cared to break.

When he got up to leave, Alana held the door open.

"Good. Thank you for coming, Ian. You needn't tell the skipper that I'll be aboard. When we're at sea, I'll get him to keep on going south. You'll see."

As Scarm started down the hill, he thought he saw someone's shadow on the landward side of Alana's cottage, but when he stopped to look again, he could not make out what had caught his eye. He sighed, resigning himself to accept what he could not change without making the situation even worse. If he told the skipper about the conversation, he broke faith with Alana. If he didn't tell, he was complicit in her scheme. And if the *Mollie* did not sail south, his suspicions would neither be confirmed nor set to rest.

That night, a northeast wind blew at Alana's door and rattled the shutter on her window that looked out over the Village towards the harbor. She stepped outside and shivered. The wind had been cooled by the icebergs of summer, so she closed her door tightly and stopped up the draft under it with a length of old rope. She wedged her window almost closed, leaving a small gap to freshen the cottage, drew the curtains, and banked the fire for the night as if it were winter. The pines on the hill above her cottage whistled and sighed in a rising wind, competing with the distant roar of breakers at the harbor mouth. Something scraped across her chimney, but she did not hear it. She checked the door and windows against the wind, and smiled wistfully at the memory of working with Astreya's father to make the cottage weatherproof.

Alana heard nothing but storm sounds. Something nagged at the back of her mind when the chimney no longer hooted occasionally, but she told herself there must have been a change in the wind's direction. She did not hear Yan carefully closing the window in her bedroom, nor did she notice that the curtains no longer pulsed with the gusts. A little smoke puffed out of her fireplace as she climbed into her bed, and the wood she had added burned fitfully, but she was not aware of it. She lay against her pillows planning how she would stow away on the *Mollie*, and what she would say to Roaring Jack when they were at sea. Beside her bed, her candle flickered and went out. Her eyes closed.

Yan crouched behind a tree and shivered in almost total darkness, watching and waiting. Clouds blew in from the northwest, blotting out the sky. He had intended to stay until just before dawn, but as the first drops of rain drove into his hiding place, he changed the improvised plan he had hatched while he was eavesdropping on Scarm and Alana's conversation.

"Just give her a scare," he murmured. "Maybe make her a bit sick for a couple'a days," he rationalized as he approached the north side of the cottage. "An' then when she's sick, an' I let out that the crazy lady wanted to stow away on the trip south, the whole thing'll blow over, an' then it'll be winter, an' Jack'll not be goin' south again."

Alana's ladder, which he had found against the north wall, was still leaning against the chimney. He climbed back up into the dark until the wind blew rain into his face, and removed the slab of wood he had placed on top of the flue. Smothering a cough from the stale smoke, he climbed down. When he was back on the ground, he could no longer see even the outline of the cottage roof against the wind-driven clouds. As he was lowering the ladder, the wind nearly slammed it and him against the window that he had closed with such care. Panting with barely suppressed panic, he put the ladder flat at his feet, groped his way back to the path and down towards his home. He was in bed, listening to his mother snoring when he realized that he had left the smoke-stained slab of wood at the foot of Alana's chimney.

Next morning, Mollie climbed up the path to find out what Alana had to say about Scarm's visit. Because it was that time of the morning when women stopped for tea, she did not knock at the door. She frowned at the shuttered darkness inside, and opened the door wide to see what she was doing. So it was that when she looked into Alana's room, there was just enough light for her to see her lying with her face in her pillow.

"Wake up, darlin', I've brought you..." Mollie began cheerfully, and then stopped. A pitcher of fresh goat's milk slid from her hands and smashed on the floor.

"No!" she wailed, as she touched Alana's cold hands and face. "No... no... no!"

She was still weeping when she reached her home. Roaring Jack frowned at her as she sobbed out the worst thought of all.

"Jack, it was smoke. I could smell it. She must'a did it herself."

"No more o' that, girl," he said as firmly as he could. "'T'was grief. An' thinkin' too much." He turned away, so that she could not hear him add, "An' 'cause Oi didn't do as Oi should'a."

Soon the whole Village knew. A few people echoed Mollie's surmise, but elders who refused to even think about suicide shushed them into silence.

"Grief," they said firmly, and grief became the explanation.

That afternoon, a line of Villagers climbed the path to the cottage, where Mollie presided over the wake. They solemnly murmured their goodbyes over the open coffin, and on their way back down the hill, they reminisced about Alana's singing, her needlework, her foreign husband and her unlucky son.

Later that day, Scarm was sadly adding one more entry in the *Born and Buried Book* when he heard a soft knock. Closing the book and sliding it into a drawer took only a moment, but the memory of what he had recorded haunted him as he opened his door, candle in one hand. He nodded a silent welcome when he saw Cam's upturned face, but when he lowered his light, he frowned because he saw that there was something hidden under the jacket that hung over Cam's left arm.

"A word in private, Scarm?"

Scarm nodded, as he had done so many times before when visited by Villagers who needed to talk in confidence. He sat back down at the table, Cam opposite him, and composed himself to listen. Cam took a slab of wood from under his much mended jacket and laid it on the table between them.

"Scarm, I found this back o' Alana's cottage."

Scarm poked the blackened surface of the wood, rubbed his finger with his thumb and sniffed.

"It's covered in soot, but it hasn't been burned," he said. "Did Mollie or Jack use it to clean out her fireplace?"

Cam shook his head. "Jack didn't go near. He didn't even go to the wake. After the viewin', he took off walkin' to the cliffs. That ain't what I'm here about. Listen, when I went to pay respects, there was too many inside, so I walked round the cottage while I was waiting my turn to say me farewells. This here was by itself, right close to the chimney."

"It's a cedar shake," said Scarm, wiping his fingers. "It's been split too thick to go on a roof, and too thin to be split a second time."

"Y'know, it's the right size to close off a chimney."

Scarm looked at Cam solemnly. "What are you saying, Cam?"

"The soot sticks," said Cam, holding up a smudged palm and fingers. "Now there's three of us with it on our hands."

"Three?"

"You, me and Yan. Both his hands. He'd tried to wash it off before he went to the wake with his ma. But I saw."

"Did he notice you?"

Again, Cam shook his head. "I don't think so."

"Then don't tell him. Or anybody else."

"Wouldn't even think o' it."

"We got suspicions, that's all."

"An' we got eyes, too," said Cam as he stood up to leave.

* * * * *

Not long after Cam left him, Scarm again heard knocking at his door. This time it was Roaring Jack who sat opposite him. The skipper had a skin of whisky with him, and they shared what little was left.

"It ain't my fault," Roaring Jack began in what for him was a hushed voice. "But Oi should'a..."

A long series of 'should'a's' later, Scarm heard what he had expected to hear when he first opened the door.

"Oi gotta be headin' south to do what should'a been done back then."

He also detected something in Roaring Jack's voice that he had never heard before, and though he could not find the exact word to describe it, 'despair' came close.

Much later that evening, after listening to many drunken repetitions, recriminations and resentful oaths directed at the unfairness of life and the fickle nature of luck, Scarm stood at his door, watching Roaring Jack start his stumbling way home. When the skipper's lantern finally bobbed and weaved out of sight, Scarm turned to go inside. He almost dropped his candle as a voice spoke out of the night.

"Scarm, I heard," said Cam softly. "So, here's my plan."

* * * * *

The next day, fresh earth was mounded over another grave in the Village cemetery. Then as was the custom, first the family, then the crew mates and finally almost everyone in the Village all trooped back down from the cemetery to Alana's cottage, where in order of their closeness of blood and belonging, they entered and took something by which to remember her. When it came to Scarm's turn, he opened the chest that Astreya's father had made. He took the bundle of drawings and writing that Astreya had studied, and as an afterthought, a little leather bag of green stones that clinked as he dropped it into his jacket pocket.

Two days later, Roaring Jack's voice echoed through the Village as the *Mollie* slipped her lines to the shore and hoisted sails. Soon her bluff bows charged the confused seas between the headlands, and she was out of sight. The Villagers who had seen her leave shook their heads, pursed their lips, and returned to whatever they had been doing. The second trip south was even less secret than the first, and it was universally judged to be beyond foolishness. They had been kept from forcibly restraining boat and crew because of their conviction that a skipper had the right to sail his boat the way he chose. More importantly, nobody wanted to be the first to tackle Roaring Jack, Red Ian, or Scarm—least of all when they were all together. And even if they had done something to stop them, nobody knew what to do next.

When the *Mollie* had cleared the harbor mouth and was dipping up and down on the steady waves of the open sea, Roaring Jack shaded his eyes against bright sunshine and scanned a sea flecked with small whitecaps.

"Ease the sheets," boomed the skipper as he pulled the tiller towards his belt buckle and then steadied his boat on course. "We're on our way."

Red Ian, Yan and Scarm bent over the main and jib sheets, glancing back at Roaring Jack for his nod of approval when the set of the sails was to his liking. As they watched, the skipper frowned as Cam climbed out of the fish hold onto the foredeck and made his way astern into the cockpit. He tossed a small bedroll pack down the companionway into the cabin, and then threw his jacket after it.

"What in the flaming blazes are y' doin' here, lad?" demanded Roaring Jack.

"Very nicely, thank you, skipper. Glad to be aboard."

"Who asked ye?"

"Well, I heard the *Mollie* was leavin' for the south. So I stowed away last night."

"Stand by to come about. We're takin' you home."

"Alana...." Cam began.

"What's she got to do with it?" Roaring Jack demanded, his blue eyes glaring. "She didn't want 'Streya to go to sea, so why would she want you to go after him?"

"I told him..." began Scarm.

"That the *Mollie* was leavin' for the south," said Cam firmly. "That was when we decided I should go too."

"We decided? We?" Roaring Jack repeated incredulously.

"Well...." Scarm began.

The skipper turned his scowl on him.

"Well what, Scarm?" he demanded

"I figured we needed another pair of hands, what with me having only one that's any use in a blow, so I..."

"Why in blazes didn't you tell me what y' were up to?"

"Do we come about now?" Yan asked hopefully.

"Belay that," Roaring Jack rumbled.

"We're just going fishing, same as before, ain't we, Skipper?" Yan's voice became querulous. "It's not about looking for 'Streya, is it?"

"Y' think?" said Cam, with a shrewd glance at Scarm.

Something between anger and bewilderment passed across Roaring Jack's face, and he spoke so low that Cam could barely hear him.

"Cam, did 'Lana think Oi'd never do the job? Is that why she..." His voice trailed off.

"Can't say, skipper," said Cam. "All's I know is she would'a wanted me to go wi' you. Could be it's 'cause I was the one that told her what the Village was sayin' about her. You know, how she was s'posed to be crazy."

"You told her that?" Roaring Jack was incredulous.

"Well, yeah. The first time I saw her, it kinda' slipped out. I was tryin' to say that I didn't think the way they did, an' it didn't come out quite the way I meant. After that, we talked a few times. 'Bout 'Streya, an' his dad, and how she missed 'em both. You know. That kind of stuff."

"You spent last night in the fish hold," said Red Ian, with the air of a man who has reached a firm conclusion.

"How'd yer know?"

Red Ian sniffed meaningfully. Cam shifted to the lee side of the cockpit.

"Oi should take y' back," said Roaring Jack slowly, choosing his way amongst impossible alternatives, "but we can use another in the crew, so Oi won't. But it'll be yourself who'll be tellin' Silver Don and the lads on the *Ronnie B* why you jumped ship on him and then stowed away on the *Mollie*."

"Suits me, skipper."

* * * * *

Favorable winds and gentle seas carried the *Mollie* southwards. This time, Roaring Jack knew from Astreya's sketches where they were, so they did not have to feel their way close to the shore, but could stand off to the eastward, where the cliffs and headlands did not roil the land and sea breezes, and as a result each day they went faster and further than before. Yan's resentment of Cam was obvious, but the cheerful competence of the younger, smaller boy made it easy for the men to appreciate his presence aboard. When he was not needed for other tasks, he found a place beside Roaring Jack, Astreya's sketches in hand, taking note of each passing headland. Towards the end of the first day, Roaring Jack grunted approval when Cam pointed to a distinctive headland that they had been looking for.

"Close hauled. We're headin' in back of that bluff."

That evening, Cam lit a driftwood fire on the sand close to where they beached the *Mollie*'s bow. He filleted a big cod that Scarm had caught during the day, rolled the portions in corn meal and fried them with some of the onions he had thought to bring with him in his bedroll. He was thanked by a profound silence broken only by murmurs of satisfaction.

As they finished their meal, the wind dropped, so that the scrubby trees along the shore stood still, silhouetted against a darkening sky. Waves hushed along the sand as the last light faded and the first stars gleamed. Roaring Jack stood, lit from below by the remains of the fire.

"T'morra', or maybe the next day, we'll stop coastin' an' strike out southwards, wind and weather permittin'. If the wind holds fair, we'll have a broad reach with the wind to starboard. By evenin,' perhaps a bit later, we'll reach the shore where we... where we lost 'Streya."

He looked down at his crew, knowing that it was one thing to run before a storm to avoid being forced onto a rocky lee shore, but quite another to deliberately sail out of sight of land in the hope that they would make the same landfall as before. Cam nodded, as did Scarm. Red Ian raised his huge shoulders in a shrug as if to say that he was ready for whatever Roaring Jack decided. Only Yan looked fixedly into the fire, refusing to meet his eyes.

"But..." Yan began.

Roaring Jack talked him down. "We'll be off at first light, then."

Scarm and Roaring Jack strolled back towards where the *Mollie* was beached. Yan sat very still for a few heartbeats, and then followed them. Red Ian took it upon himself to scour the frying pan with sand at the water's edge. He brought it back to the fire, where he stood, towering over Cam.

"Y'know 'Streya's markings?" he began awkwardly. When Cam nodded, he glanced around to be sure he was not overheard, and went down on one knee. "Well, 'Streya made a picture of me when the Skipper weren't lookin', so's I could give it to Pearl to remember me by."

"Angus' daughter?"

He nodded.

"An'... an'... an' it... um... it worked. She's waitin' for me."

"I'm happy for both of you, Red," said Cam.

"An' it's why I'm aboard. To find 'Streya. First thing when we find him, I'm gonna thank him." He stood back up to his full height. "I got the first watch," he muttered.

As he turned to go back to the *Mollie,* Cam looked thoughtfully after him. To his surprise, the big man seemed to have no doubt that Astreya was alive. He picked up the remains of supper and was about to kick sand into the dying fire when Yan returned from the boat.

"Lost my knife," he muttered. "Guess I put it down when I was eatin'."

He wandered around the fire hopelessly. Cam ran his fingers systematically through the sand where Yan had been sitting. After a few passes, his fingers bumped into the hilt, and he held it out to Yan. For the first time since the journey began, Yan had to face Cam. Hoping that the gathering darkness would shield him from his steady gaze, he reached for the knife. As his fingers closed on it, Cam caught his wrist. Yan tried to jerk away, but though Cam was the smaller of the two, he was both wiry and determined.

"Yan, tell me what really happened."

Taken by surprise, Yan tried to tug his hand away, but Cam held it firm in a two-handed grip.

"I believe 'Streya's ma, Yan. So you're goin' to have a problem tellin' me that he's dead."

Yan strove with the dilemma that had tortured him since their return to the Village. If Astreya was alive, then he was not a murderer. But if he admitted anything of what had really happened, he would be exposed as a treacherous, lying coward. Over the summer, he had been basking in the Village's pity for his misadventure and admiration for his luck in catching the big fish. There had even been some who said that it was he who had brought good fortune to the Village. Yan had encouraged both misapprehensions with modest shrugs. But on a darkened beach far from the Village, neither strategy would work.

"Yan, what really happened?" Cam insisted.

Yan squirmed. His lies had been plausible at first, but Alana's knowing had trumped them, unsettling Roaring Jack and convincing both Cam and Scarm, all three of whom believed that Alana had the power of second sight. His swiftly concocted scheme to silence Alana had been more successful than he had dreamed, but its outcome was not what he had hoped.

"There were maybe eight, ten, a dozen men, and they all ran after me." Yan began slowly, as if the words were being pulled out of him. His voice rose and he gabbled faster and faster. "They shouted like they wanted me to stop and get knocked down... like 'Streya. So I kept goin' an' I got to the boat an' they shot arrows at us, an' they hit Scarm, an' Skipper pushed me down so's I wouldn't get hit, an'... an'... an' Red wanted to go back and bash them up, an' Skipper wouldn't let him, an' he hoisted sail, an' we went back home."

His voice trailed off inconclusively. Cam looked up into Yan's face, but the fire had died and with it any chance of eye to eye questioning.

"That's what happened, fer real?"

Yan nodded so vigorously that Cam could hear his hair flapping into his face.

Roaring Jack's voice boomed around the little cove.

"Nobody ashore at night. Everyone aboard. Now."

Cam relaxed his grip. Yan tugged his hand free and ran towards the *Mollie*. "Coming, skipper! I'm on my way!"

Cam scuffed sand on the last few red embers and walked slowly to the *Mollie*. He knew enough of the craft of lying to be sure that Yan was using pieces of truth to conceal what he did not want to say.

Yan and Scarm were already aboard, so Cam tossed the pots and pans into the cockpit, and helped Red Ian and Roaring Jack push the bow off the beach. The two big men barely wetted their knees, but Cam went in to his waist before all three clambered aboard and set the anchors for the night. Yan was already curled up asleep in one corner of the cabin when Cam stripped off his wet clothes and hung them along on the boom.

"Cold and wet on the arse," said Red Ian cheerfully as he went below. "But wi' a bit of luck it washed the smell of fish off your breeks, young Cam."

Leaving the big man to stand his watch, Cam went below. In the dim light of a turned down lantern, he saw three blanket-wrapped forms that took up almost all of the available space. Soft breathing noises mingled with the tap of ripples against the *Mollie*'s hull. When his foot reached the last step of the companionway, he stepped on his blanket roll that someone had set out for him. He blew out the lantern, wrapped the blanket around himself and crawled under the hanging table. He lay awake for some time, wondering what Yan might have said if Roaring Jack had not interrupted them. Cam recalled Scarm's advice about saying nothing of their suspicions about Alana's death, and fell asleep telling himself never to be alone with Yan.

CHAPTER 15:

IN WHICH ASTREYA WORKS AS GAR'S ASSISTANT

That summer, Astreya's life became so crowded with new things to learn that he had scant time to think about the events that had brought him to the Castle, or about what might happen next.

For most of the of first few days, Gar paced up and down, glaring at the walls and arguing with himself under his breath. During that time, Learneds and sometimes students came to the hall, ignoring (or perhaps unable to read) the sign that Gar had nailed on the door. None of the Learneds would listen to Lindey, and Gar was usually too busy, so it fell to Astreya to tell the visitors that the hall had been officially declared out of bounds. He expected that they would be angry at not being able to get to the books, and so he offered to help them find what they were looking for, but almost all refused and went away muttering about not having been told.

On one occasion, two Learneds forced their way past the second door, demanding to speak with the person who had written the notice. Gar ignored them, and they ignored Lindey, so it was once more Astreya who had to explain that they should have been told why they might be inconvenienced. Their reaction was to blame him rather than their colleagues.

"I'm sorry," said Astreya, "I don't know the Learneds' names who are dealing with Gar... with the man who hired me. But if you wish, I can help you find the books you're looking for."

"Find a book for me, boy? How would you do that? By its texture and color?"

"By tasting its cover, perhaps?" said the other, his voice heavy with sarcasm.

"No, he'd find it by closing his eyes and spinning around three times," said the first, chuckling at his own wit.

The two green-gowned figures walked off laughing. Gar had heard, and took the time to clap Astreya over the shoulder.

"Ignore the insults and the laughter of fools."

"But they're Learneds..."

"Learned fools. Learned in name only. Most of them can't read."

"Really?"

"Well, they think they can, but most of them just scan a few pages, remember a few words and then go on with what they remember from when they were learning from the previous generation of fools."

Astreya wondered how much of this was fact and how much was colored by Gar's disdain for the men who had hired him.

"Gar, where do these books come from?"

"They're just about all from *Before*."

"*Before* what, Gar?"

"Didn't anyone at your Village tell you about *Before*?"

"No. They just used the word to shut off discussion. The same way they did with the word 'away'. When I asked Scarm where his books came from, he said they were from *Away*. It's the Village's word for anything that isn't... well, that isn't from the Village. My father was 'from *Away*.' Mother told me that was why they called him 'Stranger' or 'the Foreigner.' Me too, sometimes."

"Matris people do much the same," said Lindey. "We say, 'It's from *Outside*.'"

"*Outside*, from *Away*, *Before*—what do they mean?"

"They're places people haven't been, and don't want to go," said Gar. "They distrust anything or anybody who might know more than they do."

"But..."

"But I need you to help me move that scaffold. Those idiots who brought it didn't put it in the right place. *Before* comes after."

With a grunt of amusement at his own words, Gar tossed Astreya a handful of thick twine.

"Here. Untangle this. I'll show you how to lash scaffolding in a moment."

He spent a little time with Lindey, making a list of materials. When he returned, Astreya had already made a start on cross-bracing the first level of scaffolding.

"You have to triple lash each crossing of the poles and then tighten it by..." Gar began, and then as he came closer, interrupted himself. "Well, stiffen me rigid. Where did you learn that?"

"It's the way we make fish drying racks in the Village," said Astreya.

Gar's eyebrows rose and came together in a quizzical frown. He looked at Astreya as if about to ask a question, and then shrugged.

"Right. Now we'll need a lot more of these—and some planks as well for me to walk, sit and sometimes lie on."

Each day, Gar's moods and instructions ruled Astreya and Lindey. They erected scaffolds, modified them, tore them down and re-erected them under his increasingly irritable directions. Each morning, after an early breakfast with the Widow Amy, Gar would hurry them to the hall, where they stayed until evening steeped the light with a reddish glow that made him mutter about changing color values, even though they had yet to open a pot of paint. Occasionally, he would declare the light at fault by mid afternoon and go for a walk, leaving Astreya and Lindey with a few instructions tossed over his shoulder. Sometimes, the sunset would begin, build to a golden display and fade to darkness without affecting his concentration.

Gar walked the hall, climbed the scaffold, made small charcoal marks seemingly at random on the walls, climbed down and walked the hall again. From time to time, he muttered to himself. He seemed oblivious to Astreya and Lindey, but if they took more than a brief moment to rest, he always had further instructions.

Together they set out paints, pigments, brushes, steadying rods, pallets, cloths, cleaning rags, spatulas, pallet knives and all the other paraphernalia of the painter's craft on tables in the space between the bookshelves. Gar inspected, and then had them rearrange everything. Lindey was sent to purchase eggs and oil while Astreya was bidden to find or make charcoal. When he returned with a grimy bag of burnt sticks on his shoulder, there was another task, and then another. Lindey's patience guided Astreya when he grew irritated by a way of life entirely different from the ordered, traditional ways of the Village.

"Does setting things up for Gar ever end?" Astreya asked Lindey late one afternoon as he poured linseed oil through a strainer for the third time.

She looked up from the mortar in which she was grinding pigment, and shook her head.

"It's a bit like working in someone else's kitchen," she said. "You have to accept the way he does things. Gar's his own person."

"I don't understand where it's all leading. Almost all the things he has us do aren't part of any plan I can see. I can't tell whether something is Gar's way or the only way."

"My way is the only way."

Gar's voice came from above them on the scaffold, startling them both.

"For me, that is," Gar added as he climbed down. "Each cook rolls her own pastry and every skipper trims the sails to his own liking. Do things your own way or you'll never be proud of them—when you're in charge, that is. And for now, I'm in charge, and you two have to do what I say."

His words held no exaggerated self importance. They had the commanding quality Astreya knew from experience with skippers at the Village. Astreya glanced at Lindey, and fancied he could read unspoken words of agreement on her lips. He nodded his own acceptance, hoping that he would eventually understand what he was doing.

The next day, Gar began to talk less to himself, and more to Lindey and Astreya. Astreya only partially understood when Gar spoke of light, shade and composition, but practical matters such as where to stand, sit or lie to paint onto the upper parts of the walls were easy to follow. When Astreya's tentative suggestion about bracing the platforms met with approval, he found himself increasingly at Gar's elbow.

Astreya followed Gar up the creaking scaffolds, listening to him talk about balancing colors and shapes in the overall design. Astreya matched Gar's complete disregard for the height as they climbed hand over hand up and down the scaffolding. When they were back down on the floor of the hall, Gar abruptly spoke of something other than painting.

"You've been aloft before."

Astreya nodded.

Gar was about to speak, but at that moment, Lindey, who had been looking up at them openmouthed, emerged from behind her worktable.

"I've climbed a few trees," she said. "But don't expect me to swing about that spider's web the way you two do."

Consequently, Astreya spent a great deal of his time climbing up and down, fetching and carrying. Over most of one week, he helped Gar sandpaper the raw plaster. As this erased his charcoal marks, Gar returned to walking the hall, climbing the scaffold and replacing them. Astreya could see absolutely no significance to the tiny dots and lines, and Gar gave no indication of his plans.

Sometimes, after Astreya and Lindey had completed a task, as much as an hour would go by when Gar was totally absorbed. Astreya used these times to explore the head high rows of bookcases. Some stacks were entirely filled so tightly that he could not extract a single book. Others had shelves that were loose and sloppy with volumes leaning on each other, their spines crooked from long disuse. Dust was thick on everything he touched. If Gar's intentions were inscrutable, the stacks of books were even more so. There was no plan that Astreya could discern. He found books with pictures of birds beside books of maps, under books with titles so long and complicated that he could barely make out more than a few words, above books about battles, plagues, famines and floods in places he had never heard of, next to books of poems, close to books that seemed to lack both rhyme and reason. On each brief opportunity to wander and search, he chose a different dead end passage between rows of shelves, but everywhere he looked was the same jumble.

He was behind a bookcase near the entrance when the door burst open and booted feet marched into the hall. Astreya looked through a gap in the shelf from which he had just taken a book and recognized Carl. His cloak was turned back on his shoulders, revealing a long knife at his belt. He looked about him disdainfully and saw Gar standing with his head back to stare at the ceiling.

"You there, old man. Where's your black-haired helper?"

Gar turned slowly towards him and spoke softly.

"Leave now, lad, and don't come back, or you will live to regret it."

"Or you're going to throw me out, old man? Don't make me laugh. I could carve you up faster than..."

Carl stopped, hearing quick footsteps behind him. He swung around, one hand reaching for his knife, his cloak swirling behind him. He saw Lindey with her staff at the ready, and Astreya's knife sliding out of its sheath. In Carl's moment of hesitation, Gar caught his flaring cloak and jerked him onto his back. Carl's head thumped onto the floor, and the whites of his eyes gleamed briefly before they closed. For a moment, Carl lay still. When he opened his eyes, he was looking up Lindey's staff, one end of which was at his throat. Astreya stood as if frozen, caught between a sudden, overwhelming desire to bury his knife in Carl's body, and his conviction that what he felt was the insanity he had seen in Yan's eyes that day on the black sand beach.

"I did warn you," said Gar, stamping his foot onto Carl's right hand. "Astreya, give me his knife."

Astreya pulled Carl's knife out of its sheath and handed it to Gar, who stepped back and examined it judiciously as Carl flexed his fingers and winced.

"Too long, too thin, and the blade's brittle," said Gar.

He put his boot on the blade and jerked upwards, snapping the metal. Then he tossed the hilt at Carl's crotch. The stump of the blade cut Carl's fingers as he frantically tried to protect himself.

"Let him up, Lindey, he's on his way to tell his friends how an old man broke his knife while a girl kept him flat on his back... or would you rather we broke the news for you, Carl? I thought not."

Gar's last words were to Carl's back as he strode out the door.

"That was satisfactory," said Gar conversationally. "Now let's get back to work."

Astreya breathed deeply, trying to calm the rush of energy that flowed through him. He had been instantly ready for action, but Lindey and Gar had fought for him. He resented being protected, but in the same instant was grateful to them for stopping him from attacking Carl. He knew that this time he had been on the edge of losing control, whereas they had acted calmly, as they had done in previous confrontations. On top of these thoughts came a fear that they might think that he had hung back like a coward.

When the top of his head no longer felt as if it were trying to float up to the dome above him, he looked around to see that Gar had returned to staring fixedly at the ceiling, and Lindey was leaning her staff against a bookshelf. He clamped his jaw tight, determined not to be the first to speak, and strolled as casually as possible to the scaffold and deliberately checked the lashing on the poles, where he glimpsed Gar and Lindey sharing a moment of understanding.

Astreya recoiled from them, sure that they thought he had been frozen in fear. When they did not speak about what had happened, he spent several days in near silence broken only by what was necessary for the work to go on. He wanted to explain that he had hesitated when he sensed that he was planning to kill Carl out of hand, but the excuse sounded lame. Even afterwards, his moment of rage troubled him. He thought of Yan's mindless desire to kill him that day on the beach, and decided that he, too, was capable of the same kind of irrational fury. Gradually, as he accepted that there had been no change in either Lindey's or Gar's behavior towards him, his tension eased.

More than a week later, when the actual drawing and painting began, Astreya had little time for thinking about Carl. The setting up phase had been confusing, but when the actual drawing began, Astreya marveled at the speed with which Gar sketched first a frieze of animals around the edges of the wall at the level of the bookcase tops, and then above the animals, a few lines that suggested a procession of people. To his delight, Astreya was given increasingly difficult tasks: first applying the pale undercoat for Gar to paint the initial images, then filling in solid background color, then copying repeated images within the overall design. Day after day, he worked his way around the hall at the level of the window tops, painting intertwined leaves in a border a little more than a hand span wide. Astreya became so sure of what he was doing that he felt he could do it in his sleep. Then Gar had him a work on a series of birds and animals to occupy the level above the leafy border.

Astreya received his new assignment with trepidation, fearing that Gar had given him a task that was beyond him. For a few days, he checked, commented and improved Astreya's outlines, and then he simply told him to complete the detail in color, then continue the design on around the rest of the hall. Astreya worked on nervously, wondering if the old painter was looking for a chance to rid himself of a fumbling, cowardly assistant. But after several successful images, Astreya's confidence improved. He started to improvise minor changes, and Gar grunted approval.

Astreya worked with painstaking care, focusing all his attention on his task, barely noticing that Lindey seemed always to know what brush or color he would need next. She was used to producing shades and subtle tones to Gar's specifications, but when Astreya started to work on his own, she took over his job as fetcher and carrier, climbing the scaffold with a cautious determination unlike Gar and Astreya's casual disregard for height. She accepted Gar's grumbling when the pigments did not produce the effects he wanted, and gave a little smile of satisfaction whenever Astreya thanked her. She watched him carefully and brought him fresh pigments, or altered the consistency of the paint so that it clung better to the wall. It became a point of pride for Astreya that he never duplicated an image, so that each evening before they left the hall his reward was to hear Lindey name the new bird or beast he had painted that day.

After several days, when they were both assessing the results, Gar stopped what he was doing and favored them both with a thumbs up gesture of approval. Astreya's eyes met Lindey's, she smiled, and the last of his self-imposed reticence ended. When next he picked up his brush, he did so with a confidence that had been absent from his previous careful attempts.

At the end of that day, he climbed down from the scaffold to find Lindey and Gar gazing upwards at what he had been doing.

"Are they all right?" he asked. "Will they do?"

"Any better, and you'll have me out of work," said Gar.

As Astreya took breath to protest, he saw Lindey shake her head.

"What's wrong?" he asked her.

"Nothing's wrong, you silly goose," Lindey chuckled. "You're painting so well, you've got Gar working to stay ahead of you."

Her laugh convinced Astreya more than all their words. That evening, the conversation at dinner flourished, as it had not done since their first night at the Widow Amy's.

Drawing and painting wholly occupied Astreya's mind as the weather warmed to high summer. Learneds turned back their gowns over their shoulders every day, and scholars carried theirs on one arm whenever they thought that the Learneds were not watching. Inside the domed hall, Gar worked with his shirtsleeves rolled. Astreya would have done so as well, but he wanted to keep his bracelet hidden, so he contented himself by asking the Widow to enlarge the neck of his shirts. Lindey tied her lengthening blonde hair high on the back of her head, and, when she was in the hall, kilted her skirts to the knee. Astreya shaved daily.

One morning, when they arrived in the hall, the portly little Learned with whom Gar had negotiated was haranguing a party of earnest scholars about reverence, holiness and spirituality, pointing to the images of animals, birds and flowers to illustrate his sermon. The scholars stood amazed by what they saw until Gar chased them all away. On another occasion, a troupe of green-gowned Learneds and scholars appeared through the doors, chanting as they came. As they became fascinated by what they saw, their recitation straggled into silence. One of them asked Astreya about the meaning of the drawings, and when he tried to reply, their leader, a tall man whose presence was enhanced by a broad cream-colored scarf on top of his gown, gazed upwards and audibly implored his God for protection against wizardry and magic. He received a drop of paint in one eye. Trying his best to maintain his dignity, the Learned pushed his way back through his followers and led them out of the hall. As the last scholar trailed out the door, Gar laughed. Astreya and Lindey looked up at him.

"Gar," said Lindey reproachfully. "You did that on purpose."

"God botherers," he said. "So sure they're right. They make my skin crawl."

"Surely they're entitled to their faith," said Astreya.

"Sure they are," said Gar with unusual intensity. "Trouble is, they inflict their beliefs on everyone else."

Still muttering, he went back to his painting, while Astreya and Lindey shared a moment in which they both wondered what in Gar's past might have caused so strong a reaction.

As the summer settled in and the grass turned from green to yellow, they kept the doors open to catch whatever wind might be enticed into the aisles of books. As more and more images of leaves, flowers and animals flowed around the plastered walls and between the windows, Gar went back to walking, then climbing up to make a few charcoal marks on the dome, and then descending to walk again. This time, Astreya barely noticed. He was delighted to see that the lines and colors that he applied to the walls really did turn into leaves, birds and animals when he climbed down and looked up at them from the floor. Up close, he could see flaws and mistakes, which at first Gar touched up expertly, and after Astreya's technique improved, approved with a shrug. He started in a clockwise direction, alternating birds with animals, eventually working around the dome until he was back to the first animal he had drawn. He wondered whether this was to be the end of his contribution, and frittered away a day improving and touching up. Then he climbed down the scaffold to see from the floor if the first and last animals fitted together as well as those done in sequence. He was standing with his neck cricked back, looking upwards when Gar plucked at his sleeve.

"Help me move this bookcase away from the wall. Right, up you go. This is your spot. Draw me a procession of the inmates of this asylum—Learneds, scholars, and healers. When you're finished, do the same in the lower spaces between the windows, but this time in groups of the unlearned—taverners, butchers, barmaids and persons of questionable repute. I'll be working on the dome. Be grateful. It's cooler down here than up at the top."

Astreya was first elated, and then apprehensive. He had begun by copying Gar's leaves, and then had a few sample sketches of animals to guide him, but now he was on his own from the start. He began with charcoal because he had finally understood that Gar's preliminary sketch marks were a way of defining the size and limits of what he wanted.

Astreya began with a few fine marks that could easily be erased. Then he reached into his memory for the faces and figures that he had seen in the town, tavern and Castle. Deliberately ignoring Gar on the scaffold above him, he sketched men and women of different ages and backgrounds. He included the overweight magistrate who had nearly condemned him, Nock's distinctive helmet of black hair, Sandy's round freckled face, and Damon in the act of flicking his hair out of his eyes. He drew what he remembered of the two dark-complexioned men he had seen in the marketplace. He caught Carl's wide legged arrogant stride with his cloak tossed over one shoulder. In one of the lower spaces he drafted a cluster of long-nosed Learneds as they had stood during the arrival at the gatehouse, and he put Eva's face on one of four young Healers in training. He was just finishing one of the tavern girls he had seen leaning in a doorway when Gar's voice startled him.

"Well I'll be pounded flat," said Gar. "Lindey, come and look at this."

Astreya stopped what he had been doing and watched apprehensively as Gar and Lindey inspected his work. A part of him wanted to keep what he had done from being criticized. He considered asking them to wait until he had a chance to correct and improve. Instead, he stood; charcoal stick in his hand, while the two of them stared at what he had done. As the silent moments grew uncomfortably long, he considered running out the door, never to return.

"They're... they're so alive, with so few lines," said Lindey slowly.

"He's got the touch," Gar agreed.

"He's good at doing men," she added.

Astreya frowned. Was this approval? Or damnation through faint praise?

"She's right, Astreya. You can draw men, even those you've only glimpsed, like these long-haired woodsmen. But look here, Astreya. What's wrong with the girls you drew?"

Astreya winced. Gar had unerringly focused on the images about which he was least certain.

"I... I don't know," he said.

"I do," said Gar. "The men over here have legs and hips and bodies under their cloaks and clothes—Lindey saw that. But the girls are just faces on top of long gowns."

"But the men are all clothed and most of them gowned, too," said Lindey. "What's the difference?"

"The difference, my girl—and you too, young Astreya—is anatomy. What's under the cloaks and clothes."

"Yes," said Lindey, "but he doesn't have to draw all that. It's only the cloaks and clothes that we see."

Gar stared at her, then at Astreya and then at the drawings, his eyebrows dancing up and down as he focused his attention back and forth.

"They're not all wearing gowns now that it's warmer, I suppose I should..." began Astreya.

"You miss my point," said Gar. "Astreya, draw me one of these men in his skivvies. Any one of them. Here. On this scrap of paper. Do it."

Astreya obediently resketched the man he had made the center of a group of arguing Learneds. This time, the potbellied, round shouldered, knock kneed, middle aged Learned clutched a towel around his middle to preserve his modesty. Gar chuckled.

"Good. Right. Now do one of the girls."

Astreya frowned. This was more difficult. He redrew one of the girls with her cloak off her shoulders, and most of one leg peeping out of her cloak.

"You cheated, Astreya. Where's her body, for goodness sake! Let's see all of her—hip, thigh, bottom and breasts!"

Astreya raised his hand, poising the charcoal to try again, and stopped.

"I can't," he said. "I can't see it."

"Oh, my shattered oath," said Gar. "It's so obvious. He can't draw it, because he can't see it. Lindey, take off your clothes."

Astreya's eyes widened and his jaw dropped.

"What?" Lindey demanded. "Not a chance," she said firmly.

"He's got to see, Lindey," said Gar.

"Well, if you think I'm going to take off my clothes, here and now, believe me, that's not going to happen."

Gar strode forward and back in short steps, turning sharply as if coming to the edge of a cliff. He stopped short in the middle of the third repetition and stared at the sunlight on the floor below one of the tall windows. Astreya and Lindey watched him quizzically.

"Got it," said Gar.

He pulled Astreya a few steps back so that he was looking towards the sunlit window. Then he took Lindey by the shoulders and pushed her so that she stood between Astreya and the window, and then turned her until the sun shone on one side of her face.

"Stay there. Don't move, either of you."

He disappeared behind the scaffolding and bookcases and reappeared with a book the size of a small tabletop, opened it to a blank page at one end and thrust it into Astreya's hands.

"Astreya, look. Absorb. Don't draw yet."

Astreya frowned, and then blushed as he saw that Lindey was silhouetted against the window, with the light through her blouse and skirt revealing the shape of her body. Gar looked over Astreya's shoulder and pointed.

"See, Astreya. Hips. Girl hips, not boy hips. No, don't move, Lindey. See the way that when she stands with her weight on one leg, everything's feminine? Look at that sweetly curved line around her hips. Nothing like a man's waist that's built for a belt with a knife in it. You can draw a man with straight lines and catch just about all his angles and knobs—at least, a young man's. You couldn't begin to catch Lindey on paper without curves: long and smooth below, rounded above where her breasts—oh for goodness' sake, Astreya. Don't go all prissy on me. And don't you start moving, Lindey. Just because this boy is embarrassed, doesn't mean you can wander off. This is part of your education. Both of you stop blushing this minute!"

Lindey stood still. At first, she looked ready to mutiny and walk away. Then as her initial embarrassment faded, she considered that Astreya had not said anything, and she became increasingly curious to see how he would draw her. She relaxed and unconsciously slipped into the pose that Gar wanted, with her hips tilted, one arm hanging, the other arm bent with the hand cupped loosely below her chin, her head slightly to one side.

"Now draw," Gar ordered.

Astreya's charcoal scratched across the page, catching Lindey's essentially female stance. He traced the hollowing at the small of her back, the long smooth line that began just above the outside of her knee and ran up and outwards, then swooped inward and upward, before moving outwards again around her rib cage, on to the entrancing curves of her silhouetted breast, up through the halo of her sunlit hair to her face. One part of Astreya's mind drew shapes and contours, another warmed to the task of capturing not just any girl, but Lindey herself.

Behind Astreya's shoulder, Gar smiled as he watched the sketch taking shape. All three of them were locked into the moment. Later, each of them reflected that if had they not been interrupted, even more might have been said and understood. But footsteps echoed in the hall and the magic evaporated. All three reacted. Astreya dropped his charcoal stick and closed the book on his thumb. Lindey shook off the soft calm in which she had been standing, and hurried back to the painting equipment. Muttering curses under his breath, Gar strode to the door, waving his arms in a vigorous gesture of dismissal.

"Out. Out. I don't care who you are. Oh, it's you, Damon. All right. But don't interrupt the work of shattering genius that you are privileged to witness in its gestation stages, wherein none can yet tell whether it will be a masterpiece of human imagination or a horrible heap of hideous half-hearted scrawls."

Damon strode into the hall and stood with his head back, staring at the images of people, animals and birds.

"This is going to be good," said Damon. "I doubt the Dean and the God Squad will like it, but the scholars will."

Astreya ignored him and began to copy his drawing of Lindey onto the wall, wondering if he could transfer what he had learned when he came to do sketches of women who had not posed for him. Damon's voice turned into background noise, unnoticed until an exclamation of surprise broke Astreya's concentration.

"Hey! That's Lindey!"

"I can't draw women," Astreya explained, "so Gar was showing me..."

"He's learning at the feet of the master," said Gar. "I'm conducting a class here."

"It doesn't look as if Astreya needs it," said Damon.

"He knows what a man looks like under his clothes because men take off their shirts to work, and their breeks cling to their legs. But women wear skirts and blouses and whatever so that you can't see their bodies," said Gar.

"And that's one of the reasons why it's so much fun taking their clothes off," said Damon, with a practiced leer.

Almost out of sight behind a table of equipment, Lindey stirred a pot of paint more vigorously than was necessary. Gar's lips twitched.

"Looking at this," said Damon, "I'd say you draw women very well, Astreya. You've seen a lot more of Lindey than... er ... usually meets the eye."

Lindey abruptly thumped the paint pot on the table. Astreya swung around and glared at Damon, who raised both his hands in apology.

"Just a figure of speech, Astreya. Don't look at me like that, Gar. Don't reach for your staff, Lindey. What I meant to say was that Astreya has a drawn a... a speaking likeness of Lindey, and has let all us see that she's... a good looking woman. Which she always was... er... is... but... um..." his voice trailed off.

"She doesn't flaunt it," said Gar, with finality. "That's what you wanted to say, isn't it, Damon?"

Damon nodded. Lindey frowned at Damon, and then when she caught Astreya's glance at her, favored him with an expression he could not interpret.

"The reason I came," said Damon in the tones of someone deliberately changing the subject, "is to tell you that we're meeting at Bob the Swab's tavern this evening. That's me and Nock and Sandy—and Eva as well."

"Eva?" Lindey asked. "I thought women weren't allowed to..."

"There's a lot that's not allowed, but that doesn't mean it isn't done," said Damon.

"Then we should join you after we finish up here," said Gar.

When Damon left, he took with him the moment he had interrupted. Although all three went back to what they had been doing, none of them could concentrate. Eventually, Gar threw down the stick of charcoal he had been waving vaguely at the dome.

"Beer," he said. "Come on, you two. We're not doing anything useful here."

That day ended at the tavern. Robert the Taverner came towards them as they entered, and waved them to the same table where Astreya's adventure with Carl had begun.

"I'd like to thank you..." began Astreya, but Robert waved both hands in the air and talked him down.

"First round's on me," he said heartily. "Have a nice quiet evening this time," he added, emphasizing 'quiet' both with his voice and a series of meaningful glances at each of their faces.

Astreya sat with his back to the wall, next to Gar's chair, with Lindey on his right. They had no sooner picked up their first mugs of ale when Damon, Sandy and Nock arrived with Eva, who had cut her hair shorter, so that it swung across her shoulders. The four of them had just climbed over the Castle wall and were eager to explain how cleverly they had avoided the Learneds' watchmen.

"Eva, are the Healers teaching you well?" Astreya asked.

Eva responded with a brief nod before sitting between Damon and Sandy, who competed for her attention. After that, Eva took little notice of Astreya, although she glanced at him from time to time, perhaps disappointed that he gave no indication of jealousy, no matter how much she flirted with Damon and Sandy. From Astreya's point of view, the three of them had become a pattern, a composition, an event to be captured and recalled for the next day when he might draw the angle of their heads, the way they leaned towards each other, the expressions that came and went on their faces. They were interesting to him, but the moment when he had sketched Eva beside Gar's cart in the meadow was now a distant memory.

As one of the taverner's helpers brought them beer, Astreya scanned her, noting her out-thrust chest, swaying hips and bold glances. The girl noticed his gaze and accentuated her every move, bending forward so that her blouse gaped as she slid the beer mugs onto the table. She was used to being stared at, but was taken aback by the concentration of Astreya's gaze. His look was not the usual open mouthed sexual hunger that she was used to seeing in the faces of the students and young men of the town. She pouted at him, tossed her tousled red-brown hair and flounced off to another table where three scholars greeted her raucously. Gar looked on with approval, congratulating himself. He decided that Astreya's interest had swiftly matured from the bashful glances of an easily embarrassed boy to a young man with an artist's eye for what was around him.

"Just one thing, Astreya," he whispered. "Don't let 'em see you stare. That's when the boyfriends get ugly, and you find yourself in a fight."

"I know," said Astreya.

Gar's attention had been claimed by Damon, so putting aside his memories of Yan and the fight on the beach, Astreya's gaze left the tavern girl and refocused on Lindey. As usual, she was saying little and observing much. He smiled at her, and her lips moved. Astreya was certain she was asking him, "Did you like what you just saw?"

Astreya spoke out loud without thinking first. "Not really. Nowhere near the way I like seeing you."

He knew he had read her lips correctly when she blushed. There was a silent moment in which they both acknowledged and accepted what had happened.

As the evening went on, each time he glanced at her beside him, she seemed so much more real than everything else around him, and he was secretly elated that she seemed to be warming to his covert attention. When he looked at her, she did not apparently react, but he noticed a different quality in her expression. Amazed by the change, he looked away, his glance flickering over the men and women in the tavern. Then his eyes met Lindey's again, and the corners of her mouth lifted in a delicate smile. Astreya's cheeks burned, and he looked away again. When he looked back, she was still smiling, her lips curling back from even white teeth.

Gar watched these exchanges as each mug of ale led to the next. Drawing attention to himself, he once again began to rattle off still more of his improbable stories. When Damon challenged the truth of a particularly outrageous tale, Gar's voice penetrated Astreya's concentration, and he noticed that he had not been listening for some time.

"All my stories are founded on the very stuff of which great truths are made," Gar proclaimed, and launched into another.

Astreya went back to looking, memorizing and sketching in his mind. As the evening progressed, the tavern full of people seemed less interesting to him, and Lindey became more fascinating by the moment. Eventually, he did not even bother to pretend that he was listening to Gar's continual flow of words, and simply stared into Lindey's eyes.

When they all left the tavern, Sandy took Eva's arm. Immediately, Damon took her other arm. Nock, who had lurched unsteadily out the tavern door behind them, stood swaying slightly, hands on hips.

"Letsh go," he said. "We gotta get her back o' th' wall. An' you two better help me thish time."

"Comes out uneven any way you look at it," said Gar. "Hard to work it out."

"Not worth the effort," said Lindey.

Gar chuckled at Astreya's puzzled expression in the light of the tavern's open door.

Lindey's shadow fell between them. To their mutual surprise, she took both their arms and started purposefully down the road. Considerably steadier than either of them would have been alone, the three walked back to the Widow Amy's house.

* * * * *

After that day, Astreya, Gar and Lindey subtly and silently became working partners who fiercely protected each other from the rest of the world. A part of this unspoken contract was that all three had secrets that they were entitled to keep or speak of, as they wished.

As the summer ripened, the painting slowed into the painstaking work of completing images, so different from the exhilarating business of sketching the outlines of what was to come. At the beginning this process, Astreya and Gar took time away from the hall to stroll together, notebooks in hand, to capture details of faces and figures, and then to discuss what and how to incorporate what they saw into the overall composition on the walls and dome. They visited taverns and drew furtive portraits of young men and women, scholars and farmers, smiths, peddlers, tavern girls and tosspots, just as Gar had bidden Astreya to do. But now there was no further testing. They spoke—and sometimes argued—more as equals than as student and teacher. And though Gar noticed that Astreya filled many sheets of paper with drawings of Lindey, he never mentioned it.

When they returned to rework their sketches into completed pictures on the walls and ceiling, Astreya had still more to learn. After his first attempt at capturing a particular scholar with long hair and an angular body, he felt that he had been quite successful. But when he climbed down to the floor, his work looked awkward and distorted compared to the sure strokes with which Gar was finishing another figure nearby.

"I can't do it, Gar. It's all wrong and I don't know why."

"Climb up here again."

Chewing his lips with frustration, Astreya did as he was told.

"Now look."

By some magic, his drawing seemed acceptable.

"It's where you're looking from, Astreya. You have to make the feet smaller than you'd draw them for an ordinary picture, and the heads bigger, and kind of taper the middle bits between so that from up here, the figures look odd, but when you get down on the floor again, they seem right. Here, try it."

Astreya did as he was told, checking the proportions against Gar's work. Lindey's voice floated up to them from below.

"Hey, you two, haven't you noticed that it's getting to be time for supper?"

"Go ahead, Lindey," said Gar. "We'll be along shortly."

She continued to watch them from the floor, but the two painters did not notice her. After a little while, she shrugged and left them. At last, warm golden light shone through the windows, and shadows obscured what they were doing. They climbed down together and talked all the way back to their lodgings, leaving paint pots uncovered, brushes drying, and Astreya's jacket hanging on the scaffold. As they reached the door, Gar muttered in Astreya's ear.

"We're late for supper, and we left a mess for Lindey to clean up. Be very agreeable. Praise the food."

Like the evenings before, they began by taking baths, and then turned their attention to the Widow Amy's cooking. Gar teased Amy; she pretended to be insulted. He praised her cooking; she tried to make all three of them overeat. Gar never spoke of the painting, or himself, or what he was planning. Much of the time, he encouraged the Widow Amy to speak about her favorite subjects: magic and superstition, which she referred to as "medicine."

There was nothing that happened for which she did not have an explanation. Some of her beliefs were guides to everyday life: if her cat washed behind the ears before breakfast, there would be rain before noon. If crows cawed in flight, a thunderstorm would brew up by nightfall. If anyone sneezed, only ritual washing with her herbed soap would protect everyone from falling sick. If the new moon hung in the sky like a cup, the rain would hold up for a month. If you ate with dirty hands, your stomach would rumble. However, most of her interpretations of the world had to do with understanding people. One evening, she told them that Gar's wide palm foretold that he would make a generous gift of money—an idea that made him roar with laughter and make himself out to be a miser. Astreya's green eyes were because he could see into others' minds, which he found so much the opposite of the truth that he had to clamp his jaws tight to avoid a guffaw of disbelief. The shape of Lindey's ears was a sure indication that she would guide the lives of many children, after which prediction Lindey excused herself to mend brushes and cut stirring sticks for paint, leaving Gar and the Widow Amy to swap exaggerations.

Astreya followed her out onto the doorstep, where they sat in the fading glow of a rose-colored summer sunset. Lindey took a knife from her pocket and began to trim a paintbrush. Astreya found himself completely absorbed by the way that the last light caught her hair, putting a soft halo around her face. He felt that the most important thing in the world was to remember what he saw, so that he could paint it at a later date, even though he knew as he looked that he would only be able to capture a weak echo of the moment. When she eventually looked up, he looked away, and launched into speech to cover his embarrassment.

"Some of Amy's sayings sound reasonable, but I can't tell for sure which of them are right and which are foolish," said Astreya.

"She's a little like my great aunt," said Lindey. "Before she went completely silly, that is."

Astreya waited silently, hoping Lindey would tell him about her childhood. Meanwhile, he watched the sunset deepening the honey shades of her hair.

"Tell me about her," he said eventually.

After another long pause, Astreya tried another tack.

"Why don't you paint as well?"

Lindey carefully put down brush she was fixing.

"I can see what's right after you and Gar have done it, and sometimes I can tell what's wrong, too. But I can't make it happen myself."

"You mix paints and get shades that I have difficulty even seeing," said Astreya.

"And you see shapes I only notice after you've put them down in lines," she countered.

"I have so much to learn," said Astreya. "Gar..."

"Gar watches what you do and shakes his head," said Lindey.

"Then how can I fix it?" said Astreya.

"No, no, no, Astreya. It's because he can't believe how good you are. The two of you are up there on the scaffold, painting your hearts out, swinging around as if you were birds in a tree and could float down to earth on wings if you ever slipped. Neither of you believe that what you're doing is good, and yet each of you admires what the other does. You don't realize how alike you are."

"We argue a lot."

"True, but both of you would die rather than tell the other what you're really thinking."

"I don't know if what I'm thinking would interest Gar," said Astreya. "I wish I knew more about him."

"If I were talking to Gar, he'd probably say the same thing about you," said Lindey.

Even though he had come to respect Lindey's opinions, Astreya found this difficult to believe.

"Why did you leave your home, Lindey? And how did you come to be traveling with Gar?"

"It was best for my family and community," she said.

Astreya saw her lips tighten, closing off the fleeting hints of unsaid words. He wanted to exchange memories about their respective childhoods and upbringing. For the first time in his life he felt he could drop the guard that time and habit had build up around his childhood experiences of both joy and pain, culminating in how he felt about being left for dead in a strange land. He knew she had heard the facts: it was the reasons and emotions that he wanted to share. He was so caught up in this complicated longing that he was unaware of her eager look as they sat together gazing at the glow left by the setting sun.

"Come away into the house," called the Widow Amy, pulling them from their reverie. "Into bed, both of you, while there's still light."

When they went inside, she stood, hands on ample hips, watching them go to their separate rooms. Then, when their virtue had been ensured, she went looking for Gar.

* * * * *

The leaves darkened into the shades of late summer, the meadows browned in the heat of the sun, and even some of the Learneds occasionally carried their gowns over one arm. Inside the hall, Astreya barely noticed the passage of time. Each day brought new insights about seeing, watching, and painting what he saw. From Gar, he discovered touches and tricks, from Lindey he learned about colors and how to make them from a variety of unlikely ingredients. The three of them shared a focus on completing a task none of them could have done alone. The universe held its breath while they painted their version of it on the walls and ceiling of the Learneds' hall.

From time to time, Damon, Sandy and Nock visited them, looked about and then left when they were unable to enter the charmed circle that held Astreya, Lindey and Gar together. After her evening in the tavern, Eva did not reappear, nor did anyone mention her. Then, as the scent of late summer haying drifted from nearby farms across the Castle grounds, Damon and his friends showed up and made their presence more insistent than it had been on previous occasions.

As usual, it was Damon who talked most. Astreya noticed that his mustache had begun to curl up at the ends, giving him a devil-may-care look that suited his quick smiles and sudden movements. He was no less irreverent than at their first meeting, bluntly asking Gar to talk about the overall plan, the meaning of which was still unclear.

"What's it all about, Gar?"

Gar wiped his hands on a rag and sniffed.

"Above your head is a painting that will live for ages in the minds of Learneds and scholars alike." He began in the voice he used for telling stories and making exaggerated claims. Then as he continued, he shifted to the softer tones that he used to teach Astreya. "Think of it as a single picture made of many images. All around are trees, plants, and flowers. Within, animals and birds. So far, that's what you see: they're done. All around are students, Learneds and ordinary folk. They're all sketched in, and most of them are nearly finished."

"What's going in the middle?"

Astreya felt a stab of jealousy that he had not been told, and that Damon, an outsider to the three of them, should be first to hear Gar's plans. However, Gar's tone shifted back to the one he used with the Learneds.

"That you'll have to wait and see."

"But what does it all mean?" Damon asked.

Gar ran his fingers through his hair, inadvertently daubing green paint on the bare top of his head.

"The painting is about the idea I was asked to paint. The life of a Learned. The reverend sirs instructed me to paint about the urgent pursuit of understanding, the unremitting search for knowledge, and the unswerving desire for truth." He paused, sniffed and frowned. "So that must be what it's all about."

Astreya looked at Lindey, who raised one eyebrow. Her lips seemed to say, "I'm not so sure...." Gar's expression was entirely serious, but there was a note in his voice like the one he used when talking to the Widow Amy. Astreya's jealousy faded.

Damon stared at Gar.

"Do you mean it?" he asked.

Gar nodded curtly, his eyebrows raised as if offended.

Damon took a breath to tease Gar with questions about what all the birds, beasts and people had to do with the cloistered, self-absorbed and argumentative Learneds, changed his mind and took Astreya by the arm.

"Your lessons start today in the manly art of staying alive in the face of cold steel," he said. "We have to prepare you before Carl comes to call."

"I have no further quarrel with Carl," said Astreya.

"No further quarrel?" echoed Damon incredulously. "He took you by surprise from behind, he offered to cut you up, he got you hauled in front of the mayor, and you say that you have no quarrel? Astreya, if you hadn't been so quick and cool when the knives were out, I'd think you were one of those pen wielders who think fingers are for turning pages and scribbling down their own musty thoughts."

"It's all over as far as I'm concerned," said Astreya firmly, hoping Damon had not heard about how Gar and Lindey had ejected Carl from the hall.

"Well, it ain't over for Carl," said Nock slowly but emphatically. "He's lookin' for another go at you."

"For Carl, you're the one that got away," said Sandy. "He wants to take another crack."

Gar cleaned his nails with his palette knife.

"Listen to them," he said to his finger ends. "When that knife-happy bully comes back, he'll know you're slippery, and you won't be able to deal with him the same way you did before."

Astreya looked at Gar, grateful that he had not mentioned Carl's last visit, but the painter's attention was focused on getting a crust of paint from under his left thumbnail. Lindey's voice made them all turn.

"I know one important thing about knife fighting," she said. "The difference between the winners and the losers is that the winners lose less blood than the losers. Not none, just less. The only sensible approach to knife fighting is to be a good runner—or to be quick with a stick."

"There hasn't been anyone killed in years around here," said Nock, as if he regretted it.

"Of course, there's people who've been cut up a bit," said Sandy cheerfully.

"Losers," said Damon.

"Why do it?" demanded Lindey. "If you have to paw the ground and snort like randy bulls, why don't you go about it the way they do, without weapons?"

"It's not the way," said Sandy.

"Then the way is ridiculous," said Lindey, returning to her paint. "Better stay out of it, Astreya."

"Not possible," said Damon. "Not how it's done. Only a fool meets a knife with bare hands. Anyway, Carl will choose a place where running's out of the question."

"We never run," declared Nock with finality.

"Go with them, Astreya. Leave now," Gar ordered harshly. "Lindey and I'll finish up. Just look after your hands and eyes."

Astreya stared, silenced by something in Gar's voice he had never heard before: a tone of command that could not be ignored or denied. He wanted to wait, ask questions, talk over the options that might be considered, but found himself obeying automatically. Lindey looked up at him, the word ghosts on her lips so quick that Astreya could not even guess at her thoughts. When he tried to meet her eyes, she looked down, her blonde hair falling like a curtain around her face. Gar's hand touched her shoulder, but she did not move.

Damon plucked at his arm again. Astreya picked up his tunic and went with the three green cloaked scholars. They left the hall, crossed the tree-dotted Castle grounds and went out the gate in the wall, Astreya's thoughts balancing between curiosity about what he might learn and concern about what both Lindey and Gar had left unsaid. For the first time, he was sure he had seen Lindey disagree with Gar's assessment of a situation. And though for the present he was prepared to follow Gar's advice, he was uneasy.

Damon led the way. They left the town, crossed fallow fields and pushed through patches of scrubby alder that were reclaiming what some farmer had cleared many years before. Damon chose a spot where the grass had been cropped short by wandering cattle, shrugged off his cloak and wound it around his left arm. Sandy produced two wicked looking knives, each considerably longer than a hand span.

"Some people start off with a wooden practice knife," said Damon. "But you need to learn a lot in a short time. Besides, wooden blades build false confidence. Never forget for an instant that these things cut."

He took a knife from Sandy, and tossed it into the air. Steel glittered in the afternoon sun. Damon caught the knife by the handle, sighted along the blade, and lobbed it to closely miss Astreya. Time slowed. Astreya sidestepped, reached into the whirling arc of metal as it passed him, and took the knife by the handle. Nock crowed with glee and Sandy whistled.

"A natural, Damon!"

Astreya looked at the weapon he had caught. It was two handspans from pommel to tip, had a short curved guard at the beginning of the blade, and a reverse curve towards the end where it was sharpened on both edges. It balanced in his hand, and when he waved it back and forth, he automatically turned his wrist so that the cutting edge was leading. This was a weapon and nothing else. He could not even imagine using it for cooking, splitting fish or splicing rope.

"He's got some learning to do," said Damon grimly, covering his surprise.

For the rest of the afternoon, Damon led a series of repetitive drills. Each began differently: some low and thrusting, some high and slashing, some weaving from side to side. The drills were formalized. To each attack, there was a reply of knife, arm and body that, if successful, left the attacker foiled, and perhaps at a disadvantage. Each drill ended with the finishing blow feigned but undelivered.

At first Damon moved slowly. Then, when Astreya finished ahead of him, he quickened the pace. As drill followed drill, the knife became an extension of Astreya's hand, and a subtle change came over the way he moved. Damon's face reddened with exertion as he strove to maintain his advantage, but Astreya's blade began to anticipate his, forcing him to drop back.

After several such sequences, Damon fell back a pace as if to take a fresh guard, and pretended to stumble. Astreya paused to let Damon regain his balance, and in that moment, Damon threw his knife. Astreya swung to one side, hearing the knife swish through the air past his ear.

"You could have had me, if you'd followed through," said Damon through clenched teeth. "But if I'd thrown faster, you'd be wearing my blade in your eye. This isn't a game, Astreya. Try it once more."

Again, they squared off, and again Damon was late at the end of a series of feints and parries. Astreya saw his advantage grow, but did not press home an attack. As he relaxed his attention, Damon's attack took him by surprise. His foot hit the back of Astreya's knee; when he staggered, Damon's left hand caught clothes, and yanked. Astreya saw a wrestler's opening, another and another, but the knife in his hand was in the way of the holds he could have made, and as he hesitated, Damon was behind him. Astreya felt steel against his throat.

"Remember," panted Damon in his ear. "In knife fighting, there are no rules."

Astreya's eyes widened, he nodded, but his thoughts were confused. He realized that it was foolish to look for wrestling holds in a knife fight, but he was unwilling to accept that there were no rules.

"Again tomorrow," said Damon. "Now, give me a coin."

Astreya pulled a silver penny from his pocket. Damon took it from him, spun it in the air and caught it.

"The knife is now yours."

"I already have one... my father's."

"Good for cutting rope. Not a real weapon. Besides, you just bought a new one."

"It must be worth more than a penny," began Astreya.

"It's worth the first coin out of your pocket. You've bought it, so it can't cut our friendship. Here's its sheath. Wear your knife, but don't show it unless you mean to use it. Now let's find ale."

They walked back to the Jug and Bottle, three of them talking about the finer points of knife fighting, Astreya walking silently. Without thinking, he had assumed that there must be limits to knife fighting as there were to wrestling at the Village. He had behaved as if he had been learning a complicated dance, not understanding that the gracefulness and skill hid an ugly reality. The challenge of outmaneuvering someone was still an attractive test of skill to Astreya, but his Village upbringing and his own convictions made him see killing or maiming as insane and abhorrent. Knife fighting was not like wrestling, in which only pride was lost and won. Nor was it the same as the impersonal challenges set by the sea. Try as he might, Astreya could not find a neutral outcome to knife fighting like the one he had discovered in Village wrestling. At the Village, there had always been rules so basic that nobody even gave them words, much less thought of breaking them. There, he had been able to elude the shame of being a loser. Now, he owned a blade that demanded the final thrust that separates survivors from victims.

As he grappled with these thoughts, Astreya remembered Yan's treachery. For the first time, he saw how blind he had been to the possibility of attack from outside all rules. Were there then no rules at all? Astreya shook his head as he walked between his new friends. He thought of Carl, and knew that if it came to a challenge, he would have to fight to win, but he still clung to the hope of avoiding what could be a life-or-death situation.

"Ale, 'Streya. That's what you need to stiffen you up," said Sandy.

Astreya recognized that his new mentors were thinking that he had been cowed. As his time sense returned to the everyday, Astreya knew that he held not only the secret of quickness that Damon envied, but also an advantage as keen as the blades he had held—the three scholars did not understand him. Astreya started to smile, suddenly knowing that as long as people thought of him as an outsider, he possessed the advantage of the unexpected. He disciplined his lips into stillness, wondering why this had not occurred to him before.

He followed quietly as the three of them entered the tavern in a noisy, jostling group and took possession of a table. At the other end of the room were the big shadowy circles of barrels from which the innkeeper and his helpers drew jugs and mugs of ale. Three young women appeared from behind the head high barrels. Their bodices were loose, their shoulders were bare, and their hair casually unkempt. They teetered as they walked, their hips swiveling, breasts bobbing. How do they do that? Astreya wondered. One of them was the same brown-haired girl who had served them when Gar had been in the big chair now occupied by Damon. Astreya noticed that she was taller than he remembered; and he glanced down past her swinging skirt to see that her none-too-clean feet were in sandals that lifted her heels more than three fingers' width from the floor. She came towards him, stepping short, her wooden heels clacking, one foot in front of the other in an almost straight line, a hip dipping one way and a shoulder the other.

Noticing Astreya's scrutiny, she adopted a look of disdain. Chin raised, lips slightly parted, she ignored him and headed for Damon. Behind her flounced two more girls of roughly the same age. One of them, a plump, auburn-haired girl, slid unasked onto Nock's knee and took a drink from his ale. Astreya's eyes widened as he looked at the third, a tall, dark-eyed girl whose stomach was bare from her belt to the knot in her blouse that held her breasts in a loose bodice. She bent over Sandy, who slid his hands around her midriff and tried to undo the knot that only just restrained her breasts. The girl's laughing face was masked by Sandy's red hair as he gave her a loud kiss, which was followed by much head tossing and high pitched giggling as she alternated between tugging the knot tight and slapping at Sandy's hands. Astreya took a gulp from his tankard to cover his embarrassment, and turned towards Damon, only to find himself looking at long, tangled ringlets of hair the color of old copper, so close that they tickled his nose. Ignoring Astreya, even though she was very conscious of what she was doing, she draped an arm around Damon's shoulders and leaned over him, her hair falling so that it shadowed both his and her own face. Despite the tavern noises, Astreya could hear Damon murmuring something to her.

Astreya was embarrassed by the boldness of the girls' behavior, so unlike that of the Village gatherings where only those soon to be married sat together, and then under the eye of the elders. He took another mouthful of beer, thinking that all three girls somehow made him intensely aware of their bodies beneath their clothes in a way that perturbed him. He tried to recapture what Gar called the painter's eye, but the only way he could avoid staring open mouthed was to look into his beer mug.

Astreya suddenly felt a warm pressure against his thigh. The girl who had leaned on Damon was now sitting beside him, her leg pressing against his. Her fingers tickled along his wrist to the mug he held. Reflexively, Astreya drew away his hand. She sipped his beer and then as she put the mug down, slid her arm along his. On the other side of the table, Damon launched into a lengthy description of the relative merits of different kinds of knife. Each time Astreya's attention focused on what Damon was saying, he was distracted by slight changes in the pressure of the girl's hip against his side. When he shifted away from her, she slid closer. Then her hand was on his arm, and her breath fanned his cheek. In the same way as he had distanced himself from the knife fighting to ask himself about his mixed feelings, Astreya found himself examining both the girl and his own reaction to her. It was distracting, but not disagreeable, he decided. He reached for the frame of mind with which he sketched and drew, and deliberately noticed that the girl's fingers ended in close bitten nails. In the same analytical mood, he examined the gleam of fine downy hair on her forearms in the lamplight. He looked further, and scrutinized the way her hair had clumped and tangled around her neck. Then she slid one leg over his thigh, and he felt himself respond to her. At that moment, he realized that neither she nor he had yet said a word.

When Astreya leaned forward, half to catch what Damon said, half to edge away from the girl, she moved with him. When Astreya glanced at her, her lips parted in a smile that showed slightly uneven teeth. Her brown eyes did not alter their close, appraising stare. A similar moment plucked at Astreya's memory, and he recalled the dark-eyed shepherd girl whose fixed stare had disturbed him years before. Then, looking was everything and nothing further; now, he saw one of the girl's hands disappear below the table, and felt her fingers ran up the inside of his leg. Astreya' face reddened, and his eyebrows shot upwards, but when he looked around at the others, Damon's eyes were focused in his ale mug, and both Sandy and Nock were busy with the other two girls.

When Astreya looked at the girl whose hand had so frankly investigated his breeches, her blouse seemed both too large and too small for her. One moment, it hung away from her body as she reached across him to commandeer his mug, the next it hugged her chest when she tossed back her head to take a drink. Astreya had never been so conscious of or embarrassed by a woman's breasts.

He was grateful when Damon demanded his attention, talking about parries and thrusts, ripostes and lunges. The girl swung one shoulder around so that she was almost facing him, and Astreya found himself staring into the valley between her breasts. Blushing uncontrollably, he swallowed, found words, and spoke hesitantly.

"My name is Astreya," he said awkwardly.

"And that's our Elsie," said a loud voice behind him.

It was the walleyed taverner, bringing more ale in a fistful of slopping mugs. Astreya stood and reached into the pocket of his breeches for coin to settle his share of the score. The girl slid away, and turned to Damon with a flounce of her skirts and a swirl of tangled hair.

"You tell me he's good with a knife," she began as she curled an arm around Damon's neck, drawing him towards her as if to tell a secret. "But he's no swordsman. Have you found yourself a boy, now Damon?" she demanded loudly. "A tall, thin, black-haired mouse?"

Damon dealt her a loud slap on the thigh, pulled her to him, kissed her forcibly on the mouth, and then pushed her away so that she staggered.

"Your memory slipping, Elsie?" Damon sneered. "So many faces you've forgotten me? If you'd asked me nicely, I could have reminded you. But when you let your mouth run ahead of your brains, I can find better things to do."

The girl recovered her balance and shot him an evil look. Tossing her copper-colored hair back, she turned and walked off, swinging her hips.

"I think I'll be getting back now," said Astreya, seizing the opportunity to avoid further embarrassment.

Sandy and Nock protested that he had not finished his beer, but Damon slid both his and Astreya's mugs across the table to the two girls beside them.

"Take your time. I'll walk Astreya to his lodgings."

Astreya did not protest, even though he wanted to be alone, free of the confusion that the girl had aroused. Her insistent closeness had affected him, his body had reacted, but the more she flaunted herself, the more he had withdrawn, revolted by her brazen attempt to seduce him. Now he only wanted to walk swiftly through the early evening, leaving the experience behind him.

While they were still in the shadows of the alley, Damon took his arm, and Astreya tensed against him, breaking his stride and stepping apart. There had been a difference between Damon's gesture and the casual friendliness with which they had all entered the tavern.

"Hey, 'Streya!"

Damon stopped, and Astreya turned to look at him. Damon raised both shoulders and both hands in an elaborate shrug. Light from an upstairs window fell on his face, making deception impossible.

"Just checking, Astreya. I was wondering if you didn't like these girls, or whether you didn't like girls at all. Or preferred boys. Personally, I like girls. Highborn, rich and polished if the chance ever presents itself, but tavern dwelling and willing do me just fine."

Astreya did not answer.

"You disapprove of the girls in there, don't you? But you're not the scholar type that beds down with a book and dreams of righteousness. And I can't see you as a snob. So what's your problem?"

"I don't know... I don't know why they were so bold," said Astreya.

As they started to walk slowly side by side, Astreya's face was no longer in shadow. Damon studied his expression.

"Listen, Astreya, have you never met up with tavern girls before?"

Astreya shook his head.

"Then I suppose you really don't know," he said slowly. "You haven't done much town living, either, have you?" When Astreya said nothing, he continued. "Well, to answer your question, the girls are in it for the fun and the money. Some drinks from anyone with a full purse, a meal and some fun in a back room."

"But their parents, the elders..."

"Their parents are glad of anything the girls bring home—if they go home. The elders disapprove and look the other way. The softheaded girls imagine that they will find themselves a well heeled student foolish enough to marry them."

"Does that happen?"

"I've been here three years, and never seen it. That doesn't stop them believing, though."

"I thought the Castle kept women under lock and key. I've seen Eva only once all summer."

"That's the girls at the Castle. The green gowns don't even go into the town taverns, much less control what happens there."

Astreya was silent for several strides.

"The girls make love for money, then?" he asked.

Damon searched Astreya's face to see if he was being teased, and came to the conclusion that the question had been honestly asked.

"Yes, Astreya," he said quietly. "Have you never seen that before?"

Astreya shook his head.

"Well, it happens, and it happens so much and in so many places that I can hardly believe that you've never at least heard of it."

"Are they doing it because they want to?"

"Most of them, most of the time, I guess. Of course, it's not what you'd call a job with a lot of promise, but what is?"

"Do you approve, Damon?"

"Do I approve?" Damon made a noise midway between a laugh and a snort. "I accept. I can't change it, and I don't see why I should try."

"Couldn't they find some work that led to getting husbands and families and...."

"If they wanted to. Tell me, did any one of those three look as if she'd rather be baking bread, feeding pigs, caring for a baby? Besides, what's wrong?"

"I couldn't feel that...." Astreya paused to find words. "I couldn't feel that she was...a person. I felt that I was just a curiosity to her, and yet, there she was, so close to me. What I'm trying to say, Damon, is that I think a man and a woman should know each other, understand each other, before they..."

"Do all the girls in your Village understand the men they marry?"

"Yes. They share. Not only dances and lovemaking. Their lives are intertwined."

Damon raised his shoulders as he walked, his gown a dark shape billowing behind him.

"Must be a good place."

"It is."

"Everyone understands everyone else. Nobody hurts anyone. No ugly girls get ignored, no stupid boys get left out."

Astreya took breath to defend the Village, then thought of Yan, of Alana's separation from even her own family, of his own loneliness while he was growing up. Several strides later, he still had not replied.

"I thought so," said Damon smugly. "Nowhere's perfect. The important thing is to live in spite of the imperfections. Enjoy. Know you're alive. Kiss the girl and make the short moments happy. Ignore her bad teeth and don't think about what she'll look like in a few years."

They walked on in silence.

"Why are you a scholar, Damon?" Astreya asked as they neared the outskirts of town. "They all seem to be looking for something—I'm not sure what—but it doesn't seem to have much to do with..."

"With the way I live? Listen, Astreya. I'm a scholar because I was sent here. I didn't have a choice. My father's dead, and my uncle said, 'A few years at the Castle, or no share of your father's land.' Somehow, I don't think there'll be any land for me anyway, unless I fight him for it. So I'm putting my days at the Castle to a good use, though not the one he expected."

"My father is dead, and I didn't have much choice in coming here," said Astreya.

They each recognized that the other had memories and thoughts that he did not want questioned, and as a result, the silence they shared was companionable as they plodded along the shadowy street towards the town's edge. As they neared the Widow Amy's house, Damon stopped.

"Astreya, I think maybe I should be apologizing to you."

"For what, Damon?"

"Well, I thought you might be upset that I kind of took your girl—Eva. Truth is, she took me. I've been seeing her almost every day. I mean, you didn't seem to be interested in anything but painting, and..."

"Eva isn't my girl, Damon. We had—um—a moment, but really, she's in love with being a Healer, not with me."

"Hmm. Maybe she is. I hadn't thought of that. But I have to tell you that she's the first girl that's kept me interested for longer than it takes until the next one wanders past. You saw how I dumped Elsie back there at the tavern."

"Do you love Eva, Damon?"

"I'm—I'm tied up to her. She's got me in a spell, or something."

"You sound like the Widow Amy. How do you mean?"

"Well, she's quite the best lover I..."

"Lover?" The word popped out of Astreya's astonished mouth.

"Do I hear just a little bit of jealousy there, Astreya?"

"No," said Astreya slowly. "It's just that she said she wasn't experienced when we—when we kissed."

"You kissed her, then."

"Yes. Back at Teenmouth."

"Just kissed."

"Yes. We agreed that there was too much chance of her having a baby if we.... And she's—she's like the girls back in my Village. She doesn't..."

"Well, Astreya, she sure does now. And she's not likely to have a baby, either."

"How can you be sure? She's young and healthy and..."

"Astreya, the first thing apprentice women healers learn is where they're supposed to sleep. The second is how to get to the dining hall. The third is how not to have babies. And the fourth is not to talk about it."

"Oh."

Astreya felt that he had heard too much. He started down the darkened road again, but Damon's voice stopped him at his second stride.

"And there's another thing, Astreya. Our meeting in the marketplace wasn't exactly an accident. Before I met you, a fellow found me at the Castle, and told me you were coming. He promised me—oh, a bunch of money—if I relieved you of your purse and parchment and gave them to him. He even told me how much money was in the bag, so I couldn't cheat. So, that's why I was there with Nock and Sandy to meet a black-haired boy and a pretty girl from Teenmouth. Gar and Lindey were a complete surprise."

Astreya shook his head. "I thought we were friends," he began slowly.

"Well, Astreya, we are. I am. Or, I got that way. And if it makes you any happier, I'm really, really sorry that I was planning to steal from you. I'm ashamed of myself, and if you can't forgive me, that's fine, because if I were in your shoes, I'd not find it easy."

Damon spoke in bursts of words, quite unlike his usual confident speech. Astreya took a long deep breath. He was whipsawed back and forth between belief and doubt, trust and deception. Leaving Damon's words hanging, he asked a question.

"He knew how much was in the bag? I didn't know that. I never counted it."

"He knew," said Damon. "He wasn't leading me on."

"Who was he, for goodness sake?"

Damon's voice returned to his usual tone.

"Well, it wasn't the kind of meeting where people use their real names."

"Then what did he look like?"

"He was well built. You know, farmer-strong. And I remember he had strange eyes. I never saw anything like them before. They weren't just brown, they were really dark brown all over, like a dog's, almost no whites."

Astreya stood silent, remembering the young man who had wished him an ironic farewell.

"His name was Seth." Astreya muttered. Then words came swiftly, as one idea led to the other. "He organized the ambush. He only pretended to attack Eva. He wasn't covering up a blow; he was hiding his face because he knew I would recognize him. She knew all along. They must have worked it out together. She only pretended she was through with Seth to confuse me. What she wanted was the money to come here to the Castle. I bet her mother knew—and helped her. Judith said there were people who thought I shouldn't be the Teenmouth scholar. Of course. One in particular—Eva, who wanted it more than... more than... well, enough play me for a fool."

"Astreya, you have to believe me. I thought the fellow—Seth—would turn up and ask me for the money. But he never did."

"She must have known," said Astreya unhappily. "Everyone betrays me. Yan, Jack, Scarm, Judith, Eva. Now you."

Astreya turned from Damon and walked down the darkened road towards the Widow Amy's house.

"Hey, Astreya! Not me! I told you what happened. I didn't betray you. Oh, all right, I thought about taking advantage of you, but that was before I knew you. You can't blame me for what didn't happen."

Astreya kept walking. Damon's voice came after him in sudden anger.

"And thanks so very much for telling me my girl's a conniving little bitch, you self-righteous prig!"

Astreya increased speed, pounding his heels furiously into the road. After a few strides, he caught his toe in a rut and fell face down. He lay where he had fallen, breathing in the dust, trying to deal with what he had heard. The facts were plain: the feelings were overwhelming. He got to his feet and walked slowly to the Widow Amy's house, pushed open the back door and blinked at the single candle guttering on the kitchen table in front of where he usually sat. He had missed the evening meal, but Amy had left a cold supper for him. He picked up the cloth that covered a plate of bread, cheese, ham and greens, and dropped it back when his stomach knotted against even the sight of food. He had survived Yan's treachery, Carl's attack, the injustice of being accused of fighting, and had learned to think of them as adventures along a road to something important. Until now, his way had been confusing, but it had seemed to him something that was his and his alone. Now he knew that others had actually shaped his choices for him, and he felt that he had been played for a fool.

From the front room came the sound of Gar and the Widow Amy talking. His own name, mispronounced as usual, aroused him to concentrate on what they were saying.

"'Streya must be in love," said the Widow Amy.

Whatever Gar said in return made the Widow laugh immoderately.

Astreya flushed as he had when the tavern girl had touched him, and a confusion of emotions made him want to shout and strike something or someone. One hand on his new knife, he turned and walked swiftly out of the kitchen into the night, taking the road towards the town. In a few moments he slowed, the aftertaste of too much beer in his throat. Two houses crouched in the darkness, each with one window faintly lit. They were the cottages belonging to some of the town's poorest people, and were even smaller than the Widow Amy's. From one of them came the cry of a child, followed by a ringing slap, then whimpering before silence. Confused shouting in the distance disturbed the night as a tavern on the edge of town disgorged drunken revelers. Astreya looked up at the sky, seeking the familiar shapes of constellations he had learned from Scarm, finding some of them half lost in the northern sky, while to the south were stars he could not name. When he looked down again, his eyes had adjusted to the pale starlight and he could dimly see the road at his feet, leading towards the yellow lights of the town. He hesitated, unsure whether to go forward or back, and in that confused moment, stumbled on a lump of horse manure that in daytime he would have seen and avoided. He was wiping his boot against a tuft of grass at the edge of the road when he heard a soft footfall. Before he knew it, the knife Damon had given him was back in his hand, held low. A pale figure shimmered in the starlight.

"You learn knife fighting quickly."

Lindey's calm voice froze Astreya's churning emotions, and his mind cleared.

"I hope not," said Astreya fervently, aghast that he had drawn on her without a flicker of preliminary thought.

"Defense is necessary, Astreya," began Lindey as she stepped closer.

"It wasn't defense that I learned," said Astreya.

He suddenly asked himself whether he could maintain control when his emotions flared as they had when Gar and Lindey had saved him from Carl. And yet, as he stood in front of Lindey, a part of him was proud of his deadly talent, even eager to take revenge on those who had lied to him, and to make up for the fact that other people had been doing his fighting for him.

"The trouble is," he said slowly, "I enjoyed it."

"That's not all that's on your mind," said Lindey.

"No," agreed Astreya, but could not go on.

His Village training was that men did not talk of their inner troubles. He surmised this was true of his father, who had kept so much of his previous life from Alana that she could not even explain the notebooks he had left behind. Probably his inability to share was inherited.

"Walk with me," said Lindey.

They turned and paced the darkened road in silence, steadily moving away from the town, past the Widow Amy's house and on to where fields spread out on both sides, shadowy trees in the distance. Soon they were clear of the last smells from the crowded houses, and they breathed the cleaner air of the countryside. The sounds around them no longer were from people finding their way into and out of sleep, but came instead from the hedgerows where small creatures were going about their nightly adventures. The starlight, which had been so thin as to be barely noticeable, now drew his eyes upward. He took his direction from above, as he might have steered a ship, with the road ahead visible only at the edge of seeing. Step by step, Astreya silenced his troubled inner voices, leaving them trodden into the road.

Eventually, after Astreya had been striding faster and faster for some time, Lindey stopped and leaned on her staff. Astreya missed her presence beside him, stopped and turned to look at her where she stood, almost invisible in the starlight.

"We could go on," she said. "But we lack a destination."

Unexpectedly, Astreya laughed.

"Lindey, you are so practical," he said. "Where did you learn to take life so... so..."

"Reasonably?" she asked. "I learned that fear comes from not understanding, and that there really is nothing that can't be understood if you take the trouble to think about it."

"It sounds as if you didn't have much laughter around you while you were growing up."

"You're wrong. It was after I left that I seemed to lose the knack of laughing."

"There's a lot in the world that isn't funny at all," said Astreya. Her hair streaked with starlight as she nodded. "Why did you leave your home?" he asked.

"It's necessary. There aren't enough men in Matris. If a woman wants a husband, or at least a baby, she has to go looking."

"What do you mean?"

"Matris is small. I couldn't marry anyone there because I'm related to the few of them that are even roughly the right age. The elders agreed that I should leave."

"That's awful," said Astreya, a wave of dark incomprehension again sweeping over him.

"No, it's reasonable. Besides, I've been lucky. I found Gar, and learned a lot more than if I'd just found the first man who looked healthy and made a baby. Fortunately, I had more sense than that." She paused, and pointed towards a fallen tree near the road. "Let's sit for a moment. Tell me about your Village, Astreya."

They left the road and sat side by side on the tree trunk, looking up at stars that dimly lit their faces.

Damon's ironic probing of the claim that the Village was a uniformly happy place stuck like a burr in Astreya's mind, and he talked about the hardships of Village life, of the men who did not come back from the fishing grounds. Hesitantly at first, and then increasingly easily, he talked about his own loneliness and the father he had never known. He tried to explain how he and

Alana had become increasingly remote. Before he knew it, Astreya was speaking about how he felt about Yan's treachery, Eva's father's trickery, the girls in the tavern, Damon's revelation, and Eva's duplicity.

Because he talked about feelings rather than facts, what he said was often disjointed and confused, but through it all, Lindey did not interrupt as he wrestled with contradictions that made him feel both lucky and unlucky, doomed and yet somehow chosen for he did not know what. They sat side by side, the road a dark ribbon running away from them in the starlight. Then Lindey turned and put her arms around Astreya. One hand tilted his head down the slight amount needed, and she kissed him, her lips warm and soft. Sudden delight caught Astreya unaware, and he made a small sound of surprise.

"Do you think me bold?" Lindey asked, her arms still around him.

It was the same word Astreya had used to describe the tavern girl, and unwanted memories flowed back.

"Girls in your Village don't kiss boys, do they? They wait until they are kissed. Well, I'm not like that. Does it bother you?"

Astreya's arms slid around Lindey, drawing her closer. Her hair smelled of the fields through which they had been walking, and her breath was warm on his cheek.

"No," he answered, and they both moved still closer. "I like it."

"Oh good," said Lindey, "because I'll never learn to simper and pretend."

She kissed him again. This time Astreya responded, and for both of them there was nothing but their kiss. He felt Lindey's breasts pressing against him, her hand in his hair, her lips moving against his. Eventually, she sighed, drew back and picked up her staff.

"We're going back now," she said. "Logs aren't comfortable, and the ground's wet."

Astreya stood up, drew her to him, and they kissed for a time that neither of them cared to count.

"Practical," he chuckled.

He looked down into her face and saw a tranquil smile he had never seen before.

"I would like to draw you as you are now," he said, tracing his finger across her face and into her hair.

"You can't see me, that's why."

"I see you perfectly."

"Nobody would recognize me."

"I would."

They walked back to the Widow Amy's house hand in hand, stopping occasionally to kiss again. Neither of them noticed that their return took much longer than their outward journey. When they reached the house, they paused on the doorstep to kiss once more.

"This isn't how it ends," Lindey whispered. "Be very quiet on the way in, and...."

They were suddenly nearly pitched to the ground as the door was jerked open and the end of a broomstick thrust out.

"All right, you lubbers," snarled Gar's voice. "There are six more of us inside."

Astreya's hand found his knife at the same moment that Lindey's staff struck the broomstick, knocking it to the ground.

"No there aren't, Gar," said Lindey.

The door swung open.

"Well, I'll be pounded flat," he said, his voice softened. "If it isn't the returning innocents. Get in here quickly. We have planning to do. Eva just woke us out of our well earned rest with uncomfortable news. Carl has decided to pay you a visit tomorrow, Astreya, and we have to work out a way of keeping you alive."

CHAPTER 16:

IN WHICH THE HALL BURNS DOWN

Gar hustled Astreya and Lindey into the kitchen, where a candle in the middle of the table dimly lit two figures, one large, one small. The smaller of the two stood up as they entered.

"Eva!" exclaimed Astreya.

"I thought women aren't allowed out of the Castle," said Lindey.

"I climbed the wall," said Eva. "Alone."

She was at the same time amazed at her own daring and proud of the accomplishment.

Lindey's left eyebrow rose. "Well done, Eva," she said.

"Carl's got your notebook, 'Streya," said Eva. "He's been to the Learneds, and convinced them that you're up to witchcraft maybe, or what they call 'unauthorized studies,' and, if anything, that's worse. One of the women Healers was there, and she told another, who told me, and...."

"My notebook?" asked Astreya, feeling in the pocket of his tunic. "It's right here."

He pulled out the little pouch he had made, and plucked at its drawstrings. Then he frowned as he withdrew wadded up paper folded to the shape and thickness of the book that should have been there. "I left my tunic hanging on the scaffold when I.... They must have come into the hall and stolen it," he concluded lamely.

"Just what was in that book, Astreya?" asked Gar. "Since what you've got there obviously isn't it."

"I don't know," said Astreya. "It was my father's, and I have to find out what it all means. But the Learneds didn't seem exactly the right people to ask."

"Good decision," said Gar. "But what?"

"Mostly it was drawings of boats, and names. Family names. Some of them from the Village, but some that I didn't understand. And a strange poem that didn't rhyme, and made no sense that I could see. The rest of the book was in code: numbers, letters, and little symbols I couldn't read. I thought maybe I'd meet someone who'd be in the book, and then I'd know that my father had been there, and I could find out more about him, and what could be the meaning of the little circles, crosses and numbers beside the names."

Gar wetted a finger and outlined a circle with a cross in it, then two short lines side by side, then an arrowhead on the candlelit tabletop. Astreya leaned on the table to watch him.

"Anything like these?" he asked.

"How did you know?" asked Astreya. "Did you....?"

"No, Astreya. I didn't go through your pockets. I just guessed. Your face, your name, and that clasp on your arm all helped. But I just couldn't believe that you are who you are."

Astreya's right hand reached to cover his bracelet, which tingled against his skin. The Widow Amy, who had been hovering in the shadows near her stove, came into the circle of light with her lips tightly pursed between her round cheeks.

"Have ye brought some anathema on me and my house?" she demanded of Astreya. "And you, Gar. Have you been consorting with some young warlock?"

Before either could protest, she snatched Astreya's hand and pried his fingers open. From within her voluminous skirts she pulled out a small white flower with star-shaped petals, and placed it in his palm. Holding his wrist tightly, she bent over and sniffed cautiously. Then she looked deeply into Astreya's eyes as she folded his fingers tightly around the flower.

"Does it burn, 'Streya? Is your flesh burning?"

Astreya said nothing as he stared at the change in the Widow Amy. Her eyes narrowed above her full cheeks. Her dimpled face was transformed by the strength of her concentration. She unwrapped his fingers and looked carefully at the crushed flower. Her ample bosom heaved in a great sigh of relief and she stood on tiptoe to kiss Astreya's cheek, her many chins quivering.

"I had to know for certain, 'Streya," she murmured.

"And what was all that about, Amy?" asked Gar.

"He's no warlock, and there's no evil in him," said the Widow Amy. "Forgive me for doubting, but I had to make sure."

"Well, I'm glad that's settled," said Gar, one corner of his mouth twitching. "Now we can get back to what those Learneds might think, since they lack Amy's... um... infallible test. They won't understand your father's book, Astreya, and that makes me worried. Their ignorance wouldn't trouble me for a moment, save for the fact that what they don't comprehend, they hate and fear. They'll be after you."

"Not just 'Streya," said Eva. "All of you."

"How do you know all this, Eva?" Lindey asked.

"It wasn't rumors. It was Flip—he's one of Carl's followers. He saw me today, and he taunted me. He said that next time they would have you, 'Streya, right where they wanted. And Gar and Lindey, too. And then he said he wouldn't get me involved if I... um... you know."

"Bestowed gross and physical favors upon him," said Gar with relish.

Lindey gave him one of her direct blue-eyed stares, and his half smile vanished.

"It must have been very frightening for you, my dear," he said to Eva.

"It made me angry," said Eva. "I won't be used as anyone's plaything."

Gar smiled again, this time without irony. "Good for you," he said firmly. "So you climbed the wall and came to tell us. Good for you."

"I'll leave," said Astreya. "I'll meet with Carl first, and get the book back."

"Don't disappoint me with such startlingly foolish talk," said Gar firmly. "You've been intelligent so far, but that course of action would get us all into more trouble than we can handle, and what's more, you will probably end up dead in a knife fight. You want to undo what's done, and that's wishful thinking. You... we... have to move on. It's time for a moonlit walk. Lindey and I have done it before, and I had considerable practice before she met me. First off, I must get a few of my things from the Castle. If we're lucky, and the Learneds take their usual time to make up their minds, we should be miles away when they decide what they should do next."

"But the painting..." said Astreya.

"The painting is only a painting. This is a matter of staying alive," said Gar. "Besides, you and I have a lot of talking to do, Astreya, about things that are more important than my little jokes on those green-gowned simpletons. I'd like to see your little book, for a start. There's a lot I should've told you, but we were having so much fun climbing scaffolds and getting all painty."

A knock at the door startled them all.

"I didn't think they would move this quickly," said Gar softly as he picked up a bolt of stove wood and went to the door. "Still, I've been wrong before. Be prepared to douse that candle mighty quick if I shout."

The kitchen door creaked open a hand span and Gar peered out, the stick of wood held behind his back, and one foot blocking the door from opening any farther.

"Hey, uncle, let me in. It's me, Damon. I'm alone."

Muttering, Gar opened the door and pulled Damon inside.

"Welcome to the party," he said. "What brings you a-visiting?"

"You're in danger, Gar. You and Lindey, and especially Astreya. Carl stirred up the Learneds, and...."

"They know," said Eva. "I told them."

"You!" said Damon. "You climbed the wall?"

"I didn't fly," said Eva with asperity.

"Did you suddenly get a conscience about what you did to Astreya?"

"What I did to Astreya?"

"You know, having that Teenmouth fellow Seth try to get me to steal the purse with the scholar's money. You wanted it, didn't you? And then Astreya gave to you. I bet you were really surprised when he put it in your hand."

Even in the dim light of the candles, Astreya could see that Eva's face had reddened, but she still held her small chin up.

"I was surprised, yes. But I had nothing to do with Seth. It was the elders. They put up the money, but my father saw a chance to get it back, for him."

"Later for that," Gar interrupted. "It's fascinating, but right this moment, it's not productive. Our first task, as I keep saying, is to stay both alive and free. Fortunately, Lindey and I have some experience in the art of strategic withdrawal, so..."

Astreya was still trying to decide whether to believe Eva. "So it wasn't your idea," he began, gradually becoming aware that he had condemned her unfairly. "Eva, Damon, I'm really sorry that I..."

"It was my father," said Eva. "He got me to send you on your way, so that he could have you robbed. I was the bait. And the reward. Seth told me while you three were fighting. I told him to go back and say it was lost, or spent, or whatever."

Astreya nodded slowly.

"Your mother warned me, sort of. She said there were people who would like to see the whole Teenmouth scholar business undone and done differently."

"Will you all listen?" Gar demanded urgently. "It would be a good idea if Damon and Eva left now, before they hear any more. What you don't know, you don't have to lie about after we've gone."

"That's right," said Astreya. "Especially after what I said about...."

"Hey, now, Astreya, Gar," said Damon. "And miss all the fun? Besides, you need someone along who can use a knife for more than carving roast beef. What about you, Eva? You came to help, didn't you?"

Eva looked down at the table, the candlelight glinting on her swaying pigtails.

"Eva's part in this is over," said Gar. "She's warned us, and she needs to get back before she's missed. We haven't the right to ask her to give up all she's found at the Castle."

Eva's eyes came up and found Gar's gratefully. She turned to Astreya.

"Is that so terrible, 'Streya? Can you understand?"

Astreya nodded slowly. He was still castigating himself for leaving his father's book where it could be stolen, and he was amazed that Gar, Lindey and Damon seemed willing to help him get it back.

"You got me here," said Eva. "I'll always be grateful," she added almost inaudibly.

Astreya felt he should say something, but could not decide what.

"This is very touching," said Gar. "But it's also wasting time. If you really want to help, Damon, you'd better show us all how to climb that foolish wall. I'm not leaving without some of my gear, and I think if each of the four of us takes a load, I can live without the rest." He tightened his belt. "Amy, can you get Nora between the shafts of that wagon of mine?"

"Gar, I have a foretelling, but I don't know if I should..."

"Then don't, Amy. Foretellings that make you nervous shouldn't be shared. They only make everyone else nervous, too. And I have a strong feeling that everything's going to be wonderful, if you can get Nora ready to go. Can you do it with only one candle for light, m'dear?"

The Widow Amy nodded as she dabbed at the moist folds and creases around her eyes.

"I can do it in the dark," she whispered as she let herself out of the kitchen door.

"I believe it," said Gar. "She has uncanny abilities in the dark. Fortunately, however, the moon is rising. Now then, everybody, make sure that no white shirttails or petticoats are showing, and if you stub your toes, keep it to yourself. Silence and shadow are our friends. What's more, we have someone who knows the way. You lead, Damon."

Damon's face was barely visible in the candlelight, but Astreya saw his chin rise and knew that the responsibility was eagerly accepted.

"Right," said Damon, and swallowed once to contain his enthusiasm. "First, we blow out the candle, then we open the door. You won't see much at first, but your eyes will adjust to the moonlight, and then you'll all be fine. Watch my hands. I know the green gown I'm wearing makes me almost invisible. If you...."

"Good thinking, Damon," said Gar to cut short the unnecessary lecture. "We're with you," he added, as he blew out the candle.

The door creaked open, and five figures crept into the darkness, Damon in the lead, Eva close beside him. Astreya saw their heads bend together for a moment, and guessed that they had exchanged a quick kiss. Lindey passed him like a shadow, and then Gar, who was bringing up the rear, gave him a little shove.

"Leave whatever you're thinking alone for now, Astreya," whispered Gar. "We'll straighten it out later. Right now, you need to concentrate."

Astreya took a deep breath and followed Damon, who led them from shadow to shadow, first across the field to the Castle wall, and then along it southwards. When they had crossed three fields and climbed two low fences in comparative silence, Damon pointed out a deep ditch in which flowed a small stream that left the wall through a culvert.

"That's the wet and messy route," he said quietly. "We'll take the high and dry one. First, we jump the stream."

So saying, he ran and leaped, his gown flapping behind him. One by one, the others followed him, their task made possible by the fact that, as Damon had said, their eyes were now accustomed to the light of the rising moon.

"I'll be pounded flat," said Gar to himself as he prepared to leap the ditch. "I swear I can see a road, crossing this very stream by a bridge." He ran, jumped, landed awkwardly, and continued his grumble. "The lad's determined to make life as difficult as possible."

Once across the next field, Damon turned right and led them away from the flint-capped wall that was a black shadow on their left. Rough sawn boards of a head high fence halted them. A few stumbling paces, and they were feeling the side of a low shed that leaned against the fence. The creaky structure's roof was scarcely chest high.

"Up here," said Damon, as he climbed onto the roof of the shed.

"This isn't the way I came," said Eva.

"And it isn't the way anyone watches, either," whispered Damon. "They don't care how people climb out. They wait and grab you on your way back in. But they won't catch us. We go along the other side of this fence. There's a beam you can't see from this side. Hang onto the top of the fence, and shuffle along the beam towards the wall. When you get there, sit on it, and wait for me. Stay in the shadow of the big tree that's on the other side."

"Where are you going?" whispered Lindey.

"Don't fuss, I'll be right behind you."

"I don't fuss, I merely want to know what we're doing," said Lindey, a trifle louder.

"Come on," said Eva. "Damon hasn't time to explain."

"He's having too much fun being mysterious," said Lindey.

Damon disappeared into the night at a speed designed to impress his followers, who were too busy following his instructions to notice. First Gar, then Eva and Lindey and finally Astreya climbed onto the roof of the shed, over the top of the fence, and then edged along it with their feet on a crossbar about half way up the other side, which gained height as it went. Now that the moon had risen, they could see the fields they had crossed and outlying houses of the town behind, but the fence shadowed them from the neck down.

"With our heads in the moonlight like ducks in a row," muttered Lindey.

Gar reached the wall first. The top of his bald head glinting in the moonlight, he cursed Damon's enthusiasm under his breath.

"How does the lad think we're going to get onto the wall without getting cut to shreds? And what in the name of a four-eyed flounder does he expect us to do when we get there? This is no time for a pier-head leap."

"I think I can see lumps on the wall that are like steps," whispered Astreya.

"And hand holds at the top, too," said Lindey.

Still muttering, Gar felt in the darkness and found they were right. He was briefly outlined against moon-bright sky, and then his body was a hump on top of the wall.

"Not as bad as I thought," he muttered. "Someone's broken off the flints. Come aloft."

Moments later, Gar, Lindey, Eva and Astreya were sitting on the wall, their feet dangling over an unguessable drop into the shadows. Ahead of them, inside the wall, was a pine tree, its branches sawn short to put them out of reach from the wall. Damon was nowhere to be seen.

The night darkened as fast moving patches of cloud drifted across the moon. Astreya heard a faint creaking from the fence and turned to see Damon behind him. A gleam of moonlight momentarily lit the end of a plank wavering dangerously close to Astreya's head.

"Duck," Damon whispered.

They crouched as Damon slid the plank onto the top of the wall, and then extended it towards the tree. Astreya shifted closer to help, but Damon hissed him back.

"It's all a matter of balance," he said.

The end of the plank wandered from side to side as it disappeared into the deep shadow of the pine tree with a soft thud.

"Got it," said Damon. "Now, we cross to the tree, and then going down's as easy as climbing a ladder."

He clambered up to kneel on top of the wall, tested the plank cautiously, and then started across on hands and knees. Halfway across, he gestured for the others to follow. Astreya moved first, crossing in a crouch, his fingers feeling ahead of him along the edges of the board. Behind him on top of the wall, Lindey and Eva conferred quietly about the difficulties posed by their skirts. Overhearing them, Gar started to mutter once more, his words audible to Astreya, who was now invisible against the broad trunk of the pine tree.

"Here we sit like gulls on the cross trees, while the lad plays the hero. Silly codfish hasn't thought that the lasses don't wear breeks."

Astreya, one hand sticky with pine gum, started down the tree. Half of his mind worried with Gar, but beyond this was another feeling that he was discovering something significant that had nothing to do with painting or the task ahead of them. He could hear a change in Gar's voice, as if a different person was emerging from behind a carefully constructed mask.

"We can manage," said Lindey softly.

As Astreya followed Damon into the darkness of the branches, Eva swung one leg over the plank, clambered onto it and started to crawl. Lindey got to her knees on the top of the wall, hiked her skirts up and tucked them into her waistband.

"Great smoking rope ends," said Gar distinctly.

Astreya peered through the pine branches at the narrow plank from wall to tree just as the moon shone through a gap in the clouds, and he saw what had provoked Gar's exclamation: her staff held crosswise for balance, Lindey walked across the board as if it were a path. Astreya heard a quick indrawn breath from the other side of the tree trunk, and knew that Damon had also been impressed.

"You can be very sure I'm not going to try that," muttered Gar. "I'm much too old to dance and skylark along a yardarm."

When he saw that Gar was crawling carefully across on hands and knees, Astreya climbed downwards. As Damon had said, the sawn off stubs of branches were as regular as a ladder, though much thicker and rougher. "Easier than a mast," said Astreya to himself, and as he heard his own words, became aware that Gar's speech was growing increasingly sailor-like.

"Are you all right, Astreya?" asked Gar's voice softly from darkness higher up the other side of the tree. "Damon's so excited he's rowing with only one oar in the water."

Despite the seriousness of the situation, Astreya grinned. "Time you took command again, skipper," he said.

"Just as soon as we're back on the deck, you can bet I will," growled Gar.

There were more rustling noises in the night as five pairs of feet and hands felt for safe holds on the branches, garments got caught on the rough bark, and more than one set of fingers were trodden on by the person above. Eventually they were all on the ground, huddled around the base of the tree. Damon arrived last, having shoved the plank back over the wall before climbing down.

"Now which way?" asked Lindey, who seemed least affected by the crossing and climb.

Damon pointed across the Castle grounds between the trees to a dimly lit window.

"That's where Eva's going," he said.

"And I'll have to run, because they won't keep that light on much longer."

In the darkness, first Lindey and then Gar found Eva's hands in a quick farewell. A moment later, Astreya felt her tug his head down towards her face.

"Truly, 'Streya. I didn't try to steal the money. Don't forget. Whatever happens. I mean, I'm sorry, but I have to get back. Otherwise it'll all be wasted."

Astreya searched for something to say, and the echo of both their mothers' words came back to him. "We each have our road to walk," he whispered, his lips close to her hair.

"You do understand!" she said loudly. With a quick squeeze to his hands, Eva turned and ran towards the lighted window.

"She'll be seen in the moonlight," said Damon.

"What moonlight?" asked Gar. "There's cloud thickening overhead. I suppose we must be grateful it didn't happen while we were climbing up and down walls and trees. Anyway, Damon, we're glad you got us here. Now if we could see the hall, we'd be on our way."

"There, there," said Damon, pointing urgently.

A patch of moonlight scudded across the Castle grounds and briefly lit waving grasses and trees bent before the rising wind. For one brief moment, it shone on the hall. It was the farthest building, almost out of sight. They had no sooner glimpsed its dome, when the patch of cold light traveled across the grass into the distance, and was gone. The candle set in the window for Eva winked out.

"Now we can't see a thing, and there's no path," said Lindey. "How are we supposed to walk a straight line in the dark?"

"We'll have to chance a light," said Damon. "I have flint and steel, and...."

"Put it away, Damon," said Gar. "Now's not the time to tell people where we are. Besides, it wouldn't help us much anyway." He turned to Astreya. "Roll up your sleeve and let's see your clasp... er ... bracelet."

"What in the world for?" Lindey asked.

"You're in for a surprise, Lindey," said Gar. "Come on, Astreya, do it."

Astreya turned back the sleeve of his tunic. In the darkness, a green light shone from his arm, and a white spear of light was at its heart.

"It's never done that before," said Astreya. "I mean, not so bright."

"Either there's a mother ship in range, or you're a powerful wielder," said Gar, and before anyone could ask what he meant, he took Damon by his cloak and pulled him to stand beside Astreya.

"Point to where we last saw the hall, Damon. Hold out your arm so Astreya can feel where we have to go. Right. Now Astreya, think north."

"Think north," repeated Damon. "Whatever do you mean?"

"Stow it, Damon. Astreya understands."

Astreya looked down at the glowing green stone, Gar's words still in his ears. The spear of light started to waver and turn, pivoting at its center. Astreya shook his head in amazement, and the light dimmed.

"You had it, Astreya," said Gar. "Concentrate!"

Again, Astreya looked down at his arm almost as if it belonged to someone else, and the light in the stone grew brighter until the greenish glow gleamed in its bright metal cage, and lit the little hairs on his arm. The spear of white slowly revolved, and then pointed steadily.

"Swing your arm around," commanded Gar.

Astreya did so. The spear of light continued to point in the same direction, no matter how he moved.

"Power," said Damon in a shaking voice. "M - m - mysterious forces that...."

"Don't talk nonsense, Damon," said Gar. "The stone is nothing magical."

"It's witchcraft." Damon's voice rose in fear.

"Listen, Damon," said Gar. "You know those tiny lightnings you sometimes see on a cold dry night when you pull a woolen tunic over your head? The stone feeds on even smaller lightnings we all have in our bodies—and that some of us can control."

As Gar spoke, Damon shuddered, his cloak flapping against Astreya in the dark. But his objections ceased.

"Good. Now, put your hand on his shoulder, Damon. Lindey and I will hold onto your cloak. Astreya, point the light in the direction Damon showed you, hold it there, and lead us to the hall."

Astreya grasped Gar's meaning, and as he wondered whether he could do it, saw that the spear of light had swung around and now pointed to where they were going. His questions vanished as he felt himself in control, and he began to lead the way through the darkness. The distance across the grounds would have been nothing to worry about by daylight, but at night each slight hummock and curve of the rough trimmed field they crossed was an opportunity for them to lose their way, as was every tree or bush that loomed suddenly ahead of them. Using the steadily pointing spear of light to maintain his direction, Astreya was able to work his way around the obstacles, confident that he would still know his course after each minor detour.

He divided his attention between the light on his arm, and the darkness ahead. When he looked ahead to avoid an obstacle, he had to put a hand over the bracelet to stop its green and white glow from blinding him. As he walked, he saw a picture in his mind's eye of the four of them crossing the darkened field. He was aware of Damon's hand on his shoulder, and could hear footsteps rustling in the grass behind him, but these were only at the edge of his awareness. At the center of his concentration was the bracelet, but he held all that he was seeing, hearing and feeling in a delicate balance, as if he were carrying water cupped in the palms of his hands.

After he had counted several hundred footsteps, he began to worry lest he had misjudged, and they were now walking past the hall. Suddenly his foot struck something solid and his shoulder rasped against a wall. Greenish light from his bracelet illuminated stones and masonry as he lowered his arm. Damon staggered to a stop, as he, too, bumped into the wall.

"We're here," said Gar, reaching out to touch the uneven surface.

Astreya pulled his sleeve down over his bracelet, and felt the tingling diminish. Even though the light no longer led the way, his confidence did not ebb, and he continued to lead the others along the edge of the wall until they reached the main door.

"Locked," said Astreya, testing the handle.

"Let me at it," said Gar. "Locks only keep honest men honest."

Astreya moved aside as Gar crouched over the keyhole. Soft scraping noises were followed by a loud click, and then the big door swung open. Gar stepped inside.

"Come on in," he said. "Now we'll chance some light, I think. There's a candle or two with the rest of the gear, if we can get across the hall without crashing into too many things on the way."

Astreya was about to unwrap his bracelet again, when he felt a hand on his arm.

"My turn, Astreya," said Lindey. "The old fashioned way, by feel. Follow me close, and bring Damon with you."

Astreya stretched out his hand, felt Lindey's smooth hair, and let his fingers slide down to her back. He tugged at Damon's cloak with his other hand, and they started towards the collection of painting equipment, Lindey leading, her staff tapping ahead of her, like a blind man. She found her way past the rows of books and on to the table where she mixed her paints. Astreya heard her hand feeling about on the table, and at the same time, Damon struck a fire lighter. A glow appeared in his cupped hands and then lit his face. Lindey held a candle for him, and then passed the flame on to a brassbound lantern. The part of the hall where they had worked became dimly visible. Boxes, bags, the scaffolding on which they had climbed were all patched with dark shadows. The images they had drawn and painted came and went in and out of the shadows, almost as if they were alive.

"Brushes, knives and pigments first," said Gar. "After that, the smaller jars of unmixed paint. Leave the turps, the washes, rags, charcoal—anything we can replace. Let's get it all into those four boxes that fit into the wagon."

Damon stood and watched as the three of them started to collect up tools and paints. Once he had almost filled one box, and had joined Lindey in contributing to a second, Astreya stood and looked upwards.

"What was it going to look like, Gar?" asked Astreya. "Everything's there but the center. Why don't you stay and finish it?"

Gar spoke from above him on the scaffold, where he had climbed in search of brushes and knives.

"Not without you, Astreya. Even if the Learneds didn't want my scruffy neck with which to purge their shattering ignorance, I couldn't go on without you. It was you who gave me the idea."

"I did?" asked Astreya incredulously.

"You, Astreya. You admired my painting of Chatters the squirrel. That got me started. That's why you've been painting animals, birds, and plants all around the edges. But you gave me the center as well, when you noticed the Learneds walking about with their eyes on the ground. That's what I was going to put in the middle: a gaggle of foolish Learneds, staring at their own toes, ignoring the wonder around them. It was my idea of a joke, Astreya. I wanted to insult the green-gowned ignoramuses, and even have them like it. Oh well. Perhaps you and I can use the idea somewhere else."

Damon's voice came from the shadows. "These boxes look waterproof. Are they?"

"Yes," said Lindey.

"I could pull them through the wet way, and save a lot of time. And we'd be able to carry more than we'd be able to get over the wall, too. We could drive the wagon quite close."

At that moment, fitful moonlight shone through the windows, competing with the lantern.

"Good idea, Damon," said Gar. "Take a couple of them and go now while you can see. You, too, Lindey and Astreya. I'll be right behind you. There's a couple of good brushes up there on the scaffold that I refuse to leave behind."

The scaffold squeaked and groaned in the darkness as Gar climbed. Damon shuffled to the door carrying two boxes, while Astreya and Lindey packed the last two. Because there was so much that they would have to abandon, they each checked the floor along the recently painted wall for anything that might be essential. His hand on the inner of the two doors, Astreya paused.

"Lindey, did you find the...."

His hesitation saved him. A blow aimed at his head fell across his shoulders, sending him sprawling to the floor. He rolled, twisted and turned in time to see three small lanterns swinging back and forth as Carl and his henchmen emerged from behind the bookshelves where they had been hiding, their lights concealed by their cloaks. As they advanced, Astreya saw Lindey's hair gleam. Above her head were Carl's distinctive black eyebrows, and a knife glittered at her throat. Lindey squirmed in Carl's grasp, but the knife stayed in position. She gasped as a hot lantern burned her arm.

"Right, who or whatever you are," said Carl. "Come out here, all of you, or I'll set fire to this witch's clothes and then slit her throat. Come on out, keeping your hands where we can see them."

The other two lanterns came closer as Carl's henchmen closed in.

"No girls to fight for you this time, eh, stranger?" Carl taunted.

"Let her go," said Astreya. "You can fight me if you like, but let her go."

"And get cracked on the skull by her staff? Oh no. We'll tie her up and then I'll do you. Don't move if you want her to stay alive—long enough to see you dead."

Astreya stood. In the patchwork of light from the lanterns, he glimpsed hands, belts, knives, swaying green cloaks. Huge shadows slid across the walls as two figures moved towards Lindey. Her face was invisible, but her hair still gleamed in the light from Carl's lantern. Astreya knew that though Lindey was held, she was by no means helpless, and he waited for a moment when they both could move. He was aware that Gar was still on the scaffold, and that Damon was somewhere in the dark.

Astreya felt the bracelet on his arm tingle, and he subtly relaxed. Time began to slow. Shadows crawled across the walls, and the three men near Lindey seemed to move sluggishly. A hand put one of the lanterns on the floor. Another hand holding a rope reached towards Lindey's wrists. Her hair shimmered as she jerked her head up, and someone swore as his hands touched hot metal. Something fell through the air, and a lantern toppled onto its side, briefly lighting Damon's knife as he slashed at one of Lindey's captors, who twisted away, letting go as he did so.

Astreya took a quick step forward. His right foot sent the lantern on the floor twirling into the shadows. Another step and his head rammed into the stomach of Carl's helper, who staggered backwards, gulping for air. Astreya glimpsed Carl's knife as it swung away from Lindey and towards him. He clutched at the wrist that held it, caught a handful of gown instead, and yanked downwards. His attack loosened Carl's hold on Lindey. She stepped behind Carl, tangled a hand in his hair and wrenched his head back. Then Astreya lost his grip on Carl as both his arms were pinned to his sides, and two hands locked on his chest. Carl still held his knife.

"Got him, Carl," grunted a rough voice.

Astreya heard the quick words as if they had been drawled. He jerked his chin upwards and the back of his head hit something soft. Swirling one leg behind him, he hooked his foot around his captor's leg, pulled and crouched. The hands around his chest let go as the man staggered forwards, falling over Astreya, who tucked and tumbled onto one shoulder. An upward driven knife blade flashed in what light remained. Someone screamed in mingled pain and disbelief.

"Lindey?" Astreya shouted as he rolled clear and back onto his feet in the shadows below a bookcase. At the same moment, he heard Lindey's voice yell his own name back: "Astreya?" The last remaining lantern threw a patch of light on a doubled over, green-cloaked body. Carl had stabbed his own partner, and now stood shocked, the bloody knife in his hand. Astreya took a quick step and grabbed Carl's knife wrist with both hands. Now that he knew where the knife was, he forced it upwards with all his strength, throwing Carl off balance. They fell to the floor in a tangle of arms and legs, and thrashed about indecisively in the dark. Carl was undoubtedly the stronger, but Astreya had more to lose by letting go of his wrist, and neither could gain an advantage.

And then it was dark no longer. A tongue of flame licked out from one of the fallen lanterns, and fire slid in a blue trail across the floor to a half-empty jar of turpentine, where it paused, reduced to smoke. Then yellow flames erupted from the pot and leaped up to a handful of rags tucked in a crosspiece of the scaffold. The rags flickered and smoked, then burst into a gout of flame that rose to the first level of staging, where it found more rags and pots of paint, which burned blue, green and orange. A fireball swirled up the freshly painted wall to the dome; blazing liquid fell in drips and streams onto still more paint pots on the floor below. The expanding fire made its own windstorm: it sucked rags and papers up, twirled them around and threw them into the rising flames. Shadow and light writhed together on the walls, and hot air seared every throat. Flames reached up towards the dome, reddening the smoke that coiled up and around the hall.

Astreya's back was on the floor and both of his hands held the knife above him, silhouetted against the leaping flames. Carl's free hand clutched at Astreya's face. A finger pulled his mouth sideways. He bit it. He glimpsed Lindey's staff arcing downwards like a pale fan, but Carl saw it in time and rolled onto one shoulder. Lindey's blow missed, but now Astreya was on top. He lunged forward, crushing his chest into Carl's face, using his weight to force the knife to the floor over Carl's head. He hammered Carl's knuckles on the floor. Carl's other first pounded at Astreya's ribs.

Astreya slammed Carl's hand on the floor again, and felt blood-slippery fingers loosen. One more blow, and the knife skittered towards a pool of burning paint. Astreya and Carl reached for it at the same moment. Both shoulder rolled and snatched, but Astreya was a shade quicker. They came to their feet facing each other in the fighter's crouch, but Astreya held the knife. Damon was to Astreya's left, his knife a menace.

"Give up, Carl," said Astreya. "I've got your knife, and you can't take both of us."

Carl glanced from one blade to the other as the flames turned them to red tongues of glinting steel.

"That's it. I've had enough," he gasped.

Gar's voice came from above.

"The book, Astreya! Get your book!"

Astreya held out his left hand. Carl fumbled in an inner pocket of his gown, pulled out the book and threw it at Astreya, hoping to distract him. Instead, Astreya picked the missile out of the air, and thrust it into his pocket. Grunting a curse, Carl turned and charged for the door, his cloak casting grotesque shadows towards the open door.

"Astreya! Lindey! Pile up some of the soft stuff," shouted Gar from above. "I've got to jump."

They looked up to see Gar silhouetted against flames. Below him, paint pots belched flame, and fire ran along the ropes that secured every crosspiece of the scaffold. Wood twisted and creaked as Gar clutched at a stanchion. He burned his fingers on the smoking wood and let go, cursing. Two pieces of scaffolding, their lashings burned through, swung downwards, spilling fireball paint pots. The whole structure swayed away from the walls towards the space in the center of the hall.

"Too late!" he shouted. "I'll try for a bookcase."

For a moment, it looked as if Gar would make it. He launched outwards, his hands spread to clutch at the stack of shelves. But as he jumped, the scaffold crumpled behind him. Gar seemed to hang in the air before he fell into the burning wreckage.

Lindey was first to reach him, flapping at the fire with her skirt. Astreya and Damon helped her pull away the burning beams. Together, they half dragged, half carried Gar clear of the scaffold and toppled bookcases. As they bent over him, two doubled-over figures limped slowly past them, heading painfully towards the door.

"They're getting away," said Damon.

"Let them," said Astreya. "We've got to get out of here. The whole building will go up in a moment."

"He's alive," said Lindey, crouched over Gar's face. "We have to get him out of here."

Acrid smoke caught at the back of their throats. Astreya looked for something on which to carry Gar.

"Grab their cloaks, Damon!" he shouted as he ran after the two slowly fleeing men.

Astreya pulled the cloak from the first, who was still staggering from Lindey's blow to his head. Damon tugged green material from the other, whose bloody hands clutched a gash across his stomach. Astreya, Lindey and Damon paid the two fugitives no further attention. Astreya stripped off his tunic, snatched up an unburned length of scaffold and thrust it through one armhole. Grasping his idea, Lindey pushed her staff through the other arm. Damon struggled out of his tunic as well, and together they slid Gar onto their improvised stretcher.

"Put on their gowns," Astreya coughed.

Astreya struggled into one, and Damon tossed the other to Lindey. She shrugged it onto her shoulders and then held its wide sleeves over Gar's head to protect him from the hot ash that swirled around the fire-lit hall. Astreya and Damon grasped the stretcher and, gasping in the superheated air, rushed Gar out the door. They had no sooner gained the outer hall than an explosion belched out the doorway. Damon's gown billowed around him, smoking at the hem.

"It's the turpentine," gasped Lindey as they staggered through the second set of doors, which had been blown open by the explosion. "Three whole crocks of it. Now they'll never put it out."

At first, their sole thought was to get away from the blaze behind them. Their initial rush took them out of the building, where they paused, the fire still hot on their backs. Two more explosions buffeted them as hot air belched out of the doors behind them.

"Where now?" Damon asked from the back of the stretcher. "We can't take him the way we came."

"We'll go out the main gate," said Astreya. "We're cloaked like students, and we have a wounded man. The fire's behind us. If we're quick, maybe they won't look twice."

Damon looked at Lindey, who nodded. He shrugged, took a stronger grip on his end of the stretcher, and headed for the gate. Astreya led the charge, staggering on the uneven ground, wondering how long his hands would be able to grip the poles. Gar's head lolled from side to side, his breath coming in choking gasps.

Damon hesitated as they came to within a stone's throw of the gate, and figures ran towards them.

"Fire at the hall!" yelled Lindey.

She took the lead in front of the stretcher and waved the confused students and Learneds out of the way. Bent almost double by their load, Astreya and Damon followed her towards the gate, running as fast as they could. A cloaked Learned stood in their way, a torch in his hand, shouting confused instructions to put out the fire, to stand out of the way, and to go for help. Lindey charged directly at him. The torch wavered, and the Learned gave way. A few paces further, and Lindey almost ran into two men in their shirtsleeves who were opening the gates.

"Injured man! Injured man!" yelled Astreya, and put on speed.

Lindey went first, pushing the gate open far enough for the stretcher bearers. On the other side, all three of them saw why it had been unlocked: at least six men were pushing and pulling a clumsy water cart forward, lighting their way with waving torches. Lindey swerved, leading Damon and Astreya around wildly gesticulating hands and arms that sought to hold them. They kept going.

Many panting steps later, Damon faltered.

"Must take a rest," he gasped. "Put him down for a moment."

In the mouth of a deserted alley, they eased Gar to the ground. Astreya and Lindey knelt over him, listening for his breathing.

"You three... all right?"

Lindey and Astreya nodded.

"Just a scratch," said Damon proudly. "You should see the one who gave it to me."

"Get away to the south," said Gar, his breath bubbling in his throat as he tried to talk. "Careful.... There's a ship near. Find Stumpy. He'll help... find me... is a... find the duck... not the sieve... not... or... on... I can't tell you... too late."

"Don't try to talk," said Lindey. "We'll get you to the Widow Amy's very soon."

"Keep Estr... Astr... Astreya's clasp... book."

Gar coughed, rolled his head, coughed again and took a longer breath than before.

"Shush, Gar," she said. "Hang on. You'll be all right."

His words came slower but more coherently as he got enough control to whisper.

"I know better, Lindey. My ribs are stuck through my lungs. Listen. Who's that? Damon? Keep your knife hand cool, lad. Now go away. I have to talk to Lindey and Astreya."

Astreya and Lindey huddled over Gar, their heads almost touching. Gar reached up and the three of them clasped hands.

"This is not what I planned," he whispered. "Not what I expected at all. We were having so much fun! I had an idea that I'd... but... now this. At first, I thought Men of the Sea sent you to trick me, Astreya. But you're Estraella's son all right. He was always the smart one. We should have stuck together."

He fumbled with his shirtsleeve, wheezing as his action compressed his chest.

"What is it, Gar?" Astreya asked.

"Cut my shirt back to the shoulder."

Astreya slid the tip of his knife under the material and slit it from elbow to neck. High up on Gar's arm was a bracelet like his own, save that its stone was dull and lightless.

"Lindey, take my clasp. Astreya's a stone starter. He'll light it."

Very gently, Lindey eased the bracelet off Gar's arm and clipped it around her own.

"Lindey," Gar whispered. "Oh, Lindey, Estraella should never have left. But if he hadn't, the three of us would never.... It was hard to say goodbye. The Master trained us. We respected... what he knew... but we... we hated what he'd become."

"What's he saying, Lindey?" Astreya asked as Gar's voice trailed off.

"He's... he's..." Lindey began, but Gar's voice strengthened.

"Lindey, stay with Astreya, or I'll haunt you. Astreya, I should have told you more. But you're a lucky man. You'll find out for yourself."

Lindey's head swayed from side to side, her hair glinting in the moonlight as it swung back and forth across her face.

"Gar, she's shaking her head. She wants you to..."

"Right, Astreya," said Gar. "And wrong, too. Lindey shakes her head when she cries. I'm underneath, getting wet. Look after yourselves."

Gar moved his head, coughed again, and lay very still. Lindey bent lower.

"I'll be pounded flat," Gar whispered, the words catching in his throat. "Lindey kissed me. And I can't kiss you back, girl. I...." A gurgling interrupted his words, and he coughed again. "I *am* pounded flat," he said, and choked.

Astreya and Lindey realized that he had been trying to laugh. They waited for the rasp of indrawn breath, but it did not come. Gar's hands went limp in their grasp. Lindey pressed her fingers below his ear to feel for a pulse, desperately felt again, and then sobbed. Astreya slowly folded Gar's hands over his shattered chest. He stood up, took off the green gown he had been wearing, and laid it over Gar's body.

"Damon," he called into the shadows. "Come back. It's over."

When Damon reappeared, he found Astreya holding Lindey in the moonlight as she cried silently against him, all her stoic calm lost.

CHAPTER 17:

IN WHICH ASTREYA AND LINDEY JOURNEY TO THE SEA

The shadows were lengthening toward evening when Astreya became conscious of anything other than putting one foot in front of the other. For the entire day, he had been walking beside Lindey, carrying his share of their meager belongings. In the moments when he was able to feel for other people, he wished that there was something he could do or say to alleviate Lindey's grief. Although they had both been able to deal with each successive moment since Gar's death, in her eyes was a desolation unlike her usual calm. She walked unaware and uncaring for where they might be going.

Astreya could barely remember what had happened during the rest of the night after Gar's death. Somehow they made the arrangements that had put them on their way south, as Gar had directed. Now, as Astreya plodded along, he could only remember snatches of events: the sad procession back to the Widow Amy's house, the way the good woman helped them with Gar's furtive, candlelit burial in the woods behind her home, the preparations for their journey, and their eventual departure in darkness. She had outfitted them with food and such homely necessities as extra socks, and then sent them on their way with a serenity that amazed them all. Perhaps the same superstitions that made her ordinary life a mass of small worries gave her strength at a time of crisis. Astreya envied her.

He stumbled to one knee, and long grasses swished at his face. He recovered, stood up, and looked about him as if newly wakened. They were pushing their way through scrubby trees, out onto a knoll of weathered grey rock patched with shin high juniper bushes. They had left the road at daylight when it started to curve to the west, and had struck out to the south, using Astreya's newfound ability to control his bracelet. They had seen blackened skeletons of dead trees, remnants of some long past forest fire, standing like sentinels in the undulating landscape; and they had waded through knee high growth, the sun-warmed plants giving off puffs of their characteristic scents: the rank smell of aspen and the harsh, ferny odor of bracken. Astreya breathed deeply, smelling the tang of juniper. To his right the sun was declining in the west, and from the reddened cloud banks along the horizon, white mare's tails curled upward and outward toward the deepening blue of the sky. Astreya's feet and legs refused to walk further. He stood amid the bushes with his eyes and mind receptive only to the sky above and the landscape around him. In the distance, he could see low hills soft with trees. Closer were clumps of woodland such as they had been avoiding since they left the road.

"I'd need an almost dry brush to streak in the high clouds," he murmured to himself. "Then a faint pink wash, deepening into red towards the sun. Do the trees with a brush dipped in several shades of green: squash the tip of the brush down and then twist to swirl the colors together. Sketch in the tree skeletons with charcoal on top of the paint and then ink them in later. Leave the sun just outside the composition, and...."

Lindey almost walked into him.

"Are you all right, Astreya?" she asked.

Astreya nodded slowly. "I think so. But I'm not sure. Have I seemed strange to you in the last little while?"

Lindey shook her head, her blue eyes on his. "You haven't said much since we got on our way, but you planned what we had to do, kept me from getting too upset, spoke kindly to the Widow Amy, and gave Damon the leave he needed to stay behind. I couldn't have done it without you. None of us could."

Astreya shook his head. "But you're the practical one, not me."

"Not this time. You did all the thinking for us. You sent Damon back to the Tavern with money to pay Robert to say he'd been drinking there all night. And you got him to send Sandy and Nock northwards to confuse anyone trying to follow us. You stopped the Widow Amy in time before she got too emotional, and persuaded her to keep the cart and Nora. You shared out Gar's secret store of coins after I got them from the wagon, and persuaded the Widow Amy to take some of them. Then you got us on our way down the road at first, and later, across country. After that, you kind of withdrew. Since then, you've been walking, checking your bracelet from time to time, and walking some more. Whenever I asked you if you were all right, you just nodded."

"What about you, Lindey?"

"Numb. I can't think about him. I can't. My mind slips off. I expect him to be around the next bend, waiting for us."

They stared at each other as the red sunset dimmed above them, sharing their sorrow.

"I never knew my father," said Lindey. "Like you. But Gar was like...."

Her voice tailed off, and Astreya nodded, unable to speak. She had expressed his own thought, and there was no more to say. He looked around him.

"We should make camp for the night. It looks as if there's water down in the dell, and we can make a fire against one of the rocks, over there."

By the last light of the sun, they wearily trudged over a shoulder of rock patched with moss. In the dell beyond were wildflowers of late summer and tall grass going to seed. A couple of paces down slope, an old and twisted pine rose to barely twice a man's height. The tree had survived the fire that had transformed the landscape through which they had been walking for most of the day. Strong lower branches spread out from the trunk, forming a shelter. Above, the limbs ended abruptly, leaving a burned and broken stick pointing at the sky. Below was a hollow soft with generations of pine needles, in which they could spend the night. Astreya fetched a pan of water and some charred pieces of wood with which he lit a small fire in the lee of a boulder. Lindey produced bread, smoked ham and apples given them by the Widow Amy, which Astreya had been carrying in his pack. They washed down their supper with herbal tea made from the Widow's stock of dried leaves and flowers. The food gradually replenished their bodies and spirits, and as the hollow flickered in and out of sight by the light of their campfire, they began to talk softly.

"Gar tried to tell us something important, but it came out as nonsense about ducks and sieves. Then he started to make sense, but I can't get my head around what he said about my being Astreya's son. Why would he waste time telling me what I knew? Especially when he said there was so much he should have told me earlier."

Lindey did not seem to hear him. She started to speak slowly, almost to herself.

"I first met Gar only a few weeks after I left Matris—my home. I was in a little community where I'd gone to work for a farmer. Mostly that meant cows. Milk them, clean them, muck out the barn, fork down the feed. Did I say it was winter? Anyway, Gar turned up in my farmer's yard, and offered to paint things and people. I thought he was wonderful. You remember he once said that there was a farmer who wanted him to paint a cow that had died a year earlier?"

Astreya nodded.

"My farmer. Anyway, Gar started painting the cow that wasn't there. I just had to watch him, and Gar couldn't resist drawing my farmer alongside the cow, looking even more stupid than he actually was. When the farmer's wife laughed, the farmer decided Gar was in league with the devil, and off he went to get help from his neighbors. They were an awful, argumentative lot who had little in common except for their fear of strangers and belief in the powers of darkness. They decided to kill Gar and steal the cart and Nora the horse. I overheard their plan being hatched, and before my farmer could get enough of them sufficiently stirred up, I snuck out to Gar's wagon, and told him."

"Was that when you did your first moonlight flit together?"

Lindey nodded. "Yes. But in this case, we had to apply some physical persuasion first."

"Your stick."

"And Gar's club. And Gar's smokes. I'm sorry you never saw them. He had some earthenware pots filled with something he had cooked up which made enormous quantities of choking smoke."

"Convincing the good people he really was a devil."

Lindey nodded again. Slowly, the haunted look left her face, and she smiled at the same time as tears ran down her cheeks, glinting in the firelight.

"He was such a good man, Astreya."

Astreya nodded bitterly. "Gar's dead, and it's because of me. If I hadn't left my jacket, then Carl wouldn't have come after me, and..."

"Astreya, he chose to go back. He wanted to help you. The whole business of getting back to the hall convinced him he had to open up to you, and he did. He showed you how to use your bracelet."

"Why didn't he do so earlier?"

"I don't know, but when he was dying, he said something about fearing that you had been sent to take him back."

"Back where?

"Back to the Men of the Sea, Astreya. Back to your people—or at least, your father's people."

"What do you mean? My people?"

"Something Gar told me on the road to the Castle. When I asked him if he knew what your bracelet was, he said that only Men of the Sea had them. That was after you told him you'd got it from your father. He told me he was going to talk to you, but then we were attacked, and he wasn't sure if Eva was behind it. And because Gar thought you were sweet on her, he didn't speak out then, and then... well, he said it himself. You two were having too much fun."

"Sweet on Eva?"

"Well, you did give her a bag of money."

"Do you think that...?"

"Not any more, Astreya. And only a little at first."

"She sure wasn't interested in me. She started up with Damon the moment she got to the Castle."

"Yes, but the point is that Gar didn't trust Eva. He knew she faked the swing she took at the man who attacked her, because if it really had connected, we'd have been digging his grave."

"Why didn't he talk to me about it?"

"First, he wasn't absolutely sure. Not enough to accuse her. And because she ended up with the money, he was wondering what would happen next."

"So you both just let things happen? I don't understand why you didn't tell me."

Astreya threw a stick onto the fire, and a small plume of sparks coiled up. Once again, the metal of his bracelet tingled against his flesh and his fingers closed on the silvery band under his shirt.

"I need to think," he said, and stood up. "I'll be up there on the rock."

He pushed his way through crackling bracken to the crest of the hill, and stood silhouetted against the sky. He stared into the deep wells of darkness among the stars, feeling the hollowness left by Gar's death. After a few moments, he sat down, and looked out to the south, where his bracelet pointed. A cool night wind made him grateful for the cloak given him by the Widow Amy. Astreya shuddered, but not from cold. He had experienced the sudden ending of lives in the Village, but always it had happened to someone who was not close to him, and usually because of the implacable sea. He had observed grief, and even thought he understood it, but now the loss was his own, he discovered that with the emptiness came resentment.

"There's so much he could have told me," said Astreya, unaware that he had spoken out loud. "He should have..."

"He should be alive," said Lindey. "But he isn't. So, now you have to think of what he did show you. All of it. Including the funny parts. And how he let you decide things for yourself. He didn't try to make people do or be anything they didn't want to."

"He made me into a painter..."

"You already were. He just helped you get better."

Astreya looked down at Lindey, who was standing in the hollow below him, her head level with his knee. Star shine washed over them, gleaming on her skin. He reached out his hand and she took it to climb up beside him. They sat in silence.

"You've been the cause of a lot of changes in my life, Astreya," said Lindey at last.

"I've taken you away from what you had with Gar. I'm responsible for what happened to him."

"No. Or at least not so that you should feel any guilt for it. What I meant was that you've made my plans change. I don't have them anymore. Gar started me doubting, but you made the real change. I told you, before Gar..." she paused, sniffed and hurried on. "... that I had to leave Matris. I thought I'd do what was expected of me, and that would be that. Find a husband. At least bring back a baby, so that I'd really be a part of Matris, as my mother was. But now, I don't want that anymore."

"I can't believe they just told you to go and get pregnant."

"That's not how it happened. If I'd married any of the men of my age in Matris, our children would probably have been deformed or not right in their heads. The village is too small, so it needs what they call new blood. Unless, of course, I just gave up and grew old and silly, the way my aunt did. And there were other reasons my going away was necessary... people I... I offended. But that didn't make it any easier."

Astreya wanted to ask her to say more about the other reasons, but fearing she would simply fall silent, he asked a more neutral question.

"You weren't the first, were you?"

Lindey shook her head.

"Did the others come back?"

"Some of them. That's why my uncle trained me to use my staff."

"Were they happy?"

"The ones who came back? They were... changed. They didn't talk about it. Only two brought their men back, but it didn't work out. They both left after only a year. They said they couldn't have their lives run for them by women, but that was an excuse. Besides, it's silly, because some of the mothers... the elders, I mean, are men."

"Most of them are women?"

"Of course. There just aren't that many men."

Astreya pondered the idea of a village where women were leaders. It seemed to him strange, but not impossible. Lindey brought him back to the present with a jolt.

"Astreya, what do you hope to find in the south?"

"I really don't know. I suppose I'm just doing what Gar told me. Maybe I can find out what my father's book is about. Perhaps..."

He rolled back his sleeve and the green stone in his bracelet pulsed as if it were alive. The spear of white light at its center pointed steadily in the same direction as he swung his arm this way and that. Then he held his arm still, and as they both watched, the spear changed its direction until it was aimed over their shoulders at the North Star.

"Astreya, did you do that?"

"I... I think so. But I don't know how. I asked it to point north, and it did. No, that's not quite right. Gar said it. 'Think north,' he said. So I did, but it knew where north is. Why don't you try with the one Gar gave you?"

"It's not lit up like yours."

"Let's see."

Lindey rolled back her sleeve.

"Look, Lindey. It's glowing."

"It's just a gleam of starlight."

Astreya brought his arm close to hers, and when the two bracelets almost touched, the light from Astreya's stone dimmed and then brightened as if a spark had jumped to the one on Lindey's arm, which began to shine almost as brightly as his. They both gasped, Lindey in delight, Astreya as if he had taken a misstep down a dark staircase. He swayed, and Lindey took his arm. Her eyes gleamed in the doubled light from the two stones. Their arms side by side and their faces close, they looked at each other. Astreya saw wonder transform Lindey's face, and she saw excitement in his.

"You can do it too, Lindey. Think north, like Gar said."

The spear of white light in her stone wavered. She glanced overhead to the pole-pointing stars, and the light in her stone swung around.

"Right. Now close your eyes and swing your arm around."

Lindey raised her arm until it was horizontal and waved it back and forth.

"It's working! You're doing it."

Lindey opened her eyes and looked at her bracelet. "It's swinging away again."

It was as Lindey said. The spear of light was brighter and the green glow softer, so that they had to look closely to see anything but the pointing sliver of white.

"I'm going to let mine go," said Astreya.

The spear swung to point a little east of south, just as Lindey's had done. On both their arms, the green glow intensified once more, and then blinked.

"Did you do that?" asked Lindey.

"I don't think so. Just a moment. Let's do that again,"

They concentrated, and the spear of light turned; they nodded at each other, relaxed, the pale centers swung back, both jewels blinked, and they both felt a tingle strong enough for them to let go of each other and reach for their gleaming stones.

"Don't touch it!" said Astreya. "The stone burns... that is, it feels like burning, but it's not. I suppose that's why they're set in a metal cage."

They both stood looking at the gleaming stones, and at each other. Lindey's lips flickered a question whether he was all right, Astreya nodded, and they were both reassured.

"The moment we're not thinking about it, the light dims, and it points over there, towards the sea," he said.

"Then that's where you have to go," said Lindey.

"Gar said something about a ship, but that was when his speech was confused," said Astreya slowly.

"And he said he'd expected to get back to sea, just before he...."

Lindey's thought hung unfinished, while they both remembered Gar's last moments.

"He was... he certainly had been a sailor," said Astreya.

"Then we have a plan," said Lindey. "At least, we have a destination, and we're not just running away. Besides, even though it's not completely rational for me to say so, I have a feeling that there's something important you have to do."

"People keep saying that to me," said Astreya. "I never expected to hear it from you. There are times when I've felt the same way, but later it all runs away and I don't know what I should do. When I left the Village with Roaring Jack, I thought I'd find out for sure. Then I got all wrapped up in painting with Gar. There was so much he could have told me, but instead we sketched and painted, and now he's dead."

"He'd want you to get the answers for yourself. Gar was like that. He didn't tell people things, he let them find out for themselves."

"It's a lonely way to learn," said Astreya. "He could have told me something—just a few hints, maybe—and then I'd know what I had to do."

"If he had told you who you were, you'd never have believed him. And anyway, if someone tells you what you have to do, and you believe them, you're the prisoner of their words."

Astreya turned to her and looked into her face by the starlight, struck by the force of what she had said.

"How do you see me, Lindey?" he asked.

"You're a good person, Astreya. You could have killed Carl, but you didn't. You didn't run away, either. You're gentle, and maybe you think a little too much. But you do the right thing, even when it's difficult."

Lindey paused so long that Astreya thought she was finished. Then she reached out a hand to touch his bare arm, her fingers dimly visible in the light of the green stones.

"You make me feel more alive, Astreya."

The light from the stones intensified again, and they pulsed in a regular rhythm. By their glow, Astreya and Lindey could see each other's faces clearly. Her eyes were open very wide, and her lips slightly parted; his eyes were almost black in the green light. They both moved at the same moment, and their lips pressed together. They shared a sudden rush of pleasure that made them both draw back their heads at the same time to take a deep breath. Astreya leaned back against rock and drew her to him. Lindey moved her head slightly, and Astreya kissed her face, her eyes, her neck, delighting in the faint scent of her hair and body, feeling that he had found a part of him for which he had long been searching. She chuckled deep in her throat.

"I hate to spoil the moment, Astreya, but this is not a good, or dry, or comfortable place. I'm wet, and I need a bath—and so do you."

Astreya recoiled, embarrassed. She took his hand, pulled him closer and kissed him gently. They climbed down the rocks without letting go, until Astreya started to wrap his damp cloak around himself and look about him in the firelight for a flat space to lie down.

"Hey, I didn't banish you forever, Astreya. And what's more, we'll be warmer if we put the wet side of your cloak down, and the wet side of my cloak up, and ourselves in between."

They lay down in the cool night, drawing together between their cloaks. Astreya lay on his right side, wondering what to do with his left arm, on which his bracelet glowed dimly through his sleeve. Beside him, Lindey rolled over to face him, pulled back her sleeve so that her stone lit both their faces, and they shared a lingering kiss.

They slept, woke, curled closer together, and slept again. Later, neither could recall dreaming of anything.

* * * * *

When false dawn ripened the sky to the deepest blue, Astreya woke and lay on one arm, looking at Lindey. Bracken tickled her leg, and she moved under the cloaks between which they had slept. She turned towards him and nestled against his chest without waking. In sleep, the calm that he had so often admired in her expression was now a peacefulness he envied. He curled one arm around her, and the position felt right, natural, as if he had known it before.

Gradually the sky brightened, and the first rays of the sun lit the broken top of the tree under which they lay. Lindey stirred, opened her eyes and smiled up at Astreya. He kissed her, and she chuckled as she sat up. She touched the side of Astreya's cheek with her fingers and wrinkled her nose.

"It's going to be a good day," she said.

"I…." Astreya began.

She put one finger on his lips.

"I'm going to wash," she said. "I'll bring back some water if you make up the fire."

Astreya blew up coals that still glowed in the grey ash, and soon had a crackling blaze. He stood close to the fire, warming his legs and looking over the rolling, tree-clad hills. They had camped just over the crest of the highest rise in their immediate region. Ahead of them, treetops poked out of morning mist like green reefs in a cloudy sea. The valleys were pools of grey vapor that curled upwards in tendrils. To the west, the rising sun warmed the wisps of cloud into the palest pink. Fold after fold of ground-hugging fog repeated its soft lines into the distance, where hills rose like waves, one behind the other.

"Smooth strokes with a watery brush of light pink," Astreya said to himself. "Let the texture of the paper do the work; just don't let the paint run down in drips. Do the near hills with greens in the same way. Smooth strokes; they have to be right the first time—no going back. Hint at mountains in the distance: charcoal smudged with a finger, leaving the line crisp at the top. Ask Gar if…"

His mind descended into grief as the landscape darkened, and his thoughts with it. As his shadow softened, blurred and disappeared, Astreya looked east and saw the lower rim of the sun disappear into heavy clouds. Light brightened the distant mists for one last moment, and then the landscape darkened to shades of grey.

Lindey returned with a pan of water, her dress damp to the knees from the dew-wet bushes. She came to the fire that Astreya had now coaxed into a blaze, and held her skirts out towards it to dry.

"It is not going to be pleasant walking today, but at least we know we can keep a straight line to the south."

They ate a morning meal of dried fruit in silence, and packed up their belongings. Finally, they poured the dregs of their tea over the fire and stamped out the embers. Astreya rolled a stone onto the ashes and broadcast the remains of their firewood and the bracken beds. Satisfied that they had concealed where they had been, they set off southwards.

They walked down the gentle slope from where they had camped, and in a few strides the mists closed over their heads. In a cold, damp world where bushes and plants blurred together only a few paces ahead of them, they were dependent on the green stones in their bracelets. Walking while checking the pointing shafts of light was too slow, so they took turns choosing a tree or a rock as a landmark along the line indicated by the stones, then they walked to it, and then repeated the process. Sometimes the fog shifted and they could go a fair distance without having to check direction, and sometimes they could walk only a few strides. Occasionally they were forced to ford streams overhung by maples and elms. Sometimes they had to make their way around swamps where cedars clumped together into impassable thickets. Every now and then, they scrambled up a rocky outcrop, only to find at the crest that the other side fell away like a breaking wave, forcing them to angle westwards, away from their line of march. The green stones never failed to point their way, so that overall, their line of progress was southerly.

At first, they were cold. The fog hovered around them and water dripped off every bush and tree. After a while, they found themselves warmed by walking up steadily rising ground. Each time they stopped to check their bearings, they plunged on quickly, knowing that a long halt would chill them again. When it came time for the midday meal, they ate handfuls of nuts and dried fruit as they walked, and stopped only briefly at streams to quench their thirst.

A silence lay between them that neither could break. Astreya's mind churned over three questions: Where were they going? What had Gar not told him? And most of all, what had almost happened last night? Each time he started to put together words on one of the three questions, the other two poured into his mind, leaving him in a confusion of feelings. One moment, he knew a simple answer to the last: Lindey had sensibly stopped them. The next moment, he wondered why. Was it that she rejected him? Or had she just put off the moment to another time? Or was she looking for something more? Curiosity drove him forward, and loss was at his back, but having Lindey walking beside him tugged at his feelings in ways he had never imagined possible. Unlike Eva, the tavern girl and the shepherd's daughter, being with Lindey simply felt right to him.

In the afternoon, the strain on the backs of their legs told them that they were gaining height, instead of merely going up and down as they had done during the morning. The trees thinned to the occasional stunted pine, which they saw as a darker shape in the mist. The ground was stony under their feet; they glimpsed great shards of black rock on either side as the mist swirled around them. They wound their way upwards, obedient to their pointing bracelets.

Astreya wondered whether they had reached the distant ridge he had glimpsed early that morning. When lichen-covered cliffs forced them to angle away from their direction, he grew increasingly concerned that they were becoming lost. Then, almost as if it were in response to his thought, he pushed his way through a thicket of knee high juniper, and found himself on a path.

It was not one of the wandering game trails they had crossed or briefly followed earlier in the day. The people who had made this path had wanted to get from one place to another by the shortest route. Astreya checked its direction with his bracelet, even though he knew it would lead them closer to their destination than any amount of rambling around the edges of the ridge on which they stood.

Lindey had been a few paces behind him, her skirts caught in the branches.

"Couldn't we find a way that..." she began testily, and then grabbed Astreya's arm. "Oh, well done, Astreya. You've found a path."

"Blind luck," said Astreya, but he set off up the path with a confidence he could not explain even to himself.

Walking was much easier, even though they were now climbing steeply. Bushes and grasses no longer plucked at their ankles, and they did not have to duck under branches that sprayed them with droplets of clinging fog. The mist thinned as they climbed, and they felt both warmer and dryer. The sun did not appear in the whiteness overhead, but they could feel its warmth. Their cloaks were no longer necessary to keep them warm, so they took off the heavy garments that had flapped wetly against their shins and tied them on top of their packs. Lindey started to hum to herself, and the little tune she repeated over and over seemed to make their steps lighter. Where the path was wide enough to allow it, they walked side by side, their strides matching.

As the late afternoon waned, they came to a pass between two rocky hill crests. The path steepened until it led up a series of irregular terraces with rough scrambles from one to the next. They had to use hands as well as feet to climb over rock made slippery with damp yellow lichen. A stream that had flowed beside the path dwindled to an intermittent trickle that wound its way around boulders and rocks, eventually disappearing completely under tumbled stones, where for several strides they could hear it chuckling. Despite the increasingly rugged climb, they could see where rocks had been rolled away or laid flat, and they knew they were still on a path.

A wind freshened at their backs, and the last vestiges of fog blew away. Low in the west, the sun sent out long fingers of light under a blue-black cloud bank, much darker than the one they had seen at dawn. Tiredness made them stumble as they crossed a boulder-strewn saddle-shaped pass between gaunt rock on either side. Suddenly they were looking out and down on a new landscape. The downward slope was completely different from the ridge they had climbed.

Astreya's arm tingled, and when he glanced at Lindey, he saw that she, too, had put her hand over her bracelet. He shrugged, and as the faint prickling sensation died away, they both smiled. Astreya stamped his feet. Instead of the cracked and jumbled grey stone they had climbed, a darker, harder rock was underfoot. He was reassured by the way his boots crackled on little gem-like crystals as there were in the cliffs above his Village. Lindey's hand sought Astreya's, and she squeezed his fingers. Shading his eyes against a sudden gleam of sun between the clouds, he looked forward.

"The sea, Astreya," said Lindey.

Far in the distance, whitecaps rolled shoreward, catching the level light. Closer below them, the sun glanced through clouds onto a nearly circular bay, surrounded by tidal flats that blended into fields that reached to the foot of ridge on which they stood. When they looked left and right, they saw that they were on an escarpment that formed a rough circle broken where the bay met the sea by a gap between low headlands. Below them, beyond the fields at the water's edge, was a collection of houses. Boats dotted the water at their moorings and Astreya could just see the outline of wharves. As they stood and watched, shapeless masses of dark cloud drove overhead and blotted out what was left of the sunlight. The town and harbor dulled, turning to grey shapes near an indistinct shoreline, with a few dim lights glowing in the gloom. To their right, the main path took an easy route towards the town in a series of switchbacks. Ahead of them were scuff marks and scars on the rocks where walkers had taken a more direct route.

"We'll do well to get there before the storm hits," said Lindey, glancing back at the sky behind them. "Let's head straight down."

Astreya looked dubiously at the faint trail, and shrugged. Cautiously, they began the descent towards the harbor.

Chapter 18:

In which Astreya meets Adramin

The rain struck while they were still on their way down from the pass, turning their path into a water-slick streamlet. For much of a risky hour, they picked their way downward over rock made treacherous by water. Every few steps, they had to put down a hand onto the rough, cold stone, or lose balance. When at last they reached a gentler slope at the foot of the ridge, the path turned to mud before it eventually joined a road churned to mire by horses' hooves. The rain beat down, soaking through the hoods on their cloaks. Lindey's blonde hair dripped onto her shoulders, and Astreya's black curls were plastered flat, soaking past his collar and down his back.

Soon they could barely see their way in the fading light. Their heads down against slashes of rain that gusted across the road, they slogged past open fields and into the little town, their boots heavy with water and caked with mud. Rain hissed on puddles as they passed, and each step they took made wet, sucking noises. Eventually, houses frowned at them on either side, with the occasional lit window like a watchful eye. Under the eaves of a large shed or perhaps warehouse, they paused to wipe the rain out of their eyes. Astreya saw the glint of light on open water at the end of their road, and glimpsed a hunched figure with a coil of rope over his shoulder and lantern swinging from one hand. He broke into a run to ask directions, but by the time he reached the wharf, the man had vanished.

Astreya returned to the lee of the last building, waited for Lindey, and looked about him. Rain swallowed the dim light from the few windows that were not shuttered against the storm. The road they had followed led onto a wharf, studded with wooden posts and bollards, beyond which masts swayed back and forth, the wind moaning in their rigging. To his right, a line of squat two storey buildings faced the sea across about ten paces of wet, age-blackened wood. Through the hiss of the rain and the slosh of unseen waves against pilings, Astreya heard creaking timbers, the thump of fenders and the occasional slap of a rope on boats whose hulls were out of sight on the sea below the edge of the wharf. To his left, one meager pool of light glinted on the dark wood. From an upstairs window of the building in whose shelter he stood, yellowish lamplight gleamed onto a mass of wooden poles held together by knotted wet ropes, the whole affair swinging back and forth in the rain. Shading his eyes against the downpour, Astreya decided that he was looking at a curious sign dangling from the eaves. Someone had contrived to model a bed out of heavy rope and what might have once been oars, and then had hung it from the jutting beams of the inn's roof. The whole apparatus creaked as it swung back and forth.

"Here's an inn!" Astreya shouted.

Lindey made her way towards him, hunched against the wind and rain. He put out his hand, and their wet, cold fingers clung together as he led the way. The inn was a building made a long time ago by men whose first thought had been of ship-building and only later of houses. Heavy timbers held up a steep roof over a door studded with square-ended nails. By the light of a swaying lantern, its flame turned down to little more than a glow, Astreya saw the inn's name above the door: The Black Sheep. He fumbled with the latch, and when it swung open with unexpected ease, he almost fell into the tavern, Lindey close behind him. They stood on a huge scrubbed stone doorstep below a lamp hanging from one of many heavy beams, and they stared down two more age-worn steps to the low ceilinged taproom.

"Shut the hatch," growled a voice below them.

Behind Astreya's back, Lindey slammed the door, pushing hard against a gust of wind. With no draught to rag their flames, several brass lamps flared, throwing enough light for them to see that the room ran the length of the building. To their right, a fire flickered in a wide fireplace fuelled by mansized logs; to their left was a wall of barrels held in place with heavy rope. Opposite, there were doors into the back of the building, and a steep stair, almost a ladder, led up to the second floor. Sturdy wooden tables and chairs offered sufficient seating for as many as fifty people, although only half a dozen were filled, all of them by men.

Astreya pushed back his hood and looked down onto the shortest, broadest man imaginable, who was standing at the foot of the steps in front of them. His thick body had been mismatched with legs no longer than those of a small child, though no child ever had such massive, post-like limbs. Spectacularly developed arms, shoulders and chest bulged under a knitted blue shirt.

"Two half drowned wharf rats," he rumbled in a deep bass voice. "One fair, one black."

Astreya found himself being appraised by deep set eyes under heavy black brows. As he stared back, the man's mouth widened into a broken-toothed smile.

"Don't mistake me, folks. You may be high born, highbred and even highly wealthy, but you don't look it now. And you may have put together a fine explanation why a young man that's so black on top, should be travelin' with so blonde a girl, but I don't want to hear it. An' that's why I'll thank you to show me some coin before you start your bill by asking for dry clothes. D'ye catch my drift?"

Astreya turned back his wet cloak, fumbled in his pocket and counted coins with his fingertips. Carefully, he withdrew all but the gold, and held out a palm full of silver and copper for the man to see. Before he could step backwards, the man's long arm reached out and his fingers closed on Astreya's pocket. Astreya's fist doubled around the money, and he reached for his knife. The big hand let go of his pocket.

"Right," said the innkeeper. "Put the knife away, my careful friend. I have to be careful too. O' course, you may have lead in your breeks, but I doubt it."

Astreya slid his half-drawn blade back into its sheath and let his wet cloak hide it once more. As he put his handful of coins back into his pocket, his eyes widened. One of the gold pieces was bent almost double.

"Walt's my name, when you wish to call for food and drink. Now, follow me for hot baths, dry clothes and a mug of mulled ale. Oh, and let me tell you that nobody fights here. That is, nobody fights twice. And nobody's been robbed since eight years ago, when a man had the misfortune to break both his hands. Have ye taken that aboard?" He cracked his knuckles like pine branches snapping.

Astreya nodded, and Walt led the way across the room. The offer of hot baths and dry clothes was irresistible, but they wondered how much of their concealed but already evaluated gold it might cost. On balance, they were prepared to count the expense small if they could once again be warm and dry. They followed Walt's rolling gait among the tables, past heads and shoulders of men studiously attending to their food or drink. Astreya hesitated as the bracelet on his arm tingled. Beside him, he saw Lindey's fingers stray towards her left arm. They exchanged a swift glance, and then followed Walt, to the back of the room and up the steep stair like a ship's companionway with a rope handrail. In the gloom at the head of the flight of steps, Walt suddenly turned around, briefly overtopping their height.

"It would be more seemly if the young lady were to wear some clothes I can offer her. In that wet cloak, and with your hair no longer than many a seaman, lass, it's a good chance that most did not see that you are what you are... and very nice too, let me add. In a loose shirt, a pair of breeks and a tunic, you'll pass in the shadows for a young lad, and I'll have less chance of trouble on m'hands. Your friend won't need to be defending your virtue, and I won't have to be mopping up his blood."

"It'll be someone else's blood if Astreya's in a fight," said Lindey, ignoring Astreya's quick silencing gesture.

"Ho. He's capable, is he?" Walt asked over his shoulder as he led the way to the end of a short passageway, lit by another brass lantern. "Then what do you think of this?"

His long arms were a blur of motion as he seized Astreya by the belt, swung him around and pinned an arm behind his back. Beside Astreya's throat was a short-bladed clasp knife. Fast as he had been, Astreya and Lindey were no less quick. Lindey's staff lanced up to a finger width from Walt's throat, and Astreya's knife pressed inward, a little lower than the innkeeper's bottom rib. All three stared at one another, unmoving. It was clear that any first move would precipitate a bloody melee. Astreya's arm became free, Walt's clasp knife folded with a snick and vanished in his big hand. The heel of Lindey's staff met the floor, and Astreya returned his knife to its sheath.

"Very fine, young sir and lady," said Walt, his broken teeth exposed in another even wider grin. "My compliments. There have only been two others who have come up even with me... both of 'em Men of the Sea. None has been faster. Now that we all agree that we don't want to see each others' blood, we can be friends."

His big, square-ended hand came out, and Astreya took it. His knuckles ground together under the man's grip, but he did not wince. When Walt reached out his hand to Lindey, she took it as had Astreya: formally, forcefully, and with a steady gaze. They followed Walt to where a small lantern lit a narrow hallway punctuated by varnished doors. The innkeeper lifted the latch of the one closest to the stairs.

"Now, in you go. There's a tub, and I'll have hot water for you in a trice."

They stood in the light from the hallway while he lumbered into the room ahead of them, lit a lamp and hung it over a thick-topped wooden table surrounded by four matching chairs with substantial arms. He waved them in, and three heavy steps later, closed the door behind him. The room was like a well appointed cabin: everything in it had been designed for a comfort that conserved space. Polished brass knobs, hinges and fasteners reflected the light in tiny pinpricks. Dark blue curtains were pushed back at the head and foot of two white blanketed mattresses set on top of low chests of drawers. There was room to lie on the beds, but if a sleeper sat up incautiously, he would bang his head into the underside of the roof where it angled down towards the eaves. Heavy, knee high chests provided seating in the corners and under the deep set window, which was tightly closed and shuttered against the storm. In the light from a smaller version of the fireplace in the tavern below sat the lower half of a huge barrel. Before they had the chance to do more than slide out of their packs and hang up their sodden cloaks, they heard a muffled thud on the door. Lindey opened it to reveal Walt, carrying two huge buckets of water, one of which would have overburdened most men.

"Me hands was busy, so that was me head knocking on your door," he said cheerfully. "I thought ye'd like some time alone before you came below for food." He poured steaming water into the tub. "In them chests o' drawers are clothes... all clean, and in most sizes."

"How much...." Astreya began.

Walt turned and casually touched one fist to the point of his chin. Astreya felt sure he was meant to understand the gesture, but it was meaningless to him.

"From you, young sir, it'll be a pleasure to take your money, and no more of it than you see fit or can afford." Walt paused at the door. "It might be easier on everyone if you would wear one of the caps you'll find in the sea chest. Your hair is very obvious. No offense."

He moved so quickly that the door was closed before Astreya could think of words to question him.

"Did your bracelet sort of itch down there in the tap room?" asked Lindey.

Astreya nodded.

"Perhaps it was just that we were side by side—like last night."

Astreya felt his face redden, and could think of nothing to say.

"Well, there's no point in letting this room go to waste," said Lindey cheerfully. "Whatever the explanation for our luck, we might as well enjoy it. I'm going to get into that the tub and soak. Then I'll see what those chests have to offer."

They turned at another knock on the door. It opened just wide enough to admit two steaming mugs held in a huge hand at the height of Astreya's waist. When he took the mugs, the arm withdrew, and Walt's deep voice came through the closing door.

"Food below when you're ready."

Astreya covered his confused emotions at sharing the room with Lindey with the behavior he had learned from growing up in his mother's tiny cottage. He bent over and placed one of the mugs beside the tub, deliberately looking only at Lindey's feet. He then turned and sat at the table with his back to the tub, drinking his mulled ale, looking at the wall and wishing it was a mirror.

"This is a lot better than that awful Jug and Bottle at the Castle," said Lindey. "There's a water closet through that little door. Much better than fifty cold paces to an evil smelling outhouse. And a tub of hot water in the room! Marvelous."

Behind him, came faint splashes and an occasional sigh of contentment as Lindey enjoyed her bath and her ale at the same time. Again, Astreya was balanced at the center of conflicting impulses, the most pressing of which was Lindey's presence, only a couple of steps away. Should he turn? Would he embarrass her? He would certainly embarrass himself, and what then? Balanced between shyness and longing, he did nothing. Eventually the splashing ceased and Lindey came into view, wrapped demurely in a towel.

"Your turn," she said as she opened one of the chests.

Astreya eased off his wet boots, trying both not to notice and at the same time to remember every movement Lindey made.

"Go on, silly. The water's still hot."

Astreya started to unbutton his shirt. With a glance at Lindey's back as she bent over one of the chests, he swiftly pulled off the rest of his clothes and stepped into the tub.

Astreya bent his knees and lowered his shoulders under the water, noticing as he did so that his bracelet had lost the woven string Scarm had given him. The green stone gleamed as if in response to his glance, and without thinking, he held it out of the warm water while he soaked away the cold and tiredness from their long walk. Eventually, the water did not seem warm any more, and he reluctantly climbed out of the tub, splashing water onto the floor.

"You slosh, you mop," said Lindey cheerfully.

He took a step behind one of the chairs on which she had set out some clothes, and toweled himself vigorously. Lindey was kneeling to dry her hair by the fire, her face invisible.

"Now we're both clean and dry, and I've found some things that should fit you, the next thing is food."

"Good idea," said Astreya, pulling on the clothes swiftly, wishing he had the confidence to put his arms around her.

They left their room in borrowed clothes. Lindey wore a loose white shirt and faded blue breeches, and her hair was tucked into a cloth cap; Astreya had pulled a black knitted watch cap down to his ears, above a dark, coarse shirt and black, close fitting trousers. The knife Damon had given him was on his belt, as was his father's. Astreya looked sidelong at Lindey under the lamp in the hallway. She had transformed herself. As well as putting on a man's clothes, she had changed the way she moved, somehow replacing her femininity with the look and movements of a young man. It was almost a shock when her fingers found his and squeezed.

"It's a pleasure not to be wearing a skirt," said Lindey, as they started down the steep staircase. "In Matris I only wear skirts and dresses for celebrations."

Astreya found himself staring at a button that had come undone on her borrowed shirt. Lindey caught his glance and rebuttoned briskly. He blushed.

"Sorry," he mumbled.

They entered the taproom at the same time as a noisy group of five came through the main door, slapping water from their hats and shrugging off their coats. Walt greeted the men by name, suggested mulled ale before they could order it, and waved them to a central table. On his way back to the kitchen, he passed Astreya and Lindey, winked, and twitched a massive shoulder towards a quiet corner not far from the fire. They sat side by side behind the table, their backs to a wall.

Astreya looked about him carefully. Most of the men at The Black Sheep were fishermen. Their seagoing clothes were familiar to him, and also the way they held their heads and glanced around them with an alertness so unlike the Learneds' self-absorbed, downcast eyes. A moment of sorrow touched him as he remembered Gar's approval when he had noticed how the green-gowned men ignored the world around them. The emotion triggered his memory, and, as if obeying an order, he cleared his mind and looked about him with what Gar had called "the painter's eye," wanting to catch what he was seeing on paper, and wishing Gar could share his sketches, as he had done when they had prowled the town around the Castle, looking for interesting faces and figures that they could add to the design in the hall.

Here were men who reminded Astreya of the Village. Even the younger men's faces were weathered and seamed by salt-laced air, and most were bearded. It was their eyes that delighted Astreya, because every man's expression, no matter how shaped by nature, age or temperament, held a keenness that had been absent during most of his travels on land. Whether for good or mischief—as in the case of a couple of decidedly furtive looking characters near the beer barrels—everyone was unobtrusively alert to his surroundings, even when supping on a mug, ripping a piece of bread from a loaf or spooning down a chunk of the fish stew that had started Astreya's mouth watering. Noticing Lindey looking about her with what seemed to him a slightly apprehensive air, Astreya thought that maybe she was used to students, tavern girls and farmers but not to sailors, until she directed his attention with a whisper.

"Those men over there aren't missing anything," she said. "They're not fishermen, and they don't look very friendly."

He followed her glance and saw four men hunched around a table in the corner on the other side of the fieldstone fireplace. The flickering orange light from the big hearth lit their backs, and the candle in the center of their table revealed only glimpses of their faces, all of them clean shaven. The few times any of them spoke their voices were indistinct and secretive, even though the other patrons of the inn had left the tables near them empty. Astreya's attention fixed on the tallest, who overtopped the others even though they were all seated. For a moment, light fell on his angular face, and he caught a glimpse of dark, almost black eyes. Then, as the man's head tipped back to drain his mug, he saw the firelight gleam on straight, black hair, tied back into a short queue. Unlike the heads of his companions, the man's hair was not just dark, it was raven black. Astreya's fingers strayed to the cap Walt had suggested he wear.

"I'm not the only black-haired man here," said Astreya thoughtfully.

Lindey followed his glance, and nodded. Astreya's attention returned to his own table as Walt appeared, his broad hands loaded with food and drink. Astreya saw that his long stare at the four men had been noticed.

"Walt," began Astreya.

"Later, young master," replied Walt softly as he slid a plate in front of Astreya. "Pay 'em no mind. They ain't popular wi' most o' me customers."

Before Walt could be questioned further, he returned to serving other patrons, his huge shoulders rocking back and forth to his awkward, hip-swiveling gait.

"We'll finish our meal quickly and talk in the room," said Astreya.

They dipped spoons into their bowls with appetites whetted by long hours of walking on short rations. Astreya tasted lumps of fish, lobster, potato and onion in milky broth.

"Chowder," he muttered.

"It needs more fish, more herbs and less time waiting to be eaten," said Lindey.

"Do they make chowder in Matris?"

"Wait until you taste mine."

In no time, they were chasing the last drops with chunks of crusty bread, and draining their mugs. Astreya looked at her, and nodded. They chose a path among the tables as far as possible from the black-haired man, and climbed the stair back to their room. There, they found the curtains drawn, the tub removed and their clothes almost dry before the fire, which had been replenished. Conspicuously placed in the middle of the table were Astreya's father's book and the money pouch. He snatched them up, cursing under his breath for having not transferring them to his borrowed clothes, and as he did so, felt relief that Walt had used the mistake as a way to assert that he was trustworthy.

Astreya sat in a chair by the table under the light of the lamp, and pored over the book once again. He pulled off the cap he had worn to disguise his hair and tossed it in front of him, and then dropped his little bag of coins into it. The sleeves of his borrowed shirt chafed at his wrists, so he rolled them up above his elbows and leaned his forearms on the cool wood of the table, his father's book between them. The bracelet gleamed on his left forearm.

Lindey sat beside him, and he almost reached for her. Instead, he started to talk.

"I don't understand what this book is about, Lindey. Gar would have, I think, but I never asked him. For certain, it's not witchcraft."

He looked into her eyes suddenly as a thought struck him.

"Walt must have taken a look at it, while we were downstairs. I hope..."

"Let me see it," said Lindey.

Astreya pushed the little book between them, and they sat, shoulder to shoulder as Lindey turned the pages slowly.

"Astreya," said Lindey, suddenly putting her hand on his. "This is the symbol of birth... this one of the father... this one of the mother. We keep records at Matris in this way. But I don't understand the first page at all."

"Gar knew them as well, but he didn't explain, and I never got a chance to ask him about the poem, or puzzle, or whatever it is."

He turned to the page, and Lindey read the deeply scored words.

Hand of gian far draws on shore

Star sets in song where stones roll in the tide
Son of or on plots a course to the city of the sea
Where dim clasps light no stones

"The part about plotting a course sounds like sailor talk," said Lindey. "And could that be a star to steer by?"

"It makes me think of a song, 'The Wanderer's Curse'," said Astreya gloomily. "But this is even more obscure."

"Gar thought you might have been sent for him by the Men of the Sea."

Astreya frowned as he once again wished for a conversation with Gar that he would never have. He deliberately shrugged off the impossible, ignored Lindey's line of thought, and tried a new direction.

"Do you suppose the City of the Sea is where they live?"

"I don't know," said Lindey, "But my people know about sailors who stole people from us, years ago. Mothers frighten girls by telling them about men with black hair who'll sail into Matris and take away the naughty ones to be slaves. But there's another story about Men of the Sea bringing the first settlers to Matris. It's all a bit confused."

"Slaves?" asked Astreya. "Do you mean they had slaves?"

"You're thinking of slaves in chains, Astreya. Women of Matris use the word for any woman who makes her husband into a lord and master, and gives him babies until she dies of them. The women of Matris took over our village to stop that sort of thing. Besides, the Men of the Sea couldn't have been all bad, because there's also the tradition that they brought my ancestors to a good place in which to settle."

"All of them women?" asked Astreya.

Lindey shook her head. "There were more women than men, though."

Astreya was struck by an uncomfortable memory.

"Lindey, I never told you about the ship and the village we saw on the *Mollie*'s voyage south. It was huge—big enough for a hundred people or more. It had been grounded and dismasted. We first thought it was a wharf. But the village was empty, windows and doors open, and there had been a huge fire. Yan ran ashore before Roaring Jack could stop him, and he found bones. Human bones. Scarm tried to tell us that there had been a plague, but I think it was an attack that stove in the ship and then murdered all the people. Lindey, where would such people come from other than from the sea?"

Outside, the rain drummed on the window and the wind hooted under the eaves. Coldness wrapped itself around Astreya's mind. He looked down at the book and continued in a whisper.

"You're with someone who's part of that evil."

"Astreya, look at me."

Astreya brought his eyes up slowly and faced Lindey. Her eyes were very blue, and the shadows from the lamp above them accentuated her lips as she talked.

"You're not evil, and I'm sure neither was your father. Besides, you are not responsible for what your relatives did... or do. Their lives, good or bad, are their own. And like everyone, they must have had done things that anyone could take pride in, as well things that we all wish hadn't happened."

He stared at her, wanting to believe what she said, but fearing that she was only trying to relieve his distress.

"I just wish Gar had been able to tell me..."

His gaze fell to the dark tabletop, his head tipped forward and he squeezed his eyes shut. Then he felt her hands on his cheeks as she drew his face to hers, and kissed him gently on his eyes.

"Salty," she said.

"I wasn't crying. I was..."

"...thinking about Gar. So was I."

He opened his eyes, and as her lips met his, he closed them again. A long and breathless moment passed during which Astreya felt his mind slow as feelings replaced thoughts.

Three heavy blows thudded on the door of the room. He opened his eyes and drew back, his heart pounding. They both jerked to their feet.

"It's me, Walt," came a deep voice through the door. "There's men who want to meet the young master."

"Enter," said Astreya.

Walt opened the door and a tall figure strode forward along the passageway. The black-haired man had worn authority when sitting with his men; he was even more commanding as he stood in the doorway. Tight black trousers accentuated his lean height, and his jacket of the same leather-like material framed a white shirt beneath, open at the neck. Below his chin hung a silver gorget in the shape of intertwined dolphins. Astreya's appraising look froze when it reached the man's eyes. They were black, unblinking, and they had the arrogance of someone used to unquestioning obedience. Yet, there was also something restrained about him, like a sheathed knife, its point and edges out of sight for the present, requiring only an instant to be whipped into action.

Astreya stood, met the man's stare, and then slowly lifted his arm to beckon him into the room. As he did so, the loose sleeve of his borrowed shirt slid back from his bracelet, and the green stone gleamed white fire from its center. The man's black eyes caught the light as he glanced from Astreya's face to the stone, to the money pouch and open book on the table. His eyes narrowed in a slight hesitation, and his dark eyebrows drew together in a frown. He straightened his back and rocked onto his heels; his left arm curved up from his side, and his hand balled into a fist below his chin. As his clenched thumb touched his gorget, Astreya saw a green stone in a ring on the man's middle finger.

The gesture was a well practiced salute, but it left Astreya without a response.

"You are welcome," he said courteously. "Please enter."

"Sailing Master Adramin of *Cygnus*. Your name and vessel?"

"My name is Astreya."

"Liar. Men!"

Adramin strode deliberately forward to the end of the table as two men surged past him on either side, one in a brown jacket, the other wearing blue. The first shoved Lindey back into her chair, seized her wrists and twisted them behind her. Astreya heard her mutter a curse, but before he could move to free her, he felt a knife blade on the side of his neck. His pulse slowed, giving him time to realize the futility of fighting at that moment. Instead, he spoke quietly and evenly, choosing the formal speech he had read in books.

"I made you welcome, and gave you my name. You called me a liar and filled the room with drawn knives. You menace my friend. You have shown strength, but not courtesy."

His words matched the leader's manner, and both knew it. Astreya had caught the measured tone of command, but where Roaring Jack would have set everyone's ears ringing, Astreya's voice was low, and had it not been for the edge of anger, almost gentle. Adramin blinked and muttered a word to his men. The knife at Astreya's throat slid back into its sheath and both men stepped back. Lindey's eyes flashed, but she did not move. At another order, the man in a blue jacket stepped away from Astreya. The man in brown nodded respectfully to his leader, and went out the door. As it closed behind him, Astreya glimpsed Walt's squat body in the passageway outside.

Astreya took a slow breath, gestured to chairs, and sat down. Adramin chose the chair on the other side of the table, the door behind him guarded by the sailor in blue. The lantern hung above the center of the table, making eyes gleam unnaturally and leaving a dark pool of shadow in the middle of the table.

"Let us start again," said Astreya. "My name is Astreya."

"That one's a girl," said the man in blue.

Adramin nodded.

"Once again, then. My name is Adramin, sailing master of *Cygnus*." He paused and shifted slightly in his chair as if to indicate that he was bored with the formality. "This is boatman Mirak." He indicated the man in blue with a small gesture. Then he continued in a tone marked by deliberate irony. "Now, may I ask, with all the deference you claim, how it is that you, who appear to be younger than I, are using the name of a man who, if he were here, would be older than either of us? And as you think about your answer to that question, you might also be considering how to explain why you wear a navigator's clasp, something I would not dare to do unless I had earned it."

Every word was edged, making the formal politeness into a calculated insult. Lindey moved slightly beside Astreya, placing her hand on the table beside his.

"My name was given me by my mother in memory of my father, who I never knew. He died before I was born. The bracelet... clasp... my mother had from him as a wedding gift. She gave it to me when I left the Village. I wear it in his memory."

Mirak bent and whispered deferentially in Adramin's ear, he replied inaudibly, and the man nodded.

"If you are Estraella's son," said Adramin carefully emphasizing the different pronunciation, "by whomever, then you have inherited his looks. But you have no right to his badge of rank and ability until it is earned and clasped to your arm by the Master."

Astreya glanced at Lindey, on whose swiftly moving lips he read a quick admonition not to be overly impressed. His answer sounded more confident than the guess that was behind it.

"Then I judge that only the Master himself can remove it."

"Very well, even a by-blow has a right to a hearing."

Astreya stood as quick as thought. He tipped the hanging lamp so that its light fell squarely into Adramin's eyes, at the same time plunging his own face into darkness. The boatman's knife rasped out of its sheath.

"Insult me if you wish, Adramin, but not my parents."

He quickly straightened the lamp and sat down again.

Adramin pursed thin lips, as if Astreya had both confused and impressed him.

"I offer no disrespect to Estraella, or to your mother, whoever she may be," he said, conspicuously avoiding any apology to Astreya himself. He raised one hand, turned his head so that neither Astreya nor Lindey could see his lips, and whispered to Mirak.

"Now, of your own will and without force, you will accompany me to the Master."

"And my friend?"

Adramin's lips curved into a smile that was not friendly, and the heavy-browed Mirak on his left gave a little snort of derision.

"Will not be harmed," said Adramin. "We do not assault women."

Astreya looked at Lindey. Her lips and eyes moved minutely, and she nodded.

"We will go with you," he said.

Adramin stood, the door behind him opened, but Astreya did not see anyone enter.

"Young master," rumbled Walt's voice from behind Adramin. "Best you take that book. I wouldn't want anyone to think I'd had somethin' t' do wi' it."

Astreya picked up the book and thrust it into the pocket of his shirt. He rolled his sleeves down slowly, covering the bracelet on which Adramin's eyes were still fixed. Astreya and Adramin stood up at the same moment. Lindey reached for her staff, but Walt's hand closed around it first.

"You won't need that at sea. I'll keep it for you. Now about that bag of..."

"Out of the way, Stumpy," said Mirak.

Lindey frowned, but had no time to speak as Adramin turned, opened the door, and strode out of the room. Mirak and the unnamed sailor in brown waited for Astreya and Lindey to move, and then followed them closely. There was no opportunity for Lindey to do more than clasp Astreya's hand briefly before she followed him down the steep stairs. They entered the taproom, where the hum of people talking, drinking and eating ceased abruptly, and more than a dozen pairs of eyes followed their every move. Adramin and his men paid no attention to the silent watchers on their way to the outer door, but held their right hands significantly close to their belts.

In a few closely escorted strides, they were outside, and uncomfortably aware that they were not wearing either their jackets or cloaks. Mirak slammed the door behind them. The rain had ceased, but the wind had piped up and the waterfront was alive with noise: the slap of waves, creak of cordage and the incessant tapping of halyards against the masts of the boats alongside made conversation impossible. The moon glanced through torn clouds, washing a fitful light over water flecked by whitecaps. By its wan light, Astreya saw that the inn was the next to last building before the end of the wharf, where a finger dock reached into the water. Adramin led the way to the edge of the quay, where his men bent over mooring lines. The nameless sailor jumped nimbly down into a boat that had been invisible from the inn, save for its swaying mast.

"Boots off," said Mirak. "I'll toss 'em down to you when you're aboard."

Astreya nodded, bent over and did as he was directed. Behind him, Lindey fumbled with her laces.

"Step down onto one of the thwarts—that's seats in lubber lingo. If you can," said Adramin as Astreya stood up, barefoot. "Don't fall in," he added scornfully.

Astreya looked down into the gloom where he saw a slim open boat rise and fall, tended by two men who were fending it off from the wharf. He gauged the distance as the waves lifted the boat, and when it was an arm's length from the wharf's edge, he jumped, landed lightly, and sat immediately. He looked up, waiting for Lindey to follow his lead, but saw only Adramin, silhouetted against the moonlit clouds. Suddenly, he misgave, sensing treachery a moment too late.

"Lindey?" he shouted, and stood to jump back ashore at the next wave.

A heavy blow between his shoulder blades felled him to the bottom boards of the boat. Taken by surprise, Astreya got his hands up just in time to save his face, but he could only struggle ineffectively as he was rolled onto one shoulder. His arms were pulled back behind him. Two pairs of hands pinned and tied his wrists and then his ankles. Then the two men forced him into a sitting position and trussed his elbows to his knees. Helpless, Astreya saw Adramin leap into the stern, the last mooring line falling into the water behind him. Astreya felt a knee shove him out of the way so that a sail could be hauled up the mast above his head. A mooring line splashed and was brought inboard, the boat's bow swung away from the land, and the sail thumped as it caught wind.

Astreya had been kidnapped by the Men of the Sea.

SEYMOUR HAMILTON

A Sneak Peek At

THE MEN OF THE SEA

BOOK II OF THE ASTREYA TRILOGY

"Adramin, can you make another crossing tonight?"

Adramin's answer came almost at once. "No, Master."

Oron turned his face to Astreya. "You see, already we are too far away."

"Then turn this ship around!" demanded Astreya.

Oron shook his head. "Even for you, my grandson, I cannot," he said in a tone different from anything Astreya had so far heard. The tone of command was gone, and in its place was an exhausted matter-of-fact statement of circumstances the old man could not change. "Other ships claim our attention," he continued. "There is a summoning to the City of the Sea. Even for your death, Estraella, my son's son, it cannot be otherwise. The safety of the fleet and my ship demand it."

"When will you return?" asked Astreya.

"We can be back to these waters in less than a month, if the fish run true," said Adramin.

Astreya and Oron continued to look at each other, probing the relationship of blood and likeness. Oron stared at his grandson for a moment, unguardedly. Astreya's eyes fell to the table between them, more persuaded by the old man's momentary emotional weakness than he had been by his tone of command. Oron was foreign, strange, and the latest of many people to thwart him, but there was a subtle shift, a softening of his grandfather's attitude toward him, which might be turned toward agreement. While Astreya searched for something that might persuade the old man to let him return, Oron drew his cloak around him and lowered his head so that he stared fixedly at the green stone in Astreya's bracelet on the table in front of him. Astreya followed Oron's gaze.

"Put it back on, Estraella," said Oron quietly. "It's yours, even though you have much to learn before you can carry its authority."

Astreya's hand twitched, but he did not reach out. His anger was waning, and with it, his strength of purpose. Something demanded that he reclaim his bracelet, but he fought against it.

"What is it to you?" he asked.

"Badge of rank, talisman, signal of belonging, but first and foremost the heart of navigation. It points to the mother ship, where the shipstones are. And with training, it can be used to control them. When your father didn't return I watched his echo stone, knowing that when it dulled, he would be dead. It dimmed, and never showed the white light at its center that would have allowed us to trace it, but it kept the same luster, season after season, year after year. Then this year, it re-awoke."

"When I started wearing this," said Astreya, pointing to the stone.

The old man nodded. "We came north as we had done before, and it kept brightening. I hoped Estraella might be alive."

Astreya felt himself a poor substitute in Oron's eyes, and his moment of sympathy for the old man evaporated. Then, when Adramin cleared his throat as if to enter the conversation, and Oron glanced sideways in his direction, Astreya understood that they expected him to be showing some sign of distress at separation from his bracelet. His fingers strayed to his arm, where the stone had tingled so often, and he felt an indefinable sadness, a sense of loss. As he inspected the feeling, he became aware that the value of what lay on the table was far greater than he had imagined. He was sure that there was more, much more that Oron could show him. The desire to learn that Scar Arm Ian had awakened in him flared into a curiosity stronger than anything he had ever experienced. Despite his annoyance at the unfairness of the Men of the Sea, who kept secrets from men like Roaring Jack and all the other skippers who needed a way of finding their way home, there was much here he wanted to know.

Should he—could he return to Lindey, or should he learn to control the stones? Astreya was poised between the two in an excruciating moment of indecision. He had made the case for returning, but at the back of his mind, now he wanted to stay. Perhaps he could learn and take back the secret. He could carry skills and knowledge to others—to share with Lindey. She would be proud of him. She would see reason in his staying, and abject foolishness in missing the chance to amass knowledge. Besides, he had no way of returning. As Adramin said, it was too far to swim.

"Master. Grandfather. Will you put your hand on your own green stone and tell me that you will return soon?"

Oron's piercing eyes fixed on him and the old man's clasp glowed on his arm. Astreya regretted his last vague word.

"When you take your clasp and return it to your arm," he said. "And I will do as you ask later, if you still wish it, grandson."

Behind his shoulder, Astreya heard Adramin suck in his breath.

Astreya guessed that his cousin was appalled that the Master was bargaining rather than commanding. Astreya felt his advantage return as he guessed that Adramin's ring stone was not as powerful as Astreya's, which was the same size as the one on Oron's arm.

"Promise that you will return," said Astreya.

The old man's hand moved slowly to cover his stone, and he stared into Astreya's eyes. "When you know more of what you are and can do, I will ask you if..."

"When you've done whatever it is that you must at the city..." prompted Astreya.

"Very well. We will confer after the City of the Sea," said Oron.

Astreya slowly reached out his hand, took up his bracelet and clipped it onto his left arm. The green light intensified, and the white spear flashed. Opposite him, Oron's shoulders lowered as the old man's tension ebbed.

"Show him his quarters, Adramin. Outfit him as befits a kinsman and Man of the Sea. Help him learn our ways. I charge you in this."

The stone on Adramin's finger flashed as he brought his fist to his throat. "At your command, Master."

"Estraella, you will attend me tomorrow morning," said Oron.

Astreya wondered whether to copy Adramin's gesture, and decided instead to nod.

"Then follow the Law and await my command," said Oron.

Astreya recognized a formula of dismissal. He stood up, slid his chair back into place, and followed Adramin out the door.

"My father's book!"

Adramin closed the door and paused. As he turned on Astreya, the lantern lit his face in profile, sharpening its arrogant angularity.

"Forget your book: it's the Master's now. He'll tell you about it when he's ready. When he's taught you more than you've ever dreamed," he said through tight lips. "Now, grab your jacket, and follow me."

He walked swiftly down the passage, balancing to the movement of the ship with the ease of one for whom it was second nature. Astreya followed him, pulling on his jacket as he went. As the green light of the stone vanished under the black waterproof material, Astreya thought of Lindey, and his spirits sank. He had sold out. Greed for knowledge of the mystery behind the green stones had won out, and he was ashamed. And Oron had his father's book. What would he make of the riddle? Astreya slowed, stopped and stood. The words his father had written ran through his mind.

Hand of gian far draws on shore
Star sets in song where stones roll in the tide
Son of or on plots a course to the city of the sea
Where dim clasps light no stones

"Thinking of your little piece ashore? Going all teary eyed? Get a move on, lubber."

Astreya started as if he had been struck. His fists clenched, he strode forward so quickly he almost ran into Adramin, who had stopped and opened a narrow door.

"Your space," said Adramin. "For as long as you measure up to the Master's expectations. And mine, too," he added scornfully.

Astreya took a step into the gloom, staggering as Adramin's hand shoved him between his shoulder blades.

The door closed behind him with a metallic click and Astreya was alone in the dark, listening to the sound made by the ship's hull rushing through the water. He took off the waterproof jacket and light bloomed from his bracelet, illuminating the cabin. It was not much longer fore and aft than the bed that lay beside the slightly curved wall, on the other side of which Astreya knew was the sea. He turned, banged his shins on a chest against the passage wall and sat on it, grateful of the chance to relax some of his tension. Leaning his forearms on his knees, he took a deep breath and tried to make sense of the last few crowded hours. His meeting with Oron had run the gamut through anger, defiance, a sudden craving for knowledge, and in the end, a compromise that left him ashamed. That way lay despair, so he deliberately reflected on the trip on Adramin's strange, fast boat that had brought him to the ship. He recalled first sight of the huge hull in which he now was—what? A prisoner? A prodigal grandson? An unwelcome relative, as far as Adramin was concerned, that was certain. And as he mused, he again was torn by the abrupt parting from Lindey, and rueful that he had capitulated to Oron's vague promise.

He stared at the stone, noticing that the spear of light was aligned with the ship.

"I didn't ask it to do that," he muttered, and in the instant decided to rebel against whatever controlled his stone.

Astreya replayed Gar's words in his mind. "Think north, Astreya."

At first, nothing happened, and then gradually the spear of light pointed at almost a right angle to the ship's midline. Astreya smiled grimly. He did have control, even here. He tried to swing the spear of light away from north, and again was successful, although behind his eyes he felt as if he were pushing his head against a wall. He rubbed a spot above his right eyebrow, and tried again. This time, nothing happened. His head now ached, but he did not give up. The cabin darkened. He blinked, momentarily at a loss, and greenish light again flowed from the stone on his bracelet.

"That's it!" he said aloud. "I made it wink."

He refocused his concentration, and the cabin darkened again. He counted two heartbeats, willed the light to return, and it did.

"Three's a charm," he muttered.

One more time, he was in darkness, and then his stone blazed again. The pain in his head lessened, but he suddenly needed to lie down. He took off his shirt and breeks and dropped them on the chest. He stood, took the short stride to the bed, and slid between rough blankets. Once he was lying flat, he felt the soothing movement of the ship, but although he was exhausted by the events of the day, he could not sleep. Where was Lindey? Was she safe? Did she blame him for what had happened?

"Did your stone wink, Lindey? Did I reach you?" Astreya asked the darkened cabin.

There was a knock on the cabin door.

"You all of a piece in there?" The voice was neither Oron's nor Adramin's.

"I'm all right," he answered as firmly as he could.

"Word from the Master. You're not to do whatever you're doing with your clasp, because you're throwing the ship off course."

"All right," said Astreya. "I wasn't planning to do anything more, anyway."

"You'd better not. Master'll be right upset if you do, and that's something you don't want to see, take it from me."

"Um... Thank you."

"Don't mention it. 'Dramin tell you about the head?"

"The what?"

"Washplace... toilet... shitter..."

"No."

"Two doors ahead along the passage."

"Thank you."

"'Night then."

Astreya could not hear footsteps going away, but since he had not heard them approach, he did not know if the passage was empty. He sank back onto the bed and listened to the water rush past, only a hand's breadth of the ship's hull between him and the ocean. He thought to pulse his stone again, in spite of Oron's orders, but he was too tired to do more than watch its green glow until he could no longer keep his eyes open.

As he slept, he did not see his stone dim and brighten three times.

ABOUT THE AUTHOR

It took a long time until Seymour Hamilton could legitimately call himself a fiction writer, although he remembers wanting to do so when he was about 12 years old.

He studied English and Philosophy at Queen's University, Kingston, Ontario Canada, and went on to do a Masters in English at the University of Toronto. In those days, a MA was sufficient qualification to teach in many universities, so he became an assistant professor at Acadia University in Wolfville, Nova Scotia, where he married and his first son, Robin, was born. Three years later, he moved to Canada's west coast to teach at Simon Fraser University. Three more years, and he returned to Queen's to complete his PhD (on American Science Fiction) just in time for a cyclical slump in hiring by Canadian universities.

He returned to Nova Scotia and worked first as a contract writer and editor, then as a communications officer in the provincial government. He also wrote and performed radio essays and theatre reviews. It was during this time that he sailed on a friend's schooner to the south coast of Newfoundland—an experience that was the genesis of *Astreya*.

Government communications experience led to his next academic job in the graduate school of Communications Studies at the University of Calgary. After four years of teaching and much hiking in the Rockies, he returned to Ottawa, the city in which he had gone to school. He married Katherine, and they moved a few kilometers into Chelsea, Quebec and had a son, Ben. Until retirement, he taught at Ottawa University and wrote and edited extensively for both private sector and government.

Astreya had been on his mind since the 1970's, increasing in volume by fits and starts. In retirement, it became a full-time activity, growing from a short novella to a trilogy.

Seymour Hamilton is from a seagoing family going back many generations. He first learned to sail a dinghy from his father, who, like his grandfather, was a Master Mariner and Commander in the British Navy.

For more about Astreya's world, visit:

AstreyaTrilogy.com

DON'T MISS ALL OF THE EXCITING BOOKS IN THE SIR SIDNEY SMITH SERIES BY

TOM GRUNDNER

THE MIDSHIPMAN PRINCE

How do you keep a prince alive when the combined forces of three nations (and a smattering of privateers) want him dead? Worse, how do you do it when his life is in the hands of a 17 year old lieutenant, an alcoholic college professor, and a woman who has fired more naval guns than either of them? The first book in the Sir Sidney Smith nautical adventure series.

HMS DIAMOND

After surviving the horrors of the destruction of Toulon, Sir Sidney is given a critical assignment. British gold shipments are going missing. Even worse, the ships are literally disappearing in plain sight of their escorts and the vessels around them. The mystery must be solved, but to do that Sir Sidney must unravel a web of intrigue that leads all the way to the Board of Admiralty.

THE TEMPLE

Napoleon is massing ships, troops, and supplies at Toulon and a number of other ports. He is clearly planning an invasion; but an invasion of who, where, and when, no one knows. The key is a captured message, but it's encoded in a way that has never been seen before. From a dreary prison in Paris, to an opulent palace in Constantinople, to the horror of the Battle of the Nile—*The Temple* will take you on a wild ride through 18th Century history.

ACRE

Nelson has defeated the French fleet at the Battle of the Nile, and Bonaparte is trapped in Egypt. Unfortunately, Bonaparte doesn't see it that way...

Acre sets a dizzying pace, sweeping the reader from Smith, to Napoleon, to Nelson and back, until you are almost intoxicated. It is perhaps the best book written about this extremely important chapter in history.

DON'T MISS THE FIGHTING SAIL SERIES BY

ALARIC BOND

His Majesty's Ship

A powerful ship, a questionable crew, and a mission that must succeed.

In the spring of 1795 HMS Vigilant, a 64 gun ship-of-the-line, is about to leave Spithead as senior escort to a small, seemingly innocent, convoy. The crew is a jumble of trained seamen, volunteers, and the sweepings of the press; yet, somehow, the officers have to mold them into an effective fighting unit before the French discover the convoy's true significance.

Jackass Frigate

How do you maintain discipline on a ship when someone murders your first lieutenant—and a part of you agrees with their action?

For Captain Banks the harsh winter weather of 1796 and threat of a French invasion are not his only problems. He has an untried ship, a tyrant for a First Lieutenant, a crew that contains at least one murderer, and he is about to sail into one of the biggest naval battles in British history—the Battle of Cape St. Vincent.

True Colours

While Great Britain's major home fleets are immobilised by a vicious mutiny, Adam Duncan, commander of the North Sea Squadron, has to maintain a constant watch over the Dutch coast, where a powerful invasion force is ready to take advantage of Britannia's weakest moment.

With ship-to-ship duels and fleet engagements, shipwrecks, storms and groundings, True Colours maintains a relentless pace that culminates in one of the most devastating sea battles of the French Revolutionary War—the Battle of Camperdown.

Cut and Run

After leaving the Royal Navy, Lieutenant King opts for a spell with the Honourable East India Company.

It turns out to be anything but the easy option when his new captain turns is an old enemy. With the added perils of privateers, storms, and the mighty French Navy, he wonders why he ever bothered to Cut and Run.

A.D. 61 - 70
BERIC THE BRITON
A STORY OF THE ROMAN INVASION
GEORGE HENTY

CPSIA information can be obtained at www.ICGtesting.com
Printed in the USA
BVOW07s0909061214

377688BV00001B/1/P

9 781611 791907